DECIMATION ISLAND

LOST TIME: BOOK 5

DAMIEN BOYES

DECIMATION ISLAND
Lost Time: Book Five

Proofreading by Tamara Blain.
Cover by Wadim Kashin.

PUBLICATION HISTORY
eBook 1st edition / June 2019
Print 1st edition / July 2019

This is a work of fiction. Any similarity between the
characters and situations within its pages and places or
persons, living or dead, is unintentional and coincidental.
Obviously.

ISBN: 978-0-9950464-6-7

THANKS_

*To my Beta Team, especially Rob Coli, for the
excellent insights.*
*To Tamara Blain. for once again killing all the typos and
making my grammar good.*
To Wadim Kashin, for his peek into my world.
And to my family,
for letting me sit in my room and do what I do.

Control Complex

The Fractured Cliffs

Wilhelm's Final Scream

Brock's Bastion Wreck of the Seastar

Sunset Wild

Ghostwalk Cavern

Evermore Castle The Verdant Wild Leftright Towers

Gunpowder Remorse

Fort Grimdark

Aurora City

Revenge of the Treepeople

Hacienda De La Mer

Trinity Landing

Gunship Grotto Fargo's Lost Cargo Lake River Rivals

Firestorm Dean

Greenbeard

Observatory

The Caldera

Admiral Grant's Armada

Beetroot Plantation

Monorail Heist Sunrise Gulch

Skull Island

Crater Expedition

Buck-An-Ear Cove

Riverboat Race

Walter's Arena

Camp Townsend

Rachel's Reach

Sunken City Blues

Robot Junction

Crystal Coves

Zombie Freakout

Escape from Potato Mountain

Raptorwolf Rampage

Giga Prison Riot

Forgotten Son

Hostile Coast Ranger Rick's Last Stand The UnderLab

Lavafield Rescue Smuggler's Run

Tri-Force Dam

Moonbase Delta

Sky Temple Ruin

Rocket Hijack

Frost Harbor

Saigon Farm

The Shattered Dome

Water Treatment Collapse

Los Endos

Decimation Island

0   4   8   12   16   20 km

You come online already in midair, soaring in a rigid wingpack with the wind snapping at your cheeks and the ground rushing up to meet you. The sudden lurch to a strange body staggers you, and you shiver through a moment of panic before you remember where you are —and why.

A moment ago you were wearing your regular skyn and loading your rithm into the game lobby, now you're three thousand feet in the sky, a mini-glider strapped to your back, and surrounded by ninety-nine other players ready to murder you.

This is Decimation Island, and the game has already begun.

You blink your eyes clear behind your goggles and take a second to get your bearings. It's a midmorning start, and from the look of the jungle below and the shape of the coastline hurtling toward you, you've dropped from the southwest tower. Depending on how the safe-zone shapes up, the best hotspots will likely be the UnderLab, Sky Temple Ruin, the Shattered Dome, and Ranger Rick's.

Lots of players head straight for the action, but you know better than that. Trying to solo a hotspot from the drop is a prayer to RNGeezus: either you get lucky and maybe score yourself a powerful weapon or upgrade—or you die in the first ten minutes of the game. That strategy's fine for virts, you can drop hot all you want, as many times as you have the stomach for it—there's always another game waiting. But out here you only get one life.

Instead you flick your eyes to the lower right, open the map, and check the safe-zone. There's still lots of open ground for now, nine hundred and ninety-nine square kilometers of playable area, but everything outside of that is in the red, swarming with hostile bots eager to rip you to shreds the second you've burned through your safe-time. That's a concern for later though. No point in worrying about the bots when you haven't hit the ground yet.

What you need is a quiet place to scramble a kit together while you get a handle on your new body, and since you're already headed toward the ocean, you figure the Sand Hawk Apartments compound on the coast is your best option. It's low-key enough you'll stay out of the early game frag-fests and you can be relatively certain no one'll be at your back. Plus, anyone else who lands out here might be playing the long game too. You don't need a whole group, but maybe you can find a single like-minded partner without having to risk the hustle of the starter hotspot.

Yeah, it means your loot will be balls for a while, and with your back to the zone the bots will be chasing the entire round, but you'll still scavenge gear and can get aggressive when you need to. It's a big island, and a hundred hours is a long time. Finding kills will be easy—the hard part's in figuring out who to trust.

You stretch out awkwardly, struggling with the strange

fit of your arms and legs, and grit your teeth as you fight to catch the air with your wings. This skyn is bigger than yours, and the muscles more conditioned. You knew this would happen, that adjusting to the game body would take a little time, but already it's harder than you expected. You've trained your whole life for this, been gaming since you could walk, played tens of thousands of rounds of the original Decimation Island video game and spent the last four weeks simming game after game of the live version, but you've barely started and already controlling the flesh and blood you're packed into is way more finicky than the digital aspect you're used to.

For a moment, you wonder how it'll affect your aim. You've always been a good shot, but who knows how these futzy analogue nerves and muscles will react when you need them to. This game is challenging enough as it is, you don't have time to relearn how to shoot too.

There's no fooling around here. This isn't a simulation, this is what you've been training for: Decimation Island Live. Reszos fragging it out in a battle royale fight to the death, and it's the biggest thing going in sports. Every day millions of people stream it live or ghost along in the heads of individual players, watching through their eyes, and even more will catch up with their favorite gamers' daily highlights.

The game's just started but you can already feel the people watching you, the weight of their combined attention gently shimmering in your head like a sixth sense. It's faint though, your audience isn't huge—while you've got a solid tuber base, you've never played live, so no one expects much—everyone's too busy watching the high-hour players drop to bother with a firstie.

That's okay, for now. When you win it all everyone will

be watching, but you won't get very far if you can't get a handle on your skyn.

You argue with your foreign body for another moment before it finally settles down and you're able to more or less steer yourself. You scan the sky as you glide toward the row of low apartments along the water. Players are still airborne, dropping all around the island, but only two are close by, both lower to the ground and ahead of you. They've had their arms tucked in, soaring toward the coast at speed while you've been fooling around with your skyn and lost in your thoughts.

Come on, Anika, get in the game.

"Looks like we got us some competition," you say in your head, trying to fire yourself up by addressing your small audience directly. You can't hear their responses, but from the eager buzz of anticipation that trills down your spine, you get the gist. They're looking for you to start killing, and you've always tried to give the fans what they want.

You press yourself flat and angle off to the left, aiming to put a little distance between you and the other two, and land on the south side of the complex. You'll be okay for a bit, you can avoid them while you find something to defend yourself with, but after that your first priority will be finding a partner. You don't need to outlive everyone on the island, just ninety percent of them. The last ten players alive continue on to the next round, but lone wolves rarely survive that long. Sure, the odd person will snake their way into the winner's circle from time to time, but never more than a round or two in a row. You need a team if you want to survive long term, but in this game no one can be trusted, and when it comes down to winning or losing, partners are just victims you haven't killed yet.

The Sand Hawk complex is made up of six long four-story buildings along the beach, three on each side of a common pool and rec area, a dock with no boats, and assorted other outbuildings, including a guard hut at the only road in or out through the thick surrounding jungle. The other two players have already pulled their chutes, and one's headed to the rooftop of Building Five, while the other's descending into the courtyard, probably looking to loot up in the cabana. You head for the roof of Building One, the southernmost apartment building, and trigger your chute just before you hit the roof. A slap to the latch on your chest to releases the wings and chute straps, and you roll and come up running. There's a ML-23 pistol and ammo nearby, and you snatch them up and load while you head for the access door, holding the weapon ready as you swing down the stairwell to loot the empty apartments.

By the time you hit the main floor you've found level-one body armor, some water and rations, a single medpatch kit, a weapon harness, and an e-blade, and that's it. Who knows what the others found. They could already have an assault-class rifle and be hunting you down.

You'd like to loot the next two buildings close to you but can't risk it yet. There are too many hiding places, and a pistol's only good in close quarters. You're not ready for a fight, especially since you're not even fully adjusted to your skyn. Instead you play it safe, pause in the building's lobby, weapon held low, and scan out across the tropical courtyard to the beach.

No movement, but there's lots of cover out there. The other two players could be anywhere, playing it safe like you, or circling back around to put a bullet in your face. Either way, you're not all getting off this beach. Before you leave the Sand Hawk you'll have a partner or you'll have your first kills.

"*Ready y'all?*" you think, snapping right back into the role of AniK@, Queen of Carnage. The gentle buzz of attention lifts in response. "*Let's find someone to kill.*"

"You are not your meat," Shelt says, his voice echoing in the vaulted church. He's in his element, striding up and down the aisle between the curved pews, preaching the Gospel of the Restored to the three-dozen people who've come to tonight's counseling session. "You are the expression of the erratic thoughts and feelings racing through your head, of your lived joy and suffered trauma, of the unique and complex genetic interaction that created the signals bouncing around your brain—and that's true whether your head is filled with organic chemicals or pulses of light. What matters is that you exist. Right here—*right now*—you are real. You have a soul and you have agency in this world."

Murmurs ripple through the crowd. Heads nod. Everyone here is slightly less than human—or most of us think that anyway, me included. For one reason or another, through tragedy or design, we've all gone digital, and the trip from biology to technology has messed up each and every one of us.

There's only one person here who's absolutely sure there's nothing wrong with him, and that's Shelt. He's the reason why we come back every week: we all want to be a little more like him—as strange as that might seem if you knew him like I do.

Shelt would be the first to tell you he's no role model. I met him in a counseling session like this one. He was a tweaked-out shyft junkie and I was just back from the dead. I was forced to attend and resented being there, but he was already a willing acolyte of the church of the psychorithm.

We've both come a long way since then, as he's leading the sessions and no one's outright forcing me to attend— even if I'm not actively participating. I come, but not officially. Mostly I stand at the back, get the coffee and snacks ready for when the session ends, and listen. That's as far as I'm willing to go for now and Shelt knows it, but that doesn't stop him from trying.

"And with that, we'll end the session," Shelt says, and then, right on cue, he turns and calls out across the room. "Unless you have anything to add tonight, Finsbury?"

The heads in the pews swivel to face me. Shelt does this every meeting, puts me on the spot, trying to draw me out, and I always decline.

It's not like I have nothing to talk about, and he knows it. The world is changing, faster every day, careening downhill with the brake lines cut. Advancements and discoveries that would have made global headlines fifty years ago come and go with a shrug every other afternoon. Life is dizzying and disorienting and we're all caught up in it, riding the crest of the wave of progress. And being reszo only compounds it. I've got as much or more wrong with me than anyone, not that it's a competition, but I'd bet I'm the only one here with an angry stowaway in their head.

I call him Deacon. He's a malicious echo of me, a twisted version of a person I once became, and any time I get too excited, or if my rithm gets revving in fear or anger, he wakes up and tries to take over. He's quiet now, but only because of the shyft a rithmist friend of mine rolled to keep him sedated. It's worked so far, but whenever I go out in my body the shyft leaves me foggy, like my thoughts are filtered through wet cotton, so I don't go out much.

As of right now, the only way to get rid of him would be a psycho-surgery, where we'd try to isolate and cut him out of my head, but that's an iffy gamble at best, and we're not even sure if I could disentangle myself from Deacon without my rithm unraveling in the process. So for now, I'm stuck with him.

And as if living with the literal embodiment of my every evil impulse isn't enough to keep me in therapy for the rest of my life, I'm also wracked with guilt over all the shit I did when I *was* Deacon, even if I don't remember all of it.

I know I hurt people. I lied, I betrayed my friends and colleagues. I basically threw my life away—so, yeah, I have plenty to talk *about*, I'm all kinds of broken, but I've never been one to air my dirty laundry in public. So I come to the meetings, I listen, but I'll leave the sharing to others.

Not that these sessions are a complete waste of time. It's nice to get out of my head occasionally. And I mean that literally—if I wasn't here right now I'd be back in my virtual cabin in the Arctic, where Deacon can't hurt anyone, chilling with the digital ghost of my dead wife.

Which is yet another problem. Maybe the worst out of all of them.

A few years before she died, Connie trained a sprite to mimic her personality, and she gave it to me as a joke gift, and now we live together. It stays in the cabin with me. Eats with me. We even sleep together every night. I know it's not her, and I know damned well my relationship with it isn't healthy—honestly, even I recognize it's a little morbid—but I'm not ready to let her go, and there's no amount of talking that'll change that.

So no, no sharing tonight.

"Only that the coffee's hot," I call back. "And the muffins only slightly stale. Come help yourself."

Shelt rolls his eyes but smiles as people gather their belongings and wander over. I've got the folding table set up with the big chrome coffee carafe and a couple plates of snacks. Only about half the people stay to mingle—the newbies often bail right after the session's over and stalk out with their eyes pointed at the floor—but over time more and more are staying. Shelt's building a community here, a place where the broken and the ostracized and the dejected can come and feel like maybe there's a place they belong, where they're treated like humans even though their heads are full of ones and zeroes.

It's a regular island of misfit toys, but despite my being an asshole I find myself coming back, twice a week. I lost my wife and my job and every connection I ever had, including the one to my humanity, and being part of this small group reminds me that I don't have to spend every second of my life locked away from reality, hiding from who I am.

"Good turnout tonight," I say as Shelt comes to stand beside me.

"The more the merrier," he replies and chucks me on the shoulder. "Though one of these nights I'm going to get *you* up on that stage."

I shake my head. "Not gonna happen, but you're welcome to keep trying."

Shelt's wearing a new skyn tonight, one from the collection he keeps at his club: a tall female with dark skin, big brown eyes, and a tight Afro, but even though his body is a stranger, Shelt's personality still shines through. He can't stay still, keeps fussing with the layout of the paper cups and plates of muffins with his long fingers, and when he leaves me to move through the crowd, making small talk, his facial expressions are as animated as ever. I think he's trying to prove the point of his sermon tonight: you aren't your meat. I've never seen his skyn before tonight, but I still know who's inside.

Watching him gently nudge people toward doing the work to come to grips with their new lives is inspiring. He's a good friend. I wouldn't have expected we'd get along so well, but he's patient with me and I'm lucky to have him in my life, even if he's often a Jiminy Cricket pain in the ass conscience on my shoulder telling me all the ways I'm fucking it up.

Soon all that's left are the raisin muffins and the crowd has thinned to the last few stragglers. Shelt's talking to one of the regulars, there's another small group still chatting, and a girl is standing off on her own, a cup of coffee in her hand she hasn't touched. She's watching me, but trying not to look too obvious about it, and glances away when she notices me noticing her.

My heart trips a little faster, anticipating trouble, and the fog in my head thickens as the shyft keeping Deacon quiet stifles my anxiety. There's nothing outwardly suspicious about her. She's Asian, petite, with long black hair and a face like a J-Pop star, but who knows who might be wearing that skyn. I've made my share of enemies over the past few years, lots of people have plenty of reason to come after me—but for some reason, maybe the way she's standing, or the unsure look in her eyes, she makes me think of Doralai Wii, probably the one person I hurt the most.

Deacon stole her body, infiltrated her head, and took

over her life in a demented attempt to merge his rithm with mine. I've tried to repair all the damage he did, but I haven't been able to find Dora anywhere. No one knows what happened to her, or where she went, and while I don't think that's Dora, you never know.

I keep my eye on her as I tidy up, and then, just as I'm about to haul the carafe back into the kitchen to wash it, she seems to decide, and approaches me.

"Hi," she says, timid. She glances down at her untouched coffee as if she's only just realized she's holding it and takes a big swig from the cup, swallows, then continues. "I'm Sofia."

"Nice to meet you, Sofia," I say, still not sure what this is about. I don't think she's a threat but these days you can never be too sure. "I'm Fin."

"I know," she says quickly. "I mean, I know who you are. I know what you've done."

My spine tingles with adrenaline. I brace myself to heave the carafe at her if she makes a move on me.

"Oh yeah?" I say, noncommittal, still not sure what she's angling at.

"Uh huh," she says, confidence easing back into her voice. "I've been coming here the past few weeks, and I noticed you right away. I read all about how you stopped that runaway AI, and you helped catch a serial killer last month, right? You're a regular hero."

"I..." I'm used to people being interested in me because they want to take my head off. Now I have no idea what to do. "Where'd you hear that?"

I mean, I guess it wouldn't be hard to find. I've tried to keep a low profile but my name was all over the feeds for a while there. A disgraced cop taking on a rogue AI is never not gonna make the feeds. A simple dox is all it would take to find out all the things I've done. The official stories, anyway.

She smiles and shrugs and brushes a stray hair from her forehead, looking up at me with hooded eyes. "I wanted to talk to you plenty of times but could never work up the nerve."

The adrenaline swerves and turns my stomach. My cheeks flush. *She's hitting on me.* I could deal with her trying to kill me, but this...

"You can't believe everything you read on the link," I say, keeping my voice light, but finding it hard to make eye contact. I reach back and absently scratch the skin around the cuff secured to the base of my skull. "A lot of that stuff is exaggerated."

"I asked Shelt," she counters. "He said it's true."

I look past Sofia and see Shelt. Everyone else has left and he's watching us, an expectant grin on his face.

Son of a bitch. *He set this up.*

"Shelt's a smart guy, but even he doesn't always know what he's talking about."

She smiles and leans in. "Well then, maybe I can find out for myself. How about I help you clean up and then I'll buy you a drink?"

Dammit, Shelt. Why'd you put me in this position?

I press my lips together and I guess she knows what I'm about to say because her face falls. "That's kind of you to ask," I say, trying to be as gentle as I can. "But ... I'm involved with someone."

Her head jerks to the side and she glances over her shoulder at Shelt. He isn't grinning anymore.

"But Shelt said ..." Then her brows knit together and she takes a step back. "I'm sorry," she says, embarrassed. "I didn't know ..."

"It's not your fault," I say, trying to reassure her, then raise my voice so Shelt will hear. "Shelt shouldn't have said anything."

She gives me a weak smile. "Well, good night then," she mumbles, sets her cup down and rushes out of the room without a look back.

"What the hell, Shelt?" I yell the moment the door shuts behind her.

He's already walking toward me, hands raised like *what did I do?*

"My life is fucked enough as it is, how the hell do you think I'm supposed to bring someone else into it? You knew I'd have to let her down—how's a cold cup of rejection supposed to make her feel?"

Shelt sighs. "She's new to the life and having trouble connecting to the person she used to be, and I thought maybe you two could help each other. Twenty minutes of real human interaction wouldn't have killed you."

"You should have asked me first. I know you're trying to help, but all you did was make us feel like shit."

"What, you have something better to do tonight?"

"As a matter of fact I do," I blurt, but immediately wish I hadn't.

"What?" Shelt asks, suspicious. His skyn's taller than mine and he cranes his neck down to glare at me. "The only time you leave your pod is to come here. What could you possibly have going on?"

"You don't know everything about me," I say, and even I hear the petulance in my voice. I sound like a teenager arguing with his mother.

Shelt smirks. "I've seen inside your head, remember?" he says. "What could you possibly have left to hide?"

I don't respond. Don't know what to say that won't make me sound like a brat throwing a tantrum.

"*So,*" Shelt prods, "what's this big event?"

I don't want to answer, but Shelt won't let this go until I do. "If you must know, I have a date."

Shelt straightens, momentarily surprised, but then he shakes his head. "With who?" he asks, though he already knows the answer.

"Connie," I say. "At a telecafe."

I've got a reservation at a place down the street that's set up for people to have virtual meet-ups in the real world. And I know I can see Connie anytime I want, she can superimpose her sprite over my vision and appear anywhere I am, but no one can see her but me. At the cafe, I can sit across from her and have a meal like we're out on a real date. Pretend for a moment that our relationship isn't all in my head.

The telecafe's designed for people in different cities or countries to hang out, but there's nothing stopping me from using it with Connie's sprite. People do it all the time. I'm not the only one in a relationship with a virtual entity. It's only weird because it's my dead wife. If I was in love with a big-eyed, squeaky-voiced manga character no one would bat an eye.

"So you're taking this thing with Connie out into the world now?"

"Yeah, I am," I snap back. "So what? Plenty of people have virtual relationships. Why can't I?"

Shelt throws up his hands. "I'm not judging," he says.

"Sure as hell sounds like it."

Shelt's big dark eyes narrow. "You know me," he says. "I'd never tell anyone how to live their life, or who to love. Hell, be a polyamorous purple dragon if that's what you're into, I don't give a shit. I just want to make sure you understand the difference between"—he points to my forehead—"*in there*"—then raises his finger and spins it in a tight circle—"and *out here*. Confuse the two and you may never find your way back."

I take a breath and it comes out as a long sigh. He's trying to help, I know that, but he needs to back off this one. "I appreciate your concern," I tell him, "but I know what I'm doing."

"If you say so," Shelt replies. But I know this isn't the last I've heard from him about this.

"I'm late for the reservation," I say, glancing at the table. "Can you finish here?"

"Sure," Shelt says. "Say 'hi' to Connie for me."

I give him a dirty look but let him have the last word. There's no point in arguing. We both know he's right. This thing with Connie isn't healthy, but what else can I do? I love her, and her sprite is all I have left.

After everything I've lost, I can't lose her too.

I THINK Connie a quick note to tell her I'll be ten minutes late, hop on my bike, and let the battery get me up to speed. Usually when I'm feeling like this, all confused and edgy, I work the pedals myself, fight back against the nervous energy corroding my brain by exhausting myself, but the air's been hot and swampy in Toronto for weeks, with no sign of letting up, and just stepping outside is enough to overheat my temperature-tolerant skyn. I don't want to show up for my date dripping in sweat.

The green lanes are thick with Skütes and wheelz and other bikers, and it's slow going up to the virt cafe where I'm meeting Connie. I should probably just call it off. I'm already late for the reservation as it is.

There's part of me—a big part—that knows Shelt's right: this isn't natural, what I'm doing with Connie's sprite. I'm treating an artificial construct of the woman I love like we're in a real relationship, like she's the person I married and not a virtual approximation of her. A damn close approximation, but still. I know it's perverse, but I can't stop—and the worst part is, I don't know if I even want to.

It's hard to stay out in the world for long, and it's not just the heat, or my problems with Connie, or the general disarray of my life that make me want to stay in hibernation. My brain is broken, and the neural governor in my Cortex keeping Deacon on lockdown makes me feel like I'm thinking through cheesecloth, with all the fine details stripped away. I want to be out here, but it's so much easier living in my head.

In there, everything is just as I want it to be, or as close as I can get. My thoughts are clear. I can jump into any world I want—past, present, or future. Play out endless lives. And Connie's right there with me. I know I need to stay connected to reality, but how can I when virtuality is so much easier in every possible way?

One step at a time, I guess. That's what Shelt would say —get out of your head and do what you can. It's one of the reasons I set up this date. Instead of shacking up with Connie in my headspace, we can be out in the world together. It's not the same as if she was here with me, but for now it's the best I can do.

The telecafe is tucked into a short strip of stores up on Donlands Avenue., between a Mennonite butcher and a Sea Feed & Co., one of those algae-based chain restaurants, and I lock my bike to the rack out front and head inside. It looks like a typical coffee shop, with a long bar and customers sitting at an eclectic mix of old Formica tables in mismatched chairs, except all the tables are split in half by a transparent screen. Most of the tables are full, with people sitting on either side, but they're not talking to each other— they don't even see the person opposite them—instead, they're chatting with whoever's on their screen.

Connie's already waiting at our assigned table. I slide into my chair and there she is across from me. She's got her hair pulled up in a loose bun, showing off the sweep of her long slender neck, and her red top is conservatively buttoned all the way up, but it hugs her body in just the right way. She's frowning, but I know she's only playing. I don't think she could be mad at me even if she wanted to.

"It's about time," she says in a mock-hurt tone. "I'm beginning to think you like Shelt more than me."

"Never," I say as I sit. I want to reach across to grab her hand, but even as real as she seems, I know that's impossible. One more reminder that this is all a fiction.

There's a beer waiting for me, the glass wet with condensation, and I pick it up and take a long swallow.

"How was the session tonight?" Connie asks. She's got a glass of wine in front of her and she raises it and takes a sip.

"Good," I say with a shrug. "Shelt was in fine form. He tried to set me up with someone."

Connie raises her brows and leans in. "Oh yeah? Was she cute?"

"I guess," I reply. "Seemed nice enough."

"And?" she presses. "Do you have a date?"

"Of course not," I answer, maybe a little too quickly, like her question was a subtle test of my loyalty even though I know I could go on all the dates I want and Connie wouldn't treat me any differently or be upset in the least. This relationship is entirely one-sided and all in my head. I'm the only one holding us to it. I take another swig of beer, frustrated. "I'm not ready for that. Besides, I have you. I don't need anyone else."

"That's sweet," Connie says. She flashes her teeth, reaches up, and pulls a strand of hair back over her ear. "But you know, if you ever wanted to go out on a date, I wouldn't mind. It might do you some good."

"I ..." I don't know what to say. First Shelt sticks his nose where it doesn't belong, and now even Connie is trying to shove me back into the dating pool. "We only have the table for an hour. We don't get to be together like this much. Let's talk about something else, okay?"

"Whatever you'd prefer," Connie says. As programmed. "I do have something to tell you—your friend Ari Dubecki sent you a message. He wants you to help him with something."

My first instinct is to say "no" before I even hear what it is, but I fight down the urge. I first met Ari Dubecki— Dub—in the same counseling session where I met Shelt. He was only an amateur fighter back then, spent all his life savings to buy himself a top-of-the-line skyn with dreams of making it to the New Gladiators, the high-stakes reszo fighting league. Then, after everything the other version of me did, when I was restored the second time, Deacon had hijacked Dub's killer skyn and tried to use it to force his way back into my head. When that failed, Deacon walked Dub's skyn in front of a train to hide the evidence.

At first the authorities thought it was a suicide, and tried to get him disqualified from the Gladiator trials, but when I took down Deacon and everyone believed it was a rogue AI that had been killing reszos, the Gladiator Commission relented and allowed him to compete. Eventually he earned himself a spot in the arena, fighting for Humanitech's Gladiator team. I haven't talked to him in a few months, but I've followed his career, and he's racked up quite a kill streak in the arena. Undefeated in one-v-ones last I saw.

"Did he say what he needs help with?" I ask. Dub and I aren't exactly close, but we've been through a lot, and after what Deacon did to him, I'll help however I can. I owe him that at least.

"Nope," Connie says. "Just that he'd like you to meet him at the Ludus Humanitech tomorrow."

"I guess that'll give me an excuse to get out of the house again. Two days in a row even."

"Careful," Connie says with a sly grin, "you might decide you like it out here."

"I like it out here just fine," I say. "As comfortable as it is in the cabin, there's nothing like the feel of real flesh."

"Then you should get out more," Connie suggests, absently stroking the hollow of her throat with her index finger. There's absolutely nothing sexual about the gesture, but even still my pulse quickens and a tension throbs in my groin. Another reason to appreciate reality: it's analogue, and rife with contradiction. Flesh isn't always rational.

And, maybe, *that's* what we need—I could get Connie a skyn of her own.

I've been toying with the idea, just in the back of my mind, and I know it's crazy but the more I think about it... Why not?

Other than the fact I'm basically broke and skyns run into the millions, and modifying a Cortex to run a sprite instead of a psychorithm takes some doing.

What's more troubling is how fucked-up the idea is. It's one thing to cling to a dead loved one through a personality sprite, but it's a whole other level of messed up to contemplate a flesh-and-blood replacement body. I know I'm not the first person to ever consider this. I didn't come up with the idea out of thin air—there are plenty of stories about people who've recreated lost loves or dead children. Sure, no one thinks it's a particularly healthy thing to do, but who cares what people think?

I want to get back out into the world, and having Connie here to help would make that easier. So, other than the expense, and the considerable social stigma, and the questionable effect it'll have on my mental health, what's stopping me?

I sigh and take another drink. Connie's watching me, her face placid, endlessly patient. She'll wait for me forever, never lie to me, and never, ever leave me.

Arg. I can't, and I know it. I can't be that guy.

"Something bothering you?" Connie asks. "Why don't we talk about it?"

I shake my head. This isn't something she can help me with.

"Why don't we order," I suggest, but as I'm bringing up the menu there's a crash outside, then the *pap-pap-pap* of a semiautomatic weapon, and before I'm out of my seat to see what's happening, an explosion lights up the night.

You HUDDLE against the low stone wall of a balcony outside Building Three, crouched on the balls of your feet, staying silent, waiting for any hint of where your opponents might be. Unless they're complete Hanzos they'll know you're here too, know exactly where you landed and likely where you'll be posted up. They'll be waiting for you to make the first move so they can take shots at you, so you need to stay still and hope you spot them first.

You glance up and to the right and two rows of plain white text slide out from the edge of your vision. The countdown shows seventeen minutes and six seconds gone, with ninety-three players still alive. Only ninety-nine hours, forty-two minutes, and fifty-four seconds to go. For this round. Then you have to survive nine more.

That's what it'll take to win the Grand Century. Survive ten games—one thousand hours—and take home the massive prize that comes with it. No big deal, right?

Except everyone agrees it's next to impossible. Vegas puts your shot at a million to one, and that's being generous. There's a higher chance you'll be struck by lightning on the island than you'll win ten games in a row. The closest anyone's ever come is a guy called OVRshAdo. He's put in almost two thousand hours on the live game alone, who knows how many simmed, and he's still never won. He came close once, made it eight hundred and eighteen hours, until an unlucky headshot took him out early in game nine of his run.

He's a legend, best who ever played, and just your luck he's in this lobby right now, starting his three hundredth hour with this drop. For sure he's the deadliest enemy out here, his name's already graced the kill-feed twice, but if you want to win, you need to be better than the best.

Not that you have a choice. Losing isn't an option. The prize money for completing a Century is nearly twenty million dollars, free and clear, not including everything you bet on yourself to win—and you need it, need all of it. *Rael* needs it. The money will pay for the treatment he needs to survive, without it ...

Your eyes mist up and you swallow the sudden stab of heartache, fight the grief back down. You can't let the audience see you weak. Rael still has time, remember that. It's why you're here. You have the chance to save him.

It took everything for you to get here. First fragging your way up the leaderboards to earn an invite, then gambling the rest of your savings on the entry fee and the bets on yourself to win. Plus, you're still not entirely comfortable when fleshed. Even after the pregnancy and caring for Rael this past year and a half, you still prefer the cool sterility of living digital. You grew up virtual, been grinding crypto from a trodebed since you were a ward of the Alabama Foster System. And even after you escaped you chose the refuge of the digital life, immersed yourself in the virt mesh and abandoned the brutal uncertainty and ever-present pain of reality.

Forever, you thought.

At twenty-four you went reszo, sold off your perfectly healthy body for parts, and took all the money you'd earned over the years of tubing and bought yourself a one-way ticket to a purely virtual existence. Sure, you could have continued as a tuber without transitioning, even then the trodes had improved, the resolution was tight and the feedback had progressed from a simple one-way controller to completely interactive, and the implanted versions were even better, but you knew nothing would compare to living in the mesh as a native—as a psychorithm. Purely digital. Immortal. Protected from reality, and unable to be hurt by anyone.

You loved it. Released from the limitations of your sluggish blood and guts, the mesh became a fucking paradise. When you were playing a game and magical flames rippled up your arms, the cold heat and the otherworldly sense of power was like something you'd never imagined, like a drug they'd immediately outlaw if it existed out in the physic. And when you kicked off the ground and pulled yourself into flight, you couldn't believe why anyone would want to live in a world where none of it was possible.

You were happy, for a long time, and didn't once regret renouncing your flesh—until that tragedy with one of your fans sparked a fire in you, and your brain began aching for something the mesh couldn't give you: a family.

After ignoring the longing for as long as you could, and then actively hating it for a while, you realized it was the one thing you couldn't escape from, so once again you pulled together everything you'd earned, bought yourself a skyn, and had it impregnated.

They based the baby off your old DNA, added a bunch of good filler to make the kid strong and smart, and when you finally pushed it out and the bot laid it on your chest, naked and squirming, you felt the toggle in your head flip from a single-player focus, where you and you alone controlled the storyline, to a two-player co-op. And when he instinctively grabbed your thumb and nuzzled down into your breast, you felt, for the first time in your life, the power of unconditional love. The mesh never gave you that.

You're only here because of Rael, because if you don't win he'll die, and that will kill you, so ten wins it is. But you can't just stay hidden here for the next ninety-nine hours. You need to do something.

Other than the palms swaying in the gentle breeze, there's still no movement. You've already cleared the loot out of Buildings One, Two, and Three—snagged yourself a level-one helm and a small backpack with a single weapons hardpoint, a Phoenix MX-2 autoshotty, an AR comp, an SMG extended mag, a compass perq, another sixty seconds of safe-time, and a smoke grenade, but found nothing that'd let you shoot at range. There are a few bots hanging around, prowlers, the big cat-like hunter types with fangs and razor claws, but since you're still in the safe-zone, their green eyes and running lights show they're not threatening. You could try taking one out with the shotgun, they'd probably be carrying something worthwhile, but you're not ready to call attention to yourself by starting a bot war. With only a pistol and a shotgun you'll need to get right up close to engage, and if you're out here banging on the bots you'd leave yourself exposed.

So, the options are stay here and keep waiting for someone to show, or get aggressive and find some action. Your two opponents are north of you, one probably in the courtyard watching the apartments, and the other already looted through buildings Four, Five and Six. The courtyard guy's isolated. With you to the south and the other player to the north, he's got eyes on either side of him, and since the beach has the most open area, he's the obvious target. But the guy to the north will know that too ...

You know immediately what you're going to do. You can't stay here. No one likes a camper, and a big part of winning this game is getting the audience on your side. The crowd wants action, and the more attention you draw, the more likely you are to earn sponsored drops—and apart from the boss runs, all the best loot is sponsored.

"Hey y'all, *how 'bout a sick flank, come around from behind?*" you ask the aud silently, and they respond with a cheer that vibrates your rithm. They want action, so give 'em some.

You push off the wall and crouch-run across the main road cutting between Buildings Three and Four, keeping low in case someone spots you, and hug the wall as you head away from the beach. The skyn is starting to feel less like a costume you're wearing and more like *you*, and you push yourself to a sprint, see what your body can do. These skyns are above Human Standard to start, and between the muscle enhancers and the rithm upgrades and the powered armors available to loot, by the end of the game players can get downright supernatural.

You make it to the back side of the building, cut north along the rear wall, and your muscles ripple down your back as you hop the balcony railings one after the other.

The jungle's close by on your right, and you keep an eye out for movement as you race through the narrow backyards of the first-floor apartments. Someone could have slipped around and positioned themselves in the trees, but you're not expecting it, and when you hear the sharp smack of a Trident in burst mode echoing from the other side of the building, you know you made the right call. You put on speed and race to the north end of the complex, spin around the wall of Building Six, and inch your way to the corner looking out over the beach.

The shots came from the south, out closer to the water. You don't know who found the Trident, but they're hostile, whoever it is. If they're already shooting they won't want to duo up, which means they're the priority target. The trick then is to get close enough that your shotgun can take them down before they spot you and punch you full of holes at range.

Good news is, you're behind them.

And also, you're just better. Don't forget that—*you're a goddamned monster*. This may be your first live game, but you've been fragging guys your whole life. A kill's a kill, ain't no different than a virt.

There's not much protection out in the manicured paths of the rec area, nothing but trees and a couple thatched-roof walk-up bars—unless they're swimming submerged through the connected series of pools. Even fewer places to hide out on the beach, just umbrellas and lounge chairs until the docks. The kill-feed didn't ding though, so either the guy with the Trident missed or it wasn't enough to kill.

You pause and scan the edges of the scenery for movement, searching for anything that doesn't belong, then dart out of hiding, snake through a copse of trees, and go over a low hill into the rec area.

You duck behind a short trolley stacked with fluffy white towels and wait to see if anyone shoots at you. Unable to help yourself, you reach up and brush your fingers over the fancy stitching on the blue bird of the embroidered apartment logo and across the pillowy fabric. It's hard to believe the detail of this place. The apartments are all decorated, made up with beds that'll never be slept in and stocked with food that'll never be eaten, the grounds are well-maintained, and the bars lined with bottles. It's all real, but still it's all an illusion, set-dressing for the one thing this place was designed for—reszos killing each other for sport.

It's strange, all this happening in the real world and not running on a server somewhere—though nothing about this place is natural. The entire island is controlled by one man: Jefferson Wood, the reclusive billionaire who created Decimation Island. He's the CEO and Game Director and lives here full time, on the small island off the north-west coast, where he monitors the game states and devises new hotspots and makes sure everything runs smoothly.

The island itself is completely AI controlled—the bots and the NPCs and everything else that isn't a player. It's as much a participant in the game as anyone else, and it's also doing its best to kill you. You can't forget that—even when you think you're alone, the island is watching. It's the most dangerous thing out here.

You pick yourself up and move from cover to cover as best as you can, keeping your footsteps light, and by the time you get back to Building Four and haven't spotted anyone you wonder if you might have overplayed this, but then there's another shot and the crash of bottles shattering.

Near one of the bars, just ahead, not more than forty feet away.

"Come on out, be-atch," someone yells. A female voice, high-pitched and ragged with attitude—probably the one who's been shooting. "You know how this ends, don't make me waste ammo chasing you."

There's no response, neither verbal nor violent, and you

wonder if maybe the guy staying quiet is a live game virgin, yipping out under the pressure of their first drop. Though no one who makes it to the live game can be underestimated. Could be they just didn't find a weapon that'll stand up to the Trident and are doing their best to get away.

You creep up the path, staying low, with your shotgun loaded and level, ready to fire, and catch sight of the female player just ahead of you. You recognize her immediately. Should have known from her squawky voice. All the skyns are similar in build and height, no real difference in the performance between male and female, but by the shock of bright pink hair poking out from under her helmet you know you're looking at lucyFurr. She's a fixture on the live game circuit, with thousands of hours on her record, but she's impulsive, never making the decimation more than once or twice in a row. She plays style over longevity. Take her pink hair. It's a liability, makes her stand out—but that's her schtick and it works for her. She's always got a good audience, but you'd never partner with her. Neither of you would last very long, not the way she plays.

She's got her back to you, and doesn't have much in the way of protection—a helmet but no vest or other armor— and her gaze is fixed down the sights of her raised weapon as she stalks toward the shredded bar. You're close enough to hear the artificial click as she thumbs her weapon to single fire before she squeezes a few rounds into the bar, hoping to get a lucky hit on the guy on the other side. More bottles explode and glass goes flying everywhere, but she doesn't seem to hit anything else.

"That shitfucker's hiding," she says to the air, playing to her fans straight up out loud. She doesn't think she's in any danger, or doesn't care who else hears. "Come out and let me kill you, why doncha?"

Something smashes off to the right, and when lucyFurr snaps her weapon at the sound the guy on the other side of the bar—male, sandy hair, with a backpack that looks full of gear, but no weapon—makes a run for it, racing in the other direction. He jumps over a row of recliners and zigzags toward the shelter of a nearby stand of palms, trying to avoid the bullets he knows will be coming.

He's fast, but he won't make it.

You shoot before she does, punch a crater through the dark grey DI jumpsuit and into lucyFurr's back. A bright plume of blood mists the air and she screams as she's thrown forward and bounces off the bar. She hits the ground hard and her weapon skitters across the concrete.

A sudden unexpected gut-punch staggers you, and you take a step back.

You just shot someone—for real put a massive hole in someone's back—and now you're about to kill them. You've done it a million times in your life, caused far more bloody squibs than this, but that was all virtual, and somehow the reality of it is shocking, almost unbearable.

You tighten your grip on the shotgun to keep your hands from shaking.

It's a game. No different from a virt.

No one really dies here. You're all reszo, the only lasting punishment for losing is you don't get to keep the memory of your time on the island. Everything that happens here is property of the island, so when you lose, you return to your headspace as if you'd just loaded into the game and came instantly back. You get to find out how your run went by watching it secondhand, just like everyone else.

The only way you keep your memories is to win the Century, and no one's ever done that. So, if you planning on coming out the other side of this intact, you better get used to killing, 'cause that's the only way through.

lucyFurr pushes up to her hands and knees—she isn't dead, these skyns are hard to kill— and you fix the shotgun at her back and shoot again. She screams as a chunk of her shoulder blows off, but keeps fighting, rolls to her back with a pistol in her hand and rage in her eyes, and you put her lights out with a pop to the face that blasts a crater in her scowl. Her Cortex cracks with a blue-white flash through the gore, and just like that she's out of the game.

The initial shock has crystalized to exhilaration, and the trilling of your audience mixes with the tang of blood and gunpowder and the adrenaline pumping through your skyn and sends a rush straight to your head.

Damn that feels good.

Maybe a little *too* good.

You glance up and to the right as the kill-feed updates.

AniK@ downs lucyFurr. 92 remain.

Your head jangles as you absorb lucy's safe-time and the soft white photoo on your inner wrist spins up to show you've collected twenty-three minutes.

As you lower your weapon, the guy whose ass you just saved pops his head out from behind the tree and sees lucy-Furr spread out on the ground.

"Yo," he says, smirking. "So, you wanna group, or what?"

"Everyone stay low," I yell over the sudden confusion in the telecafe. If there's more shooting I don't want anyone to catch a stray round. The explosion was down the street, and no one in here was hurt, but we need to evacuate just the same. Smoke's drifting past the window, could be a fire or who knows what else going on out there. If it's a targeted attack we might be safer staying put, but if they're shyfted-up reszos out on a spree, shooting up the street for kicks, they could go building to building assassinating people. We're not safe here.

It's hard to concentrate. My adrenaline-boosted thoughts slam against the neural governor with a jittering de-sync. I push back against it, try to keep calm, stay focused, but it feels like my head's full of pudding. Deacon's contained, but he's still finding ways to make my life difficult.

I gather my wits, take a breath, and think next steps. First one's obvious: evacuate the scene.

A waiter stands shocked in the aisle behind me, staring out the window as frightened people flee past.

"Hey," I say to him, but he doesn't hear me. I give him a shake and he snaps his head around. "This place have a back entrance?"

At first I don't think he understands, but then he blinks and seems to come back to his senses.

"Into the alley," he says.

"Get everyone out," I say. "And don't stop running until you're clear. Got it?"

He nods, and I turn to tell the crowd to follow him, but they're way ahead of me; people are already hurrying to the back of the cafe. Another burst of gunfire erupts outside and the press for the exit intensifies. The shots are quieter though, like they've moved away from us.

As the cafe empties I turn back to Connie. "What's going on out there?"

She already has the answer for me. "SECNet reports three armed reszos just blasted their way into a building down the street. No identified fatalities, but a man has been shot and is bleeding heavily. Other injuries reported due to vehicle collisions and debris from the explosion."

"ETA on first responders?"

"The Police Service AMP says five minutes for a lawbot drop, with a tactical response team not far behind," Connie answers. "Fire and Emergency Services en route. Drones should be here any second. Everyone has been ordered to evacuate the scene." She pauses. "But you're not going to do that, are you?"

At least five minutes until help arrives and someone's out there bleeding. He could be dead by then.

Dammit.

"Doesn't look like it," I say.

She doesn't even pretend to be surprised. "The fighting has moved inside the building and the wounded man is to the south, on the sidewalk. Gunshots to the thigh and lower abdomen," she says. "From the way he's bleeding it's likely a bullet nicked the femoral artery. A tourniquet above the wound—"

"I can handle that much," I say, whipping my belt off and wrapping it around my fist. "Thanks for the help. See you at home?"

"I'll be waiting," she says and blows me a kiss as I run out the front door.

The sidewalks have cleared and the few cars that had drivers sit idle where their occupants abandoned them. Down the street the security gate surrounding a three-story brown-brick building is still smoldering, the front doors are wide open, and the deep whoop-whoop of a security klaxon pounds from inside.

Service drones arrive and take up a perimeter around the building, watching it from all angles, acting as scouts for the approaching lawbots. The drones ignore me as I sprint down the sidewalk, and once I'm south of the building entrance I cross the road and find the wounded man. He's a black guy, probably in his mid-fifties, and he's lying on the concrete, moaning shallowly in a pool of blood, fluttering in and out of consciousness. An umbrella and a bag of spilled curry containers lie beside him. A moment ago he was just grabbing take-out and now he's barely alive.

One of the drones turns its attention to me. "Clear the area," it orders, but I ignore it and kneel beside the wounded man.

"I got you," I say as I gently check his wounds. His gut's messed up, but probably won't kill him in the next few minutes—the blood pouring from his leg will. His eyes snap open as I try to shift his leg, and his face contorts in pain. "I'm sorry," I tell him, "but this is gonna hurt."

He groans as I snake my belt around his thigh just above the bullet hole and pull it as tight as I can. The man's eyes widen, then roll back in his head as he passes out—which is probably for the best. He can wake up in a hospital, full of painkillers.

There's a wad of napkins in the take-out bag, and I press them against the hole in his leg, trying to staunch the bleeding as much as I can. Sirens wail in the distance, an ambulance by the sound of it. Shouldn't be long now.

Another burst of gunfire clatters nearby, but it's louder again. They're back outside the building, off in the parking lot to the side. If my head were clearer, I wouldn't think twice about heading into the building after them. There could be more people injured inside, people who need help, but I can't risk it, not with my thoughts fogged up like a bathroom mirror. Besides, I have to move this guy. I don't want him to end up a target again if the shooting comes back this way.

Good thing he's unconscious, 'cause I have to grab him up under the arms and drag him, smearing a trail of blood behind us. I only get about ten meters before the air starts to quiver as the heavy drones arrive and drop three blue-and-white lawbots into the street. They hit with cushioned thuds, then rise, check their bearings, and launch forward on their powerful legs, shoulder lights flashing, headed for the building. They leap over the security gate, weapons out, and when met by shots, they return fire.

A fourth bot drops behind us, unfazed by the back-and-forth shooting. "This area is not safe," it says in a cool voice. "Please evacuate."

"He's been shot," I say, glancing down at the injured man. "He needs an EMT."

"First responders have been notified," the bot responds.

Then it bends and gathers the wounded man in its arms. "I will take him to safety. Please follow me."

The bot takes off, running smoothly while cradling the man in its arms. The ambulance is approaching from a side street. Red and white lights blink from the intersection just south.

I turn to follow the bot but whip around at the sound of a big six-wheeled cargo truck crashing through the security fence and out of the parking lot with a lawbot pinned to the front grill. The truck skids out onto the road and revs silently up to full speed. The bot can't hold on and falls under the truck's wheels as the big vehicle swerves around abandoned cars, heading north toward the highway.

One of the reszos must be driving, and another hangs from the handles on the rear doors, with a great big smile on her face like she's enjoying herself. But Connie said there were three of them. Where's the third?

There's only one lawbot left moving, and it's in bad shape. It limps over the downed fence, still firing, but can't keep up as it drags a ruined leg behind it, and that's when the third reszo appears.

He's in the air, having leapt off something on the other side of the fence, and now he's twisting to fire down at the lawbot with machine pistols in each hand as he passes overhead. Streams of bullets shred the bot's armor and it collapses. The reszo tucks and rolls on the concrete and comes up running, vaults over an abandoned car, and sprints flat out until he catches up with the speeding truck. Then he effortlessly springs up onto the roof, spins, around and looks back at the wreckage.

He notices me watching as they pull away, and he flips me a lazy salute as they wheel around the corner and out of sight.

My jaw hurts. I've been sitting grinding my teeth in frustration as the crime scene slowly evolved into an investigation. It feels like all I do lately is spend hours waiting around to talk to the cops after something goes to shit while I'm next door. I used to be part of this, and I was good at it, but now my head's so messed up I can barely exist out in the world.

At least tonight, after I give the constable my statement, instead of sweating my ass off on the curb she lets me chill in the back of the cruiser with the AC on until the detectives arrive. No one's exactly sure what the attack was about, but they're assuming it was a robbery. I checked in with Connie while I was waiting, and she told me the building is owned by CycloCode, a niche nanochip encoding company who does specialized work for a bunch of different customers all over the world. Nanochips are microscopic, usually smaller than a speck of dust, and are used in sensor swarms and security implants and consumer goods packaging and hundreds of other everyday things. They aren't valuable, and as far as I can tell, hardly worth the effort to fence. The truck they stole was probably worth more than the barrels of chips it contained.

The facility is mostly automated and no one inside was hurt, but the security bots were all blown to pieces. The robbers were systematic and took them all out, even ones they didn't need to. From a robbery standpoint, it doesn't make much sense. Seems more like they were in it for the kicks.

I heard the guy who was shot will survive though. He's in surgery now but is expected to pull through. The paramedics said I probably saved his life, though I'm not sure he'll ever feel safe going for take-out again.

It's infuriating. This kind of thing is happening too much. In gaining immortality, reszos have lost their sense of consequences, of right and wrong. The woman on the back of the truck was smiling, and the guy waved at me on his way out. Like it was all a game. If this is the way the world is heading, maybe I shouldn't be trying so hard to get back out here. I can find a nice virt to ride out the final years of civilization while the world kills itself.

Ugh. I'm being dramatic, feeling sorry for myself. I was here, and a man is alive because of it. That's something at least. I'll have to take what I can get.

I've been expecting a detective from the Psychorithm Crime Unit to arrive at any time but they're taking forever. Reszos were involved in the heist, but it doesn't seem like a Standards issue, so I expect the PCU will catch the case.

Usually that means Detective Karin Yellowbird, though it could be anyone. I've been out of the loop long enough I don't even know who's working there anymore. Still, I hope it's Yellowbird. I haven't seen her in a few weeks, not since that thing with Winter.

The detective arrives a few minutes later, and I'm

shocked when, instead of Yellowbird, my old boss, Inspector Chaddah herself, arrives. She's wearing a loose-fitting light purple suit, with her dark hair tucked under a darker purple-and-gold hijab. The constables snap to attention as she approaches for an update, but she must be already up to speed because her thick eyebrows remain impassive and the conversation doesn't last long. Then she comes to see me.

I get out of the cruiser and meet her and the air wraps around me like a hot, wet fist.

She looks at me and her lips set in a thin purple line. "You have a startling tendency of appearing at my crime scenes," she says, but continues before I can say anything. "You've been keeping well, Finsbury?"

"Can't complain, Inspector," I answer. I don't know what it is about her, but I always feel like I'm talking to a disappointed step-parent.

"Glad to hear it," she says, then the pleasantries are over. It's all business now. She glances over her shoulder at the CycloCode building. Constables are still milling about, keeping the bystanders outside the line of showtape while the forensic techs and their drones are sniffing for evidence. "How'd you come to be involved in the incident here?"

"I was across the street having dinner," I tell her. "Then the shooting started and I came to see what was going on."

"You simply happened to be in the area?"

I shrug. "I didn't plan on getting in the middle of a robbery, if that's what you mean."

The corner of her mouth twitches. "You heard shooting, and your first instinct was to run toward it?" she says. The cool detachment in her voice has eased.

"It wasn't my *first* instinct," I confess.

Her lips spread into a faint smile. "I understand you saved a man's life."

"Just slowed the bleeding. The paramedics did the hard work while I stood around and let the bad guys get away."

For just a moment her eyes narrow, then she says, "His name is Wallace Adi, he is a husband and father of two. You risked your life for his, and for that you have my personal thanks. I'm sure his family shares my sentiment."

There's a moment of quiet between us. We have history, Chaddah and I, and she knows more of it than I do.

I still don't remember everything about when I was Deacon, but there was a time that Inspector Chaddah and I had a decent relationship. She tried to help, and Deacon threw it back in her face.

I know I've lost her trust, and I don't blame her, but even though I was kicked off the force, I've never stopped feeling like a cop. Maybe that's why I'm having such a problem returning to the world: I used to help people, used to have a purpose, but what good am I to anyone now?

Though after helping Agent Wiser hunt down that psycho Winter, and now tonight, maybe there's a chance for me to regain some of what I lost.

"An idea what all this was about?" I ask, hoping Chaddah won't immediately shut me down.

She seems to be wondering the same thing, because she considers a moment before saying, "The skyns were unregistered, black market, and well Past-Standard. Any hope of identifying the occupants is slim, and their motives are unknown."

"What about the nanochips they stole? They're not valuable, why would anyone go to the trouble?"

She shakes her head. "We have to assume the chips had some value other than monetary; otherwise, why risk their skyns?"

"I don't know how much risk there was," I say, remembering how easily they took out the lawbots. "They were in and out like they'd done it a thousand times. The bots hardly slowed them down."

The frown returns to Chaddah's face. "Indeed," she says, noncommittal. There's something she's not telling me.

"There's more to this than souped-up skyns stealing tech, isn't there?"

Chaddah reaches up and smooths her eyebrows, then says, "You have connections on the street." It isn't a question. "Have you heard anything about a new shyft? They're calling it Killr."

"No," I say. "But I can ask around. What's this one do?"

"We're still not one hundred percent certain, but it seems to impart weapons knowledge and enhanced combat abilities, enhances neural response times. Effectively turns anyone who uses it into a lethal weapon."

"Jesus ..." I was generous thinking civilization still had a few years left, looks like we'll all be dead way sooner than that. "So now any asshole in a rented skyn can take out an entire TAC Team?"

"So it would seem." Chaddah's eyebrows press together. "My understanding, however, is that the shyft's targeting algorithms select against noncombatant casualties. Perhaps Mr. Adi was more than an innocent bystander."

"Or maybe it mistook his umbrella for a gun."

Chaddah only sighs. Shit her job sucks, yet I still wish I was back here with her.

"Do you have a source?" I ask after a second. "The shyfts have to be coming from somewhere."

"We don't."

"Does Standards? They must be all over this. What's Agent Wiser have to say?"

She makes a frustrated noise in her throat. "Nothing. So far."

There's a shyft in the wild that turns reszos into murder bots, and neither the cops or the feds know anything about it. *Great.* As if things weren't bad enough.

"So how can I help?" I ask.

Chaddah turns her head away, scans the crime scene again as if confirming that everyone's still where they're supposed to be, then takes a heavy breath and looks me dead in the eyes.

"The Service appreciates everything you've done since your last restoration, Finsbury," Chaddah says. "*I* appreciate it. Terminating that superintelligence, aiding in the apprehension of a serial killer, and now with your efforts tonight, I see you possess the desire to do good, and certainly the propensity or bad luck for finding yourself with occasion to act on it." She pauses, staring me down. "But you went bad once. I'm still not convinced you won't follow that path again."

She's right to be worried. It could happen, easier than she thinks. She doesn't know the truth about Deacon, at least I don't think she does, but I'm only standing here because of a convenient alibi. If she knew the truth, that it was Deacon and not a superintelligence who was responsible for all those terrible things—the mindjackings, the weapons charges, the lost time—she'd have my head in a stock and throw away the hash key. Crimes committed by a previous restoration aren't wiped out just because that version dies. I'm still me, and whether I like it or not, so was Deacon, which makes me responsible. Doesn't matter if I was there or not.

Tell her about Deacon.

The words leap to my tongue but I bite down on them

before they can escape. I've thought about it, long and hard. It eats at me. I know I should confess, tell her everything that happened. Deacon's dangerous, I've seen it. I can *feel* it. Every second I'm out here I put people in danger.

Do the right thing. Tell Chaddah now before something else terrible happens. Come clean, and if they have to wipe your Cortex to get rid of him, then fine, you've been dead before. It's not so bad, it's not anything—

"It won't," I say. "I'm not him."

Coward.

Chaddah smiles, but it doesn't reach her eyes. "I'm afraid that's not good enough," she says, then pauses, and suddenly this is an interrogation. The change is subtle, but I've run enough of them to sense it. Maybe she does know something after all. "I know you," she says. "Even if you're not the *you* I knew. He came to me angry, conflicted, and when it mattered he made the wrong decisions. Every time. He made the *selfish* decisions, until one of them got him killed. And then *you* came along."

My stomach clenches up and wants to argue, but I can't. She's right.

"I can't tell you what happened, I wasn't around then, but the man you knew became a person I don't understand. Whoever that other version of me was, I'm nothing like him."

At least that's what I keep telling myself. It's the only reason I haven't turned myself in.

"I've been watching you, Finsbury," she says. "I keep your case file on instant access. How you managed to best a superintelligence is a thing of wonder. The details are almost unbelievable. If the story wasn't so neat, so highly plausible based on the overwhelming physical and digital evidence, I'd find it difficult to believe."

I don't say anything. There's no point in arguing a question she hasn't asked.

"As I say, I'd like to believe you, Finsbury, but I've been over and over your file, and there's one thing doesn't sit well with me."

And there it is. I fight to keep my expression neutral. She's got a bomb to throw, and she's just lit the fuse. Maybe I won't need to confess after all.

"What's that?" I ask, playing along.

She pauses for effect, then studies my face as she says, "Doralai Wii."

Dora. I get a flash of her standing in my doorway, sweating, and then she's in my arms—but it's not me, not *my* memory.

I push the image from Deacon's life away, try to keep it from reaching my expression. Of all the people Deacon hurt, Dora got it the worst. First she and Deacon had an affair, then he hijacked her entire life to get to me, wore her body and assumed her identity for months while scheming to get back into my head. I've made amends with everyone else, everyone who'd let me anyway, but I still haven't heard from Dora. As far as I know no one has. Of everything Deacon did, what he did to Dora is my single biggest regret.

"Do you have something to tell me, Finsbury?" Chaddah asks.

I must not have hidden my reaction as well as I'd hoped. She could even be running an interrogation shyft, analyzing my micro-expressions.

"I'm just—have you talked to her?" I ask.

"I haven't," Chaddah replies, eyes fixed on mine. "And I've made considerable effort. She gave a brief statement after her mind was returned to her, but disappeared before she could be properly questioned, and now she's gone off-grid. Even SECNet can't locate her. Which leads me to ask, Mr. Gage, do you know where Doralai Wii is?"

Does she think I had something to do with her disappearing?

"No," I say, which is the one truth among all the lies. "I know she and the other version of me were involved and she was mindjacked because of it, and it makes me sick to think of what she went through. I've tried to reach out to her, but ... I get why she wouldn't want to talk to me. If I was her I wouldn't want to talk to me either."

Chaddah's nostrils flare, and I'm not sure which way this is going, but then she takes a breath, purses her lips, and says, "Okay, Finsbury. I'm going to choose to believe you."

"Thank you, Inspector," I say, feeling like absolute shit for how I'm abusing her trust. "And I'll ask around about that shyft. Someone has to know something."

"I'd appreciate that," she says, and turns to leave, but hesitates, catching my eye one last time. "Just so we're clear. I'm still watching you."

"I wouldn't have it any other way, Ma'am," I say.

She nods. "Be good, Fin," she says, adjusts her scarf, and strides away across the pavement.

You END up leaving the Sand Hawk pretty well geared. You keep lucyFurr's Trident and the fourteen rounds she had left and give LinkerJayyyy—your new squaddie—the automatic shotgun. Then, after you've spent twenty minutes weaving through the jungle ahead of him and he hasn't tried to shoot you in the back, you give him the ammo for it.

There are downsides to teaming, the most obvious being you can't trust anyone out here, but there are other little balancing penalties too. Like if you're grouped you can't use heals on yourself—if you get shot, someone else in your squad has to administer the medpatch, and if your partner is pinned down or too far away, you could bleed out with the meds still in your pack—and safe-time is pooled and shared out automatically, so there's no hoarding, but still everyone knows you're better off running as a group than alone. Having someone to watch your back can be a literal life-saver, and the safe-time clock runs out slower when you're teamed. Plenty of games end with geared-up four-man squads hunting each other through the red while relying on their safe-time to keep the bots at bay.

After you fist-bumped yourselves into a squad, you pulled up your sleeve and watched the photoo on your inner wrist shimmer as your safe-time jumped up another ten minutes. Linker found a twenty-minute chit, and you got half. It's not much, but you can work with it.

"I've seen your feed," Linker says as he brushes a large fan-shaped leaf aside. He's wearing lucy's helmet, scraped the pieces of her skull and Cortex out of it and strapped it on when you were divvying up her loot. "I'm glad *you* found me."

"You're just lucky lucyFurr had the Trident," you say. "Otherwise she'd be here instead of you."

She wouldn't though, no way you would have teamed with lucy, but it sounds cool. The audience eats toxic shit like that up.

You and Linker are creeping along a game path through the trees, stepping over vines and ducking around heavy green leaves. It'd be way easier to walk along the road, or better yet take one of the vehicles in the apartment garage—but players dropped all over. Someone could post up just out of sight off the road and wait until you drove into their crosshairs and that'd be game over right quick. So you're in here with the birds and the bugs and the bots. And while the game could make your skyns chemically invisible to the mosquitos, that'd make hiding in the jungle just that much simpler, so of course the little buggers are biting like they haven't eaten in weeks.

At least the bots are docile. It's still early and you're in the green, so you don't have to worry about them yet, but the zone's always shrinking, and getting caught in the jungle when you're out of time is also a good way to get killed. You can't hide forever. You've got a partner, now you need a plan.

"This is your first game, right?" he asks over his shoulder, then snaps still and swings his shotgun to the left, listening hard. You take a knee immediately. You're wearing armor, but you're not invincible. If someone starts shooting you want to make yourself as hard to hit as possible.

After a few seconds of typical jungle soundtrack—birds squawking and insects trilling—Linker shakes his head and continues.

"Yeah, you?"

"Second."

"How far'd you get last time?"

"Just under thirty," he admits. Thirty hours out of a hundred. Not great.

"Ambush?"

He hesitates. "Got caught sleeping," he finally says, and you can tell he's still not over it. He nodded off and woke up dead, not the most glamorous way to go. Sleep is another thing the game forces on you—all players need to go into a rest cycle for an hour out of every ten, that's ten whole hours a round spent helpless. Plenty of promising runs have been cut short because a player put off rest for too long and the game switched them off in the middle of a firefight. There's no reason for it—these skyns could go a hundred hours easy without needing a break—but it keeps the game interesting, and more importantly it's a great source of revenue. Millions of people are riding along in the heads of the Decimation Island players, and sponsors love a captive audience. Most players opt to rest a few minutes at a time, here and there. Long enough for the game to run an experiential ad, but not long enough for the audience to bother jumping heads.

There are perqs to shorten or eliminate the need for sleep, and security bots that'll stand guard and wake you up if enemies approach, but the best option to surviving a rest cycle is to have someone watch your skyn while you're out. The game does everything it can to encourage teaming, right up until the end, when it forces you to fight each other to the death.

But all that's something you can deal with later. You need to get there first.

"Let's hug the zone edge for a while," you suggest, but don't expect Linker to object. It's a standard, if conservative, play, especially for the early game. Keeping the bots at your back is solid insurance no one's behind you. It's also a good way to get pinched: someone holds you at bay while the zone washes over you and then you're fighting the bots too, but you've got time before that becomes a problem.

"Fine with me," Linker says. "We need better loot though. We could take out some bots—"

Sounds like a good way to get killed.

"Not in here," you say, keeping your snark to yourself. Don't want to piss your partner off right away. "Prowlers are made for the jungle, we're not. We shoot one and they'll all come running."

"What then?"

You've been thinking about this, got a plan in mind already. "Let's loot up at Ranger Rick's."

Linker stops and turns to face you. "You just said you wanted to play it safe and now you want to run Ranger Rick's? That's hardly keeping a low profile."

You know why he's worried. Ranger Rick's Last Stand would be a challenge for only two of you, and it'd take hours to complete, calling attention to yourselves the whole time as you shot your way through the storyline, but the loot at the end is well worth it. And you don't need to run the entire story to get there.

The hotspot contains a quest line featuring Space Ranger Rick, his plucky deputies, and their army of ragtag robot sidekicks trying to protect their jungle colony outpost against the waves of invading hostile bandits and their cybernetic wardogs. The Space Rangers and the bandits are all AI-controlled skyns, while the wardogs are roughed-up versions of the prowler bots that roam the red zone.

Most of the hotspots are like that, AI controlled bioSkyn NPCs, or bullet-sponge bots. Gives the players something to shoot at other than each other. More action to keep the audience entertained.

There are a bunch of different ways to play the Ranger Rick quest. If you go friendly, you'll need to find a way through the line of bandits surrounding the outpost, earned the confidence of the deputies manning the walls, then go on a series of errands for Rick—clear out some bandit camps, grab supplies from a nearby crash site, stuff like that —then help defend the outpost as the bandits stage their final assault. It's about a four-hour run, all in all, but not so hard a well-looted duo or even a competent solo couldn't finish it. And after you've fought off the bandits, Ranger Rick will open his armory and let you pick something from inside. Usually a killer piece of loot—a personal defense bot or an advanced weapon or skyn upgrade.

But there are other ways to get the loot, ones without all the busywork. Another popular tactic is to go in hot, shoot everything you see, bandits and deputies alike, until you get to the bunker, kill Ranger Rick, and loot his armory yourself. Fighting through the bandits *then* assaulting the outpost *then* beating Ranger Rick is no joke. The deputies are all skilled, and Rick's super hard to kill. It's usually a tactic for later in the game when teams are fully armored and carrying more powerful weapons. But unless you're at least a trio of survivors from last round coming in already geared, trying that this early in the game is just dumb.

Then there's the third method.

"Trust me," you say as you resume walking. "We got this."

FINALLY, nearly three hours after I met Connie at the tele-cafe, I get back to my room at In the Flesh. Shelt's been letting me squat in his playground designed for virt-locked reszos, people who went digital and never came back. Here they can rent a body for a few hours and indulge in a dose of reality. Real skin and bone, real food, and real sex.

Even the most dedicated virt-heads crave a bit of the physic now and then.

Shelt's got a bunch of themed rooms set up: an Old West brothel, a stateroom in a luxury space cruiser, a fantas-tical Middle Eastern sultan's tent, a bunch more. He's letting me stay in the Detective Room. It's got a worn desk and a cracked leather sofa and a window overlooking a busy 1930's L.A street scene, full of men in hats and bulbous vehicles. He thinks it's a huge joke, slides into a clipped newsie accent whenever he walks through the door. I don't mind though. Truth be told, I appreciate the irony of it.

There's a medpod hidden in the closet, but I just sink down onto the creaky couch, zone into my head through my cuff, and cast back into in my headspace in the Arctic.

I arrive on the stone pathway leading up to the log cabin. It's night but the stars are blazing. The cabin windows glow an inviting yellow and smoke wisps out the chimney. Behind me a seal barks as waves crash into the shore.

A tension I didn't know I'd been carrying in my chest loosens. Finally, I can relax.

This place is a lot different than the first house I had here. After my tangle with Winter I got rid of that Spartan concrete box and replaced it with this ramshackle two-room cabin. I built it myself: installed a crafting mod in my head-space, cranked up the speed of time, and went to work. The mod cheated a little and grew me a forest nearby—which, sure, isn't exactly true to geography, but whatever. It's my head, I can do what I want.

I spent weeks living in a tent and cooking over a camp-fire while I worked from dawn till dusk. I felled trees with an axe, then hewed them into notched logs and used a pulley system to place them, one by one. I laid the roof with lumber I planed myself. Then I mortared it all and I put in windows and a rustic kitchen and a wood-burning oven. I even made the furniture. Connie picked out the drapes and bedding. It's simple and rugged and smells like pine and smoke and dirt, and of all the places I've ever lived, this feels the most like home.

Connie comes out of the bedroom as I close and latch the front door behind me. She's only wearing a flannel shirt, with no makeup and her hair braided back in a ponytail, but she looks amazing. She pads over and gives me a hug, and I let myself sink into her arms.

"Are you okay?" she asks a moment later, after she's let me slip out of her grasp.

I walk to the kitchen and draw an ice-cold glass of water from the pump. It stings all the way down my throat.

"Better now," I say.

She just stands there, watching me, and without thinking I walk back over and kiss her. She melts into me, instantly responsive. Her arms wrap around my neck, and the feeling of her body against mine makes me dizzy. I know this isn't real, that none of this is real, but it feels right and that's all that matters.

I only wish we weren't stuck in here all the time. It would be so much easier transitioning into the world if only Connie was out there with me ...

So, I guess I've made up my mind.

I'll get her a skyn. On a trial basis only. Maybe Shelt will lend me one from the club. It doesn't have to look like Connie, I'm getting used to seeing past the surface to the person inside. Might even make it easier.

I break off the kiss, pull my head away, and look her in the eyes, and she looks back at me with all the love and warmth I remember from our life together.

"You're sure you're okay?" she asks. "Do you want to talk about it?"

Only hours ago I was wrestling with the idea of taking her into the world, but it makes so much sense. I'll ask Shelt about it tomorrow, after I get back from seeing Dub.

"Maybe later," I say, and she just nods. She'll never press. One of the small differences between her and the real Connie.

The side of her mouth curls up as she takes my hand and leads me into the bedroom. I know all this is unhealthy: our relationship, us having sex, all of it—especially bringing her out into the world—but I don't care. If I'm wrong, then so be it.

I want start rebuilding my life, but I can't do it by myself.

I need her with me.

PaulTheBaker defeats Ranger Rick.

THE KILL FEED dings with a good news/bad news situation. Ranger Rick just died, so you know you guessed right —someone's already running the hotspot—but the person who killed him is PaulTheBaker. TheBaker's a popular tuber with a big audience, and he's always flirting with the top of the leaderboards.

He's good. This might be harder than you thought.

Soon enough voices echo out from the open metal doors, sounds like three of them. They're shushed, but still loud enough you can hear them all the way inside the bunker. They've beat Ranger Rick and now they're jacked up on the kills and attention and flush with new loot. They're trying to be quiet, but they're excited, feeling invulnerable, and hopefully won't expect anyone to be waiting for them.

You're tucked back inside the gloom of the General Store, the Trident steadied on the shop counter and pointed out over the public square to the bunker.

You steady your grip on the weapon, double-check to be sure the safety's off. Normally the area inside the outpost is a PVP-free zone where killing other players isn't allowed, but now that the boss is dead all bets are off.

"Get ready," you tell your chat. *"Game's about to get spicy."*

Steady aim and quick reflexes aren't enough to win Decimation Island. You need every edge you can find to last a full ten rounds, and getting off to a strong start with good gear is one of the surest ways to set yourself up for the long game. Before you joined the lobby, you studied the leaderboards, learned as much as you could about the players you'd be facing in your first game—where they liked to drop and the weapons they preferred. It's the one advantage you get to bring with you into a new game: you know who your competition will be. After that your contact with the outside world shuts down and every round is a surprise until you die or you survive game ten.

There are plenty of familiar survivors in this round—OVRshAdo, Sp!ceWrack, GRadeeM, PaulTheBaker, Nitro-nguyen, KitKatMoxie—and all of them into multigame runs. You know PaulTheBaker is currently on a two-game streak and carried over an upgraded Cortex and a beefy DR-17 battlerifle from his past games—plus whatever he just looted from Rick's safe.

Your hands are sweating, and there's a fly buzzing around your head, but you can't let your concentration slip. You only get one shot at this.

You followed the trail of NPC corpses on the way into the outpost, and while you didn't find anything better than the Trident, you gathered up a whole bunch of ammo for it. Linker picked up level-one body armor and a light SMG to supplement his shotgun. In a fair fight, you'd be easily outmatched, but you don't plan on having a fair fight.

Linker's posted up close to the bunker entrance, hunkered down beside a stack of crates just outside the door, ready to rock. When PaulTheBaker and his squaddies emerge, you'll grab their attention with a burst from the Trident, hopefully deleting one of them instantly, then open fire as Linker shoots them in the back.

That's the plan, anyway.

"Wait for my shot," you silently say to Linker though teamspeak, and he nods in return. You're outnumbered three to two. The only way this works is if you catch them by surprise. Backup plan is you run, out the back door of the General Store and over the outpost wall into the jungle, hope Linker loses the coin flip and they chase him instead of you.

PaulTheBaker emerges first. You recognize his pale skin and white-blond hair even under the level-three helmet and armor. The long barrel of a sniper rifle is poking up from behind him—that'll be the Redeemer, Ranger Rick's personal weapon, and one of the best sniper rifles on the island. It's deadly, a mag rifle with massive range, a 16x zoom and aim-assist. It can pick off targets a mile away, but it's useless up close. That's why he's got it on his back and a bullpup carbine—an LX-7 with variable sights—in his hand. Too bad for him he's got it down at his side, not expecting he's about to need it.

He steps out of the bunker entrance into the bright early afternoon sun and raises his hand to shield his eyes. You're well hidden. He won't see you until it's too late.

A male and female you don't know follow him out. They look like they're having fun, joking around. They're well-geared too, both armored up. The female is dark-skinned, with a decent assault rifle, and she looted herself a level-three vest and helm, while the male is Asian, has the DR-17 Paul dropped with, and is wearing a tactical combat helmet—level-four protection with a full-face visor, a heads-up display, and sensors that'll instantly ping an enemy's position the second they start shooting.

He'll need to go first, that helmet will spot your position the second you start firing. You're playing guerrilla—if they immediately know where you are, you're done.

You raise the Trident and take a breath, aim down the sights at the Asian's unprotected neck. Usually a headshot is the way to go, but even with the Trident set to burst fire, his helmet would deflect too much damage, so you need to thread the needle between his chest plate and his helmet. You have one shot to take him out. Miss and this goes south real quick.

Before you can fire PaulTheBaker stops short, holding up his hand for silence, and they all freeze and immediately scan around them, searching for threats. Something's spooked him, maybe his audience reacting to your pending ambush, or just a game sense that something isn't right, but whatever it is only serves to do you a favor.

The worst thing you can do in this game is stand still long enough for someone to get a bead on you, and the Asian does just that. The Trident barks and the Asian goes down, clutching his throat as blood sprays through his fingers. If his friends survive they might be able to patch him up, but he won't last long.

The other two instantly whirl in your direction and open fire, their faces pulled to grimaces, but they don't know exactly where the shot came from and you're already out of sight, moving through the gloom of the General Store toward the back door. Their bullets smack into the wooden

ANIK@   63

boards and shatter the front windows, but don't come close to finding you.

You're already clear of the building when Linker opens up with the shotgun, six rapid-fire blasts, and by the time you've sprinted around the side of the building and have a sight line on the clearing, you see the female is hobbled, her legs useless and staining the dirt with black blood as she tries to pull herself into cover. Paul's all by himself now, but Linker has exposed himself.

AniK@ downs Glittrgun. 90 players remain.

Your wrist tingles as you absorb his safe-time.

"Anika!" Linker yells, frantic, as Paul's bullpup spits bullets at him. Your partner's only hiding behind a few crates, and all Paul needs to do is swing out to get a better angle and Linker is screwed.

But Linker's shout warns Paul that you're coming, and just as you move around the side of the General Store, Paul spins and empties the rest of his clip at you and you're just able to duck back behind the corner of the building as the bullets chew holes in the wood.

Then his weapon clicks dry, and you dart out, pressing the attack. Paul drops the bullpup, knowing he won't get the chance to reload, and tries to get the sniper off his back instead. His eyes go wide as he sees you step into the clearing, and he swallows hard, as if he can taste his death approaching.

That's two games down the drain.

"Hold up!" he cries, raising his hands as you step out, your Trident dead set on his chest. "We can work together."

You don't even consider it, and the instant after you pull the trigger Linker does the same.

LinkerJayyyy downs PaulTheBaker. 89 players remain.

The female is still alive, dragging herself away on her elbows, but her legs are ruined, and even if she applied meds it'd be a few hours before she'd be walking again. She knows she can't escape.

You bend over and collect Paul's bullpup, eject the magazine, load another, then ratchet back the slide.

"Fuck you!" she spits.

"You're not going to offer a team up?"

"Fuck no," she answers as her eyes dart around looking for something, anything, to save herself.

You bend and unfasten her helmet. "Let's not ruin this," you say, and she glares at you in defeat as you stand back up and blast her Cortex to plastic shards in the dirt.

AniK@ downs makeitrhymesister. 88 players remain.

You drop the helmet for Linker, then move back over to Glittrgun's corpse and take his. Thankfully it isn't full of blood, and you pull it over your head and lower the clear faceplate. It runs through the calibration process, then highlights Linker in green. The built-in tactical recognition system will immediately recognize weapons fire and show you where it's coming from. It won't help to survive the first shot, but after that it'll give you a good sense of where your enemies are. A useful tool in the jungle.

"Can I have this?" Linker asks. He's bent over PaulThe-Baker's body, stroking the Redeemer like he wants to fuck it. He knows how powerful that weapon is. It's point and click, can kill from a mile away. In the right hands it can win games, and you know you could use it well. But here, in the jungle, it's all but useless. The sight lines through the trees are shit. Might as well let him have it.

For now.

You shrug like you don't care one way or another, and he flinches slightly, like he was expecting an argument, but then seems to forget all about it as he gently brings the stock to his shoulder and settles in behind the optic, making a *pew* sound as he mimes firing.

You keep the helmet and PaulTheBaker's bullpup, leave the DR-17 for Linker if he wants it. The Trident is decent at medium to long range, the three-bullet pulse does major burst damage if you can hit, and the bullpup's shortened barrel is good up close. In addition to the weapons and full sets of level-three armor, you collect a bunch more safe-time, putting you and Linker over an hour each. PaulThe-Baker and his crew must have found a trove of chits when they looted the bunker.

Just over four hours into your first round and you're already fully geared and carrying a decent safe-time cushion. Not a bad start.

Only nine hundred and ninety-six more to go.

You give yourself a second to think of Rael, try to imagine the way he smells, then just as quickly push the thought away.

Out here emotion is a distraction, and distraction will get you killed quicker than any bullet.

Dub lives and trains at the Ludus Humanitech downtown, and I pull on my workout gear and huff my bike over to meet him. I figure there's no point in dressing up, Dub sure as hell won't bother. I work my frustration out through the pedals, trying to come up with reasons not to pull Connie's sprite into the real world, and quit once I hit an even dozen. There are plenty of reasons not to, but none of them matter. My mind's made up.

It takes forty minutes of weaving through the bike lanes to get to the arena. My workout clothes do their best to keep me cool but can't compete with the humidity and the heat my body is generating, and I arrive breathless and sweaty.

Sponsored by Humanitech, one of the richest gentech corporations on the planet, Dub's ludus is spread across most of a city block. They've got more money than God, but why they chose to spend it designing their New Gladiator arena to look like a massive crinkled tinfoil semi-sphere is anyone's guess. It's impossible to miss. The reflective surfaces catch the morning light, and the arena shines like a crumpled mirror ball.

I pause inside the wide front entrance and luxuriate in the frigid air blasting from the vent above the door. Once I've cooled down I take a few more steps into the lobby and a bot trundles up to me, lets me know I'm expected and that Dub is waiting inside. It shows me down a long curved hallway and out to the deep red bowl of the arena killing floor.

The lights are off except for intense spotlights shining down on Dub and the six red-and-white combots he's sparring with. Dub's skyn is huge, a black hole of muscle absorbing all the light in the arena. The rows of curved seats stretching up and around the circular arena are dark. It's like nothing exists but the fight.

The last time I was here Dub wasn't yet a gladiator. He was a novi, still auditioning, and Deacon had just dropped his mindjacked skyn in front of a train. Dub asked me to prove it wasn't a suicide, and I did, pinning it on that phantom superintelligence like everything else.

When I'd come that time, another novi named Nyx had been on the floor, running a clinic on how to dismember the lithe combat robots. She'd been all arrogance and flash, taking risks to prove how badass she was.

She made the team before Dub did, but flamed out spectacularly only a few months later when it turned out she was boosting her Cortex with a banned reaction-enhancing shyft before matches.

Now Dub's the one training, but he couldn't be any more different. He's all alone, doing this for himself, not an audience. The only thing they have in common is he's got a half-dozen long-limbed training bots trying to murder him too.

He's barefoot, unarmed, wearing only a pair of compression shorts. His skyn is a rich brown tone, so dark it's almost black, but offset by glowing photos in purple and green and teal. His face is a stone mask of concentration, and his body moves like molten ebony as he spins and whirls around the bots, keeping out of their reach but never attacking himself. I think he's just warming up.

I stop at the sloping arena edge to watch, but without taking his eyes off the advancing bots he calls out, "Come help," in a deep baritone that echoes in the cavernous arena.

He wants me to fight a combot? My head may be messed up, but I'm not stupid.

"Not without a big gun," I call back.

He shifts his legs, pushes a diving bot past him to the floor, smoothly glides around to face a second, then stiff-arms past a tight jab meant for his head.

"I promise I won't let them hurt you," he replies. "It'll do you good. You look like you need to work thorough some shit."

I roll my shoulders, flex my toes in my shoes. He's right. If pushing myself through traffic helps blunt the edge of the tension, I bet sparring with a bunch of deadly machines will blast it smooth. For a while at least.

"What the hell," I say as I jog toward him. "Never too early to die." The bots angle their sensors at me as I approach, but freeze their movement.

"Safety protocols engaged," a voice announces from above. Probably the training program. "An unknown combatant has entered the ring."

"Authorize for engagement," Dub says as he bounces from foot to foot. Even though the bots have suspended their attacks, he never lets down his guard. "Set new player for novi-level difficulty."

"Novi?" I say as I get up next to him and bring my

hands up in loose fists in front of my chest. "Taking it easy on me?"

"Arena easy is real-world lethal," Dub responds with a smile. "Just means they'll do their best not to actively take your head off. Ready?"

"I guess," I say, my confidence wavering as I stare down the six sinewy robots silently calculating how to dismember me.

Dub cocks his head, taking his eyes off his opponents for the first time since I arrived. "Don't guess," he growls. "Commit yourself to the fight, or step away."

I take a breath, get up on the balls of my feet, and tighten my body to react the second he gives the go ahead. "Ready."

"Resume training," Dub says, and the bots snap immediately into motion.

Everything else fades. Connie, Dora, Deacon. My fractured psyche. All of it recedes as four of the bots move to focus on Dub while two set their sights on me. My brain kicks into high gear, and I settle in to ride the wave of adrenaline but feel myself lurch as the neural governors kick in, preventing Deacon from finding a crack to exploit, and I nearly stumble.

Shit, I should have expected that. I'm playing with one hand tied behind my back.

My thoughts run in place as the bots swing around me. One moves to flank while the other immediately launches at me, trying to disable me with a blow to the solar plexus. It's fast, damn fast, and I barely dodge the jab and Dub has to save me from the follow-up roundhouse by stepping into the kick.

He grunts as he takes it on the arm, then whirls around with a flying heel that surprises two of the bots moving in.

"It's not enough to avoid the first blow," Dub says as he fends off another flurry of attacks, "if you're not prepared for the second."

He snaps his attention to a bot swinging around to get behind him, and I brush aside a left hook coming for my nose, then twist out of the way of the next bot's snap-kick and return with a kick of my own.

My foot catches the bot in the back and unbalances it, drives it away, but before I can get too pleased with myself I'm already retreating as its companion steps into me, knee raised. I block it with my forearm and hit it with a left-right combo that gives me enough space to slip away, but by now the other bot has returned and they stalk around me, searching for an opening.

I flick my eyes over to Dub. He's already downed two of his opponents. I've been playing patty-cake over here while he's been systematically disabling his attackers.

"I love this," Dub says, then roars as he takes two steps and leaps at one of the bots circling me. The bot instantly changes its stance to intercept him but somehow Dub's even faster. He slams into the bot with his shoulder, and as it falls backward he grabs it and slams it into the arena floor, then rolls over it and comes up facing back the way he came.

While I'm watching Dub show off I let the bot attacking me get too close, and it jams me in the side with a sharp blow. Pain flares up my abdomen and blanks out my vision, and my head's rocked back as it hits me again.

"Get your arms up," Dub yells. "Don't let it ground you."

With my eyes still foggy I sense more than see the bot's next kick coming, aiming to break my nose. I skip aside and catch the leg under my arm, and giving it everything I've got, lift the bot off its other leg and force it backwards. It hops, whirring on artificial muscle as it tries to keep its balance, but I press forward faster than it can adjust, driving it up the slope of the curved floor, and it finally topples over and lands on its back. It tries to get up but I kick its feet out from under it before it can rise, and then again, and just as I'm about to bring my heel down onto its head, Dub stops the fight.

"Halt program," he calls out, and the bots immediately power down. I lower my foot, but don't ease off the throttle, keep myself revving just in case this is another of Dub's lessons.

"You beat it," he says with a big grin. "But let's not cave its head in. Those things are expensive."

I'm dazed, breathing hard, but apart from the fuzz protecting me from Deacon, my head is clear. It's like I just power-washed the inside of my skull. Amazing what a few minutes of concentrated adrenaline will do.

There's no room for guilt and regret when you're fighting for your life.

Dub walks up out of the bowl into a dugout along the arena's edge and tosses me a towel from a stack.

"You're unfocused, but I could make a gladiator out of you," he says. The big white towel looks like a washcloth in his meaty fist as he rubs himself down.

"Thanks," I say, "but enough people try to kill me in real life, I don't want to make a hobby of it too."

Dub chuckles. "You do seem to get your nose stuck where it don't belong."

"It's my curse." I say as I finish drying myself and toss the towel into the nearby receptacle. "Which I assume is why you asked me here. You sure didn't need a workout partner."

He wraps the towel around his neck and glances at the

ceiling as if we're being watched. There's no one around, but that doesn't mean anything. I'm sure the ludus AMP is listening to every word we say.

"Not here," he says, and he leads me off the curved floor to the dugout and through the exit at the far end, then through a security gate and deeper into the building.

He doesn't say anything as we pass a training room and a kitchen and down a long hallway to door with his name on it. It opens ahead of us, and he waves me in. The living quarters aren't big, but this room is luxurious compared to the closet he was living in when I was last here. He had a small, ascetic room with nothing more than a cot, but it looks like he might have loosened up a little. Not as far as you'd expect, being one of the New Gladiator's biggest stars and boasting a legion of fans, but at least he's allowed himself a bedroom.

Still, Dub being Dub, he's kept his apartment simple, with high ceilings and no windows, bare beige walls, and the only light coming from a wallscreen radiating a yellowish glow. There are a couple chairs, a couch, and a kitchenette, but no decorations or personal effects save for a single shelf adorned with the various prizes and trophies he's collected over the years.

He waves me to the low couch and pads off toward the kitchen, his massive body a jarring contradiction in this sanitized domestic space.

"You're moving up in the world," I say as I drop down onto the light green couch.

He flashes me a lopsided grin. "Everything I need is out there," he says, waving back the way we came. "Want something to drink?"

"Water's fine," I reply. He pulls a jar of something thick and milky from the fridge and swallows until it's gone, then wipes his mouth with his towel. "Go off the record, please," he says to the air as he fills a glass with water and ice at the fridge and carries it over to me.

"Off the record confirmed," a disembodied voice acknowledges.

"Why all the secrecy?" I ask and take the glass from him. I can't help but shake my head at the size difference between our hands.

He lowers himself into a wide chair that groans under his weight. "I need you to do something for me."

"Name it."

He leans forward. "I want you to check someone out."

My first instinct is to say "no," that I'm not in that business anymore, but Connie made me promise to at least hear him out.

"You want this done quietly, I assume?"

"Silently," he replies, and his massive face droops. The confidence he exuded a few moments ago in the arena is gone, replaced by a pensive reluctance.

"I'll be as discreet as I can," I say, "but I can't promise anything."

Dub sighs and rubs his bald head with the towel once more. "We're auditioning for a new gladiator," he says. "The novi are settled, and the trials are coming up, and they all seem like good kids, mostly, but..."

"But?"

He takes another deep breath. "I've got a bad feeling about one of them."

"And this is who you need checked out?"

He nods but doesn't say anything else.

"Look, Dub, I get you're conflicted about this, but you must have had good reason to call me, right? I'm sure you thought long and hard before you did. It's just us. You can trust me."

Even with the AMP leaving us alone, he's reluctant to answer. "What if I'm wrong? What if she makes the team and it got out I had a novi investigated? We have to work as a team. No one can know, Fin. You have to promise me."

It's obviously eating him up. Dub is as pure-hearted as anyone I've ever met, and he wouldn't have called me here unless he thought he had no other choice.

"The only way I can guarantee no one will find out is if you drop it and I walk away right now."

He shakes his head. "I love the gladiators, and I love this team. I'd do anything to protect it. Especially after how Nyx flamed out. I don't want any more surprises hurting our reputation."

"I won't tell anyone," I say. "But it's a risk. The only way we can be sure you won't end up involved is to stay out of it."

"I can't do that."

"Then tell me what's going on, and live with the consequences."

He studies my face for a moment, his big nostrils flaring, and then nods. "Anika Reyes," he says, and waits for my reaction.

I don't usually keep up with sports, but even I've heard of Anika Reyes, A.K.A. AniK@. She was all over the feeds a few weeks ago. She was a tuber superstar, but then she retired and there was something about a sick kid and she returned to gaming and fought back through the digital ranks to qualify for the Decimation Island Live Game.

Against all odds she nearly survived a full ten-match run, placed in the top ten nine games in a row, and in the last hour of her tenth game, moments before becoming the first person to complete a century and earning herself a fortune, she blew her own head off, live to feed, and forfeited it all.

No one knows why, or what caused her to do it, and she isn't talking. She didn't get to keep her memories when she lost so she might not even know herself.

I didn't realize she was trying out for the Gladiators, but that's not a surprise. I don't get out much. Still, from what little I've heard, she was something of a phenomenon. I imagine she'd fit right in here.

"What'd she do to make you suspicious?"

"She offed herself in front of the world!" Dub says, frustrated, but catches himself. "Who knows what she's gonna do next? She's unpredictable and could be dangerous. How am I supposed to trust her not to pull that shit again?"

"I'm sure the ludus security team did background checks ..."

"Of course, tip to tail," Dub says, shifting in his seat, agitated. "She wouldn'ta got this far otherwise. They cleared her, but I know there's something going on with her, in my gut, and my gut is never wrong."

I'm no stranger to hunches, I've followed enough of my own down sketchy rabbit holes, but he needs to give me something to go on. "I need more than a feeling to work with, Dub."

He shrugs. "That's the problem—there's nothing. Just, like someone's behind me every time she's around. I see her looking at me. She knows I know she's up to something."

"But you *don't* know anything. Maybe she's worried about you watching her all the time. Are you sure you're not being paranoid? You were hurt by Nyx and you don't want to let it happen again and you're jumping at shadows.

Besides, I don't know how I'll find anything the security team didn't."

"Work your magic," he says.

Magic? What magic? I take a sip of water, trying to figure out my next move. Most likely he's just let his imagination run away with him, but I can't discount him entirely. I don't really want to get involved, but he's clearly distressed and I should help him if I can.

"How about this: let me talk to her. Maybe I'll see what you do."

Dub shakes his head. "She doesn't do interviews, won't talk to you—won't talk to anyone. She only comes out of her room for team practice; otherwise, she's grinding frags eighteen hours a day."

"You could set it up, say it's something official."

"Nope. Then she'd know I was involved."

"Look, Dub," I say, raising my shoulders, "I want to help you, but you need to understand—you've got absolutely nothing here. She passed a background check. You said yourself there's no evidence. We're friends, but I'm not about to tear through an innocent person's life just because you ask. If I can't at least talk to her, there isn't much I can do."

"But—" he starts, and has nothing to follow it up with. He rubs his towel over his head again. He still hasn't stopped sweating from the workout. Or maybe it's not the exercise, maybe he's just that anxious.

I set the glass on the couch armrest and stand. I'm willing to help, but not without more to go on. "I'm sorry, Dub. If you find anything else—"

"Wait," he interrupts, standing to block my path. Not that I could get past him if I wanted to. "I have an idea.

Tomorrow night Humanitech is unveiling this season's line of skyns. I can get you on the guest list."

I freeze in alarm. Parties scare me more than the combots did. "I don't want on the guest list."

"Trust me, this is perfect."

"Look, Dub, that's not my thing. Besides"—my mind immediately begins formulating excuses and I glance down at the workout gear I'm wearing—"these are the nicest clothes I have."

"Come, talk to her. Just for a few minutes. If you don't see what I do, I'll let it go."

"It's *really* not—"

"Please," Dub says. "Go and prove me wrong. I hope you do."

I don't want to, but how can I say no?

"Fine," I say. "But you're buying me a new suit."

"Done," he says, and reaches out to grab me in a big, damp hug.

Ugh. I was planning on spending the weekend in with Connie. Now I'm gonna spend it hobnobbing with the one-percenters.

All that, plus now I have to go shopping.

Every year the big gentech companies release their new lines of bioSkyns, from the cheap and cheerful standard models that'll need replacing in a decade when their hastily scafed joints start to fail, to the Standards-busting military jobs you'll only ever see the instant before they kill you.

As far as the public is concerned the arena models are the top of the line, and they're stuffed to the gills with the latest genetic and cybernetic enhancements—literally in some cases. One of last year's new features was integrated organic gills. But even though they're highly regulated, they're not classified, so Humanitech makes a big deal out of showing them off.

This year they rented out the glassed-in ballroom of the Hotel Mundi downtown for their reveal gala. The Mundi is stratospherically exclusive, and even as I'm approaching on foot I can tell security is thick. The sidewalks surrounding the hotel are closed, and bots, drones, and guards wearing combat skyns and tactical armor patrol the perimeter. I've seen less hardware deployed for presidential visits. I can't imagine anyone would be stupid enough to try to crash the party, but Humanitech isn't taking any chances in protecting their new line of flesh.

There's a full-on red carpet affair at the front entrance, and I hang back for a bit, stalling as I watch the wall of paps call out to the influencers and all-star tubers and gladiators from every ludus around the world as they spill out of the slow-moving train of limos to take their turn mugging for the cameras.

I've been dreading this. I told Dub I'd help him, and I'll do what I can, but the prospect of an evening of schmoozing agony has my gut in knots. Forcing me to get all fancied up and play socialite is my perfect torture. I'd confess anything right now if it meant I didn't have to go inside.

Connie was excited though. When I got home yesterday and told her what Dub wanted me to do she immediately ordered a new suit, didn't even ask, like she'd already had it picked out and was only waiting for an excuse to pull the trigger. I didn't even mind, it spared me the ordeal finding one myself.

A drone dropped it at Shelt's this morning: a perfectly tailored three-piece in dusky blue with narrow lapels, a copper vest, and shoes to match. I don't want to know how much it cost, but I know I didn't pay for it, so I guess it doesn't matter. It's by far the nicest suit I've ever owned, and as far as I'm concerned it's disposable. I don't plan on wearing it again.

I linger on the sidewalk until the heat becomes more unbearable than the prospect of what's waiting for me inside, then dodge through the road traffic and push through the crowd to the carpet. A security bot moves to intercept me but must match my biokin to the guest list, because it just as deftly steps aside to let me pass. Here I'd been hoping Dub might forget to add me and I'd be turned away. No such luck.

The ballroom's just off the hotel's lobby, and after another biokin scan by an imposing reszo in a black suit with eyes to match, I'm waved in.

The gala is roaring and the buzz of a thousand conversations compresses my chest as I step inside. The room is a giant glass box, like a terrarium stuck to the side of the hotel, and big enough for a massive banyan tree to grow up in the middle of the floor. The tree stands like a big green umbrella, and flittering wisps of light dance among its dense, leathery leaves. The tree looks like it must be a hundred years old, but it can't be. The hotel didn't exist five years ago, and banyan trees aren't known for naturally occurring in downtown Toronto. Some clever genitect must have figured a way to grow a century's worth of tree in a few years. Sounds crazy, but these days, with enough money, nothing is impossible.

And the other guests, they're just as impossible as the tree. Almost everyone here is wearing a body they weren't born with. The crowd must be ninety, ninety-five percent reszo. I can tell because each and every one of them is gorgeous and styled to within millimeter tolerance. This must be the largest group of beautiful people I've ever seen gathered in one place.

It even smells expensive—woodsy but salty, like someone scrubbed the sea of all the dead fish stink, mixed it with the peppery pear of a desert flower, and made a perfume out of it. A wide doorway in the far wall is open to the enclosed patio beyond, and the smell seems to be wafting in from out there, probably from some newly invented flower they grew for the occasion.

A band performs under the banyan's canopy, swaying in

time, five identical female skyns with long raven hair and blood-red evening gowns playing a light Asian jazz—taiko drums, a saxophone, a long narrow banjo, and a squeaky silver instrument that looks like a cross between a trumpet and a flute, with the fifth member singing high-pitched chirps and whistles and warbles like she's some kind of human-bird hybrid. Bars are set up at each end of the room, serving both alcohol and shyfts, and bots glide around holding trays of champagne and hors d'oeuvres: little foam cakes and cubes of glistening red meat and spoons filled with iridescent edible pearls.

As stunning as the guests are, the true stars of the evening are Humanitech's new skyns. They're all up for display on raised platforms, skyns so arresting in their perfection they barely look human, like an Italian master carved them from marble. They're naked, save for the modesty bands around their groins, each platform containing two skyns apiece, male models and female models and models with aspects of each. They vary in color and ethnicity, including some Humanitech must have made up themselves, like the narrow features, elongated limbs, and particularly subtle shade of purple one pair is sporting.

While most of these new releases are already available for preorder, and eventually will be worn by the elites of the reszo world, the real showstoppers are the skyns designed specifically for the New Gladiators. These are the Formula One models, built with every genetic and biotech-nological advantage Humanitech can offer—carbon fiber musculature, reinforced bone structure, sub-cu armor sheathing, lightning-fast optogenetic neurons, quick-healing cells, and who knows what else. They're incredibly dangerous, not even close to street legal, and only allowed to exist at all because the New Gladiators get a pass from

Human Standards to produce skyns for the games, and only for the games, and only under the tightest of restrictions.

If one of these things were to escape into the wild it'd be shot on sight, and it wouldn't go down easy.

The skyns aren't set up just for show either. Human-itech has them wired to let the guests take the bodies for test drives—even the gladiator models. Beside each platform are two seated stations with direct neural connections to the skyns, and anyone can sit down and cast in and get a feel for what it's like to live inside the latest in cutting-edge flesh.

The skyns jerk around on the platforms, hopping and flexing and running in circles as host after host takes their turn, but as bad as some of the inhabitants are, none of the skyns ever falls over the edge or jumps off the platforms or does anything too off-putting. They must have an auto-mated backup control system in place to keep them from going too far, which is a good thing, especially if some troll got inside one of those arena models and decided to see what kind of damage it could do.

The crowd is thickest near the arena models, and so I retreat to the other side of the room, and that's where I spot Anika, standing alone at a high table, staring at the rising bubbles in her drink. She doesn't look much like she wants to be here either.

Her skyn is as tall as mine, muscled but not obnoxiously, and her hair is short and shaggy and the color of fired brass. A shotgun blast of freckles disguises her narrow square nose, and her lips are thin and pale. In a room full of impos-sibly beautiful people, she's the only one who looks real.

The only thing that gives her away as reszo are her eyes. They're too big and too intensely green to be anything but artificial. She's wearing a floor-length, curve-hugging green dress and an expression that makes it clear she wants to be left alone.

I recognize her from the research I did yesterday afternoon while Connie was suit shopping. I knew a little about her before, but Dub didn't tell me she had such a tragic story. Someone cut a doc together about her life, and after watching it I'm sure Dub's concerns about her are all in his overprotective head.

She was born in flood-ravaged Alabama, abandoned by her parents, and raised in a foster home where she'd spend half of every day plugged into the link, grinding video games for crypto to pay her room and board. She found she was good at it, and angled her skill for fragging-out into an early release, and then went on to become a tuber superstar.

By the time she was of age to go digital, she'd earned more than enough to cover the cost, and with the benefit of an untiring Cortex, her fame exploded. It was then, at the height of her popularity, that she gave it all up to start a family. She had a kid grown from her stored genes, and eighteen months after he was born, when her son's genetic code began to unravel, she threw herself into trying to win Decimation Island to raise the millions it would take to pay for a life-saving re-sequencing. He died while she was in-game, and then, days later, and only minutes from taking home the biggest single purse in sports history, she killed herself in front of the world.

That was only a month ago, and now she's here, a New Gladiator novi, and she looks like she'd rather be anywhere else.

I grab a flute of champagne from a passing bot, settle in at a nearby standing table, and study her over the rim of the glass as I pretend to sip. She isn't alone for long though. People obviously know who she is, and more than one confident reszo sidles up and attempts to strike up a conversation.

She shoots them all down, men and women both. Some with curt, single-word snipes of rejection, but most with long, withering looks that make it clear she won't be responsible for what happens if they don't immediately back off.

One guy doesn't take the hint to disengage, and she leans in and whispers something, and whatever it is she says to him makes him scurry off with his face drawn like he's about to be sick.

Anika doesn't want to talk to anyone, including me. She just wants to live in her pain. I get it, I felt the same way when I first restored. I didn't want to talk either, and made it very clear to everyone who tried. After learning more about her I can only imagine the suspicious behavior Dub sees is simply a case of barely masked grief. She's just lost her son and is still in the middle of one of the biggest controversies in sports history—she blew her own head off in front of the world. He must know all that as well as I do. He can't be blind to what she's going through.

I think Dub was scarred by Nyx's betrayal and he's being hypersensitive now, searching for problems where none exist. I know Dub's intentions are pure, but I don't need to investigate Anika to see she's hurting and curled into a ball to protect herself. That'd explain her behavior better than any sinister motive Dub's cooked up in his head.

Still, I'm here. I'll give it a shot and try talking to her, just to be sure, so I can go back to Dub and tell him his fears are unfounded with a clear conscience. Lucky for me it shouldn't take long. I figure I'll last about two seconds before she's done with me and I can get out of here.

She watches me approach, and her eyes grow narrower

with every step I take, but I do my best to ignore her deepening glare and stop at her table.

"Finally worked up the nerve to make your big move?" she says in her drawn-out Southern accent. Her green eyes flare as she steps back from the table, lowers her hands, and squares her shoulders. "You stood over there and watched me send everyone else packing, and still you thought you'd impose yourself on me, like you're somehow better than everyone else. Which means either you're a moron and anything you say would only waste my time"—she lowers her head, and her voice tightens to a snarl—"*or* you're so sure of your own fucking importance that beating you to a hardlock right here, in front of everyone, would be a public fucking service. So, which is it gonna be?"

Jesus. She's packing some anger.

"Dub said you were tough," I say, with a smile I hope is covering the anxiety bubbling in my guts. "But he was way underselling it."

I can hold my own in a fight, but I don't want to take the chance, especially not with someone on the verge of becoming a gladiator. She's close enough to the edge as it is, I don't want to be the one who pushes her over.

Dub's name pauses her, but only for a second. She makes a disbelieving noise in her throat. "Name dropping, *really*? That's your play?"

"It's not a play," I say, surprised we're still talking. I hadn't planned this far ahead. "I saw him this morning at the ludus."

"Bullshit," she says.

I shrug. "Check it out for yourself. I'm Finsbury Gage." I stick out my hand, but she just stares at it until I put it away. "Check with the ludus, it'll tell you I was there. Dub gave me his ticket," I say, then huff out a breath through my nose, like this is all a big joke and I'm the punch line. "Gave ... *Insisted*, more like." I glance at the carnival around us. "I didn't want to be here at all. I had to go out and buy a suit I'll never wear again so I could go to a party I have no interest in attending."

This seems to throw her. Her shoulders relax a bit. I've won a reprieve from a beating, but only for a few more seconds.

"Then why come?" she asks. "I drew the short straw and I *have* to be here, but I don't see a gun to your head."

"You know Dub, right?"

She wiggles her head, noncommittal. "Only a little."

"Once you do, you'll understand. I met him in restoration counseling, back before the Gladiators, when he was fighting in unsanctioned basement matches. I was in a bad place, and he helped me out, so when he asked me to do him a favor and come tonight in his place, I couldn't say no. And believe me, I tried."

The anxiety's got me talking fast. I haven't said that much all at once since I can't remember when.

"And why was he so insistent?"

"Two reasons," I say, my lips working on their own. "He thinks I spend too much time in my head, hiding away from the world, and thought a little forced socialization would do me some good—like immunotherapy for the soul."

She shakes her head. "You do everything you're told?"

"Not usually," I say. "But that brings me to the second reason."

"Which is?"

I hesitate, then just go for it. "You."

Her face hardens as she steps back, putting distance between us. "What the fuck does *that* mean?"

I raise my hands in immediate submission. "Only that

Dub said you'd be here by yourself, and that you'd be miserable, and he figured we could be miserable together. He felt guilty, you being here on your own."

I know Dub wanted his name kept out of it, but at this point I've got no other cards to play. Besides, a half truth is better than any lie.

"So this is, what? A setup? I don't give a shit who he is, I don't need Ari Dubecki playing matchmaker."

"No, no," I shake my head. "It's not like that. More like someone you could stand beside and scowl at all this nonsense in silence with."

"Well, thanks, but you can fuck off home now, and you can tell Dub to stay out of my business. I don't need anyone to look out for me." She looks up and out at the crowd. "Now it's time for you to find somewhere else to stand."

Fine with me, I'm breathless and light headed as it is. Besides, I figure I've got what I came for. She's miserable and pushing everyone away, but that doesn't mean she's up to something. It only means she's broken, just like the rest of us. Dub should have sent Shelt instead. He's the one she needs to talk to.

"Fair enough," I say, figuring we're done here. "Nice to meet you—"

I'm stepping away from the table when a sudden noise from outside on the patio stops me in my tracks. Then there's a rattle of gunfire and the thunder of fast-moving fabric and three loud *whomps* like something hitting the ground at high speed.

My stomach clenches as a black-clad figure strides in through the patio's wide doors, a compact assault rifle in each hand, and fires them into the ceiling, drawing everyone's attention. The bullets smack off the inside of the bulletproof glass and the room's buzz shifts an octave toward panic as the band squeaks to a halt. The guests on the other side of the ballroom still don't know what's going on, but those closest are retreating, pushing back toward the lobby doors.

"This," he yells, "is a robbery!" His face is hidden behind a mirrored black visor and his accent is shaved flat. He could be anyone, but no doubt he's reszo. Two more follow him in, just as anonymous, both strapped up and armored, guns raised, ready to rock. They're each running double fisted, like the leader.

There wasn't much visible security earlier, but lawbots have already appeared and are stalking toward the intruders from the lobby, and a few grey-suited guests have drawn weapons and are swimming upstream against the crowd.

The lead guy sees them coming. "Anyone allergic to high-speed tungsten should hit the deck in three...two..."

I crouch even though the high table won't be much cover, and glance up at Anika. She hasn't budged. Doesn't so much as flinch as the bullets fly, only lifts her glass and takes a sip of her drink, watching it all go down.

The screams start the instant after the firing does, as the security and the invaders open up on each other. Half the crowd hits the floor while those nearest the doors surge harder toward the lobby. Even though most of the people in here are immortal and not in any real danger of dying—at most they'd lose any memories not secured at the brain bank —their bodies are super expensive, and getting shot still hurts.

I glance back up at Anika again. *What's she waiting for?* A gunfight's popping off not twenty meters from us and she hasn't moved, doesn't seem bothered in the slightest. Instead she just stands there and watches, ignoring the flying bullets like she's certain nothing could ever hurt her.

"You're from Mississippi, yeah?" Linker's voice whispers out of the darkness as you creep through the black jungle night. "Biloxi?"

You've been moving for hours but haven't gone far. Skipping though the jungle in careful spurts is the safest way to travel, but doesn't cover much ground. The stars are bright powder across the sky when they peek through the canopy, but that doesn't happen often, and there's no moon. Fireflies flicker in the air and bioluminescent flowers glow on the jungle floor, but still you can barely see. A low-light perq would be useful right about now.

"Alabama," you correct him. "Mobile."

You and Linker don't talk much, but you're good with that. Mindless chitchat is the hardest part about teaming with randos. The kid's cool though, not too annoying. You'd never be best friends but there's a give and take. He knows the game and wants to win and you figure you can trust him, might even be able to keep together for a few games if you both survive this one.

"Close though," he says. "I had a cousin in Biloxi. Rachel. She came to live with us in Nashville after the floods got too bad down there. You remind me of her a little, your accent anyway."

Your throat catches in a momentary blaze of anxiety as Foster Mother's face scowls at you from out of the darkness. The floods ruined your life too, left you in the care of the foster system. If only you'd had a cousin to live with, who knows what might have been different?

Though, then you wouldn't be here. As bad as it was, it made you who you are.

"Were you close?" you ask after a moment, and you're relieved when your voice sounds relatively normal. Even after all this time you still have the occasional nightmare where you're sent back to the foster system.

"Nah," he replies. "She was older, ran away not too long after. Haven't heard from her since."

"How long ago was that?"

"Going on a decade now," he says, his voice even softer.

You both know what that means, most likely anyway, and the conversation dries up.

A moment later a tropical bird squawks out a warning from the trees close by, and you both drop low, holding your breath, hearts racing and weapons ready, but nothing else follows but the nighttime quaver of jungle insects you pick yourselves up and resume walking.

"You don't sound like you're from Tennessee," you say a few minutes later. As much as you usually hate it, a little mindless convo doesn't seem so bad right now, gives you something other than what's going on back home to think about while you creep through the darkness.

"Had it removed first chance I could," he says. "I

thought it made me sound like a hick, but I'm kinda regretting it now. At least I had some character, you know? Now I come off like a Canadian news reader."

You muffle a laugh, because that's exactly what he sounds like—like he's from nowhere in particular. "Nah," you say, "give yourself a little credit—you could pass for a Californian math teacher, no problem."

"Oh thanks," he replies, but you can hear the smile in his voice. "Much better."

It's a good thing you're getting along, because you've still got thirty-two hours left together, and who knows how many more after that. With a solid duo you could recruit a third and a fourth and stick together for a while. You don't want to jinx it, but so far things are looking good.

Now's the time to start thinking about next moves. The zone is shrinking, seems to be collapsing toward Sky Temple Ruin. The question now is, should you abandon the protection of the bots and head deeper into the safe-zone, where you're sure to run into more players but might find a compound to defend and turtle up in for the endgame, or keep with the plan and stick to the zone edge?

"We could head down to the coast," Linker says, almost as if he's reading your mind. You've been keeping a low profile for a long time and you're both getting antsy. "Troll through some of the trash spots and see if we can loot something good."

"Either we run a hotspot or we keep with what we're doing. Not worth exposing ourselves for crap."

He's itching for some action, and you know exactly how he feels. The constant desire for better gear is instinctual, one of the driving forces in Decimation Island. It's hard to resist the urge to check one more hut, loot more crate, down one more bot. Maybe you'll find a top-tier item, something to leverage for a deeper spot in the game.

By the time hour eighty rolls around there are usually still forty or so players left standing, and most of them have found at least one legendary weapon like the Redeemer, or maybe a chameleon cloak or a full CEA suit, and some have two or three. Almost everyone has upgraded their skyn with muscle unlocks and tactical perqs. By hour ninety the remaining players are killing machines who can turn invisible and see through walls.

The problem with getting geared so well so early is the mid-game drag. It's necessary, you get that—the game skyns heal fast, but not instantly. Players need time to recover from their wounds between hitting hotspots and picking fights. And while the kill zone is always closing, pushing players toward each other, sometimes it feels like it takes forever. Sixty-seven hours and four kills in and you're already jonesing for the end. But you're in a good spot. No need to push it. This is only the beginning, there's plenty of hours left ahead of you.

You've taken turns cycling through your rest time so you don't have that to worry about. One of the sneaky game rules is you can't rest in the PVP-free areas—that'd be too easy, just close your eyes and power down where no one can hurt you. After all, the game wants sleep to be dangerous, and while having a partner makes resting more reliable, resting is a gamble, even when teamed.

Linker could blow your head off while you're unconscious—team killing is always a valid tactic—but he'd be marked hostile, and his position made visible on the game map for two hours. Anyone who wanted a free kill could come clean him up. It's a play usually reserved for the last minute, when there are only a few players left and bots are closing in and you've got nothing left to lose. For now, you're better off together, and you both know it.

"Saigon Farm?" Linker suggests. "We can scout it out and if the coast is clear raid the stockades, load up on go juice. We've got good gear but our skyns are still stock."

Staying quiet has worked so far, but the tension is gnawing at you, and with your skyns beefed up with the muscle enhancers you'd have an edge once things get tight.

Everything in you wants to fight. You didn't come here to keep your head down, and so far you've only come across one team of four and a solo. You took out the solo, but she was playing the edge game too and didn't have anything worth taking, and you shut your mouths and ran in the other direction when you spotted the four-man.

Neither you or Linker were interested in a four-v-two fight in the middle of the jungle. Way too easy to get outflanked. But your audience has been dwindling over the past day, and keeping them on your side is the only way to get the good sponsored loot.

"Saigon Farm," you repeat, mulling the idea over. Might not be such a bad idea. It's still in the safe-zone but won't be for long. Down on the south coast the jungle gives way to grasslands for a short stretch before it hits the beach. The sightlines will be good, Linker could use the Redeemer to scan for hostiles, make sure the area is clear before you loot the outlying farms. And the movement speed increase you'll get from the go juice will come in handy. "You'd finally get a chance to whip out that beast on your back."

"Oh God, I want to get a kill with it," he purrs. "Hear it bark, just once." Like everyone else who's devoted their lives to this game, he's got a thirst for violence, and not getting to use that one-shotter on his back is eating him alive.

"Well, let's go make that happen," you say. "Then we

can kill some time in the farm hub and decide on our next move."

"Fuck yes!" Linker says, and springs ahead with new purpose. You've got probably ten hours before things get spicy. Might as well make the most of them.

"GET DOWN!" I hiss from under the table. My thoughts stutter as a spike of adrenaline batters against the brakes in my Cortex, but I've still got sense enough to duck when shooting starts.

Anika glances down at me, as though she forgot I was even here, and rolls her eyes.

"I want to see what happens," she says. Is she so far gone she isn't worried about catching a stray?

"You can see from down here," I say, jutting my hand out at the nearby female attacker just as she whips around and catches a charging bot with a long burst from her weapons.

Anika rolls her eyes but crouches down beside me, still holding her champagne.

"Better?" she asks.

"Much," I reply. "I just got this suit, I don't need you bleeding all over it."

She flicks me an odd look but just takes another sip from her glass.

After two more back and forth volleys of fire the

shooting stops and a hush falls over the room. The fighting lasted only seconds. The internal security is down, and the attackers are barely breathing hard. Reinforcements will be here in moments, but for now we're trapped.

Why does this shit keep happening to me? I was in the middle of a gun fight just two days ago.

Chaddah's right, I'm a trouble magnet. I should have just stayed home.

As I'm mulling my bad luck, the lead guy strides into the center of the room, waving his guns around. He's putting on a show. He does a little twirl, then grabs one of the musician's microphones.

"Ladies and gentlemen," he croons, "no cause for alarm. We're here for the flesh, we intend you no harm."

"*Nerd,*" the other male attacker calls, and the female laughs.

"For the loot," the leader cries. "And the *lulz!*"

"And the beerz!" the other male adds.

The leader spins around. "What do you mean '*beerz*'?" he asks, the humor shaved from his voice. "Who said anything about *beerz*?"

"Loot, lulz, and beerz," the guy says, defensive. "Like you said."

"I didn't say '*beerz,*'" the leader says, agitated, then spins back toward the crowd. "Loot and lulz," he yells, as if trying to make sure everyone understands. "That's it. No *beerz*. I don't even like beerz."

"Would you two knock it off," the female voice scolds. "Half the cops in the city will be here any second and you two are out here trolling."

"Okay, *Mom,*" the leader says, and they all laugh, just kids clowning, but then he flicks his head and they go to work, moving with purpose. The female heads straight toward the arena skyns while the male runs back outside and ferries in four bags they must have dropped in with, then joins the female at the platforms.

The balls on these guys—they're going for the arena skyns. I get why they'd want to, with the tech they're packing, the Gladiator skyns are worth hundreds of millions on the black market. *Each*. Drop one into a country and kill the population of a small city kind of expensive. But how the hell do they plan on hauling those skyns back out?

The building is surrounded by well-armed bots and security, and they'll all be rushing in here. The cops'll be on their way, with TAC teams trained specifically to handle souped-up reszos. Even if these guys are running that Killr shyft, they'll be way outnumbered.

Plus, the overrides won't even let the arena skyns off the platforms. Do they plan on hefting the skyns on their backs and running away with them? No way they get out of here.

A moment later the woman stops in front of one of the platforms and points her thumb at a pale-skinned duo with ice-blond hair and crystal blue eyes that look like Nordic brother and sister twins. "These two."

"They sure are pretty," the guy says, then they take seats in demo chairs and after a second their skyns go slack as they cast into the two arena upgrades.

Up on the platform the female skyn rolls her new, slender shoulders then leaps up, clears two meters off the surface, and lands without a sound. Her face splits into a wide grin and she looks across at her partner. "Zeef!" she shouts, then jumps and flips twice in the air before landing in a splayed crouch like a dancer.

The male seems just as happy. He's running the skyn in circles, taking long, looping strides, like a caged tiger. Then he stops and she steps up to him and grabs him by the back of the head and pulls him into a long, wet-tongued kiss.

Beside me Anika makes a little retching noise and I feel the same way.

"And release," the lead guy says, and the skyns break their kiss, grab each other's hands, and leap off the platform.

Oh, shit. That's not supposed to happen.

They suit up from the gear they carried in with them, zipping the near naked skyns into simple black jumpsuits and arming themselves with assault rifles, with extra ammo strapped on belts around their chests, then it's the leader's turn to pick.

He heads straight for a pair of a densely muscled skyns with photoo-covered, light brown skin, dark wavy hair, yellow eyes, and perfect white teeth—like lab-grown Maori warriors. He sits in the demo unit and casts into the male, then spends a second up on the platform stroking his thick beard and gazing out over the crowd before jumping off.

He doesn't bother with the jumpsuit, just pads to a bag barefoot, with only the modesty band around his groin, grabs a weapon, and takes up position behind the banyan tree.

By now the crowd has thinned and security is arriving through the lobby. The pale duo split their focus. The woman races outside while the male turns his attention to the lobby doors and raises his weapon, and between him and the Polynesian male they make the oncoming reinforcements think twice.

Sirens warble in through the open patio doors. Won't be long till the lawbots arrive. But still I don't think more bots will slow these guys down. It's gonna take the big guns.

"We have to do something," I whisper. "Give the TAC teams time to get here."

"That so?" Anika says, her tone making it clear she knows just as well as I do we're powerless here. Hers skyn may be built for combat, but it's no match for those next-level jobs, and mine isn't close. Plus, we're completely out-gunned. We try anything and they'll put our lights out before we've moved two steps.

And even if we had guns, with the fog in my head, I wouldn't trust myself to take on an angry drunk let alone three heavily armed arena skyns. We can only sit here and take it like everyone else.

A shrill whistling rises from outside, then more shots and finally three crashing thumps—probably the hot-drop-ping lawbots shot out of the sky by the female before they could land. A moment later a heavy whirring vibrates the windows and grit kicks through the open doors as two big hovering loaders settle in above the patio.

"Ride's here!" the woman yells.

"Roger that," the leader responds, and he backs away from the tree, keeping the rifle raised at the lobby, firing as he goes. He moves back to the platform he got his skyn from, leaps up, and hefts the female version over his shoul-der. That's a fourth skyn they're getting away with.

As he jumps down and moves back toward the patio doors, the black-suited bodies they rode in on stand in unison and reload their weapons. They must be running an automated control system. Two race past the leader toward the cover of the banyan tree while the other stays with him as he retreats toward the patio.

Just before he leaves he stops and turns in the doorway and raises the gun in his giant free hand and bows, keeping the female on his shoulder the whole time. His lips spread in a wide, pearl-white grin. "Thank you for your coopera-tion. We'll see you next time!"

The loaders hovering above the patio have lowered cabled harnesses, and the attackers are strapping themselves in.

They're getting away.

I've got to do something.

I half rise, moving to go after them. The leader is just on the other side of the doors, has his back to us. Maybe I can run fast enough to tackle him before he can get a shot off... but Anika grabs me by the coattails before I get anywhere.

"What are you doing?" she asks, amused disbelief in her eyes.

"Going after them," I tell her.

She shakes her head. "They'll turn your Cortex to confetti before you get anywhere close."

I know she's right, but either way, it's too late. The male and female are already airborne, and the leader has his stolen female skyn strapped in. A second later he's ready too and whoops as the loader shoots into the sky. He fires as he rises, disabling the Service drones attempting to follow, then the vibrating quiets and they're gone.

The black-suited skyns keep their posture for another moment, then collapse, like someone pulled their plugs. It's over.

Anika stands, brushing herself off, and I rise with her. She looks at me, finishes her drink in a long swallow, and sets the glass down. Security's flooding in. There are a few more scattered shots as they pump bullets into the invaders' discarded skyns, just to be sure, but she barely seems to notice, just keeps staring at me.

"What?" I ask, feeling the weight of her eyes on me.

"You were about to run out after them."

I shrug.

She studies me for another second, then the stone mask of her face softens.

"Crazy fuck," she says, then laughs once through her nose before turning and striding across the nearly empty room. She ignores the shouted commands from the incoming TAC forces and disappears through the lobby doors.

I take a breath then pour the rest of my drink down my throat. The bubbles burn in my nose. How do I keep getting myself into shit like this? Bad enough I end up in the middle of another shootout, but worse, I'm starting to think there's something to Dub's suspicions about Anika.

Either she's so dead inside that even an armed robbery isn't enough to get her pulse racing—or she knew it was coming.

She wasn't surprised. At all. And though it's much more likely that everything she's been through has dulled her to the world, what if there's more to it than that?

I need to tell Dub there's a chance he's not imagining things.

Which means he's gonna want me to keep digging into Anika's life.

Dammit.

I knew I should have stayed home tonight.

I don't hang around the hotel long. The TAC team clears the ballroom and I let myself be herded into the commotion outside. Seems like every response vehicle in the city is here, and the air is thick with the buzz of feed drones fighting for camera position. A few thousand people flooded out of the hotel and onto the streets and the entire road is blocked. It's chaos.

After I push my way through the crowd I duck into an alley and zigzag my way south until I'm free. Someone probably will want to talk to me—I'm sure Chaddah will come knocking as soon as she sees my name on the guest list —but she can come to me. I'm not spending another night in line behind a thousand other witnesses waiting for my turn to say the same thing. I don't know anything more than anyone else, other than I have a distinct knack for being in the wrong place at the wrong time.

I'm about to hop a Sküte home but Dub calls before I can even get one hailed. He's heard about the heist and wants to make sure Anika and I are safe, and he sighs with relief when I tell him we are. Or at least Anika was when she left. Who knows who might have pissed her off on the way home.

He wants to talk, in person, and I know there's no point in arguing, so I tell him to meet me at Avenue Open Kitchen, a little hole-in-the-wall diner to the west of downtown.

I get there before him and take a booth in the back, slide into the cracked, green faux-leather banquette, and when the bot rolls up and places a paper napkin and glass of water on the table I order a coffee and smoked veat sandwich. It's still early, and the place is only half full, but it'll steadily fill up as the drunks stumble in to line their stomachs with something greasy before they call it a night.

Dub rolls in fifteen minutes later. The restaurant is small, just a single row of booths and six stools at the counter, and his beefy skyn seems to cast a shadow as he stalks down the aisle.

"Thank goodness you weren't hurt," he says in a loud voice as he drops into the seat across from me. Everyone in the place is looking at us, and I shush him with my hand. He glances around in apology and hunches over the table. "What happened?"

"Somebody ripped off Humanitech's arena skyns," I say. "Took four of 'em. Flew right out the window."

His mouth drops open. "You're sure? *Four?*"

I nod. "Somehow got through the safeties and walked out with them."

"Shit. That's ... that's not good."

"Nope."

The bot comes to drop off my sandwich and tries to take Dub's order but he shoos it away. I don't think his skyn could even digest the stuff they serve here.

"They won't get far." He pats his chest. "Humanitech has their skyns tagged. Standards will track them down."

"Maybe," I say, thinking back to how efficiently the heist went. They were prepared. In and out like clockwork. They were showoffs, but they didn't leave anything to chance. "Wouldn't surprise me if they had a workaround already figured for that."

Dub sinks further into his seat. He's feeling this like it happened to him personally and not to a massive multinational corporation. He's quiet for a moment, then looks up, a sliver of hope in his eyes. "What about Anika, though? Did you talk to her?"

The answer won't make him feel any better, but I should tell him.

"Yeah," I say. "We chatted."

His head perks up. "And?"

I take a moment and choose my words carefully, stall by picking the top slice of bread off my sandwich and slathering it with mustard. I'm still ninety-five percent sure she's just messed up from everything she's been through—losing a kid and finding out you killed yourself but not knowing why is sure to mess you up—but there's a chance there's more to it. Something's niggling in my gut.

"There's a chance, a *slight* chance, you might not be imagining things," I say.

He winces and his broad shoulders slump further. "Gosh, I was hoping I was wrong."

"Likely you still are. But I was standing beside her when the shooting started and she didn't blink. I served with some hard guys back in the Forces, but I never met anyone who doesn't at least flinch when bullets start flying."

Dub processes this, then his eyes widen. His voice rises. "You're saying she might have been in on it?"

I raise my hands. "I'm not saying anything. Who knows what's going on with her, but something is. She's been through a lot—I know they don't just let anyone become a novi. You're sure she passed the psychological tests?"

"Of course," Dub says. "But no one who tries out for the gladiators is totally sane. You think she could be dangerous?"

I pick up half of my sandwich and take a bite of the salty imitation meat, chew and swallow while I consider my answer.

"I don't," I finally say. "But she sure wasn't worried about catching a bullet."

Dub makes a noise in his throat and I take another bite. I know what's coming next.

"So you'll take the case?" he asks.

Case? What case? I finish chewing and take a swig of water, stalling, but I can't ignore his pleading look. "Like I said before, I don't know what I'll be able to dig up that background checks didn't."

"But you could try—"

I take a breath. "Her psych workup, can I see it?" I ask, half-hoping he'll refuse and give me an excuse to beg off, but he doesn't hesitate, and a moment later I get notification he's sent me a trove of documents. Looks like interviews, a detailed history, psychological profiling—the whole deal.

"That's everything I have," he says. "But keep it to yourself. I could get in trouble for sharing it."

I send a thought to Connie and get her reviewing everything, but I'm not expecting much. "And I'll need anything that comes up from the investigation into the stolen skyns."

"Whatever you want," Dub says.

Now what? "I suppose I could review Anika's feed history, dig through her tube archives, first-person her Decimation Island run, see if something happened to her in-game that triggered her suicide—though I'm sure it's been relived a million times by now, and if no one else has found anything ..."

"Great," Dub says. "Whatever you can do."

The Decimation Island sub fees aren't cheap though, and I'll need the platinum level to rewatch old games. I could try to use the ad-supported route for Anika's tube history, but it'll tack days onto the search. He sees me hesitating.

"What is it?"

"I don't want to ask, but I'll need to sign up for a DI season pass, and the subscriptions to Anika's feed, and I know you already paid for this suit ..."

He blinks, then realizes what I'm saying. "Done," he says a moment later, and a notification tells me I'm rich. There's a million crypto in one of my accounts.

"No, Dub. That's way too much. I only need a few thousand for the fees—"

"Keep it," Dub says. "I have more than I need."

"I can't. You know I can't."

"Why not?" he asks, leaning in, his voice hushed like he's upset. "You need it and I have it to give. You don't need to be here, helping me, but you are and I appreciate the hell out of it. Besides, I've got more money than I'll ever use in a hundred lifetimes. I'll never notice the difference."

It would help. I could get my own place again, let Shelt have his room back. I could even start saving to get Connie that skyn. My pride's fighting me, but what the hell.

"Okay," I say. "Thanks, Dub, that's damn generous of you."

Dub smiles out the side of his mouth, playing it down.

"It's nothing. Besides, a million dollars ain't what it used to be."

"I'll do some poking around, let you know what I find out."

He nods. "The novi trials are on Sunday. We need to know before then."

"On it," I say, though honestly, I hope I don't find anything. I barely know her, but Anika seems like a good kid trying to hold herself together the best she can after all the shit she's been though.

At least that's what I want to think, but even still there's a part of me that knows this won't end well.

It never does.

ANIK@_
99:53:23 // 11 PLAYERS REMAIN.

You're trapped in the red, squatting in the shadow of a deep green fern, with only two minutes of safe-time left before the prowlers quit their snarling and pounce. Eleven players are still alive, and everyone's fighting to stay that way. The next one to die will end the round, and no one wants to go out in eleventh place.

The kill zone closes in one square kilometer hex at a time, ten hexes an hour, until there's ten minutes left and only one hex remains open. After that the zone pushes in from the sides until it either closes at hour one hundred or only ten players remain. Once in the red, only the players who still have safe-time are spared from the bots immediately going aggro, and squads start to consider whether one of their members is expendable.

You've tried everything you can to find a way into the green, but the zone's centered on a clearing around one of the excavated tombs of Sky Temple Ruin, just some tents and the low stone walls, and OVRshAdo and his team have it on lockdown, every angle of approach covered. Anyone who's tried to sneak in was cut down, and their corpses are sprawled on the grass.

With OVRshAdo's foursome commanding the center, that leaves five enemy players in the red with you and Linker. Who knows, maybe you two have the most time left. You could stay in the red and hope to run out the clock, but you never know. There's a good chance you and Linker could be at the bottom of the safe-time pool and doing nothing could lose you the game.

"We need to move," you hiss, trying to keep your voice down. In the thick jungle it's nearly impossible to see more than a few feet, but you know there's a team of three around to the north, and probably a duo out on the other side of the circle. The duo would be the best team to challenge but at this point they're too far away.

You grit your teeth, frustrated. *Not like this. Not so soon.*

You should have been more proactive with your hundred hours, gone for kills, run hotspots to get better loot. It seemed like the best idea was to play conservative, but now that you're stuck at the end, about to lose your very first game, if only you had filled up your safe-time reserve, or found a camo cloak or a drone to spot enemy locations ...

"If we move we're dead," Linker hisses back, his eyes jigging in the low jungle light. This is his second game and he's never been so close to winning—only one player away—and the tension's eating at him.

"I'm not dying to the zone," you tell him. Only ninety seconds before the bots attack. You need to go now, by your-self if necessary. Maybe you can get a lucky shot on some-one, or hold off the prowlers long enough for someone else to die first.

You lift yourself up to a crouch and scan your surround-ings through the visor over your face, searching for a clue as to where the other teams might be, but with nothing to go on you can only swallow and roll the dice. You ADS the bullpup and pick your way forward, hope you spot someone first.

A prowler's been stalking you for the past few minutes. You're in its territory and it knows you'll soon be vulnerable. You keep it in your peripheral vision as you peer through the broad thick leaves of a rubber plant, searching for any sign of movement, for a hint of something that shouldn't be there.

You flick your eyes to the countdown at the edge of your vision—twenty-seven seconds. It's a long way around the edge of the zone, and the other players could be anywhere. You're not going to find them.

There's only one player you for sure know the location of ... *Linker*.

He's the only option left.

And the second you think it, you know he's decided the same thing.

You leap instantly to the left, startling yourself with a dodge that happens before you've even decided to move, like someone's pulling your strings, just as a shotgun blast rips a hole through the rubber plant you were looking through. You land in a roll and dive back right, avoiding the next shot that thuds in the wet earth just as you clear out of the way, and the next leap puts you behind the thick trunk of a tree that absorbs the third shot.

Blood roars in your ears as you catch your breath. Thank Christ you went after the muscle juice—if it weren't for the extra speed he'd have caught you. Behind you the prowler barks—that's the twenty-second warning. Its green eyes will be pulsing red, counting down the seconds until it charges. You can't worry about the bot though, Linker's crashing through the jungle, trying to swing around to get an angle on you. He's moved far enough the targeting assist in the visor lost track of him, and he's still got seven shots left before he needs to reload

You slide a cylindrical grenade from the strap over your chest, cook it for a second, and toss it. It bounces through the jungle and Linker must hear it coming 'cause the crashing gets frantic as he scrambles to avoid the blast. You circle around to the front of the tree, away from where Linker will expect you to be, just as another cannon of pellets blows through the place you were hiding.

The visor lights up, revealing his position, and now you've got the flank on him. He's lost track of you and you keep circling, shadowing his movements through the jungle until you've crept up behind him and got him in your sights. Then you empty the bullpup's magazine into him.

Your throat tightens with a momentary pang of remorse as the bullets tear through your partner's armor and into his back. He whirls with a shriek, wild-eyed, and tries to get the shotgun on you, but he's lost control of his arm and the blast goes wide.

Linker drops to his knees, embedding the shotgun barrel in the dirt, trying to keep himself upright, but he's done.

He looks up at you, no regret, but no hard feelings either. You worked well together, but of everyone you faced out here, he's the one that came closest to ending your run.

Maybe partners aren't such a great idea after all.

"GG," he chokes, and blood sprays from his lips.

"Good game, pal," you reply. But the game isn't over, he isn't dead yet, and you only have five seconds left before the bots come for you both.

You draw your pistol as you cross the jungle and step up next to him. He watches you, knows what's about to happen. And he doesn't try to stop you when you take the Redeemer off his back. Survivors get to take one item into the next round, and this will be yours.

"See ya in the next lobby," you say, then flip off his helmet, and just as the prowler behind you flexes to leap, you blow out the back of his head.

AniK@ betrays LinkerJayyyy. 10 players remain.

Round complete.

I'm in Decimation Island, ghosting Anika's run through her eyes. She's got a pistol braced to fire in her outstretched arm, only a twitch of her finger away from surviving her tenth game in a row, with one last enemy to finish before she wins it all. She has nothing to lose by hesitating, but she doesn't pull the trigger.

"What are you waiting for?" a male voice calls from behind. He's confident, with an accent slanted toward British. OVRshAdo, her partner for her last two games. They've made it to the end together. Worked hard to get here. This is a win for him as much as it is for her.

But she doesn't answer. Doesn't take her eyes off her target.

Even the guy standing across from her, his weapon empty on the ground next to him, the guy clutching a bleeding stomach wound and about to be eliminated with a bullet through the Cortex, is excited. You can see it in his eyes. People will know his name for this, even if he'll never remember it himself. GrUNchuckoo—AniK@'s final victim. The last player defeated on her way to glory.

Her eyes flick to the display in the upper corner of her vision. Time is running out. Only eleven players left and the bots are closing in. Their warning growls grow louder. Still she doesn't shoot.

Why doesn't she shoot?

"You want *me* to finish him?" OVRshAdo asks, amused. He cocks his weapon, *click-clack*, and ejects a live round out of the chamber.

Anika's head shakes but her eyes don't move. "No," she says, speaking slowly, like her lips are heavy.

Is this when she decides to do it? Or did she intend it all along?

It's the first thing people ask her, and she's been asked dozens of times since, but not even Anika herself claims to know why, instead of pulling the trigger on the easiest shot of her life, in her moment of triumph, she twists the pistol up under her chin and ends her own run.

I've relived this next moment over and over. I've watched it from the spectator view. Lived it through OVRshAdo's perspective. I've even played GrUNchuck-oo's POV, and the way his mouth drops open as he watches Anika's Cortex burst out the top of her head in a bright blue flash is never not grotesquely satisfying. But mostly I've inhabited her, played through this moment in first-person, watched it through her eyes. I've lifted the weapon in my hand, felt the cold cylinder press against my skin, and trembled through the second's hesitation before I squeezed the trigger. Replayed it a dozen times now, but no matter how many times I relive it, without the benefit of knowing what's going on inside Anika's head, it's impossible to know why she does what she does.

I can only guess, and there's only one answer that makes sense.

After the bullet tears through her head I let the playback run, but the game only lasts another moment before the round ends.

So why'd she do it?

The obvious answer is she knew her son was already gone, and what was the point after that? But she'd known that for days by this point. OVRshAdo had already told her two games ago. Why wait until now to give up?

I consider jumping back and running through it again, but it won't help. There's nothing obvious that explains her actions. I don't feel so bad about not finding anything though, no one else has either—and it's not for lack of trying. People have cast themselves into this moment by the millions to live it for themselves, hundreds of articles have been written, hours of investigative feed produced, conspiracy theories hatched and discarded and re-litigated with every new scrap of information.

A convincing rumor took hold claiming that somehow Jefferson Wood himself, the Decimation Island Game Director, overrode Anika's skyn and forced the suicide at the last second rather than pay out the win. It made sense, and it fit the facts. After all, he had the most to lose. How else to explain the second's hesitation before Anika ends it? What could it be other than an override? The story trended long enough that Wood made a rare public statement and put the story to rest.

He stood on the glass balcony of the Decimation Island Live Control Complex, with his thick sandy hair waving in the breeze and the sun shining red in his beard, and promised there had been no interference, then to prove it, he released Anika's internal Cortical telemetry for this moment to the public. Every biokin examination of Anika's movements indicates she acted of her own free will, but still there are conspiracy groups who think somehow the island itself was behind it.

I can't find any proof though, and neither can anyone else. I think the better explanation for her hesitation is she reconsidered it one last time, then went ahead with it anyway.

I've been through her entire run, and most of her life before that, playing through the archives, going through her thousands of hours of tube feed at 100X normal over the past day and a half. I feel like I know her, and find her low-key brand of tubing oddly charming.

Even back when she first started playing games for an audience she wasn't the bubbliest of personalities, but she was clinical, strategic, and had supernatural aim. She won a lot, almost effortlessly, and when she interacted with her fans it was always cordial. And when the trolls came at her, she gut them easily enough, but she never seemed to take it personally.

Over the years she evolved into a low-key badass in the gamer scene, and she didn't much care if she was popular, which is probably why she ended up there. Even going reszo didn't change her. It just made her better at what she was already great at.

Then she walked away from it all to have a kid, and when she returned to gaming to save his life she came back a different person. Not completely, but enough to be notice-able. She was no longer in it to entertain—even the cutting sarcasm was gone—she was playing to win, and solely to win. She was playing for her son.

This drive continued into the live game. It started rough, and she nearly lost a bunch of times, but once she got her feet under her she came back to herself a bit. Then she teamed up with OVRshAdo, and that's when things changed again. I don't know what caused it, but something in her turned the closer she got to winning. She went sour.

I've been through her entire life, and just like the ludus security team, I've come up with nothing. Her early childhood records are spotty. She has no family, and the orphanage she grew up in is long gone. She's lived her entire life online, everything exposed. There's no one to track down and interview. No hidden scandals to uncover. Any secrets she's hiding, somehow she's kept them buried.

Which means the only way I'll find out what they are is if she tells me herself.

And the only way to do that is to ask her.

I'd rather not, but I guess that means I'm leaving the house again.

ANIK@_
POST GAME 1 DOWNTIME

A FEW SECONDS after the game finished, the jungle went black as you were pulled you from your skyn and you found yourself standing alone in Camp Paradiso, the virtual holding area where the survivors' rithms are stored between games. It's styled like a beachfront tropical resort, complete with swaying palms and tiki torches and thatch-roofed huts, always at sunset. There's a whole banquet table filled with simulated food and alcohol, anything you could want, but you're not hungry. You'll have about an hour to recover and compose yourself before the next drop.

First, though, you need to get through the confessional, and that means talking to Jefferson Wood himself. You turn and he's behind you, his perfect smile doing its best to put you at ease. You've been dreading this. Fragging's way preferable to the chit-chat part of the game.

"Congratulations on your performance, AniK@," he says. "How does it feel to survive your first live game?"

You won, you should feel great, but your chest hurts and the audience pressure in your head is growing as news of your win spreads. Rather than excited and energized, you're exhausted, wrung out. Simulated games are one thing, but one hundred hours constantly on edge, fighting to survive, is a long slog and harder than you'd expected. And that was only game one. You still have nine hundred hours before this is over, and each one you manage to survive only makes the next one harder.

"I did my best," you reply, keeping your tone light. This is all part of the show. Jefferson Wood always interviews each of the winners himself. It humanizes you for the fans, and performing well with him can be just as important as getting kills. "I hated turning on my teammate, but he left me no other choice."

"And no one could fault you for it," Wood says. "Your play throughout the game was adept, particularly your ploy to eliminate the PaulThe Baker and his squad at Ranger Rick's Last Stand. Did you expect it to work so effectively?"

"I hoped it would, but out here nothing's guaranteed. We got lucky."

Wood runs his fingers through his thick hair. "In our opinion, luck had nothing to do with it. You have shown yourself to be a formidable contender."

"I'll try to keep it up," you say. Humility's always a good option for the confessional. Makes you relatable.

The Director pauses, and when he resumes its voice is lower, tinged with concern. "We all know you're playing for your son, Rael. Is there anything you'd like to say to him?"

You can't help it, even though you know Wood is manipulating you, your heart clenches and you bite back a sob. Now that you're in game seclusion, you won't get to see him until either you die or win it all, but at least you know he's still alive. Wood wouldn't ask otherwise, right?

"I just—" you start, but choke on your own thoughts and

take a moment to compose yourself. "Just that his Mama loves him, and she'll be home soon."

"Perhaps not *too* soon," Wood adds. "Until the next round then, AniK@. We'll be watching."

Then the resort shimmers and Wood fades away as the other survivors appear, scattered throughout the dining hall like they've been here all along and you're the one late to the party. The other survivors are congregated together, laughing and toasting each other in celebration. OVRshAdo and his crew—Zara-Zee, HumanBacon, and HuggyJackson —are leading the hours race with four hundred each. They came in together and have done this plenty of times. There's a surviving threesome who just finished their second games, and this is the first win for the remaining duo, but you expect this isn't their first time at Camp Paradiso.

They all seem like they've been here before and fall into a loose banter while they crowd around the bar. You know you should join them, playing off the other survivors is part of wooing your aud, but you don't feel up to it. Instead you head out to the long wooden dock that stretches out into the azure water and stare at the blazing sunset.

Your chest loosens as you watch the yellow-and-orange light ease into pinks and purples, but for some goddamned reason you still feel bad about turning on Linker. Even though you've done it countless times in virt games, even though it was self-defense, and all part of a fucking game, you still don't like how it ended.

The salt air tingles your lips as you suck in a breath. Doesn't matter, you made it. That's what matters. That's why you're here. You're a survivor, and now the game truly begins.

"You doin' okay out here, firstie?" someone says from behind you.

You spin around and see OVRshAdo on the dock behind you.

He's dressed the same as everyone else—just a light linen shirt and pants, and the aspect he's wearing is as absently attractive as everyone else's. His hair is light brown, swept up in a wave and shaved to a fade around the sides, his eyes are deep brown, and his face is halfway between angular and chubby, like a fat kid after six months of daily running.

You were so wrapped up in self-pity you didn't hear him approach. Lose your head like that in the game and you could lose your head for real.

He cocks his chin out to the side when you don't respond, and a grin worms its way across his lips. "You got that look. Real thing's harder than you expected, huh?"

You respond with a nod. OVRshAdo's your biggest competition out here and you don't want to reveal any weakness in your voice.

He laughs. "So it's like that, huh? You gonna play the hard-ass? That's cool, I'm vibing." He raises his hands like he's waiting for something. "Go ahead, ask."

"'Bout what?"

"You gonna make me come out and say it? You want to team, right? But you thought you'd come out here and play hard to get." His accent's vaguely British, but also sounds artificial, like he's putting it on.

"I don't want to team with you," you say flatly.

His eyes go narrow. "Of course you do," he says. "I get it, you took down three survivors in the first few hours of the game. You're a real 'press W' kinda girl, am I right? But you're a solo and you'll go into the next game with a target on your back. You want to win as bad as anyone, so go ahead —*ask*."

He's already got a tight four, he doesn't need you. What's he on about?

"Pass," you say, and he takes a step back, runs his fingers over his chin, and pushes his lips out in a self-satisfied pout.

"Good," he says, "'cause I only came out here to tell you we're full up." He does a little dance and spins on his toes. "And I know for a fact Zara-Zee wants that Redeemer, so I guess we'll probably be seeing you soon."

"Great," you say, then turn your back on him and stare out into the ocean.

This is the real game, the game within the game. Now that you're a survivor you're playing against the other nine. The other ninety that'll drop in fresh next round are dangerous, but not nearly as deadly as the players starting the game already armed and with hundreds of hours to lose. They'll be coming for you from the jump, and if you want to stay ahead of them, you'll need to play smart.

Last game teaming nearly got you killed. This next one you're gonna be the lone wolf, let the Redeemer be your backup, and take the head off anyone who gets too close.

Let 'em come. You'll be waiting.

I spent hours behind Anika Reyes' eyes, but nothing I saw got me any nearer to understanding her. I checked in with Dub and told him I had nothing, but he wouldn't let me off the hook, said she'd closed right up since the heist, and he's convinced she was in on it. As far as he's concerned, our only way forward is for me to get close to her and get her to open up, then find something, anything, to prove him wrong before it's too late.

My first reaction was to tell him not a chance in hell and ship him his money back, but spending all this time in Anika's head's got me invested. There's just something about her I can't let go of. I'm not ready to give up quite yet —not that I'm thrilled about what moving forward requires.

He suggested I try talking to her again, and even though she rarely leaves the ludus, she does slip out of the building once a week: every Tuesday morning she leaves before training starts and spends ten or fifteen minutes in a nearby park, sitting alone on a bench, watching the sun rise over the playground equipment.

That's why I'm standing outside the ludus' rear

entrance at the ass crack of dawn, waiting for her to emerge —so I can pretend to casually run into her. It's a shitty idea, I know, but it's the only one we have.

"I'm excited," Connie says. She's waiting with me while I loiter next to the ludus' mirrored exterior. My Cortex doesn't have the processing power to render her reflection in the building's surface or adjust her appearance to account for the early morning light, but it's nice to have her here all the same. "I've never been on a stakeout before."

"We've only been here a few minutes," I reply in my head. "The excitement wears off when you get to hour twelve and your pee bottle is full."

"What are you going to say to her?" She knows why I'm here and what Dub wants me to do, and it's a good question, one I haven't got completely figured out.

"I'm not sure—" I say and then the back door swings open and Anika steps out.

She's wearing a grey Humanitech warm-up suit with a baseball cap pulled low over her short hair. She stiffens when she sees me.

I keep my distance—if she triggers on me I'll want a head start when I make a break for it—and flash her what I hope is a disarming smile.

"Hey," I say, "remember me? Finsbury Gage—we witnessed a felony together."

Her eyelids twitch and she glances from side to side. "I know who you are," she says. "What are you doing here?"

She doesn't sound angry, or look like she's about to lunge at me. But I'm sure if she did I wouldn't see it coming. She seems more annoyed than anything else.

"I wanted to thank you for saving my skyn the other night. If you hadn't been there to stop me I would have done something stupid." I smile again, trying my hardest to be charming without seeming like it. "I'd be all ones and zeros right now if it weren't for you."

She considers me for a moment, but her shoulders relax. "Dub told you I'd be here?"

I nod, and she makes a little growl in her throat.

"I know," I say, commiserating. "He's frustrating. But he's a good guy. Wouldn't hurt anyone."

"I've seen him rip a guy's arm off," she counters.

"That's just his job. At home he's a pussycat."

She licks her lips, swallows. "Well, then you're welcome, I guess. Next time send a text."

She turns to leave. "Wait—" I say, but don't have anything to follow it up with.

Anika gives me an expectant look, but there's something there. The steel is gone from her eyes. "There's something else?"

"Yeah, I..." I toss a glance at Connie and she just shrugs. I'm looking to the ghost of my dead wife for dating advice. *What am I doing?* "I didn't send a message because I wanted to thank you. In person."

"Which you've done..." she leads.

"And to ask you..." *I don't know how to do this.* "To have a meal with me. As a thank you."

Meal? Why did I say "meal"? Who says "*meal*"?

What the hell is wrong with me?

"A meal?" Her face cracks, almost to a smile but not quite. "Well isn't that precious?" Then she closes right back up again. "But not necessary. Besides, I have a fight coming up. Not a lot of time for *meals*."

"How about coffee? Fifteen minutes," I suggest. "I'll even splurge on real beans."

I glance at Connie once more, and from the look on her

face she's enjoying this. For some reason she likes watching me squirm.

"Thank you, Mr. Gage—"

"Fin—"

"Thank you, Fin, but my life doesn't have room for coffee dates right now."

Of course it doesn't. Why did I think this would work? She isn't interested in socializing, she's training for the biggest fight of her life. I'll just tell Dub I did my best, but I'm out of ideas. He'll just have to live without knowing if she's shady or not.

But she's still standing there. Could she be waiting for me to say something? One last shot.

Connie's still smirking at me, and without thinking I blurt, "I know this isn't a great time, but when is it ever? And I'll be honest with you—I could use the company. It'd be nice to talk to someone other than the sprite of my late wife for a few minutes."

She blinks at me, and her head dips to the side while her mouth purses in a confused smile. "For real?" she says.

I shrug, give a little nod, and feel my cheeks tingle. *Why did I tell her that?*

"You made a sprite of your dead wife?"

"I had nothing to do with it. She did it, thought it'd be funny. And it was— at the time."

Guilt stabs me in the guts and twists. This isn't right. I shouldn't have said that—I'm using Connie's memory to worm my way into a stranger's life. It's not fair to either of them.

"Is she here now?" she asks, looking around.

I dart a look off next to me, and she follows my eyes then barks out a laugh before she can cover it with her hand. She stares at me for a second.

"I'm sorry I laughed," she says, her green eyes wide, "but that's fucked up."

"No shit," I say. She's right, no point arguing. Mental note: never use the fact that you still live with the ghost of your dead wife as a pick-up line.

But again, she's still standing there. For longer than I expected.

Finally, her lips part in a tentative grin. "Okay, Fin. But I wasn't lying, I don't have room for coffee." She considers me for another moment. "I'll be tubing tonight though, after practice. I'll send you an invite if you want to join me for duos."

She wants me to game with her? I've spent plenty of time in virts, but not a lot gaming. I won't wow her with my fragging skills, but it's a start.

"I'd like that," I say, still surprised she agreed.

My stomach twinges as she gives me a last, quizzical look. "I'll ship you the invite," she says before taking two steps and launching herself into a full-on sprint down the sidewalk.

"Way to go, slick," Connie teases. "Looks like you got yourself a date."

Ugh. At first I felt bad about taking Dub's money for this.

I don't anymore.

I HEAD BACK to my room and spend most of the day lying on the couch with my head in a game. Growing up I was more of an outdoor kid and didn't get into video games much, but since my head went digital I've had plenty of time to catch up. I've played through a bunch of narrative sims, and I've basically lived in a survival virt for these past few months. They've grown on me, so shifting into pure action games isn't too much of a stretch. Over the day I take runs through Anika's favorites—Decimation Island of course, plus Underlook Champions and Warfire 1944. She's a pro and I know she'll kick my ass at whatever we do, but I don't want to come off like a complete potato.

The games are all first-person sims, and while each is wildly different—from the visuals to the body mechanics to how much it hurts when you die—some are more compli-cated than others. It takes all day, but after the initial learning curves I'm at least passable in all of them. Mostly.

Enough, anyway.

I don't hear from her until later in the afternoon, when I get a message from someone called GulfGaytR—which turns out to be one of Anika's alt IDs. It says she'll be running duos in Decimation Island at eight if I'm still interested. You'd think after all she's been through she wouldn't want to play that game ever again, but it's still the most popular content on her feed. People want to see her challenging the game that beat her, and she tubes it like a champ on the regular.

DI's fine with me. Out of everything I played today it's the most straightforward. Collect weapons and gear and kill anything that moves. Bots, players, NPCs—doesn't matter. It's easy when everything's an enemy. Even better, the body mechanics and the weapon simulations are the closest to realistic of anything I've played. There are no real special abilities or super powers or team economies or complicated itemization paths to learn. Point and shoot, I can do that.

I reply, telling her I'm looking forward to it. Then that's it—it's a date.

Connie smiles at me. "I think you'll have fun."

I don't. I was never good at this, even when it wasn't all based on a lie.

"This in no way will be fun," I say. If I had a body right now it'd be drenched with anxiety sweat. Now that this is for sure happening I want nothing more than to cancel.

"We'll see," she says over her shoulder as she disappears into the bedroom with an inviting look, but that's the last thing I'm interested in. It isn't even her that wants me to follow, it's her algorithm, pulling her strings to give me what it thinks *I* want.

I know she isn't real, and I'm reminded all the time, but here I am, all the same, feeling guilty about going out with another woman. And not only because I'm betraying Connie—but also because I'm running a game on Anika.

What if she figures out what Dub and I are up to? Dub

seems to think it's justified but ... what if he's wrong? There's a very good chance this is all a misunderstanding, and here I am messing with her head.

I need to relax, pull myself together. It's not a big deal, we're just gaming. We're not even going to be in the same room together. No one gets hurt playing video games, right?

After a few more rounds in Decimation Island, I spend the rest of the evening pacing in the cabin until suddenly it's five to eight. I call up Anika's invitation and hit accept and a second later the air above me twists open and a beam of light sucks me up and leaves me standing in the DI lobby, right on the edge of the floating drop tower.

I stagger backwards, my heart in my throat. Even though I've played a few dozen games, the vertigo of arriving on the drop tower still gets me every time. I'm up high, standing on the hexagonal launch deck. The floor's only a thin grate with nothing under me but the ground far below. I've never been great with heights. The first time I cast in here my guts heaved so hard I nearly had to bail back to my headspace. It's a good thing that for whatever reason bursts of sudden adrenaline don't rouse Deacon when I've got my head in a virt. If this was out in the real world my brain would be thick as cold soup right now as the governor tamped him down.

I'm getting used to the height now, but my stomach still hitches once before it settles down. No one else seems to have a problem with it though. Players regularly pop in and immediately jump from the ledge, casting into their selected lobbies without a second thought.

The tower's hovering in the dead center of an island, and each side of the hexagonal deck leads to a different level, each a unique game scenario with specialized environments and NPCs. This week's rotation offers a mining and shipping island occupied by a despotic general, a manufacturing center overrun by renegade bots, an uninhabited tropical island infested by zombies, one that recreates the island from the live game, a prehistoric tropical map with dinosaurs, and one with hostile aliens on the moon I still can't play—even though I don't have a stomach in the game, somehow the lowered gravity setting makes me queasy.

Anika shows up right on time, except I don't know it's her. I'm watching a heard of sauropods grazing in the dinosaur level below when a guy in a union jack jumpsuit, white cravat, giant mirrored sunglasses, and thick blond hair hanging in what I can only describe as "locks," taps me on the shoulder.

"Hey big boy," he says, and his voice is musical. He flashes his eyes. "Lookin' for someone?"

It takes me a second but then I realize it must be Anika. We couldn't look any different. I'm wearing the game's basic starting gear, grey fatigues and black boots, and she's walked straight in from a Swinging Sixties nightmare.

"*GulfGaytrR*, I presume?"

"Oh this ol' thing?" she says, putting on a voice. "I've had him forever." She shrugs. "It's my dickhead camo."

My aspect's confused expression is detailed enough I don't have to come right out and ask.

"Fewer assholes hitting on me," she explains, "and the ones that do tend to take rejection better."

"Got it," I say, and can't help but laugh. "Something I've never much had to worry about."

"Come on," he says, and leans into me. It's weird, this is all just in my head, but I can almost feel her. She's smiling as she whispers, "You're telling me you've never slipped into a female aspect? Never pulled on a pair of long legs and a tight dress and strutted around the Hereafter, just to see what it felt like?"

The sudden intimacy startles me and my thoughts go blank. All I can think to say is a version of me hijacked a woman's skyn and rode her identity for six months. But I don't think that counts.

"Not the Hereafter," I say after a second, deadpan, and she winks and pushes me away. "You're not tubing now?" I ask, changing the subject. I half-thought this might all be going out live.

She smirks. "I figure we're gonna do this, we should do it right. I haven't been on many dates, but I'm still pretty sure they shouldn't have an audience. Besides, I haven't had a night off in months. You'd better be worth it."

A low-voltage tremor quivers through me. The game trying to replicate my throat tightening.

What am I doing?

I shouldn't be here.

Anika thinks I'm interested in her. I made off like I wanted to get to know her, like I'm not just another asshole who wants something from her. She's been through a whole fuck-ton of tragedy, lost someone she loves and a bunch of memory in the process, and must be struggling with what to believe.

I've been through it myself, I know how disorienting it can be. Plus, she's got the tryouts in a matter of days, a shot to become the next Ludus Humanitech novi—a huge step in her career—and I'm contributing to the mess in her head, all in the service of some vague notion in Dub's overprotective mind.

This isn't fair to her. I shouldn't be doing this...

Except—I saw it myself, at the gala. Violence is supposed to be shocking, and she didn't so much as rustle the bubbles in her champagne when the shooting started. Either she's dead inside, or she knew it was coming. And whichever she is, neither of those people should be given a lethal skyn and a stage to use it.

If we're wrong, I'll own it and apologize. But I don't think it'll come to that.

This isn't a date, it's not *supposed* to be fun. I have a job to do.

So do it.

She's waiting, her eyes starting to narrow. "I can't promise anything," I say, matching her energy, "but I'll do what I can—even if it means strutting around in a long pair of legs."

She angles her head. "Well, let's hope it doesn't come to that," she says, then looks out across the map selections. "Have a preference?"

"Anything but the moon."

She smirks. "Vanilla it is," she says and walks to the edge of the decking facing the slice of island swarming with bots, then looks at me over her shoulder. "Ready?"

"I'll follow your lead," I say as I step up beside her. "And try not to hold you back too much. Any pro tips for me?"

"Stick together." She spins around and her heels hang off into space. "Quickest way to die is alone."

Then she tips over backwards, watching me, and she only falls for a second before her body disappears.

No getting out now.

I wait a beat, then follow her in.

GAME 2 DROPS from the East Tower, and while the zone completely cuts off the island's coast, it opens up hotspots in the lava fields to the south, the coniferous forest to the north, the mountains to the west, and the river plains directly east. Other than in the heart of the forest, the sight lines work well for the Redeemer. It's a good sniper game, you should be okay.

The tower launch shoots your fresh skyn out facing toward the ocean but you immediately bank the wingpack around, checking to see where the other survivors are dropping. You don't care much about the hour zeroes, but you want to keep as far away from the returning players as you can. You angle upwards, maintaining altitude until you know where everyone is.

One at a time the survivors pop their look-at-me red parachutes, first the trio then the duo, until only you and a team of four are still cutting through the air—must be OVRshAdo and his crew. You spot them to the south and just behind, but they're paralleling your path, almost as if they're waiting for you to open your chute before they do.

Shit. This could be a problem.

"Well y'all, looks like we're being hunted," you mutter in your head. Being a newly crowned survivor, your aud has blossomed between games, and you feel their presence like an overinflated balloon in your skull.

Your plan was to pop your chute early and float as far as you could toward the foothills at the base of the dormant volcano at the center of the island. You wouldn't have to fight for real estate, there's only one reason anyone goes there, and that's if they plan on hitting the caldera hotspot at the very top, but not many do because it's basically impossible.

The Caldera Warbot Fortress is the single most risky hotspot in the game, and almost never attempted—it can take up to thirty hours of straight fighting into a warbot-defended factory built deep into the volcano, and unlike the other hotspots, it doesn't reset. It's a constant lure—defeat the bot overlord at the heart of the fortress and you walk away with a tank-like robot protector of your very own. It's a walking target, and draws all kinds of attention, but it's lethal and damned hard to kill. It's not transferrable to the next game, but any team who's able to secure it is all but guaranteed a spot in the top ten. Plenty of people attempt it because the reward is so OP, but never straight off the drop.

You'd planned to find somewhere quiet to hunker down, watch for potential targets through the Redeemer, and pick them off from afar. It'd be hours before anyone found a weapon that'd outrange you, and by then you'd have a good idea where everyone close by was, and you could move with a sense of security.

Instead you've got OVRshAdo and his squad on your ass. You'll need to do something to dissuade them.

All at once you push yourself into a dive, plummeting

head-first toward the ground as fast as you can. There are a few hotspots nearby—Robot Junction is the starting zone this game but there's also the Monorail Heist or Crater Expedition—and most of the mottled grey parachutes are headed toward one of them, but you pick a block of grey concrete buildings directly below that you don't think anyone else is aiming for and head straight down.

A flick of your head shows OVRshAdo and his squad in pursuit, but still above you and a kilometer or so to the south. If you push the dive as hard as you can, you'll land thirty seconds before them. That should be enough.

Weapons don't work in the air—it wouldn't be fair for a survivor carrying over an AR from the last round to get twenty kills on unarmed freshies before they even landed—but once your feet hit the ground all bets are off.

You skid to a stop on the concrete surrounding a cluster of square two-storey buildings, cut your chute, and immediately pull the Redeemer from your wingpack. It only has six shots left after the last game, but six is enough.

Even with the optic set to maximum zoom you can't quite tell who's who in the squad zooming down toward you, so you settle the crosshairs on the head you think belongs to OVRshAdo, wait for the aim assist to zero in and account for movement and wind, then flash green when it's ready.

You exhale and squeeze the trigger and the target's head blows off. The body tumbles in the air, then spirals as it plummets toward the ground.

AniK@ downs survivor HumanBacon. 99 players remain.

"*One-tap dirt nap, y'all,*" you say to the crowd. "*Make 'em think twice about gunnin' for me.*"

The remaining three scatter in different directions and swerve erratically to avoid the next shot, and at the rate they're coming you only have time for one more. By the time you settle in on your next target and the Redeemer calculates the trajectory they've put some distance between you, and even when the assist glows green and you pull the trigger, the shot goes wide. Then they're below the tree line and you lose your angle.

You've bought yourself some time though, and quickly scout through the buildings, looting a level-one helmet and vest and snagging a backpack and a light SMG before you rotate north, heading toward the forest and away from where OVRshAdo and his crew landed.

It'll take them a few minutes to regroup and get themselves looted. Especially knowing that you could be anywhere, watching them at range and ready with a headshot. They'll need to be cautious as they move, which means you should be able to outpace them.

You keep to the trees, stopping every few hundred feet to sweep the Redeemer behind you, checking for any signs of pursuit, and by the time you've gone an hour and haven't seen anyone, you figure they must have given up. For now at least. OVRshAdo's down a teammate and he'll be pissed, no way he'll let it slide.

But that's something you can consider later, once you're geared up and have the luxury of considering how you might potentially die, instead of worrying about what's immediately behind you.

Not how you wanted the game to start, but you sent OVRshAdo a message, and you're still alive.

Now you just need to keep it that way.

THIS ISN'T GOOD.

"His wards are about to drop," Anika yells, ducking a swipe from a blazing tentacle. "Get ready to hit him with the glaive."

I grab the star-bladed weapon from under my cloak and incant a charge into it, and the blades radiate ancient runes in a brilliant green light. Anika's ahead of me, wearing a muscled-up purple-skinned behemoth warrior and swinging a flaming sword that's bigger than she. Her target's a floating black kind of squid monster—the raid boss, supposedly an incredibly powerful inter-dimensional priest-god, but she's kicking its ass.

I'm an elf. A tall, female elf. I'm wearing form-fitting armor, carrying a bow, and have the power to sing spells and charge up weapons with my songs. Anika chose her for me, and every time she looks at me she laughs. I think she likes seeing me strutting around on long legs, and every time she smiles at me I forget why I'm here.

This is not good.

We played *Decimation Island* for almost seven hours,

made it to the survivor's circle twelve times, and even had a six-round continuation streak. Turns out we work well together. She called the shots and I did what I was told and watched her back. We didn't talk much at first, but after a few kills we loosened up. She's quick and dry and very good at what she does. The last time I felt this comfortable with someone I was in the Forces.

And with Connie.

How did I let this happen?

We quit DI and it was three in the morning but we both got the sense neither of us was ready to call it a night, and Anika suggested hopping into a Chronophase raid.

I'd never played it—it's a long-form roleplayer with a convoluted storyline about time traveling wizards that seemed kinda like nonsense to me—but she had enough XP bonuses and legendary gear lying around to level me up a character high enough to join her. We've been playing ever since.

While we haven't talked a lot—neither of us are what you'd call chatty—we've talked enough. There's lots of downtime in DI when you're looting or chasing the zone, and I told her about my time in the Forces, and Connie, and sketched out a retelling of the official version of all the shit that's happened to me since I went reszo.

It's all public record. She already knew most of it though—she'd looked me up. I think it might be why she agreed to meet in the first place: she saw living digital had fucked me just as hard as it had her.

This was supposed to be a job.

She told me about growing up in the foster system and condensed her decade of rising through the feeds to become a tubing superstar and then going reszo into three sentences. She talked a little more about deciding to walk away from her tubing career to have a kid, and how his death feels like a dream, like it happened to someone else. She's missing forty-four and a half days' worth of memory, all the time she spent in Decimation Island, and her son died while she was playing.

She woke up back in her body after ending her own run, and even though a thousand hours had passed and her son was dead and she was at the center of a media frenzy, it felt like she had just closed her eyes the moment before. Her entire life changed in the blink of an eye.

At least now, with the Gladiator auditions, she has something to focus on. She can put everything else out of her mind and take each day one step at a time. Sounds like something Shelt would say.

The only time I ever felt even a twinge of doubt about her was when I asked about OVRshAdo. We were talking about her run and I asked if she was still in contact with him. They'd nearly won the game together, and I figured they'd want to keep that going. She paused for just a second, and I don't know if it was a trick of her avatar or what, but when she answered there was an odd hitch in her face. She said he'd left her a message, inviting her to tube together, but she hadn't responded, and when I asked why she just shrugged and said she just wanted to put it all behind her, OVRshAdo included. Then she changed the subject.

Other than that one slight hiccup, in the twelve hours we've spent together I haven't seen one thing to explain what Dub would be worried about. And I don't know why she didn't react to the invasion back at the Humanitech gala, but I can't believe the woman I've spent the last half-day with is hiding something. No more than anyone else, anyway.

She's stoic, sure, and she doesn't take shit from anyone,

but that doesn't mean she's plotting something. After tonight, I'm positive she's clean. The question is: where do we go from here?

The sound of rending spacetime pulls me back to the game. The squid-priest's shields are down and Anika's yelling at me to finish it with the enchanted glaive.

I reach back and hurl the bladed weapon, and it streaks through the air and smacks the squid straight in its single dinner-plate-sized eyeball. The black flesh quivers for a second then explodes in purple fire, sending chunks of goo everywhere and leaving behind a black-metal sword hovering a meter off the ground.

"Nice shot, soldier," Anika says. "You want the loot?" She means the sword. From what I understand it's fairly rare and could be worth something in the auction house.

"It's all yours," I say. "Besides, you did all the work. I just stood here singing at it."

"And what a lovely voice you have," Anika says as she plucks the sword from the air. It shimmers for a moment then disappears, and a silvery portal opens in its place. We've been fighting on a hunk of rock hovering in space, surrounded by a purple-pink nebulae haze, and the portal's our only way back to the quest hub where we started.

"That was fun," I say. Exhilarating even. But I figure most of that had to do with the company.

"Yeah," she answers. "It was."

Then things get weird. It's like I'm back in high school— she looks at me, and even though I'm staring back at an eight-foot-tall wall of purple muscle and jagged teeth, I can read her intent clear enough. She likes me.

And dammit, I like her too.

Shit. This wasn't supposed to happen.

"We should do this again," she says.

"We should," I agree. "After your fight, maybe?"

She hesitates. "*Before*, maybe?"

"Yeah," I say, and the words come out almost against my will. "Even better."

"Cool," she answers, then looks down at her big hairy feet. "Well, I gotta go. Training starts in three minutes."

"Right," I answer. Twelve hours gone and I barely noticed. "You'd better get out of here. I'll talk to you soon then, I guess."

"You will," she says, then blows me an awkward kiss from her meaty lips and springs through the portal. A moment later I see GulfGaytR's status switch to "offline."

I stay behind for a moment, listen to the cosmic wind blowing through the craggy rocks, stare out at the neon night, and try to make sense of what the hell just happened.

I'm back in the cabin, my head swimming with a potent mix of shame and infatuation. When I returned, Connie came out of the bedroom to greet me and asked me how it went and I didn't know what to tell her. It's like I'm cheating on her except she's eager to hear all about it, encouraging even, and I can't take it. I mumbled something about it going fine and she didn't press and after a few minutes disappeared back into the bedroom.

Now I get to figure out how to handle this mess I've made.

At this point I'm ninety-nine percent sure that Anika's clean. Apart from her reaction at the heist, I've seen nothing to back up any suspicions that she might be up to something. If anything, it's the opposite.

While I haven't known her that long, in the time we spent together I found her to be even-headed and deliberate and remarkably self-aware for someone her age. Yeah, she's aggressive, but not mindlessly. And, no, none of that means she can't be running an angle of some kind, but I don't get the sense she is. I think she's a naturally reserved person who's been through a ton of shit. We all have. We're all fucked up, and she's no different.

When I was restored the second time and woke up as Gibson, people called me shady too, thought I was hiding something—though in the end it turned out they were right. I was, I just didn't know it.

And if I was, she could be too. That's the one percent. If it could happen to me, it could happen to anyone. I'm not quite ready to go back to Dub and exonerate her, but there are only four days until the novi trials, and if she's hiding something she's a good enough liar I won't get anything out of her before then.

No, I've only got one lead left to work: OVRshAdo. Anika's wound tight, completely in control, but her momentary hesitation when I asked about him was a radio burst in a sea of static. It's the one thing that stood out. Maybe it's a holdover from them spending time in the game but not remembering it—there are plenty of rational reasons to explain away why mentioning his name would give her pause, but I have to be sure.

Especially now that I've gotten to know her, I'm worried if there is something going on she might not be involved voluntarily. Could be she's mixed up in something she can't get out of. I haven't done a deep dive on OVRshAdo, but I've seen enough to know he's a proud asshole, arrogant and self-serving and skilled enough to get away with it. He's been implicated in a few scandals over the years—there was an early accusation of cheating at a tournament, and he was banned from more than one game for item duping—but nothing overtly criminal.

When they were competing against each other in DI he ended up knocked from the game and used every resource he had to get immediately back in to join her. Maybe he's still trying to work her somehow. It's slim, but I need to be sure.

I get Connie to dox him, but she doesn't come up with anything, not even his real name or what country he's from. He's a gamer who's spent most of his life on the tube—days in a row at times. As a matter of fact, he's only been offline four times in the past month, and only for a couple hours each time. Except last Saturday when he was dark for a whole six hours, the longest his feed has been down in weeks.

Six hours that line up neatly with the heist at the Hotel Mundi.

It could be a coincidence, sure, but …

"Connie," I call out, and she comes in from the bedroom, barefoot, wearing a flannel shirt and jeans. "I need your help."

"What's up?" she asks.

"Can you run a biokin cross-reference between the reszos who ripped off the Mundi and OVRshAdo? I want to see if any of them line up."

After a moment she shakes her head and says, "Based on the movements and his speech patterns, OVRshAdo's a 73.4 percent overlap with on the guy who was doing all the talking. Close, but not a match."

"But close."

"—*Ish*," she finishes. "I could find you thousands of people who'd score higher. Starting with someone who has a British accent, which OVRshAdo does, and the man at the heist didn't."

"Accents are easy enough to mask. There's still a chance. It *could* be him."

"Sure," she says with a shrug, giving up the fight. "Could be."

Good enough for me.

"Is he tubing now?"

"In *Decimation Island*," she says. "Nine hours running."

I've got nothing else to do today. Maybe I'll see what he's up to.

Just to be sure.

THE REDEEMER WHISPERS, and a mile and a half away a
player's head explodes.

AniK@ downs MilkDonor. 79 Players remain.

His safe-time rolls onto your wrist, another thirty-five
minutes. Puts you up to nearly the hundred-minute maximum. Should be enough to see you through the final zone.

You're into round three, and this time the game dropped
from the Northwest Tower, with the safe-zone open all the
way north to the cliffs and along the west coast of the island
to the marshes around Pirate Bay. The terrain is flat, and the
tall broad-leafed trees provide plenty of cover, but you're
managing to find kills here and there.

And you're still alive, that's what matters.

After you took out HumanBacon, OVRshAdo kept his
distance for the rest of his game, and you shot your way to
your second survivor circle. The last hour was rough, once
the zone tightened and the fighting got close, but you'd
racked up enough safe-time over the course of the game you

could skirt the edge of combat and hide among the bots long enough for someone else to go down first. Not the prettiest win, but a win just the same.

It's exhausting, lonely work playing the snake game—always on alert, sleeping in stolen minutes—and your audience drained away as the fragger they'd signed up to watch spent a hundred hours perched on rocky crags waiting for someone to walk past her crosshairs, so you didn't even have the comforting buzz of attention to keep you company. Instead your squadmates were the salt breeze and the night insects and the endless thoughts of Rael, dying in a clinic back home.

You see him every time you close your eyes to rest, his body lying scrawny and fragile, tubes keeping him alive. He must miss you so much. You're all he's ever known and you've been away from him for three hundred and sixty-nine hours—more than two weeks without his mother, his only person in the whole world.

Does he need you in the night? Do his tiny fingers search for your breast, while his weak cries beg you to come?

You feel the tears threaten and you press your fingers into your eyes, like you're massaging them after hours of staring down the Redeemer sights and not trying to keep them from spilling over.

Don't do this to yourself.

You're out here for him, doing this to save his life. In a few years, after you win and he's recovered and he's healthy and strong, you can look back on this time and know you did the right thing. Even though it was hard, even though you wanted nothing more than to jump in front of first player you saw and beg him to put a bullet in you so you could go home, you stuck it out.

At least that's what you need to keep telling yourself. Whatever it takes to get your through.

He isn't suffering, that's what matters. He isn't in pain. The bots take good care of him, and the nurses promised someone would come hold him once a day.

You gotta stick it out, for just a little while longer. You gotta be strong 'till it's all done.

You fill your lungs with air, puff out your chest until your armor's tight across your torso, then let it out and try to push the negativity out with it. You can't finish this if you're second-guessing yourself the whole time. You thought this all through before you came here, and you knew it was going to suck. You knew there'd be moments like this, when you wanted to give up, but there's no other way this can end.

So suck it up, Anika. You're gonna survive no matter who tries to stop you—and that includes yourself. Most of all.

"You ONLY CALL me when you want something," Yellowbird says as she walks up, playing wounded. "I'm not your mother."

She puts her hands on her gun belt and squints at me. She's wearing a dark green vest over a white shirt with standard-issue grey slacks. Her head is shaved on the sides and the hair on top is long and pulled back from her face, but for once it's all one color, deep black.

"My mother thinks I'm dead," I quip back, and offer her a plate of tacos. They're only ground veat but they smell great all the same, lots of cumin and green chilies. "If I called she'd think the devil was on the line."

I messaged Detective Karin Yellowbird a few hours ago, asking for help—while very little stays private for long these days, the Service still has its trove of secrets, and since I can't find anything about OVRshAdo on SECNet or the wider link, maybe she can. But she wouldn't agree to meet me until I promised to buy her lunch first. We compromised on stand-up tacos, and I got to the row of food trucks parked down by the lake before her and ordered for both of us.

"For real?" she asks, serious now, and for some reason I tell her the truth.

"Last time I talked to her she made it clear her son was dead. Then my dad told me never to call back. So I haven't."

Her lips press together and she holds my gaze. "That sucks."

I shrug. "Is what it is. They're old. If it's easier for them to believe I'm living in the clouds with Jesus and not a few hours down the highway, who am I to take that away from them?" But by the time I finish the sentence I realize it bothers me way more than I knew, and by the way Yellowbird's eyes have gone all soft she can see it too.

She cocks her head at me. "You want to talk?"

I miss my mom and dad, boo hoo. Pull yourself together, man.

I don't feel right. Gotta be this thing with Anika, messing me up. I've got a little crush and it's hitting me like a drug. Or maybe Vaelyn's shyft to keep Deacon quiet is screwing with my rithm. Or it could be both. Who knows.

"Forget it. I don't ..." *How did we even get into this?* Change the subject. "Thanks for coming. I know I'm not good at keeping in touch"—I glance down at the taco plate —"but I bought you tacos to make up for it."

Yellowbird rolls her eyes. "Remind me why we're friends again?" she deadpans.

"Because you demanded it," I tell her, mirroring her tone. And while it comes off sarcastic, it's true. I don't know if I would have made it this far if it wasn't for her insistence that I'm not a complete write-off. Even after all this time, and I still have no idea why, for some reason she seems to care what happens to me. "And because you're an incredible person," I mumble.

"A what?" Her eyes go wide and her lips spread in a

surprised grin. "Is that a moment of genuine affection? What's wrong with you?"

"Don't worry, it won't happen again."

She studies me for a second then shakes her head, grabs a taco from her plate, and takes a bite.

"Cod?" she asks through a full mouth of tortilla and deep-fried flaky white veat.

"They said haddock," I answer, and try a bite from mine, but I don't know if I could tell the difference. It all tastes like deep fried fish to me.

We carry our plates over to a nearby bench and sit, balance them on our laps, and stare out at the water.

"Chaddah said she ran into you," Yellowbird mentions, nonchalant, then takes another bite of her taco.

"I picked the wrong place for dinner and one thing led to another. How's the guy who got shot doing?"

"Still in the hospital, but won't be much longer."

"And the crew that shot him?"

"Who knows," she says with a shrug. "Unregistered skyns, no match to biokin. We don't even know what they were after—could have been nothing. For some of these guys armed robbery is a game."

Skyns are still expensive, but they're getting cheaper. And the explosion of unregulated fleshmiths cranking out an endless supply is only making things worse. There's a whole underground of immortal, anonymous bit-heads who've escaped the notion that actions have consequences, and no one knows how to stop it. Even with the Standards' rapid response teams and lawbots constantly at the ready, the cops are barely keeping a lid on it.

"You guys any closer to finding the source of that Killrshyft?"

"All we know is it's super easy to get, growing more

popular by the day, and we have no idea where it's coming from. It's been used in three more shootouts in just the past two days, and who knows how many more we don't know about. At the rate the violence is increasing, if we can't put a lid on it soon, the city will end up a warzone."

"Sounds rough," I say, and again I find myself missing the job, but the feeling doesn't last long. It's not like I could do any better than they are. I'd be just as powerless, trapped by bureaucracy and going out of my mind with it. At least out here I can pick and choose what to beat my head against.

"Swimming against the current, but we're keeping our heads above water."

"Maybe I can help," I say.

Yellowbird hesitates a beat. "Is this about you witnessing that heist at the Mundi?"

Here we go. "You know about that?"

"Your name was on the guest list, Fin."

I shove the last half of my taco in my mouth, buying myself a moment. Yellowbird watches me chew and swallow.

"Well? You want to tell me why you had front-row seats to two shoot-outs this week?"

I shrug. "Shitty luck?"

"I'll need more than that."

"I'm friendly with Ari Dubecki—the Gladiator Dub, you know him?" She nods. "He gave me his ticket. I was just there for the free drinks and the eye-candy and then everything went to hell."

"No way you'd get all prettied up to attend an event like that without good reason. You're working on something, aren't you?"

I don't want to say too much, but I need her help, so I

can't just deny everything either. "Maybe ... I'm not sure." She purses her mouth at me, impatient. "I need some information—"

"Christ, Fin," Yellowbird says, and drops her plate beside her. "Is this why you called me? I'm not your personal information faucet. I can't keep opening Service intel to you. If you know something, tell me what it is and let us look into it."

"It's sensitive." I don't want anything getting back to Anika. The last thing she needs is the cops banging at her door. The link would go nuts.

"No shit it's sensitive. Someone stole four lethal skyns and no one knows where they are or when they might turn up, but we're all perfectly clear about the damage they're capable of. Think what could happen if someone ran Killr and then took one of those bad boys for a spin."

"You think it'll come to that? They must be too hot for public use, right? SECNet would hit the panic button the second they showed up on the streets."

"We haven't heard a peep from their trackers, so they're being kept off-grid somewhere. Or shielded from the link. Fin, so help me, if you know something about where we can find them ..."

"No, nothing like that."

"But there's something?"

"It's probably nothing..." Might as well just come out with it. "There's a gamer, calls himself OVRshAdo—"

Yellowbird straightens, and her high cheekbones become even more pronounced as she squints at me. "From Decimation Island? What about him?"

"He's a chronic tuber, spends his entire life online, but his feed was on highlights when the heist went down."

"You think *OVRshAdo* stole the Humanitech arena

skyns?" Yellowbird asks, obviously skeptical. "He was probably taking an hour off, or linked under an alt."

"Maybe, but I don't know any of his alts. And I checked
—there's a 73.4 percent biokin match between him and the
guy who was leading the raid."

She sighs. "That's not near enough for a warrant and
you know it."

"It's close though," I counter, which isn't much of an
argument but it's all I've got—at least it's all I can tell her.
"Look, I know it's thin but I'm asking you to trust me.
You've got nothing to lose."

"Except my job," Yellowbird says.

Fair. "How about this. Is there anything in his record
that, if he *were* a person of interest, would trigger as suspicious for you?"

She sighs but her pupils flare blue-white as she activates
her lenzes. Her eyes dart around in her head for a moment
and then she shakes her head. "He's clean," she says. "Not
so much as a parking ticket. What aren't you telling me?"

I ignore her question. "Can you at least tell me his real
name?"

"Finsbury, no," she answers flatly. "You want his Union
ID too? That's protected info."

She's right. She has to play by the rules—but I don't. I
could get someone from the link to work up a full dox on
him. It'd probably take a few days and it wouldn't be cheap,
but it'd likely be just as thorough as anything the Service
has on him. I was hoping to avoid the hassle.

"Okay, I get it," I reply. "I should know better."

"You should," she says. And then my head thrums,
Connie telling me I've just got a new message—from
Yellowbird. I give her a look and she flashes her eyes at me,

warning me to keep my mouth shut, and I nod in return. *Best she can do.*

I open it and see it's a list, link ID names from the looks of it.

QwenTastic, CaFFeFreak, phatcawk, aimBott69, and a bunch of others including the highly inventive notSHAD. They're OVRshAdo's alts. If can cross reference all these, maybe I'll come up with a better picture of what he's been up to. It's not his real name, but it's something. And if I don't find anything at least I can feel like I did everything I could.

"Want another taco?" I ask, glancing down at her empty plate, but she shakes her head.

"I better get back to the station," she says. "Thanks for lunch."

"Anytime," I say and then open my arms and give her a hug. I think it surprises her as much as it does me, because her first reaction is to flinch, but then she leans into it. Her head barely comes up to my chin.

"Something is definitely wrong with you," she says as she pulls away.

"Shut up," I say back. She turns to leave. "I'll try not to be such a recluse."

"Yeah you will," she says as she walks away. "And next time tacos ain't gonna cut it."

THEY FOUND YOU.

You knew it had to happen eventually. After two games of playing hide and seek with OVRshAdo and his crew they've finally caught up with you. He's back to four strong again. No matter how many of his squaddies you kill, he just recruits more. For some reason, he's made killing you his personal side quest.

They come in hot, bouncing across the grassy plains from the west toward your hiding spot high up in the skeleton of a comms tower, two on motorcycles with a buggy close behind. Problem is they're moving faster than the Redeemer can project a firing line, and the third time the aimbot throws an error you're forced to switch it off and take the shots yourself, picking your moments as the targets become visible in the rolling terrain.

You try to take out one of the bikes and whiff the first few shots, but the fourth connects on one of the riders and they nearly lose control, but don't go down. It's late game and they're armored up, probably level-four adaptive head to toe, and they just tank it, reset, and keep coming.

The buggy might be easier to hit, and you sight in on it, thinking maybe you can take out a tire or put a few shots into the windscreen and hope you get lucky. You've only got a few seconds left, they're only a mile away, and once they hit the line of trees surrounding the compound you'll lose line of sight.

The optics keep the buggy steady as you lead your shot, aiming for the driver, but then you realize something— there's no passenger. There are only three of them.

This is a trap.

Your head ripples with adrenaline. *"Fuck, fuck, fuck, y'all. I think we're dead."*

You anchor the Redeemer to your back, hook yourself into the rappelling line you set up, and slide down from your perch, scanning all around for any sign of the missing enemy. Someone's here already, one hundred percent. Send three of them at you in vehicles while the fourth sneaks up from behind.

They probably ran the Observatory hotspot and scanned for you. It's one of the quest rewards, gives you three codes to ping out player locations. You've been camped here for hours, plenty of time for them to set up an ambush.

This is your fault. You got comfortable hiding behind the long reach of the Redeemer, and now you're gonna pay for it.

You hit the ground and dash immediately inside the antenna building, put a wall to your back and switch out the Redeemer for your assault rifle. It's not legendary but still good, with a high-capacity magazine and low recoil. You've got level-three armor with a full visor and your skyn's muscled-up, plus the reflexes and the aim to take just about anyone one-v-one, but their teammates are only seconds away.

You stashed an escape truck in the garage on the north side of the compound, got it ready to bug out, but for sure that's where they'll be expecting you to go. You could run, try to lose them in the trees, but the forest around here is thin and you're on the edge of the zone as it is. Even if you managed to evade them you'd have to spend your safe-time to hide in the red, and if you burn it all now you'll have nothing left for the endgame, when solos are the first to get picked off.

You're not moving but still your breath is ragged. You're pinched. Death is certain unless you can miracle yourself out of here.

The engines grow louder as they roar up the tree-lined road toward the compound. They're almost here. You need to move—*do something*. If you're just gonna sit here waiting for them to surround you, you might as well end it yourself. At least then OVRshAdo won't get the satisfaction.

Your ears burn with sudden anger. Screw OVRshAdo. No way you let him win. You push up off the wall, weapon ready, switched to full auto. You've still got time. That fourth goon's got to be around here somewhere—if you can take him out before his buddies get here you just might have a fighting chance.

You jiggle peek out of the doorway, keeping your head moving, searching for any signs of movement, but come up empty. Nothing in sight and all you hear are engines. The other guy could sneak right up on you and you wouldn't hear him coming. They'll be crashing the compound from the west side, so you move east, skirting around the edge of the building toward the garage.

The good news is you're not entirely defenseless. You

set up a proximity charge across the west entrance to the compound, and that'll slow at least one of them down, if not give you an outright kill. It's not over yet.

The compound is small and surrounded by trees—just the antenna building, the garage, and two boxy guardhouses on each end of the road splitting through the middle. Not many places to hide. You swallow, then kick off into a sprint across the open area, aiming for the garage. OVRshAdo's fourth could be anywhere, set up to snipe from the trees or even waiting for you to get in the truck, but you make it into the cool shadow of the garage without a problem, and other than the truck, the place is empty, just the way you left it. The big open door looks out east through the thin line of trees to the rippling grassland below. It's a straight shot out of here, down the road and away to safety. All you need to do is get in and drive. You might even make it.

But they knew you were here, went to all this trouble to find you. No way they'd let you just drive away. OVRshAdo's too good a player to set all this up and not have a better plan than that.

Then you realize you don't hear the engines anymore. They should have breached the compound by now, should have set off the proximity charge...

Your spine tingles. There's something else going on.

You jump into the truck, drop your backpack and weapons on the passenger seat, and power up the engine. You grab the wheel and squint out into the sunlight, ready to full-throttle out of the garage, but at the last second you change your mind—*this isn't right.*

The audience pressure in your head builds as you switch the truck to auto, pick a random destination on the nav screen, and set it to drive. Then you grab your stuff and jump out the second before it pulls out of the garage and angles onto the road. You strap your pack back on and follow the vehicle out, watching your best chance at survival drive away, and only seconds later a figure materializes out of the tree line, blurring from invisibility as their camo disengages. There he is—OVRshAdo's fourth.

You pull up your AR as the figure raises something—a detonator—and an instant later the truck *whomps* up in a fireball on the road, spewing flames and wreckage into the sky. So that's what they were up to, flush you out of your hiding place and booby-trap your escape. It almost worked too. But it didn't, and now you have a chance to react, but you need to be quick. When your name doesn't hit the kill-feed they'll know something went wrong and come looking.

You take the target presented and pump the guy holding the detonator full of bullets. You've got the extended mag on your weapon and from this distance you don't miss. Forty-two bullets later his name pops onto the kill-feed.

> *AniK@ downs survivor HuggyJackson. 43 players remain.*

The others will be coming now. You imagine OVRshAdo will be furious—he had to have spent the entire game planning this out, finishing the Observatory hotspot to find your location and then running through Walter's Arena to get the camo unit. He put a lot of resources into taking you down, and all he did was deliver you another powerful weapon.

Right on cue you hear engines fire up somewhere close by. They're swinging around the compound to come in on the east, probably aiming to overwhelm you, but you won't give them the chance. You race over to HuggyJackson's

corpse. Luckily the camo unit's undamaged, and you disengage it from his armor and plug it into yours. It's still got half
a charge, and his backpack's got three extra cells. That's
nearly two hours of near invisibility.

The unit hums as it engages with your armor, and then
chimes ready in your helmet, and you engage it immediately. Your dropsuit shimmers as the built-in active camo
function engages, and you disappear. Everything except the
weapon in your hand.

Dammit! You should have thought. The rifle isn't built to
integrate with the camo, and neither is the Redeemer. You
need to drop them or the camo is useless. A floating sniper
rifle makes for an easy target.

You resist the idea of losing your most powerful weapon
but know you have no other choice, and toss the Redeemer
and the AR into the trees away from HuggyJackson's body
just as two players come sailing into the compound on
motorcycles, controlling the bikes single-handed. You just
get clear before they spray their teammate's body and the
surrounding area with high-velocity metal shards from the
flechette launchers strapped to their wrists, probably hoping
to catch you looting.

The air sings with the whistling of a thousand knives
cutting the air, slicing through wood and leaves, but you're
already out of the line of fire, moving back around the tree
line toward the west entrance. The invisibility isn't perfect,
more like a fast-changing camouflage, but it's enough to
keep you out of sight, and you play silent as OVRshAdo
barks out frustrated orders to his team.

You pull yourself up into a tree, climb as high as you
can, and stay still as they search the compound. At one
point OVRshAdo walks right under you, and you hold your
breath for dear life, but he moves right on past.

After fifteen minutes, when you could be long gone, they give up, load back onto their vehicles, and roar away.

Once you're sure they've cleared out and aren't playing another trick, you clamber down out of the tree and search the woods for the Redeemer, but it's gone. No doubt they found it. OVRshAdo may not have caught you, but he didn't walk away empty-handed.

You figure they'll probably set up somewhere nearby, hoping to catch you in rotation as the zone pushes you, but there's still lots of safe-zone left to hide in. And with the camo unit, you should be able to avoid them until you run out the clock.

It looked rough there for a minute, and you lost your legendary weapon, but you might just survive another game.

Dub was wrong about Anika.

I was wrong about Anika.

Chalk it up to the thick shell she's built around herself, to a childhood that didn't leave much room for vulnerability, and to the raw agony of losing a child.

There's nothing wrong with her. She's awesome.

And I kinda hate myself right now. A little for how I suspected her in the first place and got us into this under false pretenses, but mostly because every second I spend with her I'm betraying Connie.

I know I'm not doing anything wrong, but the buzz I get from being with Anika is hollowed out by guilt. Just a few days ago I was ready to defy nature and decency and drag Connie back from the dead, transplant her sprite into a replica body and dive head first into the lie of being with her—and now I can't stop thinking about a girl half my age I've known for less than a week.

There's nothing going on with her except her dogged pursuit of a place on the Gladiator team, and as far as I can tell OVRshAdo is clean too. I checked into the alts Yellow-

bird shared and there's nothing I could find that would indi-
cate even a hint of foul play. He's a self-important dick, sure,
but that's not against the law. Dub was being overcautious
and I got caught up in it, started looking for problems—and
yeah, I found problems, but they weren't what I expected.
Honestly, I almost wish she was up to something. It'd be
easier to deal with that way.

"So you'll be my guest at the fight on Sunday?" Anika
asks. "I have twenty tickets, I might as well use one of
them."

I don't even hesitate. "Definitely. I'd be honored."

"You don't need to be honored," she retorts. "Just
show up."

We've spent another evening together, but this time
scrimming while she streamed for her fans—a quarter of a
million people watched as we slayed duos in DI. I knew
Anika was a celebrity, but I didn't fully understand the
weight of her following until it crashed over me. I had five
thousand new contact requests in the first ten minutes, and
had to have Connie put my inbox dark after the hundred
thousandth. My rep's bumped up two full points, and it was
already pretty high to start with. I don't know how she deals
with it, this constant level of scrutiny. The weight of it must
be astounding, but she barely seems to notice.

We left Decimation Island and hopped into a private,
high-poly virt. I think she picked the location at random. It's
an alien landscape—a blue-grassed meadow under a brilliant green sky—but we're finally alone. And while our presence is completely artificial, I can still feel the warmth of
her body standing next to me. The aspect she's wearing is
different than her current skyn, her hair is longer and darker
and she's a little shorter, but I can still see her through it.
She smiles, bashful, but then leans in and kisses me, and

even though our lips pressing together are artificial, the pleasure is real.

She leans into me, and I grab her around the small of her back and return the kiss. My head is whirring. I'm giddy and horny and ashamed of myself all at once. I know I shouldn't be doing this, that it's all built on a lie and I'm betraying Connie, but none of that matters as her tongue flicks mine and her pelvis grinds into me. I want to drop her down in the grass right now and take her, and I think that was her intent in bringing us here, but I pull away instead.

She squints at me. "Is there a problem, Mr. Gage?"

"Yeah," I say. "*You.*"

"Is that so?" she says, stepping back and crossing her arms.

"I ..." I don't know what to say. This was supposed to be a job, but I can't stop thinking about her. Only yesterday I was planning on Frankenstein-ing Connie's sprite up into a new skyn, but now ...

Jesus I've fucked this up.

I wave my hands, trying to come up with the words, and finally blurt out, "I just—I'd forgotten what it feels like to not feel like shit."

This makes her laugh. "Is that your idea of a compliment?"

I like her. When I'm with her, that's the only place I want to be. She knows who she is, doesn't have anything to prove, doesn't need to fill the silence. It's easy and it's fun. I know there's something wrong because, even though I don't have a stomach in here, still it's all clenched up. The last time I felt like this I was married a month later.

"I wasn't expecting any of this," I say. "I'm still ..." I don't finish the sentence, but she knows.

"Your wife," she says, and I nod. "And you feel guilty." I nod again.

"I know it's stupid—"

She puts up her hand, presses her finger against my lips. "It isn't stupid. If anything, it's sweet." She locks eyes with me and for a moment her thoughts are far away. "I've always dreamed of being loved like that. You were lucky to have it."

I take her hand, lean in, and kiss her again, and this time I don't think about it. I like her, and I think she's feeling the same. We're both broken, shattered by loss, but somehow our cracks line up.

Eventually she pulls away and gives me a big grin. "Hard to believe this is all just in our heads," she says, and she grabs my hand and strokes my palm with her fingers. A jolt of electricity throbs between my legs.

I suck in a breath. "Imagine the real thing."

Anika gives me a coy look. "We'll have to test that out sometime."

"I'm up for experimenting ..."

Her mouth twists up in a smirk. "I'm busy for the next day or so, have this thing Sunday night, but whichever way that goes, I still get Monday off. Pencil you in?"

"Can't wait," I say.

She squeezes my hand once then lets go. "I should get going," she says, drawing out her words. "I've got a midnight training slot booked."

"Those asses aren't going to kick themselves."

"See ya, soldier," she says, her voice canted like she's quoting something, and just as she's fading away a bubble in me bursts and suddenly I don't want her to leave and I reach out to stop her but she's already gone and I stumble forward and nearly fall into the long blue grass.

I'm an idiot. Zero Chill Gage, *that's me.*

I'm no good at this, never was. I know I should let it be, play it cool, call Dub and tell him he has nothing to worry about, then cast back to the cabin and figure out what the hell I'm supposed to do.

Can I start to entertain the idea of a life without Connie? And if I can't, what the hell am I doing kissing someone else? But I don't do any of it. Instead I think up Anika's contact, still not sure whether to send her a note or try to lure her back here—but she's showing offline. She's gone, I already missed her, which is probably just as well. At this point I should just leave well-enough alone. Anything else will likely only mess things up.

I start to trigger the cast back to the cabin but have another thought, and before I can think better of it I call up Anika's alt, and there she is—GulfGaytR. She's in *Decimation Island*, probably one last solo run to warm up before training. I want to send an invite or a message or anything for the excuse to spend a few more minutes with her, but hold myself back. I don't want to come off clingy.

But that doesn't mean I can't kick back in spectator mode and watch her frag bots for a bit. No harm in that, right?

I call up the spectator console and zero in on Gulf-GaytR. She's in a vanilla DI run, just landed from the drop tower, but she isn't playing alone. She's running a squad and teamed up with three others, and instead of one of the hotspots, they've landed near the edge of the zone, away from the hostilities, and from the looks of things they're just standing around talking.

Curious, I check out the others she's teamed with. Two of them I don't know—RainBowWow and XeroFacks—but the third …

My chest vibrates with a numbed shock as I reread the name to make sure I'm not imagining things. By the fifth time I've gone over it, breaking it down letter by letter and comparing it to the list Yellowbird sent me, my infatuated light-headedness has compressed down to a tight nugget of anger in my gut.

The third name is *notSHAD*. One of OVRshAdo's alts.

Anika lied to me.

She told me she hadn't talked to him since DI, that she didn't want anything to do with him.

So what the hell are they doing partnered up in *Decimation Island*?

THEY WERE IN ON IT, OVRshAdo and Anika, both of them together. That *was* OVRshAdo at the heist. I may not be able to prove it yet, but now I'm sure of it.

Anika didn't react because she knew it was coming. It's the answer that makes the most sense and I knew it from the start, but I let her convince me she was someone she wasn't.

Some detective I am. All it takes to scramble my instincts is a pretty smile and a bit of attention. My stomach is churning and I can barely see straight. Even sitting next to the fire in my virtual cabin I'm shivering.

I'm a fucking moron.

This is what I get. For letting my guard down. For ignoring what was right in front of me. For thinking I could let someone in.

I let her play me. She must have known from the beginning what my intentions were. Whatever her game is, I'm no more than another NPC to her. Well, at least I don't have to feel bad about how this all got started anymore, I'm not the only asshole here. We played each other.

But what if I'm wrong?

Of course, there could be another explanation. I'd barely known her for a few hours when I asked about OVRshAdo. There are plenty of reasons she might want to hide her contact with him. She told me people ask her about it all the time, think they should be a couple, or at least running pro duos, and it's the first question pinned on her AMA feed. She thanks him for helping her get to the end, but makes it clear she isn't interested in a partnership, professional or otherwise.

But that's for public consumption. I've seen what they went through to get to the end of DI; they formed a bond, everyone watching could see that, and neither of them have any memory of it. That'd weigh on anyone. There must be plenty of reasons why they could be meeting up in secret.

Or could be I just want to think she's innocent because I've got feelings for her.

Dammit, she's in my head, got me second-guessing myself.

I don't know what to do, but I need to talk this through with someone, and it can't be Connie.

Even though it's after midnight Dub answers my call and a second later he's standing in my living room. His aspect is identical to his skyn, and moves like silk, no off-the-shelf animations for him. He's even wearing the same uniform of tight black T-shirt and compression shorts, and his purple photoos ripple in the firelight.

"What's wrong?" he asks, his forehead furrowed. It's the middle of the night, he must know this is bad news.

"Your gut was right," I say, struggling to control my voice. "You remember OVRshAdo? Anika said she hadn't talked to him since DI, but I just saw them together."

Dub's head bobs as he processes the news. "So you're saying—"

"OVRshAdo stole your arena skyns, and Anika was in on it."

His eyes narrow as he works the implications over in his head.

"That scans," he mutters after a moment, his deep voice rumbling in the small cabin. "The stolen skyns' safeguards were hacked before the gala even started—and the techs say it had to have happened at the Mundi, or somewhere en route. Had to be someone on the inside."

"Anika."

Dub growls, and the tendons in his neck go taut. I've never seen him mad, but I've seen him fight, and I sure as hell wouldn't want to be on his bad side. "We need to get her off the ticket," Dub says. "Confiscate her skyn before she hurts someone."

I take a second to enjoy the feeling, knowing she's caught, but it's fleeting. Mostly I'm disappointed, like I discovered something precious and immediately had it stolen from me.

And still there's a chance I could be wrong.

"Wait," I say. "Just hold on. We need to be sure."

"But you just said she was in on the robbery—"

"And I think she was, OVRshAdo too—his biokin's a 70 percent match to the leader—"

Dub hesitates. "Only 70 percent?"

"73.4."

"Still," Dub says, uncertainty in his voice.

"That's the problem, a lot of *what ifs,* but I can't prove anything. All we've got is her dead-eyeing through an armed robbery and then lying to me about talking to OVRshAdo. It's thin and it's circumstantial. We need more than that. We need to be sure."

Dub slumps down on the couch and buries his head in

his hands. "I don't know, Fin," he says, his voice muffled in his big palms, then he looks up at me. "What if we wait and she does something else? Then it's on us."

"Or we can launch an accusation with nothing to back it up and then how's that help the ludus?" Dub drops his head back into his hands with a meaty slap. "We need something concrete. Something tangible."

"Like what?" Dub asks, raising his head once more.

"Those skyns they stole, still no leads on them?"

He shakes his head. "Standards makes the ludus run passive location tracking on all the arena skyns. The second one of them comes near an active link signal they'll ping the Ministry, but so far nothing."

"Could they have removed the trackers?"

"No way, they're built right into the Cortexes. It'd take a full cortical replacement, and reseating the diganics with the skyn's nervous system would be next to impossible."

"That doesn't mean anything. They'd have known about the trackers. They wouldn't have gone to the trouble if they didn't have a way around them."

"Humanitech has them lowjacked too," Dub says, his voice low, as if someone might overhear. "A secondary tracking system even Standards don't know about. It's distributed, wouldn't show up on scans. I doubt anyone who wasn't looking would know it was there."

"Does Anika know about the second tracker?"

Dub shrugs. "Could be, though I only found out by accident. I think they want it kept quiet."

"So if the skyns had been out, we'd know about it."

"As far as I can figure, yeah."

"That's something at least. We'll see them coming." We both fall silent, neither of us sure what to do next, but then a thought occurs. "Let's say I'm right, and OVRshAdo and Anika stole them. What I still don't understand is *why*."

"To sell, don't you think?"

"From what I can tell, you and Anika share a similar problem—neither of you need money. No, this is something else." Or I'm wrong and this is all a giant misunderstanding. I need to come at this another way. "There were two other people grouped with them tonight. XeroFacks and Rain-BowWow. You know who they are?"

"Not a clue," Dub says. "Never been much of a gamer."

"Connie," I call out, "can you run SECNet for two aliases: XeroFacks and RainBowWow. Get as much as you can, dip into the funds and use the back channels if you have to."

"On it," she replies from the bedroom. If Dub thinks it's weird I'm talking to Connie he doesn't show it. A few seconds later a screen pulls itself open above the fireplace. "Not much to report. Even the undernet's dry," she says.

They're both basic profiles. Reps just high enough to make the IDs useable, limited link traffic and associations to a bunch of games, but no ties to biokin or any useful real-world data, no profile pictures. Their birthdays are both set to Jan 01, 2000. RainBowWow has their location set to Beverly Hills, but apart from that they're generic and impossible to narrow down.

No help there. "Thanks anyway, Con."

"Here if you need me," she answers back, her voice chipper. I'm stung by sudden remorse. How could I have thought about letting Connie go? She's the only person I can count on—she'd never, ever lie to me.

Because she can't. *Her programming won't let her.*

I slam the lid on my warring thoughts. I've got enough going on right now, I don't have the energy to get into this particular clusterfuck. Thank Christ Vae's shyft is keeping Deacon quiet. With the way my head's already spinning, I don't know how I'd keep him down otherwise.

I sigh and Dub looks up at me. "I have to tell Coach, and then go to the team GM. After Nyx ..." His throat catches. "Whoever stole those skyns already set us back a season. We had a good chance of winning the cup this year, but we needed those skyns. No way can we let Anika compete in the trials. What if she wins and joins the team? She could be working for another ludus, who knows? I can't let anything else hurt us."

"We need proof. If you go to your coach now, what'll you say?"

"That Anika ripped us off."

"Based on what?"

"On"—he cocks his big round head at me—"on what you just told me. That she knew about it ahead of time. And she lied about that OVRshAdo guy."

"None of that means anything. She'll have easy enough explanations—yeah she kept her cool during the heist, it's what she does for a living, and so what if she was gaming with OVRshAdo, that's no crime, besides, everyone expected that anyway after the DI live game. Plus, I bet there's no physical evidence she sabotaged the skyn safe-guards. She's clever, and she'll have covered her tracks. If I hadn't happened to be standing beside her when this all went down, no one would have suspected her at all. It'll be your word against hers."

"And *yours*," Dub says.

"Trust me, you don't want me as your sole corroborating witness."

"Then what?" Dub says, launching back to his feet and

throwing up his hands. "You want I should sit on my hands and let the ludus go to crap?"

"No, but we need something more than we have now."

"So what then?"

Good question. I could confront Anika, but she'd deny it. Toss some perfectly reasonable excuse at me and I'd never see her again. And I already know I can't find OVRshAdo. No one knowing who he is or where he came from is part of his whole schtick.

All that's left are those other two IDs. They're working as a team, and if I can find out who's behind them, maybe that'll lead us somewhere. It's not much, but I don't have anything else.

"Give me forty-eight hours, just until Sunday morning. If we don't find anything by then, one way or another, we can go to your coach. That'll still leave them most of a day to decide what to do."

"I don't know, Fin—"

"We need to be sure. Anika's trending right now. If we come at her and we're wrong, the public backlash could hurt the ludus even worse."

"*Arg*," Dub moans, and his shoulders slump. "Fine, Sunday. But I really don't like this."

"Trust me, I don't like it either," I say. "But this is how it has to be."

So that's it. I've got two days to get to the bottom of all this. Two days to figure out if the woman I've just fallen for is secretly involved in ripping off a few hundred million dollars' worth of lethal bio-tech.

Fuck my life.

You're only halfway across the road when your camo battery finally dies and an instant later the bullets start flying.

"*No, no, no, no, no,*" runs like a chant through your head as you serpentine the rest of the way across the hardpacked dirt, fists out. Your armor takes a pounding but holds up long enough for you to crash into cover behind the back wall of the concrete hut you were sneaking toward.

Armor's shredded and you've used the last of your camo, but it bought you another sixty seconds. Maybe. But there's nowhere to go from here.

You're up against it, staring down an execution line. There's only six minutes until the zone closes, and fourteen players still alive—two full four-man squads, a trio, plus OVRshAdo, Zara-Zee, and you.

The hut's on the edge of a small town nestled in a sunny valley on the east coast of the island, up north of the Smuggler's Run hotspot. All the NPC villagers are gone, and the bots are pacing, waiting for their chance to strike. The red's at your back and closing fast. This is the last slice of protection between you and the center of the safe-zone: a spot in small village made up of two- and three-story buildings. To get there you'll need to cross a wide, open-air viaduct, and the other teams are perched in the buildings' upper windows, ready to cut down anyone who tries.

Looks like you're gonna die, but the audience is eating it up.

The two squads holding positions overlooking the viaduct aren't working together, 'cause officially that's against the rules, but they're not shooting at each other either. They're after meatier targets: OVRshAdo's stuck on the edge of the zone too, just on the other side of the concrete wall from you, inside the shack.

At this point you're just a side dish—everyone is gunning for OVRshAdo. If he makes it to the survivors' circle this game, it'll put him at seven hundred hours, only three games from winning the Century. At this point the bounty on killing him is already worth risking a low-hour run on. It's one of those unwritten rules of the game: when you have the choice, always shoot the guy with the most hours. It's not enough to win, part of the game is making sure everyone else loses.

It's kinda funny. The only reason he's in this shitty position is because he wasted so much of his game chasing *you*. If you don't make it, at least you'll have the thin comfort of knowing he won't either.

But you don't want to lose.

"Anyone home?" you call out, and slap your fist against the concrete. You know it's only OVRshAdo and Zara-Zee in there. You downed HuggyJackson back at the comms tower and you saw on the kill-feed they lost their third an hour ago, and they must know you're out here. No way they didn't hear the bullets thudding into their hiding spot.

A muffled laugh comes as reply. "Well look what we got ourselves into," OVRshAdo calls back. Then after a second, "So how you wanna play this?"

You skip right over the idea of fighting. Even if you somehow took both of them out you'd still be sitting at twelfth. Since the zone will hit you before it does anyone else, your safe-time will start to tick down first, and after you were forced to ditch the Redeemer, the only weapon you've found that'll integrate with the camo is a pistol, so there's no chance the bots don't get you.

You hate the idea, but there's only one way you survive, and that's working together. Even then it's a long shot, but at this point you've got no other choice.

"What do you have in mind?" you ask.

"We've got a cell for your camo," OVRshAdo's muffled voice replies.

"In exchange for?"

"We group up and you share your safe-time," he says. "You got a full hundred stocked up, right?"

You do, and you need it, every second. "What do you have?"

"Thirty-seven."

Shit. Thirty-seven minutes. And after the zone fully closes safe-time runs down at an increased rate. That's less than three minutes before the bots overwhelm them. You could just wait out here and live longer than OVRshAdo. Granted, only by a few minutes, but it'd be something.

"There's a window around the corner," he says. "Come on in when you're ready."

"How do I know you won't shoot me?"

"You don't," OVRshAdo answers, "but we could have already, if we wanted."

It's probably true. You were lying prone out in a

defilade on the edge of town while the zone came in. You knew he and Zara-Zee were in the hut, and there's a good chance he saw you coming.

Even though he's been hunting you for the past few games, you don't think it was personal. Cold-blooded, sure, but all part of the game. An hour ago killing you might have gotten him further in the round, now it won't. Basic game math.

He'll put a bullet in your back the second it's in his best interest, but you figure you're safe for now. Still, you take a breath before you announce, "Coming in," then slip around the side of the hut and vault in through the window.

OVRshAdo and Zara-Zee look like shit. They lost their other squad member, myfriendtimmy, a few hours ago in a four-v-three and haven't fully healed up from the fight. They're well geared though, fourth-level armor with full visors, and they killed Primus and looted his Archive four times over two games and they're both double fisting Stingers—two-muzzle SMGs that don't have much range, but shred up close.

Zara-Zee has your Redeemer resting beside her, and as much as you resent her having it, right now you'd straight-up trade it for the Stingers. They're built to integrate with your camo unit and would go invisible along with the rest of you.

You stare at each other for a moment, feeling each other out. After all, you could have tossed a grenade in here instead of jumping through the window—you don't have one, but they don't know that.

OVRshAdo seems happy enough to wait, as though you're not all about to be torn apart by rampaging bots, and he watches you with his visor up and a vague smile on his face. Zara-Zee's expression isn't as contained. Her pale lips remain set in a tight line, but her brown eyes don't stop scowling. She isn't happy you're here, but when no one moves for a weapon you let yourself relax.

After another second of staring you down, the guy who's spent the past three games trying his best to kill you flashes a wide smile and holds out his hand, palm up, and offers the camo energy cell. That's half an hour of invisibility, plenty of time to sneak into the safe-zone and carve yourself into the top ten, even with sharing your time—but how's that help him? They'd still be trapped out here.

He knows he's handing you the win, so what's his play?

You move to take the cell but he closes his fingers over it and flips his fist over. The pulsing white ring on the back of his hand signals the offer to team. Before you can change your mind, you fist-up and punch-in and a trickle runs down your arm as your collected time drains away to your two new teammates.

They loaded up on tactical upgrades, and when you join the squad their battle-lens shyft automatically loads and layers over your vision, outlining each of them in green. You'll be able to see them through walls and read each other's vitals. Plus, you've got the wind speed, ambient temperature, and other info you could get to if you needed it. But most importantly, red triangles mark the enemy positions around you. OVRshAdo must have a wasp drone flitting around over there, scouting out movement. They know exactly where everyone is.

"Welcome aboard," OVRshAdo says in your head as he opens his fingers, dropping the cell, and the smile never leaves his face. You snatch it before it can hit the ground and quickly replace the empty one in the camo unit on your chest. By the time you've got it switched out you've run through OVRshAdo's options, and you know exactly why

he's smiling. He just bought his way into the top ten, and all it cost him was a battery.

He and Zara-Zee are pinned, but you're not. You've got the enemy positions, and now he expects you to camo up and go kill them. And the thing is, you know it's your best chance too. He's not getting off that easy though. It'll cost him.

"I need two Stingers and all the ammo you have," you say matter-of-factly, like there's no expectation they'll argue.

"No." Zara-Zee takes a step toward you, then silently adds, *"I'm not giving her my guns. This wasn't part of the deal."*

"I can hear you, dumbass," you say. *"One each. You want me to one-v-four a whole squad or not? If I die we all die."*

OVRshAdo shrugs, flings out his left hand, and lets the Stinger twirl around the trigger guard to offer you the grip. You get to keep one item with every win, and you didn't carry over anything last game. The Stingers count as sidearms toward your loadout, so if by luck you somehow scrape your way out of this, you can keep them both. Two Stingers plus the camo unit? If you can survive this round, the next one'll be a walk.

You toss your pistol and take the compact assault rifle from him, then wait for Zara-Zee to hand hers over.

But she isn't so sure. "I don't trust her," she says out loud.

"You're just mad she killed your boyfriend."

"Which one was your boyfriend?" you ask. "Human-Bacon or HuggyJackson?"

She doesn't answer, just stares daggers.

"Huggy," OVRshAdo says, nudging Zara-Zee with her elbow. "Come on, Zee, get over yourself. We've been trying to kill her for three games now, can't get pissed at her for not dying. All part of the game, right?"

You glance back at Zara-Zee and raise your eyebrows from behind your visor. She screws up her mouth in a scowl but finally tosses her weapon to you. OVRshAdo hands you a bunch of extended mags and you strap them to your thighs and empty everything you don't need out of your pack.

Then there's nothing else left to say. These aren't your friends, this is purely a transaction. There's not gonna be a final pep talk or teary goodbye, but one last thing before you go. You glance down at the Redeemer. "That's mine," you tell Zara-Zee, "and I'm gonna get it back."

She strokes the long barrel with her fingers. "From my cold dead hand, sweetheart," she replies, murder in her eyes.

"Any time now," OVRshAdo says, pointing to the digits on his wrist. "Tick tock."

He's right. You've got a job to do, so move.

"*Either I'm about to get wasted,*" you tell the audience, "*or y'all are about to see something cool.*"

You feel the pulse of excitement in response as you engage your camo, climb back out through the window, land in a crouch, and creep along the edge of the hut toward the viaduct. The red's right at your back now, and with your diminished safe-time that means only minutes until the bots come off the leash.

"*Anyone got a smoke?*" you ask the team.

Two canisters whip out of the hut in response, hit the ground halfway toward the buildings, and kick out a dense blue fog. The red dots marking the enemy positions shift in response, expecting OVRshAdo and Zara-Zee will be moving, and you use the distraction to crouch-walk into the open, away from the distraction of the smoke. The only

problem with the camo is its refresh rate. It's not instanta-
neous, and works best if you move slow, so you're forced to
agonize your way across the open dirt, ease yourself into the
shallow aqueduct and then up the incline on the other side,
hoping the whole time no one notices the slow-moving blur
stalking toward them.

The decision now is who to kill. There's three squads
left: a trio and two foursomes. The trio's holed up in a
building one up from you, and one of the foursomes is
camped in a two-stack just up from that. It'd be easiest to
take out the trio, they're closer and three-v-one is slightly
better odds, but there are fourteen players left, and even if
you wiped the entire team you'd still be one spot out of
placement. You'd still need to take on a full four-man,
except then they'd know you were coming.

So a one-v-four it is, and all you have to do is eliminate
an entire squad by yourself. No biggie. At least you have the
wasp updating their positions. You can do this.

You get almost all the way across the open field before a
rattle of fire rolls out from one of the windows and the red
icons superimposed on your vision shudder and stop
moving.

"*Wasp's down,*" OVRshAdo states, and the bottom falls
out of your stomach. It was gonna be hard enough taking on
a whole squad with the benefit of knowing where they were,
but now ...

You're screwed.

OVRshAdo doesn't say anything, doesn't try to be
encouraging, and you appreciate it. His voice in your head
right now is the last thing you need. Your thoughts come in
a jumble, searching for any other way out of this, but there's
no time. Nothing to do but muscle up and fight. You've still

got the camo and the Stingers, and they won't be expecting you.

Surprise and overwhelming firepower. It'll have to be enough.

Once you're across the field and into the shadow of a building you pick up your pace, hurry along the concrete wall, skip across a narrow alley between the neighboring building, and travel its length before you cut left, swinging out and around the foursome's position so you can come at them from behind.

You move quietly, slinking through the shadows, and spot movement in an upper window of a three-story building ahead, in the dead center of the zone.

It's the other four-man squad. It wasn't the team you were gunning for, but they'll do. Even better actually. They probably figure their spots in the top ten are a lock, which means they're your best target.

You skitter across the laneway and get right up next to their building, then skirt around the perimeter, glancing in windows, trying to find an opening. The safe-time on your wrist is already dropping. OVRshAdo and Zara-Zee are in the red, and as they use up their time it comes off your shared pool. It's reducing slowly right now, but the red has nearly caught up with you and the second it closes the rate it drops will spike and you'll all be vulnerable. You need to end the fight before that happens.

Thirty seconds later you find a way in. As far as you can tell there's one guy on the main floor, one on the second, and two on the third. The one on the bottom is sticking mainly to the front of the building, alternating peeks out of the two windows that give him the best angle on anyone who might be approaching. You settle in under one of the windows, a

Stinger in each hand, and the next time he peeks you pop up and spray him down through the window. He's quick enough to get a burst off, but the high-velocity metal eats through him and spins him around and he goes down.

Then it's on. You leap through the window and empty the Stingers into the groaning figure on the floor.

AniK@ downs TinkleTaint. 13 players remain.

You reload the Stingers, keeping the camo active. It won't do much now that you're moving at speed, but it won't hurt. There are three more players above you, and the only way up to the second floor is a single narrow staircase, a choke point they can easily defend. They could always be stupid and rush you, but they won't. They'll be expecting it's the other foursome, not a single player. They'll also be positioned away from the top of the stairs to give them open sight lines to take out anyone who tries to breach. Trying a full-frontal assault would be suicide, camo or no.

Instead you grab the two flashbangs TinkleTaint had on him, duck back outside, and lob them up through two of the second-story windows. Before the glass has even hit the ground you're racing up the stairs, and just as the two bangers pop you crest the stairs and dive to the left, roll to a crouch, and come up shooting.

It's an open floor, and the two waiting to ambush you are staggered by the flashbangs, unable to focus. They shoot anyway, yelling in fury as they aim for the blur coming for them, but their shots miss high, and you rake your weapons across their flailing bodies, downing them both.

AniK@ downs LuvMunkee6969. 12 players remain.

AniK@ downs Crumplestilskin. 11 players remain.

"*Well, shit,*" Zara-Zee says in your ear.

"*Ain't over yet,*" you reply.

But it is. You got this all zipped up.

For just a second you get the urge to drop from the squad. You're at the center of the zone, your spot's secured, and you could leave the guy upstairs alone, let Zara-Zee and OVRshAdo fight it out for tenth, but you don't. Eventually you'll have to stop OVRshAdo from getting his thousand hours, but now's not the time.

There's only a minute left before overtime as you loot the two corpses. They're loaded up, probably been here a while and haven't needed to spend their utility. They had a handful of grenades, a choking smoke, even an assault drone. You've got options. More than enough to take out your one remaining opponent.

"Let's talk," the guy upstairs calls, his voice trembling. His guaranteed win just got shot to shit and he's feeling the pressure. "It doesn't have to go down like this."

"Oh yeah it does," you yell back as you prime three grenades. "Ready or not, here I come."

I PACE back and forth across the cabin's uneven pine floor with the fire warming my legs, and work over the past few days.

I start from the beginning, reviewing everything I've learned, trying to make pieces fit, and it isn't until I get to something Dub said that it comes to me: I've been looking at this all wrong, concentrating on the heist and the stolen skyns and going by what SECNet can tell me, but SECNet only sees the physical world—Anika and OVRshAdo live on the mesh. While SECNet's got ties into the global communication system, it's mostly blind to what happens inside the tens of thousands of public and private virtual worlds. I've been coming at this like a cop, but I need to think like a gamer, and since I'm no gamer, I need a specialist, a *virtling*, a digital native who knows their way around.

And if anyone's gonna know someone who can help, it's Shelt.

He doesn't ask any questions and an hour later I have a meeting with someone called Jace. From what Shelt says, Jace is a true bit-head, an original gamer, been living purely digital for years and has renounced everything to do with the real world—including the concept of a personal gender. He also says Jace has maxed-out characters on half the virts in the mesh, knows everyone, can find anything, and is willing to take commissions. The catch is they'll only meet face-to-face. Digitally, of course, but it still means I have to go to them.

A few minutes later I get a link to a private virt and when I cast through I arrive in a room surrounded by mirrors, with all the reflections showing different people— and not all of them are what you'd consider *people*. I glance down and my stomach lurches for a second when there's nothing under me, not even my feet, but I know better. This is my first time in this virt, and I need to pick a body before I can go any further.

Based on my choices, I guess this must be a fantasy-based world, elves and orcs and shit. I've got a wide variety of options—a red-haired woman with a bow and a dark purple cloak, a blue-green skinned aquatic thing with webbed feet holding a trident, a guy in full plate mail armor, and plenty more—twelve in all to choose from, plus the option to customize my own. I pick the redhead for no reason other than she's directly in front of me.

The room fades to black and when the lights come up I'm sitting in the back of a wagon, bouncing over cobblestones as the horses clip-clop up a wide, heavily trafficked road toward a tight packed, fairy-tale port city. The sun's high in the sky, glittering off the ivory spires of what I guess must be the royal palace or whatever. The wind is blowing clean and clear off a wide shimmering bay strewn with high-masted ships anchored at the docks, and even more out in the water. Wouldn't surprise me if there were dragons around somewhere. Everyone loves dragons.

I've never been much for wizards and flaming swords and prophesied chosen ones and all that, I prefer my fantasy a little more grounded, but I get the appeal. Who wouldn't want to live in a place where magic was real?

I'm not alone on the wagon. Along with the driver there are others on the back with me, all travelers huddled under their cloaks, but I don't know who's human and who's background ambiance. For all I know I could be the only person in here.

We pass through the slums on the outskirts of town, my ass growing steadily numb, and a few minutes later we've entered the shadows of a bustling commercial section leading up from the docks, with vendor's carts and colorful stalls and squat wood and stone buildings lining either side of the road. Eventually the cart stops in front of a canted wooden tavern. The windows are dark, but warbling music seeps from the rickety door, and a swinging sign hanging from the rough-wooden slats reads "Harold's Barrels Tavern."

The grizzled driver gives me a dirty look until I take the hint and leap off. I'm barely on the ground before he flicks the reins and the wagon trundles away.

Inside is warm and dark and smoky, with a long bar and a dozen square tables lit by weak lanterns and a smoldering fireplace. It's still midmorning and the room is only a quarter full, but the people in here are drinking like they've made a career out of it. A stout, dark man sits on a stool near the fire, plunking the strings of a stout, dark instrument. No one looks up as I cross the floor, searching the patrons for Jace. I'm not sure what they look like, I only got their name, but when I spot them I know I've found the right person— they're the only one in here whose eyes are glowing.

Jace's aspect is strikingly androgynous, with sharp,

narrow features and a shock of messy, silver-white hair. They're sitting alone in the corner, wearing a purple leather jerkin and tight white leggings, leaning back on the bench with their slender silver boots up on the table like they own the place, and they don't move them when I approach.

"Jace?" I ask, and the word comes out in a soft-pitched, lilting drawl. I'd already forgotten I picked a female avatar.

Jace puts their arms behind their head and narrows one silver eye at me. "*Mistress.* We don't often see your people this far south. Your quest must be dire indeed to bring a northerner such as yourself to our sunny isles."

Jesus, they're in deep. I'm sure they expect me to play along but it's not gonna happen. I'm not feeling especially generous toward people wasting my time right now, and unfortunately for Jace my patience is in short supply.

"Wouldn't be here otherwise," I say. "Can we get to it?"

"Why so hasty?" Jace purrs, like they're trying to seduce me. "Join me for a flagon of summer ale, won't you? Wash the road dust from your voice before we speak."

Nope. I knock their feet off the table and they sit up with a lurch. "I'm not playing this game with you," I tell them. "I have a job. You want it or not?"

Their voice hardens. "This virt is strict RP," they say, like that's supposed to mean something. "Play your role or I'll bounce you."

"I'm about to pay you twenty grand, that buys me an exception. Now, you working or do I need to find someone else to give my money to?"

Their silver eyes glare at me, and the light briefly intensifies, but then they slump back on the bench. "Yeah, I'm working."

"Good," I say, and drop down on the chair across from

them. "I need you to run a couple gamertags for me. Find out everything you can."

"That it?" they say, the cockiness returning to their voice. "Who you looking for?"

"OVRshAdo," I say, and wait for a reaction, but they don't show me anything. "Plus XeroFacks and RainBowWow."

"I can do that," they say. "Half up front."

I hesitate, not sure if I can trust them, but then I figure it's Dub's money anyway, ack my bank account, and transfer ten grand. "When will you have something?"

They lean in, flick their shining eyes back and forth over my shoulders, and raise an eyebrow. "Is now soon enough?"

"Now? *Already?* Don't you need to go research or something?"

Their face twists up into a bewildered smirk. "What? You think I have the movements and interactions of millions of bit-heads stored in neat paper files back in my *office*? Or maybe a warehouse of punchcards I need to sort through?" I shake my head. Okay, stupid question. "You wanna see it or not?"

"Show me," I say.

They rub their fingers together.

"Prove you're not full of shit first," I counter.

Their grin widens. "RainBowWow's real name is Elmer Kham, but he goes primarily by HuggyJackson." I remember that name. He was partnered up with OVRshAdo in DI and Anika took him out of the game. Even money XeroFacks is Zara-Zee. "He's twenty-six, went rezso two years ago but still runs a skyn. Parents Philbert and Willomena, residing in Laos. He hates onions and has an extensive collection of hentai. Want to know his address?"

Shit. This person *is* good. Way better than SECNet.

I send them the other half of their payment, then they reach into their cloak and pull out a crystal that glitters as it hovers above their outstretched palm.

"What's this?" I ask as I take the rock with my thumb and index finger. Silvery light dances across its surface.

"Your answers," they reply as they sit back, a satisfied smile splitting their face.

"If you're fucking with me—" I start, but then the crystal flashes and all is revealed as knowledge dumps straight into my head.

"OVRshAdo's a mysterious fella," Jace says, almost to themself, while my Cortex ripples with fresh information. "Not much to find on him, but those two others are open books."

I'm right. Zara-Zee and HuggyJackson are a couple, which makes sense, based on how they were acting when they stole the skyns. They both went reszo in their early twenties to further their gaming careers, and they both still run skyns, and like HuggyJackson's profile says, they live in California. Not only that, but Jace scanned back through Huggy and Zara's entire network, cross-referenced their teaming habits, figured out their primary IDs, tied those profiles to their skyns' biokin, and tracked them down on SECNet.

A shipping drone running on a private network tagged them less than an hour ago. They're in the Louisiana flood zones, in Lost Orleans, which fits. No cops to worry about and isolated from the link. It's the perfect place to hide a bunch of red-hot skyns.

I can't suppress my grin. I'm impressed, and Jace knows it. "This is very good stuff."

"That was nothing," they say.

"You have done the North a great service today," I intone as I stand. "Your skills truly exceed your, ah, lofty reputation." They came through, and as ridiculous as this all is, I'm happy to indulge Jace's game. They've earned it.

They start, then lean back and put their feet back up on the table, with their silver eyes flashing and their grin set back to mischievous. "Should you or the North require my services again, good lady, you must but call."

"Until then," I say with a courteous nod, then yank myself out of the virt and back into the cabin.

Zara-Zee and HuggyJackson are moving the arena skyns, I know it. Why else would they pop up in a literal backwater like Lost Orleans? The place is mostly underwater, no one down there but fishes and people who don't want to be found.

I've only eighteen hours left, and I need to get to Louisiana before Zara and Huggy can make those skyns disappear again.

Let's hope I haven't already missed them.

THE UNION ABANDONED Louisiana's south coast to the rising waters a decade and a half ago. It wasn't the only place in the world ravaged by the rising ocean, but it got hit hard. By the time the world started giving a shit and made efforts to curb the carbon pollution, the battle had mostly been lost. It's only now, after years of actively pulling carbon out of the air, that the climate's settling back down, but the damage has already been done.

They tried their best to save New Orleans. They threw engineers and bots and money at it, built a massive sea wall and huge pumps to keep the water out, but the ocean was relentless, hot and angry, and between the flooding and the constant hurricane batterings, maintaining anything resembling modern infrastructure for a city built mostly below sea level became impossible. The Union declared the entire Mississippi Delta a disaster area and ordered its evacuation, suspending all essential services and pulling the region off the grid.

But it didn't die. The city went feral, and survived.

The tributaries of dry land still clinging to the banks of

the Mississippi became a place to hide from the Union's ever-present gaze, and New Orleans morphed into Lost Orleans, a post-apocalyptic, antebellum Venice. A city of unintended canals through submerged urban sprawl, rooftop communities connected by floating walkways, and all powered by the sun and the wind and the water, driven by the electric charges of anarchy and avarice.

It's a refuge for artists and outcasts and madmen and hustlers. The rotting buildings provide refuge for genitects frustrated by the limits of Union-imposed morality and fleshmiths constrained by Human Standards. It's a hub for smugglers, and weapons traffickers, where people shill anything you could ever want and everything in between.

Somehow it's even a vacation destination—a billionaire reszo bought the entirety of the French Quarter, domed it off, and now runs it as a 24-7 self-contained resort for bachelor parties and conferences and exuberant corporate retreats.

Sure, the murder rate is astronomical, every few weeks another building collapses and kills a bunch of people, the only way in and out is by boat or drone or hopper, the mosquitos get thick enough to block out the sun, and there's always the danger of running out of water or food if a hurricane roars in and sticks around too long, but no one worries about the cops knocking down doors and interrupting the flow of commerce, and that's all that matters.

It's not completely lawless—troublemakers are handled swiftly and harshly. But for the most part people mind their own business and work together to keep the peace. All things considered, I couldn't imagine a better place to arrange for the sale and transport four white-hot skyns, no questions asked, but OVRShAdo could have run the operation remotely, anonymously. There's no reason for Zara-Zee and HuggyJackson to be down there too.

Maybe the buyer insisted on a face-to-face exchange. Or maybe there was a hitch in the shipping—someone could have discovered the skyns and figured they were worth a bribe and OVRshAdo sent Zara and Huggy to deal with it. Or maybe he just prefers the personal touch. Who knows? Either way, they've shown themselves. Now maybe I can find out what they're up to and how Anika's involved.

Lost Orleans keeps itself cut off from the link, and there's limited local bandwidth and only basic internet, so I can't cast my rithm directly there. Instead I cast into a rented skyn in Baton Rouge and once I'm there charter a hopper to fly me to a floating pad anchored to the river-wall protecting what's left of downtown.

The landscape outside Baton Rouge grows more ramshackle the further we get into the disaster zone, and the scattered pockets of half-hearted civilization thins until there's nothing but swamp passing below. The ride takes about an hour, and when I land the heat is stifling and the mosquitos immediately form a shrill cloud around my head. Luckily the skyn I rented is built for the humidity and chemically invisible to the bugs. It'd be unbearable otherwise.

Jace sent an update while I was en route with a new location for HuggyJackson and Zara-Zee. Whoever's running the drone network must be selling the real-time sensor data on the open market. It's a lucrative side hustle, sure, but one likely to get whoever's operating it killed as soon as someone finds out.

The last drone ping had the couple at a loading crane down the boardwalk, waiting next to a small cargo ship sitting low in the water, and I head straight there.

With Lost Orleans free from SECNet's ever-present eyes, Huggy and Zara probably think they're running under the radar. They won't expect anyone to be looking for them, and I'm not too worried about being spotted. I'm running the Gibson ID and this is a rented skyn, but I play it careful just the same. I'm just here to observe, not engage. I couldn't do much more anyway, not with Deacon ready to take over the moment things get too exciting.

I weave over the gently bobbing dock and head up the ramp to the boardwalk running along the top of the river wall. Vendors line the boardwalk, hawking live seafood and imported goods and street foods of every kind, with their stalls built directly into the structure to keep them from blowing away when the winds get too strong.

The river is busy. Moored ships transfer cargo and more idle just off shore, waiting their turn to dock, while the heavier ships hauling cargo up to the Union port at Baton Rouge stick to the middle of the churning brown river. Downtown's on my left, just inside the wall—all that's left of it anyway. Only a few thousand people live there, but even from up here it's obvious the place isn't abandoned. Drones and bots are everywhere, and the market on Canal St. is doing a steady business. There's life in this old city yet.

A few hundred meters ahead a jazz quartet blasts brass at the guests arriving at the French Quarter resort. The wall is busiest there, but thankfully I don't need to go that far. I only stroll about a hundred meters, walking like a tourist checking out the city, until I find Zara-Zee and her boyfriend right where Jace said they'd be: on the dock, posted up beside an aging cargo skiff.

I step up to the railing and pretend to watch the river while I study them. They're clearly reszo, and both armed, but so are most people around here. I probably should have rented a gun before I left Baton Rouge too.

Zara-Zee's skyn is closing in on two meters tall, and she stands with her shoulders back and her head straight. Her jawline is long and masculine and she's got her long curly hair pulled into a high and tight ponytail. She's poking at a tab in her hand and doesn't look happy about what she's seeing.

HuggyJackson is shorter and a little more fidgety. His skyn is boyish, with soft blue eyes and smooth cheeks. He keeps checking out over the water, hand shading his eyes like he's searching for something.

The ship they're next to looks well-tended, but rust spots are starting to show through the layers of blue paint. A green tarp on the deck is strapped down over something big, a large boxy octagon about four meters tall, and beside that three smooth metal cylinders are secured and waiting to be wrapped. I bet those are medpods, should be the stolen skyns. But there are only three. Where's the fourth?

Zara-Zee and HuggyJackson seem to be wondering the same thing. They're impatient, fidgeting like they've been here a while. Every once in a while, Zara shoots an exasperated look at Huggy like he's the reason they're waiting, but only they can hear whatever it is they're saying to each other.

I've found them, but now what? I just came down here to prove that Anika was in on it with OVRshAdo and these two goons to steal the skyns, and now I'm sure of it. We've got their IDs, can tie them back to their gamer tags and to Anika meeting them in-game. I can go to Dub, it'll have to be enough to trigger an investigation.

Anika will lose her novi shot, but that's on her, right?

She's mixed up in all of this, helped steal highly lethal biotech. She deserves the consequences, right?

Right?

I watch them for a few minutes, flexing my dark-skinned hands in the sun and rolling the muscles in my back while I let my mind wander. I don't hop skyns much—I prefer to recognize my reflection when I catch sight of it—but I've spent enough time in loaner flesh and inhabiting virtual bodies that I'm not too hung up on my outward appearance anymore.

Sure, I've grown attached to my face and I'm comfortable with how my skyn moves, but bodies are functional necessities at best. For lots of reszos the skyn they wear is nothing more than a facade, a relic of a time when people were trapped by the random chance of genetics.

If I'm being honest with myself, this is what bugs me the most about the idea of moving forward with skynning Connie's sprite. Even if I were to commission a skyn that looks exactly like I remember her, no matter how convincing the illusion is, I'll still know there's nothing underneath. I may not think about it for short stretches of time, but I'll never be able to forget she isn't real.

And then there's Anika... She's a real-live woman, but she's a fake too. Yeah, her appearance is fluid—she lives virtual and changes it all the time—but that's to be expected. Underneath though, where I thought I'd met someone special, she's just another phony. No matter how I may feel about her, there's no denying she lied to me.

Whatever the reason she got involved in this, she's a product of her hidden desires and impulses, just like Connie is a product of her sub-routines and neural mimicry. Neither of them are real. They're both projecting, showing the world a carefully constructed persona—so what does it matter if Connie isn't "real"? At least I can trust her.

Still, there's a splinter of doubt in my mind, a plausible series of events that could explain away Anika's participation in all this. Maybe it's one giant circumstantial coincidence. And I can't swear those cylinders contain the stolen skyns. I mean, what *else* would they be, but I don't have actual proof.

I need to see for myself, which means I need to get close. The question is how?

Eventually someone comes off the boat, a woman with a dark tan, wearing dingy orange coveralls and her greying hair tied behind her head with a piece of yellow nylon rope. The way her jaw is set shows she's impatient too. It's loud out here, and with the chugging boats and the people and the jazz piping from the band playing at the French Quarter entrance, I only catch snippets of the conversation, but I get the gist. The boat's ready to go, they're already late and the window to meet their delivery deadline is closing, but Zara tells her to wait, they can't leave until the last part of the shipment arrives. They don't say it but it's obvious what they're waiting for—the fourth skyn.

The captain shrugs and makes it clear she's not to blame if they blow their schedule, then turns and pads back up the ramp and disappears belowdecks.

If Huggy was agitated before, he's morose now. He slinks over to Zara and stands in front of her, head bowed. If they're talking I can't hear it. At one point Huggy flinches, like he's expecting Zara to hit him, but she just lays her hand on the back of his head, then turns and stalks away down the dock.

Once she's out of sight he spins around and kicks a piling, then instantly grabs his foot and hops in place, his mouth set in a pained grimace. He grumbles to himself for a bit, still balanced on one leg and rubbing his foot, then drops it, yells "Fuck!" at the sky, and plods off, nearly in tears, heading in the opposite direction from Zara, leaving the ship completely unattended.

I wanted proof those were the stolen skyns in the medpods.

Well, now's my chance.

I KEEP my head on a swivel as I retrace my path along the wall, down the ramp, and over the dock to the cargo skiff. Once I get close I loiter around for a bit, waiting for Huggy or Zara to return or for a crew member to show themselves, but while the dock is busy, no one pays the skiff any attention, and no one says anything when I step across the gangplank and down to the ship's deck. I skirt around to the front of the big octagon, keeping myself hidden should anyone glance out the bridge window. The tarp is pulled tight, and I can't get through it to see what's underneath, so I crouch down next to the cylinders instead. They're smooth metal, probably faraday cages, shielded to keep the skyns' trackers from pinging, and when I press my ear against the warm surface I can hear them humming. Right shape and size, no question they're sealed medpods, but when I tap the control panel it prompts me for a password and I can't get any further.

I should find the captain, tell her what she's got on board—but then again I bet she already knows, and if she doesn't she'll want to keep it that way. I can't force her to stop, and I didn't bring a weapon, so I can't confront Huggy or Zara, and even if I did it's two against one, and these two shoot people on the regular for fun.

But I can't just let them go, can I?

HuggyJackson makes up my mind for me when he comes back and catches me bent over the cylinders.

"Hey," he yells at me from up on the dock. "What the hell are you doing?"

I jerk up and turn to face him, not sure what to say. Deacon's staying quiet, but that could change at any second.

"I'm, uh..." *Think of something.* I set my face to clueless. "Is this the Big Easy booze cruise? I was told it was down here but I think I might be on the wrong boat."

Huggy's eyes harden. "No it fucking isn't."

"My mistake," I say, stepping toward the gangplank to make my exit, but he blocks my path and crosses the plank to meet me.

"Yeah it was," he says, and for a second I think he's going for his gun but instead he unsnaps the sheath on his belt and draws a long knife. "'Cause I am not buying your shit."

I take a step back and glance around for something to protect myself should he charge, but the captain keeps her deck tidy and there's not much at hand. Nothing but a few buckets at the edge of the deck and a coil of heavy strapping waiting next to the cylinders.

Huggy keeps advancing, knife held low.

"We don't need a problem," I say, and risk a glance over my shoulder to the other side of the ship. I can always jump. I don't fancy a swim, but it beats a stabbing.

"Should have thought of that," Huggy replies, flipping the knife up so he's holding it in an overhand grip.

He's closing, backing me across the deck. I'm beside the last cylinder now, only have a few more steps before I'm up against the railing and have to vault over the edge, but I figure since I'm already caught, before I get wet I might as well see if I can get him to talk.

"Okay," I admit, "you got me, but you don't think I'm about to let you float away with that stolen wetware, do you? You must know you've got every government agency in the hemisphere searching for you."

He tries to hide his reaction, but the way his mouth briefly drops is enough to tell me I wasn't wrong about what's in those cylinders.

"I ... I don't know what you're talking about," he says, but we both know he's lying.

"Sure you do. You're HuggyJackson, right? Or do you prefer I Elmer?" His eyes flicker when I mention his alias, but they go wide when I use his real name.

"Who the fuck are you?" He stutters, but he's stopped advancing.

"That's least of your worries right now, kid," I say, playing confident. "We know everything. You and Zara-Zee and OVRshAdo and Anika, you're done."

He backs off with his jaw clenched and doesn't say anything, but the expression on his face is as good as a confession. Then his face flickers and his eyes harden. "You think you can take me in all by yourself?"

I give him a smirk. "You don't think I'd come down here on my own, do you?" I look over his shoulder and yell, "Converge, now!"

Huggy spins away from me, searching for the direction of attack, and that's when I move. I bend and grab the coil of rope next to me and heave it at his back. He turns just a second too late and the heavy coil catches him in the side, unraveling as it hits him. Following right behind, I grab his knife hand and step into him, knee him in the groin and use my other hand to snap his wrist and take his weapon.

He stumbles away with a cry but with the rope coiled around his legs he can't get far, and falls to his knees, tears running down his face. But he must shut down his pain receptors because he's only dazed for a moment.

Huggy fixes a glare on me. He's done being stupid, and goes for the gun strapped to his hip.

This gets Deacon interested. My eyes go unfocused as the governor in my kicks in, and I stagger, but I'm too far away to stop Huggy anyway. Without thinking, I pull my arm back and flick the knife at him, aiming just like I used to in my backyard when I was a kid. The blade twirls through the air, spinning end over end, and embeds itself in Huggy's neck. Which is a lucky shot—I was aiming for his chest.

His face wants to keep fighting but his head is no longer talking to his body. He gurgles as his knees buckle and collapses down into the rope. Shit, must have severed his spinal cord.

His eyes stay open as I get up next to him, take his gun, and tuck it into my pants. There's nothing left in his lungs to make noise with but his lips are still moving, breathlessly cursing me out.

I glance up and down the dock, checking for witnesses. No one seems to have noticed, but that could change at any second. I need to get rid of the body before someone gets curious. Huggy's cloudy eyes follow me as I wrap him in the heavy rope and fasten the steel clamps. His eyes go wide when he realizes what's about to happen. His flesh is fading, but his Cortex won't quit for a long time and his thoughts will keep right on ticking. I hesitate and reconsider what I'm about to do, but only for a second.

After all, he *was* about to shoot me.

And besides, he won't lose any time. *Probably*. Eventually someone will fish his Cortex out of the river.

I check the dock again, and Zara's on her way back. A heavy drone's out on the water, kicking up spray with a big metal cylinder slung underneath.

Shit, gotta move.

I get Huggy up, take two steps, and heave him over the edge. He hits with a heavy splash and I follow him in. I land on his chest and kick him down as I push off under water, letting the current carry me away from the skiff. I stay under as long as I can, then pull myself to the surface next to the metal hull of another long cargo ship further down the river, and gulp in a breath. There's no sign of HuggyJackson. He must have stayed sunk and been swept away by the river.

Treading water, I watch as the fourth skyn arrives and is lowered to the deck of the waiting skiff. I can't see Zara from down here, but I'll bet she's up there directing the transfer. They'll be shoving off within minutes. I need to stop them.

But first I need to get out of the water.

By the time I find a ladder and get back to the skiff, I'm already too late. The ship's pulling away, already nosing out into the river. Zara's standing at the railing, searching the docks—probably looking for her boyfriend. She didn't spend any time waiting on him though, pushed right off the second the skyn was unloaded.

Last chance before you lose them.

I reach down to pull the gun I took from Huggy, but it's not in my waistband. It must have slipped out when I jumped overboard and I didn't notice. All I can do is take note of the ship's name and registration number and watch it float away.

The skyns are gone, but now I know for sure: Anika's

involved. No question about it, Huggy's reaction when I confronted him was enough.

So what am I gonna do about it?

ONCE AGAIN YOU find yourself alone in Camp Paradiso with Jefferson Wood, and while you're starting to get used to these inter-game chit-chats, you still don't like them.

It's not just the mindless interview either—you've always found something off about Wood. He's too polished, pixel perfect. All at once self-effacing and superior. And the few minutes you've spent with him have done nothing to change your opinion.

"We continue to be impressed by you, Anika," the Wood says, cocking his head in appreciation. "You have managed to survive yet another difficult game. The world wants to know: how are you holding up?"

You're still fresh from the game, pumped from the fight, and if you were still in your body you'd be dizzy and breathing hard but already the excitement's fading. So what if you just wasted an entire squad by yourself? All you've been through already and you're still not halfway done. There's still a long way to go and plenty of ways it could end.

"One second at a time," you reply, keeping your composure. "It's all you can do out here."

"You seem to have considerable competition amongst your fellow survivors. OVRshAdo in particular."

"He's a gamer," you say. "Tryin' to win like everyone else."

"As you say, and he has you to thank for his continued place in the game. Without you he would have surely been eliminated in the last round."

"We both would have. Working together was in our best interest."

"You make a potent team. Have your thought about formalizing it?"

"No," you say flatly. "I plan on killing him."

Wood's lips part in a grin. "Spoken like a true warrior," he says and gives you a little bow. "Until next round. We'll be watching."

His voice fades away and once again the other survivors materialize around camp. You immediately head to your spot out at the end of the dock and lean down against the polished wooden railing to watch the orange sun sink into the ocean. It's always the same time when you arrive, just before sundown, and so far your ritual has been to come out alone and watch the sky paint a picture while you wait for the next game to start. Other than that brief chat with OVRshAdo after game one, you haven't spoken to any of the other survivors for more than a word or two and that's the way you like it.

The others stay inside, pouring drinks down their throats. It doesn't matter how drunk they get here, the second the next game starts they'll be instantly sober. Everyone's talking about the ending—how you wiped a four-man to win the game. You took their congratulations as you walked through the covered dining area, but didn't engage, and no one followed you.

As much as you love the pulse of the crowd in your head, downtime is the one chance you get to spend a few quiet moments without an audience watching your every move. You let your guard down, just a hair, and that's all it takes for the fear and the grief to come rushing in. You squeeze the railing as hard as you can, but can't keep the feelings from crashing over you.

Every second you're out here means Rael is one more closer to dying. The doctors said he didn't have long—there was time, but not much. It could have happened already ...

Then why are you still here?

You take a breath and squeeze the railing again, clamping down on your tears. Even though there's no one watching directly through your eyes, the game still streams out a spectator's view of the camp. You've got millions of people watching you right now. Gotta keep up appearances. Think happy thoughts.

You conjure up a memory of the bug-eyed face Rael made the first time he tried a lemon, and that's somehow even worse and your heart caves in on itself and for a brief second you consider giving up, running home to him, sweeping him up in your arms and promising you'll never leave him again, no matter how little time he has left.

But then what? He'd still be dying. What would you do then, if you give up now? You'd be right back where you started.

Your spine straightens. That's what you need, remember why you're here. You can get through this, just a little longer—

Someone clears his throat behind you, interrupting your

pep talk, and you instantly know it's OVRshAdo. You're surprised he waited this long.

You give yourself another moment to pull yourself together, then jump back into the game. So much for your peace and quiet.

"You gonna keep to yourself? After *that*?" he says, his voice loud, buoyant with success and all the drinks he downed in the past ten minutes.

"You're welcome," you say, not turning around. You may have been forced to team up, but you're not a team.

Zara-Zee snorts. Great, she's here too. "We save your ass and now you're too good to talk to us?"

"Yeah," you respond. "No offense."

"Offense *taken*," Zara-Zee says, posturing. God, people are exhausting.

You sigh and turn to face them. Zara's licking her lips, up on her toes like she wants to fight. Probably still mad you killed her boyfriend.

"Don't be toxic, Zar," OVRshAdo says, putting out his hand as if to hold her back from coming at you, but it's a useless gesture. Camp Paradiso is PVP-free. She can throw as many punches as she wants but they'll never land. No, it's a show, a drama for your benefit. He's taking your side over hers, subtly conditioning you to make you trust him. They want you to join them next game.

And why not? Even Wood thinks it'll happen. You three players have the most hours, and that means you're each other's biggest rivals. OVRshAdo is going into his late game, of course he wants to keep his most dangerous enemies close. Can't sneak up on him that way.

Eventually, when it makes the most sense for his game, he'll be the first to pull the trigger and off you and Zara both, then solo through his last hundred hours all the way to the Century.

Teaming with him would almost certainly guarantee you another two games. The lone wolf play has been working, but only just. You almost lost that last round—*should* have lost that last round. Running solo is a gamble, and each time you play the odds of winning go down. Eventually your luck's gonna run out. Linker put you off teaming at first, but you know you can't get to the end alone.

Not with OVRshAdo, though. He needs to die, and it'll be easier to kill him if you don't get to know him first.

"We helped each other because we needed to," you say. "Pragmatic, nothing more."

"You don't want to win?" OVRshAdo asks. "I know you don't trust me, and, sure, I get why, but haven't I been honest with you? It's the game, nothing personal. Let's try it out for one round. After that, you want to walk away and resume doing our best to kill each other, that's cool too."

That math works way better for him than it does for you.

"I can't let you hit the Century. It'll take years for the prize to build back up. I need the money now."

The light in OVRshAdo's dark digital eyes flickers. "It *is* a lot of money," he says, then gives you a sideways stare. "Help me win, and I'll split it with you."

"You're talking three ways, *right*?" Zara says, turning her attitude on OVRshAdo.

"Three ways," he amends, turning to include her. "The pool's up to near twenty million. Even split three ways that's more than any of us could ever spend."

There's nothing stopping him from sharing, but nothing holding him to it either. Others have tried this strategy, promised shares of the prize to get to the end, but no one's ever had to make good on it.

And while six million and change is a lot of money, even if you could trust OVRshAdo to keep his end, it's not enough. Rael's a genie kid, built in a lab, and not covered under the Union's guaranteed health care. After the re-sequencing he'll need a lifetime of genetic maintenance, checkups, and probably yearly treatments. Even what you'll take home from a solo win might not be enough to keep him alive past his eighteenth birthday.

"Thanks, but no," you answer. You can't keep running solo, that's true, but you're not about to help OVRshAdo steal the Century from you. You've got three games to knock him out and clear the way for your win. Can't give him the first one for free.

"What?" Zara snaps. "Why the fuck not? This is real money we're talking about."

For a moment OVRshAdo looks like he might try another stab at convincing you, but that's not his style, and he shifts tactics. "Fair enough," he says. "I respect the deci-sion. I'd probably make the same in your place."

He swings his chin at Zara-Zee, directing her back to the dining hall, and she glares at him but turns and stomps off.

"Hey, Shad," you say as he's leaving. "Nothing personal. See you out there."

You don't hold any grudges, it's just the game, and you want to win as much as he does.

"Not if I see you first," he answers, then follows Zara up the dock.

Alone again, and it's getting exhausting.

You turn to catch the last few moments of the sunset but

you've already missed it and the sky is a bruised purple smear. The next game will be starting soon.

You're not interested in teaming with OVRshAdo, but you know you can't do this alone anymore either.

Looks like it's time to make some new friends.

I KNOW I should call Dub immediately and tell him everything—that I just missed the skyns and have proof Anika's involved—but I don't. Instead I catch a hopper back to Baton Rouge in my soaking clothes, dreading the thought of what'll happen to her after I do.

This will end her. Destroy her career, tarnish her name forever. Then Standards will get involved and she'll likely end up in a stock—can I do that to her?

Anika's supposed to be on comms blackout, but the second I'm reconnected to the link I send her an invite to my headspace, telling her we need to talk and it can't wait.

By the time I get to the skyn rental shop, drop off the loaner body, and cast back into my own skyn, I still haven't heard back from her. What if she doesn't respond? How long can I wait?

Connie's standing at the front window as I materialize in front of the crackling fireplace. She's sipping from a steaming mug and watching the icebergs float by, but she doesn't say anything, just flashes me a smiling glance over her shoulder as if reminding me she's here if I need her.

If only it were that simple.

I plop down on the couch to wait, and Anika gets back to me an hour later. She says can make ten minutes around seven, but only ten. *Not enough time for anything good*, she adds. *But I'll see what I can do.*

She has no idea her life is about to change forever.

My stomach skips at the thought of it—*if only things were different*—but she doesn't know what's coming, doesn't know I know she was involved in the heist. Maybe she's playing me, maybe she's not, but it doesn't matter anymore. After I confront her she'll never want to talk to me again.

I know I should go straight to Dub and let him decide what to do, but I can't just rat her out. She needs to hear it from me first, give her a chance to prepare for what's coming. I owe her that much at least.

The next two hours drag by, but right after seven Anika knocks at the front door and I get up and let her in. She's wearing her default aspect, the one with the athletic figure and short copper hair, and she smiles as she leans in and hugs me, but I think she senses something's off as I pull away and step aside to let her in.

"I like what you've done with the place," she says after she's given the cabin a once-over. "It's old fashioned, kinda like you."

"Thanks?" I say as I move away from her, back into the kitchen, and put the island counter between us.

Anika squints at me, crossing her arms. "What's up with you?"

I'm not sure how to start. I've been sitting here for hours and still don't know what to say, so I just look at her, take a breath, and launch into it.

"I know what you're doing," I say, keeping my voice neutral, and for a moment she thinks I might be teasing her, but when I don't follow it up with a joke the smile fades from her eyes.

"What are you talking about?" she asks, her expression flat.

"The arena skyns." I pause for a second and wait for a reaction but she doesn't give me one. "You said you hadn't talked to OVRshAdo since DI, but I saw you together. With HuggyJackson and Zara-Zee. You were the inside man, right? You implanted the code that let them override the safeties and walk away with the skyns. I tracked them down to Lost Orleans, but Zara got away before I could stop her."

Finally, her face shifts as conflicting emotions dance across her face, but she doesn't deny it. She turns away, like she's going for the door, but then changes her mind and spins back to face me, finger raised.

"*I knew it,*" she says, anger seeping into her voice. "All that bullshit about your dead wife—"

"Not bullshit."

"Ha!" she snaps back. "You've been playing me from the start, from the second we met you had an agenda. Dub put you up to this, didn't he?"

I don't answer, but I don't have to, she already knows. "What I don't get is *why,*" I say instead. "Why get involved? Why throw your life away? It's not like you need the money. Does OVRshAdo have something on you? Did he force you into this?"

"Fuck you," Anika seethes. "You have no idea what you're talking about."

"Then tell me. Help me understand. Maybe there's a way out of this for you..."

"I don't want out," she says. "I'm not a victim, and I'm not a little girl. I don't need a big strong man to ride to my rescue. Especially you."

"What am I supposed to do then? You tell me."

Anika laughs, a short exasperated burst of air through her nose. "I'm not your fucking conscience, Finsbury. And I'm not your dead wife telling you what you want to hear. You're gonna have to figure this out all by your lonesome."

I press my hands against the countertop, fighting through my frustration. I should just give up on her, take it to Dub and let Humanitech and the cops sort it out, but I can't. Not yet.

"Don't you get it? You're done. Whatever this was you and Shad were planning, it's over. He may have gotten away with the skyns, but the Gulf isn't that big a place. I've got the boat's registration—it won't be too hard to find. Zara will be easy enough to track down, and Huggy is feeding the catfish right now, but they'll dredge him up eventually. The truth will come out."

"You killed Huggy?" she asks, her surprise knocking down the anger.

"He isn't dead. Might be hard to find though." She exhales sharply but throws daggers with her eyes. "He started it. I was just supposed to stand there and let him gut me?" Why am I on the defensive here? I don't need to justify anything. "Look, I'm doing everything I can to throw you a lifeline—"

"Keep your goddamn lifelines. I don't need your pity." The anger's completely gone from her face, but her chest is heaving and her hands are clenched into fists.

"You conspired to steal a few hundred million dollars' worth of highly restricted biotech. That's way up there on the Standards Offense scale. They'll stock you for twenty-five years."

"I'll end it myself before that happens." Her lips twitch as she glares at me, defiant. "Better for everyone that way."

She's hurting and she's stubborn and I know exactly how she feels. She's got a plan, and nothing I say to her will get her to back down, especially now. She's too stubborn for that. But even if she'll never trust me again, I don't think she understands just how much trouble she's in.

"They'll pull your backup out of storage and she'll get the stock," I say, my heart raw. I know it's only been a few days but I've grown attached to her, and even knowing she's been lying to me I don't want to see her suffer. "I've been inside one of those things. It's torture. They strip every sensation away, every feeling of joy and hope. You're looking at twenty-five years of grey-toned monotony, and maybe you're thinking that right about now it sounds like a blessing, the way your head must be wound up, but I promise you you're wrong. It doesn't have to go that way though. If you get ahead of this, maybe they'll be lenient."

She just stares at me, working the angles, trying to reach a different conclusion, but she'll have to see I'm right. There's no other way out for her.

Turns out she's even more stubborn than I thought. Her face settles into a steely calm, and she says, "You do what you gotta do."

I drop my palms back down on the countertop and lower my head. What is she into? All this can't just be about money. That's the one part of this that doesn't make sense—she's already rich, the risk isn't worth the reward. So what's it all about?

I raise my head and she's still staring at me. "Why does OVRshAdo want those skyns?" If she wanted she could have left by now, I'm not holding her aspect here, but she hasn't. Maybe I can get her to talk to me. "Somehow I don't expect it's the payday."

"I don't give a shit about money."

"Right, so what is it then? The only other use for those skyns is killing people—"

Anika shakes her head. "You're out of your depth, Finsbury. I know you think you're some great detective and you've got it all figured out, but you don't have a clue what's going on."

"Then tell me."

"What? So you can run to the cops?"

"So I can help you."

"You want to *help* me?"

"I do."

"Then walk away and forget we ever met. I promise you no one's gonna get hurt."

"One thing I can't do."

She growls in frustration, then screws up her face and leans into me. "What do you want from me? Why'd you even invite me here? To fuck with me before you give me up?"

"*What?* No, goddamit. I want to know *why*. I want you to give me one fucking reason to explain all this, something other than you did it for the fucking kicks—because if the person I just I spent the past week with, the one who had me questioning every fucking thing in my life, can fool me so easily, then I might as well give the world up and watch it crumble from inside the safety of my head. At least in here I know what's real."

I'm out of breath and huffing and she's just glaring at me.

"Don't flatter yourself," she says after a long minute, but the fight's gone and her shoulders slump. "You don't know me."

"I know enough. You're not that good an actor."

She chews on the inside of her cheek for moment, then

cocks her head at me. "You want to know *why*? Fine. I'll tell you." She takes a long breath in through her nose. "I spent forty days on that island, forty days away from my dying son, and I want to know what happened. Winning meant everything, no way I killed myself the second before I won it all. *Not a chance.*"

I've been there, watched myself do things I never imagined myself capable of, but it happens. Easier, I think, than any of us might expect. But still, what's that got to do with the arena skyns?

"Trust me, it happens," I say. "A lot can happen in forty days."

Her eyes narrow. "I've relived every minute I spent there, and I don't see how I'd ever make that decision." She hesitates, pressing her lips together. "Even once I knew my chance to save Rael was"—her voice hitches but she keeps right on going—"once it was too late, I never would have given up. Jefferson Wood stole the win from me, that's the only answer."

"He released your skyn telemetry from those last few seconds. The link's been through it. No question your rithm shows you raising your hand and pulling the trigger."

"Which is why I need to know for myself. Either the island cheated me, or it only took forty days for me to become a person I can't recognize. If you'd done something you couldn't explain, wouldn't you do whatever you could to understand why?"

I haven't told her much about my previous restoration, when I turned into a monster, so she doesn't know I did the same thing. He blew himself up to take out Eka. I'll never know if I would have made the same choice, and it's just something I get to live with.

That still doesn't answer the bigger question. "So what does all that have to do with the arena skyns?"

"I need them to get my memories back."

"From Decimation Island?"

She nods as if no further explanation is necessary.

"*How?*"

"Shad."

"*Go on...*"

"He's got a plan. We're gonna hit DI, and we're gonna get my memories back."

"With the arena skyns?"

"It's a hostile island full of lethal robots. We need all the help we can get."

That's...

I can't even process how insane that idea is. "All this to get your memories back?"

"No." She pauses as she works through what she's about to say. "My memories are just a side quest. Shad's running the main story."

I'm almost afraid to ask. "Which is what?"

She fixes me with a defiant look as she says, "To beat Decimation Island, once and for all."

It's a Western Tower launch, and you rejoin your skyn as it's soaring over the bay toward the coast. You've got the marshes to the north and the jungle to the south and all the pirate stuff in between, but the Sunken City Blues hotspot in Elephant Bay is one of your favorites in the whole game. It's a retro-futuristic city built fully underwater, and features a quest line about a charismatic madman and the downfall of his egomaniacal aquatic dream. It's hell to get in and out of, the enemies are hulking bots and NPC psychopaths, and it ends with a terrifying race to escape the flooding city, but the loot is totally worth it. Completing it grants a full set of level-four armor, a buttload of safe-time, muscle tonics, and a good choice of weapons. They aren't the best guns in the game, but for a single run it's well worth the trouble.

If you can survive that is.

It's not solo-able though. You can't just drop straight in and hope to finish it, even as well kitted as you are. No, you need a team.

There's no other option, eventually you need to trust someone.

You angle your wingpack down toward Skull Island in the middle of the bay. As you blaze toward the ground the stream of parachutes continues above you, players stretching to land directly on the far side of the bay in Buck-An-Ear Cove, this lobby's starting location. You're headed there too but not quite yet. You want to give them time to land before you make your entrance.

Once you hit dirt you ditch your wings and gather your gear and spend a few minutes looting up the basics before you hop a boat across the bay to the town. You pass three tall solar ships anchored off-shore, each of them representing a different faction you can choose to align yourself with in the Buck-An-Ear Cove storyline. Or Admiral Grant is further out, off the coast, if you prefer playing with the "good guys."

Buck-An-Ear is nearly vertical, built up and down a craggy slope on the edge of the island. The buildings are an assortment of stacked shipping containers with rickety spun plastic rope bridges and ladders joining them all together. The main road is a wide wooden scaffold that zigzags up from the dock to the top of the incline, where a town square and a high stone watchtower look out over the bay.

Every game has a starting town, but survivors don't often make an appearance in them, so when you stroll into the square with the camo unit on your chest and Stingers on each hip and four hundred hours in the bank, the crowd takes notice. The NPC pirates don't care who you are, but the players do—you can tell by the looks you're getting and the excited buzz that rises in the square. Some of them want to kill you, you know that for certain, and some pretend they don't even notice, but most see you as their best chance to make it through their first hundred hours.

The LFG board's outside the Rusty Screw, a ramshackle tavern overlooking the bay, but you blow right past it, feeling every eye in the place following you. Sure, you could pull some names from the looking-for-group board, but you prefer the personal touch. Besides, it'll play better with the fans this way, and right now the audience in your head is massive and expecting bold moves. After the end of the last game your following must have tripled, and it feels like everyone in the world is riding along with you. You'll need to hit a few sponsored drop locations this round —with this many people following you, the loot's gonna be sweet.

You step up onto the front porch of the tavern, spin on the wooden boards, and face the crowd. They all stop what they're doing and watch, hushed.

"I'm looking to run the sunken city," you call out to the crowd. "Anyone want to join me?"

A good number of them toss up their hands and rush forward, hoping to be chosen. They'll have seen you play, know what you can do. And you're only on game five, so that'll give them plenty of time to surf in your wake before they'll need to turn on you. Teaming with you will get them to game three at least. A deal like that—they'd have to be fools to pass it up.

The crowd pushes forward, jostling for position, all wanting to be chosen. You've been successful in your tubing career, but you've never been popular like this.

If you're not careful, you just might get used to it.

| 19:11:35. Friday, July 11, 2059.

"Hold up," I say. My head's spinning. Anika's glowering at me but I don't even know what we're talking about. "How do you 'beat' Decimation Island?"

She sighs, steps over to the couch, sinks down, and stares into the fire. I come out from behind the countertop and take the chair beside her, wait for her to continue.

"You know the entire island's run by an AI, right?" I nod, not wanting to say anything to derail her. "Shad's figured it out—Jefferson Wood has opened it up and is selling access to it."

I'm still not following. "What's that mean?"

Anika purses her lips. "Every day millions of people play Decimation Island, billions of hours over the years, and the whole time the AI has been watching, learning how to fight, how to kill, and now Wood's selling those skills to anyone who wants them."

She can't be saying...

"You're telling me the AI running Decimation Island is behind *Killr*?"

She blinks at me. "You know about that?" Her lips part in a faint smile. "How am I not surprised?"

"I've seen it up close. A squadron of well-armed reszos running that stuff could take on the whole Union Army. The cops don't have a clue where it's coming from."

"Wood's covered his tracks, but Shad traced the shyfts back to their source. It's the island, he's sure of it."

"And he's decided to take it on all by himself?"

"Not by himself—Zara-Zee and Huggy and I—though I guess we're a man short now, thanks to you."

"That explains the stolen skyns, but how do you figure you'll survive an island full of hostile bots? And how do you even get them on the island? From what I understand that place is locked down, no one in or out."

"Private rocket launch," Anika answers, as if the solution were obvious. "Shad sourced a surplus Chinese warbot drop module, but instead of bots it'll carry the skyns. We'll come in from low orbit and blend in with the drop from the next live game. Believe me, he's got the run all planned. He's been working on it for months."

It's almost too much to believe, and for a second I wonder if she's still playing me, but I don't think she is. It's a story too far-fetched to be made up. "That's insane."

She smirks at me. "Isn't it?"

"Why's OVRshAdo care so much? All the planning, the expense, what's he getting out of this?"

She just shrugs. "The whole world's a game to him, and he's seen the new meta. Decimation Island is putting its finger on the scale, making it too easy for anyone to win. He doesn't like cheaters. If beats the game at its own game, he becomes a legend."

"He's in it for the glory?"

"For the *lulz*," she clarifies.

Jesus. "When's all this supposed to happen?"

"Next live game starts Sunday at midnight local, three in the afternoon DI time. We drop then."

"Sunday? What about your novi fight?"

Her shoulders rise and fall. "I never wanted to be a Gladiator. Too real life for me."

I sit back in my chair, watch her watch me. "Well, shit," I say eventually. "Now what?"

She rolls her eyes. "You tell me. The only way this works is if we take the island by surprise and cut off the transmission tower before Wood knows we're there, and broadcasts the AI off the island. If you go to the cops we're done. For now, the AI is confined, but if Wood finds out it's in danger he'll have time to get it off the island and all this will be for nothing. I'll lose the chance to regain my lost time, and the Killr shyfts keep right on flowing, forever and ever, amen."

Dammit. This was hard enough when it was just about Anika stealing the arena skyns and putting Dub's ludus jeopardy, but shit got complicated real fast. She's staring at me, waiting for a decision, but I have no idea what to say to her. She figures that out for herself a second later when I still haven't answered her.

"Guess I'll be hearing from you, one way or another," she says, furrows her eyebrows, and then winks away.

My vision stays fixed to the place she was standing, her somber face still clear in my vision. What the hell am I supposed to do, now? Turn her in, condemn her to a stock, *and* risk losing a shot at shutting down the source of the Killr shyft—

Or trust her, and risk being wrong about her again?

Huge raindrops slap against the broad green leaves of the jungle surrounding the village. It's been raining for hours now, and while your dropsuits are designed to handle heat and moisture, you're still soaked through. The sky is a slate grey and the light is washed out, shading everything with a sense of foreboding doom.

Your rain-soaked skyn is the least of your concerns right now though. You're on the hunt, deep in the final stage of the Raptorwolf Rampage hotspot. You've tracked the animals to a small settlement near the lab and they're close. There isn't much to the village, only a dozen or so buildings in a clearing in the jungle, right near where the salt marshes begin. There's a small open-air market and a church and a community building at the north end, two rows of four rectangular concrete longhouses down the middle, and a large barn and fenced-in stockyard at the south. The buildings of the muddy village are abandoned, and the villagers are clustered in the church, hoping you'll save them from the vicious raptorwolf pack.

Your team came in from the north and took up positions

on opposite sides of the church, you and Warrack on the west, Gerbil-Of-Doom and AVmei on the east. There are six raptorwolves, and even with your full squad that's no joke.

You're moving slow, playing cautious. Raptorwolves are designed to be smart and ferocious, and given the slightest opportunity they'll have your guts in the mud. They hunt in packs and come armed with razor-sharp teeth and sharp metal front claws that'll rip straight through even your level-four armor. They're prowling somewhere through the village, searching for food, but you have no idea where. With the gloom and the deafening patter of rain all around you, you can't see far or hear worth shit, but the mud is chewed up with claw marks. They're close.

Luckily you don't need to see them—you've come prepared. Taking out the raptorwolves won't be a cakewalk, but no one should die in the process.

"*Launch the drones,*" you think, and through your team vision you see the green outlines of Gerbil-Of-Doom and AVmei on the other side of the church pull bots from their packs and toss them into the air. The copters hover for a moment while they adjust their sensors, then zip straight up to give you eyes in the sky. The rain will mess with their vision, but their radar will still work. They should help find the raptorwolves before the raptorwolves find you.

It's taken half the game to get here. After you and your new team finished the Sunken City run, you hit a few sponsored loot pylons to collect the drops, then fought your way to the raptorwolves hotspot and picked up the quest line here in the village. You've spent the past eight hours running through it, collecting the samples and saving the missing child. You fought artificial predators through the halls of the renegade scaflab and finally made it to the end, where you defeated the rogue fleshmith and genitect team and their cybernetic animal protection. Now all that's left is to clean up after them.

You pat the pouch hanging at your side, reflexively making sure you still have the pheromone darts you looted from the lab. They'll make fighting the raptorwolves less suicidal. The animals are drawn to the pheromone's pungent smell, and once you lure them out it shouldn't be too hard to finish them off from range.

You shudder as you anticipate the fight to come. This hotspot has always hit a little close to home for you. Most of the Decimation Island hotspots are complete fabrications created for the game. The desolate black rock lava fields surrounding the Moonbase Delta hotspot may give the sense that it's set on the moon, but being able to breathe ruins the illusion right quick.

But the story behind Raptorwolf Rampage isn't far-fetched at all—shit like this happens in the real world with a shocking frequency. Even as far back as when you were a kid, slogging your way through the foster system, you'd hear stories about crackpot scientists moving down to the flood-ravaged swamps in southern Louisiana to perform all kinds of genetic experiments, using nothing more than bathtub sequencing kits and basic mobile scaflabs to produce monsters and release them into the wild.

Foster Mother used to threaten to send the naughty kids out into the swamp, where she said they'd be food for the horrible creatures living there. She didn't need to invent something like the boogeyman to make you do what you were told, not when monsters were real.

Nowadays the Ministry of Standards has a dedicated team for tracking down renegade genitects and fleshsmiths and the horrors they produce, but somehow making a game show out of it still feels wrong. You usually avoid running this hotspot, but as geared up as the Sunken City left you, the team needed better weapons, and the reward for finishing off the raptorwolves is a cache of top-tier assault rifles. Not legendary class, but the next best thing. Variable loadouts with armor piercing and explosive rounds. You're still only half done this game, but when you're finished here your team will be ready to take on anyone who challenges you. And that includes OVRshAdo.

You haven't seen him all game, but you know he's out there, somewhere. Probably hunting you right now. You can't worry about him though, you've got dinosaurs to kill.

The drones scout above, their whirring rotors muffled by the clatter of raindrops on tin roofs as they search down the length of the settlement. It only takes a moment before they spot the raptors—they're all the way on the other end of town, feeding on the village pigs.

A bolt of irritation shoots through you, and for a second you almost forget where you are, have to remind yourself that this is just a game, that the pigs and the raptorwolves and even the villagers are all artificial. Bodies printed in tanks and operated by an AI. All just part of the story. Props, designed to be killed.

"*Targets pinged out,*" Gerbil announces over the comms. "*Moving in.*"

"*Confirmed,*" you respond. "*Warrack and I'll approach from the west along the huts. You two come in from the east. Once we get close we'll lure them out with a dart.*"

"*Got it,*" Gerbil says, and she and AVmei race across the open road between the church and the huts and make their way south, following orders without hesitation. Ever since you recruited them in Buck-An-Ear Cove they've been happy to take your lead. Having five hundred hours in the bank must give you some authority—to the newbies anyway. And as uncomplicated as it was to lone wolf it, having a team around you isn't too bad.

You pull the Stingers out, ready to obliterate anything that comes at you, then turn to Warrack and motion for him to follow. After you move out of cover behind the church and sprint to the other side of the village, you hug the hut walls, creeping south toward the pens. Your heart's thudding but the raptors seem occupied with the pigs. As long as the meat lasts, you should be able to take them by surprise.

Your confidence is shattered a moment later, as you're passing the third hut, when Gerbil and AVmei spin and open fire.

For a second you're pissed they started shooting without you, but when you glance over at their green-outlined position on the other side of the huts across the village, you see they're still not within sight of the red-marked raptors in the animal pen. Instead they're turned around backwards, firing in the direction of the swamps.

It's not the raptorwolves—another squad's trying to third-party your quest.

"*Warbot!*" AVmei yells in your head, and for a second you're not sure you heard her right, but then a reverberating whine purrs from the other side of the village, and you know that sound instantly: a multi-shot mag rifle. Someone's finished the Caldera Fortress and won themselves a walking tank.

"We need help—" Gerbil yells, but her words are cut off as an explosion rocks the village, spitting dust and bits of concrete into the air.

OVRshAdo downs Gerbil-Of-Doom. 74 players remain.

Your throat closes. OVRshAdo's got a warbot, and he's come to get you.

"Find cover," you call into the comms, but you're already screwed. Gerbil's gone and your team display shows Mei must have been caught in the blast too. Her vitals read multiple wounds, she's hurt bad. If you don't get her a heal in a few minutes she'll be done. Might even be too far gone already.

A frazzled anger burns in your chest. *Fuck that guy.* Why's he got such a hard-on for you?

You haven't spent long with your team, but you've come to like them over the past two days, and now they're about to have their runs cut short—all because they made the terrible decision to join up with you.

You glance over your shoulder to the jungle behind you. OVRshAdo and his team are still on the other side of town. They aren't far, far but with the camo you could run, might even get away, but you know OVRshAdo won't let up. He didn't go through all the trouble of fighting through the bots in the Caldera to back off now. He'll hunt you right out of the game if you don't push back against him. Time to make a stand—though up against a two-v-four plus a warbot, you don't especially like your chances.

You order the drones to move, have them scout the east side of the village for OVRshAdo's team, and they ping out two enemies moving up on Mei's position before they're spotted and shot out of the sky.

"Hold on, we're coming," you say as you press forward into the village, but there's an electric rattle and then Mei's gone too.

Zara-Zee downs AVmei. 73 players remain.

"*Request orders,*" Warrack says from behind you. He takes the game seriously, but even unvocalized you can hear the tension in his words. And it's not unwarranted. You're outnumbered and way outgunned. The two of you would have a hard time taking out just the warbot.

Then through the rain you hear a snarling bark and a chorus of reptilian howls.

The raptorwolves.

It's not over yet.

Someone on OVRshAdo's team yells a warning. They would have known what you were out here to do, had to expect the raptors would be active, but they came anyway.

"*Watch my back,*" you think to Warrack as you activate the camo. "*I'm gonna get us some reinforcements.*"

Warrack hefts his rifle and nods, even smiles a little. Death's coming for him from all directions but he's keeping it together, at least on the outside. Good kid.

Too bad he's probably gonna be dead soon. And you along with him.

I can't turn Anika in, I know that much. But I'm not walking away either. Problem is, the only way I can see to go forward requires doing something incredibly stupid.

I know what she's going through, I've been there too. She's had a glimpse of herself—someone she's never been—and watched her do things she can't understand. She's got her mind made up the island forced her to kill herself, and maybe it did, but she won't ever have peace until she knows for sure.

She needs to find the truth and she won't give up until she gets it, no matter what she needs to risk. Eventually it'll destroy her, like it destroyed Deacon. I know firsthand what happens when your self-image is fractured, and how impossibly sharp the pieces are when you try to reassemble them.

Yeah, she lied to me, but I understand why. I'd have done the same thing.

So how can I blame her?

Dub's left three messages with Connie, asking what happened in Lost Orleans, and even though his voice has grown more and more frantic with each one, I still haven't called him back. I know he's under the gun for a decision on Anika. Media for the upcoming match is in full rev and the Humanitech marketing people won't want anything fucking with their plans at the last minute. We're getting close to showtime, and he needs to know if the ludus needs to pull the plug and slot in a replacement for Anika.

I send him a quick message, text only, telling him I can't talk but that it might be a good idea to start prepping Anika's replacement, and I'll get back to him by tomorrow morning like I promised. I don't want to give him so much he sounds an alarm and has Humanitech security lock Anika down, but since she has no intention of going through with the novi fight, Dub might as well start getting the next in line ready to sub in.

Then I call Anika and tell her to meet me on the corner of Bloor and Avenue, that we need to talk, face-to-face. And I'm not taking no for an answer.

She doesn't reply for a few minutes, and I'm starting to think she might not, but then she sends a two-word response. *"Or what?"*

"Bloor and Avenue. 8:30," I send back. I see her read it, but she doesn't send anything else. She'll come. I know she's pissed at me, but I also know she'll be there.

I arrive early and she keeps me guessing, but in the end, she's only five minutes late. She comes wearing her lean arena skyn, with her short hair messy and her bright lips set in a pissed-off scowl, but she looks amazing. Like a superhero.

"This way," I say, and lead her down Bloor past the university stadium. She stays a few paces behind me, but follows.

I turn down Philosopher's Walk, the tree-lined path leading down from the high traffic of Bloor Street through the university grounds, and after only a few steps into the leafy canopy the city noise falls to a hush and it feels like we're in a different world.

Anika stops, stretches her arms out, and scans the surrounding rooftops through the trees. "This your way of getting me out in the open so the Standards snipers have a clear headshot?"

"No, I'm getting you out in the open so no one over-hears us discussing your plan to crash Decimation Island."

She lowers her arms and tilts away from me. "What's to discuss?"

"You're down a man," I say. "Put me in, coach."

She starts, as if stunned, but then her eyes bulge and her lips spread in a surprised smile. "*What?*"

"Take me with you. HuggyJackson is floating out to sea, and you've got an empty skyn loaded onto a rocket and ready to drop."

Anika shakes her head like she can't believe what she's hearing. "*No*," she says, and her voice sounds definite, but she's still smiling. I think I caught her off guard. "Just—*No*. I couldn't ask you to do that."

"You didn't. I'm offering."

"Then I reject your offer. I don't trust you."

She doesn't trust *me*? "You helped rip off Humanitech! You're a criminal and I'm a liar—that makes both of us assholes, but it doesn't mean I'm not willing to help you get your head straight. And if Jefferson Wood is dishing out helpings of a killer AI like OVRshAdo thinks, and we shut down in the process, even better. We work well together and you know it. What have you got to lose?"

"I—"

"Don't think about it, there's nothing to think *about*, just agree with me so we can figure out how we sell it to OVRshAdo."

She huffs, squinting like she's doing long division in her head. She needs to work it through herself, but she'll see it my way. Yeah, she's mad I lied to her, but it only hurts because she'd become invested. We both know she isn't blameless in all this, and me joining the squad is a practical answer to their missing teammate. It'll be reluctant, but she'll come around.

I give her space and after a long minute she shrugs. What other choice do they have?

"We don't need a fourth," she says, but the frost in her voice is dulled. "Shad's already changed the plan to run a trio. He's got a warbot operating system to plug into the fourth skyn. It'll shoot what it's told"—she hesitates, glances up into the trees for a moment, then looks back down at me—"but we only get one chance at this. I'd much rather fight beside someone who doesn't *need* to be told what to shoot."

"I can do both," I say. I'm smiling at her, for some reason I can't help it. I guess we're a team. "But will Shad agree?"

"I think we can bring him around. He's a dick but he wants to win. He's not who we need to worry about."

"Zara-Zee?"

"She'll be a hard 'no.' She's salty Huggy isn't coming and won't want anyone on short notice. But my vote makes it two to one."

"What's our story then? I don't think he'll appreciate the truth."

"Your idea is more *lies*?"

"You think OVRshAdo's being completely honest with you? Who do you trust more?"

Her nostrils flare, but she looks me in the eyes when she says, "You," and just that one word is enough to make my stomach flip.

What am I getting myself into?

No, this is definitely not good.

WE SETTLE on telling ninety percent of the truth, and Anika does all the talking. She starts with how we met at the Humanitech gala, but doesn't mention how I secretly uncovered their plot to invade Decimation Island and then dropped HuggyJackson in the Mississippi. Everything else sticks to what really happened. We gamed together, a lot— and her feed can prove it. We've got a rapport, and Anika vouches for me, says I can frag out.

She doesn't bother to hide the fact I'm an ex-cop, mostly because she couldn't—it's the first thing that'll come up when OVRshAdo doxxes me—but she also figures he'll get a kick out of it, think it'll make me seem like a badass, being kicked off the force the way I was. He's the kind of guy who'd see it as a positive career move.

I've got a good resume, but still not enough to win him over.

"You seriously want us to hire your new boyfriend?" OVRshAdo asks.

We're gathered in a private virt, Anika, Shad, Zara, and

me. It's nothing fancy, the setting picked at random—a big stone room with a long wooden table and flickering torch-light casting shadows in mid-fi detail. Our aspects are dressed in medieval costumes and move with the grace of tanks, but we're only here to talk, and it works fine enough for that.

"We haven't discussed our relationship status," I answer back. It's the first thing I've said since we cast in. I've been half-leaning against the table while Anika's been talking, and I step up next to her. "But if and when we do, I promise you won't be involved. Now, let's discuss your preference to run a job on an AI who's distilled killing down to an art form with a bot instead of someone who's actually done it before. You know I already beat a superintelligence once, right?" I didn't, but the link says I did, so that makes it true.

Shad only shrugs. "Yeah, impressive as shit, mate—*Finsbury*—whatever kind of name that is. But here's the thing: I don't *know* you," He glances at Anika. "I *do* know the bot."

Zara's pacing up and down the length of the room, but she stops and whirls around with her finger leveled at Shad. "Why are we even discussing this? A day away from jump and we're recruiting? We don't need the bot—and we sure as fuck don't need this guy, doesn't matter who he is. You're wasting time I could be using to find Huggy."

"We've got people on it," OVRshAdo says, not looking at her.

"Fuck those people!" Zara moans. "You should be down here yourself."

"I've posted a generous reward for his recovery. Someone will find him, but until then the bot's taking his place. Like you said, 'we're a day away from jump.' The job is what matters."

Seems like they've had this conversation before, because Zara just growls and goes back to pacing.

They won't find Huggy in time, I'm pretty sure of that. I don't know what their timing is for insertion, but his skyn's got to be somewhere in the Gulf by now. By the time someone traces its ping and recovers his Cortex and then his rithm is cleared by Standards, his ride will be long gone.

As it is there's barely enough to get me up to speed on what they've spent weeks planning for. If we're doing this, we need to get started now.

Anika steps up to him. "He's better than a bot, Shad," she insists.

"How long you known this guy?" Shad replies. His tone is still light, but there's an edge to it. "A week? And you've already told him all about us? You know what we're about to do, right?"

"I do," Anika replies.

"How do you know he won't yip out on us? This is hardcore mode we're talking—one life, no respawns, no save points. We lose and we lose it forever, lost time for everyone and Jefferson Wood goes right on converting the world to pay to win."

"Fin fought in a real war, Shad," she says, taunting him. "He's solid." Then she tosses me a hesitant sideways glance. "I trust him."

Shad throws his arms wide, splashing drama from his outstretched fingers. "Based on *what*? 'Cause he shot a real gun thirty years ago? Because he used to chase around after bad guys? Or is it some deep personal shit you can only feel in your *heart*?"

OVRshAdo's lucky he makes his living in digital. I don't expect he'd last long in the real world before someone busted him in the mouth for running it too often. But for now, he's in charge, and that means his rules.

"How about a test then," I suggest. OVRshAdo won't listen to anyone else, he needs to see it for himself. "A one-v-one, me against the bot. Whoever gets the most kills joins the team."

Shad swivels his head around to face me.

"Now that's interesting," he says. "But no, not against the bot. That'd hardly be fair—"

I see where this is going. "I can't beat you," I say.

It's not flattery. His personality sucks but he's grown up a gamer, he's a natural. No way I can beat him on his home turf.

"Well that's what makes it so much fun, doncha think?" Shad replies.

"We don't have time for this," Anika says, raising her voice. "You just lectured us about what's at stake, and you want to waste your time playing games? You know we can use him, but you need make it about yourself. No one's watching, you don't have to stir the pot every chance you get. Why don't we skip it all this time, huh?"

Shad stops, and while the expression on his face barely changes, his mood shifts, and just when I'm starting to think he might have a vein of common sense running through him after all, he laughs and his face broadens into a jagged grin.

"Uh-uh," he says, fixing his pupil-less black eyes on me. "You and me, buddy, we gonna game, and I'll show you just how easy you are to kill."

"Fin, you don't have to do this," Anika says. "Shad, knock it off. There's no need—"

I don't expect to win, but no way I'm walking away. "I'm down. But if I win, I'm on the team."

He laughs as if the idea itself is ludicrous. "Sure thing. *You* win, and you can take the bot's place. I win, and you walk."

"Then stop talking and spin up a server," I say, faking a confidence I don't feel. "Let's get this over with."

You CREEP around the edge of the village, camo unit humming on your chest as you slide from shadow to shadow and let the pattering rain mask your movements. The warbot's coming for you, probably straight down the center of the village, taking point and looking to flush you out. OVRshAdo and his team will be spread out behind it, using it as a distraction while they clear the buildings searching for you.

Once you get to the last hut before the open area around the animal pen you stop again and listen. A snuffling wheeze chortles nearby. It's a raptor, and it's close. You inch along the concrete wall and peer around the corner and nearly smack into a long, scaly snout.

You freeze, not daring to breathe. The animal is big, perched up on its powerful hind legs with the fur on its head and back rippling and its claws in the air. There's blood on its lips and it smells like raw meat. Its nostrils flare, sniffing the air, but it's confused—it smells food but can't see you. You back off slowly, a pixelated blur edging toward the jungle, still not breathing, and as you retreat you gently slide your hand into the pouch on your hip and pull out the pherodart gun. The raptor shakes its head, but doesn't follow. Its five friends are just beyond, finishing off the pigs in the stockade, but they still look hungry.

Metallic clapping rises above the rain, and Warrack's vitals spike but he doesn't seem to be hurt. A boom sounds in the distance, a frag grenade.

"Diversionary tactics," Warrack says.

"Good," you respond. *"But get ready, it's about to pop off."*

Still invisible, you swing wide of the raptor and skirt the edge of the jungle to the rear of the pen, and once you're around back you can see straight down the lane between the rows of huts. The warbot's marching down the middle of the village, its heavy footsteps squelching in the mud. The raptors have seen it too, but it's not made of meat, so they're not interested. And while you can't see them, you know OVRshAdo's squad is spread out, moving from cover to cover, letting the bot take the lead. No way you and Warrack can take them. Even without the warbot it'd be a tough fight.

Unless you even the odds.

You raise the launcher, aim down the sights at the warbot's chest, and pull the trigger. The pherodart fires with a hiss of compressed air and splashes against the warbot's red torso, coating it with a highly volatile chemical the raptorwolves are trained to seek out and attack.

They all come at once, turning instantly from the animal pen to gallop toward the warbot. The bot senses the coming attack and responds instantly, fires once with the magcannon on his left arm to blow the lead raptorwolf into red mist, and then follows up with pulses from the magrifle on its right, ripping through two more, but then the raptors are on it and the muscled beasts drive the bot to the ground.

The warbot's lethal, but not on its back, and while its armor is tough, it doesn't hold out long against three ferocious raptorwolves. It thrashes on the ground, trying to knock away the three-quarter ton sacks of teeth and muscle, but can't.

One of OVRshAdo's new squaddies pokes out from behind a hut on the east side of the village, trying to get a shot on one of the raptors, and I snap a shot of pheromones at her. The dart smacks her right in the faceplate, and she stumbles back, frantically trying to wipe it clean. She knows what's about to happen.

The bot's barely moving, its torso chewed out and no meat inside, so when the new burst of pheromones hits, the raptors lunge toward the fresh prey. She empties her rifle into the beasts as they converge on her, and Zara-Zee swings out from a hut further to the north to help, but the bullets aren't enough to slow down the frenzied artificial dinosaurs. Her screams don't last long.

Raptorwolf downs JennjaminFranklin. 72 players remain.

Then it's a full-on panic. OVRshAdo's fourth teammate pops out of the same building Zara was hiding in and fires a full magazine into the closest raptor, and while that's enough to kill it, the other two now have new targets.

You run along the fencing and cross the open muddy path back to the nearest hut. You've got eyes on three of the enemy squad. One's dead, but you still haven't seen OVRshAdo, which means he's behind you. You load your last dart and get ready to use it.

He's coming for you, you know he is. It's how he thinks. Send the rest of the team out front as a big noisy distraction while he sneaks around to get the job done. You huddle under the overhanging roof, invisible and sheltered from the rain, and wait. But not for long.

A shadow emerges from the jungle, the rain sluicing off something that isn't there. He found himself a camo unit too. Except he's moving, and the camo doesn't work great with movement, especially in the rain.

Shots come from behind you, followed by a shuddering squeal. That'll be another raptor dead. But only one. There's still one left somewhere.

Raptorwolf downs HotFannySandwich. 71 players remain.

Yes! Just Zara-Zee and OVRshAdo left. Odds are all even now. That's more like it.

The audience is eating this up. You've been so focused on surviving you haven't noticed the pressure swelling in your head, and now the attention is making you dizzy. Your aud has grown steadily this game, the crowd likes a proactive player, but now that the top three survivors are having it out, everyone's watching. One way or another, this fight right here is gonna blow the game wide open.

OVRshAdo's picking his way across the mud toward the back of the stockade, blurry water cascading down his armor. He's still got his Stinger, and the black circle of his gun's muzzle is floating along in midair. He isn't keeping it down, he wants to be ready to fire the instant he sees you. That's why you need to hit him first, but you're only holding the pherodart, and it's out of sight behind your back, as he's sure to notice you if you try to swing it out and fire. Wait until he turns his back, and then you can draw your Stingers and put him down.

"Two left," you think to Warrack. *"OVRshAdo's here with me, and Zara-Zee's in the second hut from the north on the east side. Plus a raptor somewhere around here too."*

"Roger—" Warrack answers, and just as he does OVRshAdo freezes, then spins directly toward you and fires, as if somehow he can hear your thoughts.

You dive to the side, trying to avoid the spray, but even with the muscle tonics juicing your body you're not fast enough. Bullets thud into your armor, knocking you off balance, and you bounce off the hut wall and fall to your knees. The pherodart gun spins from your hand as you hit the mud, and you abandon it as you roll, trying to stay out of the line of fire.

OVRshAdo whips around, drawing a light machine gun as he does, and this time when he fires the bullets hit you square in the chest, driving you back against the concrete wall. The camo unit sizzles as a bullet shatters it, and your invisibility winks off.

"Followed your footprints in the mud," OVRshAdo says, easing off the trigger for a moment to answer the question you hadn't asked.

You try to get to your feet but the mud slows you down, and when OVRshAdo fires again he doesn't miss. The adaptive armor takes the brunt of the bullets, but they come so fast it doesn't have time to reform around the weak spots and you feel tugs of pain in your abdomen as hot metal embeds itself in your flesh.

Then his weapon clicks dry. "Betcha wish you were on my team right about now," OVRshAdo taunts from behind his faceplate as he reloads.

Shit, shit, *shit.*

"He's on me," you call out to Warrack, but a fresh round of shooting in the distance tells you he's busy with Zara-Zee. You're on your own.

Fire burns through your abdomen but you ignore it, and you whip out the Stinger and let fly with a return stream of metal, and this time it's OVRshAdo who hits the mud.

You get up and run as you shoot, hunched over from the pain, but the bullets go wide as you prioritize moving over accuracy. Chunks of concrete explode from the wall behind you as you slide around the corner and out of his line of sight, but you won't be safe for long. You glance up and see a shuttered window and react without thinking, take a step back and dive straight through the wooden slats. You crash into the room, roll awkwardly, and tuck yourself next to an empty bookshelf, guns up, ready to shoot.

Blood is pouring out of your gut. You feel it, warm and wet, streaming over your groin and down your leg inside the resealed armor. The wound isn't fatal, you've got a medkit in your backpack that should seal it up and keep you going until the endgame, but until then it's gonna slow you down, and that could be enough for OVRshAdo to finish you off.

A metallic clank rings out as something hits the concrete floor, and you barely have time to hurl yourself into the next room before the frag detonates, throwing dust and shrapnel everywhere. Your ears are ringing but you keep moving, thud out the front door and stumble through the mud across the main path through the center of the settlement, right past the ruined warbot.

A quick glance north toward the community hall shows the coast is clear, but Zara-Zee could be anywhere. Warrack's outline is two huts up on the west side of the village, crouched with his back against an outside wall, and who knows where that last raptor is, but you don't have time to worry about it as you shoulder your way through the front door of the hut, stumble inside, and slam it behind you.

"*Zara-Zee's closing in,*" Warrack reports. "*And I've lost contact with the raptorwolf.*"

"*Run,*" you answer as you move deeper into the hut. "*Lose them in the jungle.*" He's right on the edge of the village, a short sprint and he's in the trees.

"*I'm not abandoning you,*" Warrack replies.

"*That's an order,*" you tell him, though you have no authority to give one. "*OVRshAdo's after me, but he won't chase you—*" You don't think.

You hop out a side window, grimacing as pain flares in your stomach. You can't stop moving, can't let OVRshAdo get close, but you can't run blindly either. One wrong turn and you could end up face-to-face with Zara-Zee—or that raptor.

The rain is letting up now, retreating as quickly as it blew in, and the clouds are parting to reveal bright blue sky. You pause, listening for any sound of movement, and a throaty growl ripples out in the village. Zara-Zee shrieks in surprise, somewhere off to the northeast, then lets loose with a barrage from her weapon. The raptor squeals in pain but you don't think it's dead.

"*You have any frags left?*" you ask Warrack as you force yourself to move again, tiptoeing closer to the western edge of the huts. You need make a break for it, no way you can fight your way out of this one.

"*Three,*" Warrack replies.

"*Toss 'em.*"

"*Where?*"

"*Anywhere,*" you say. "*Just not at me.*" Who knows, maybe he'll get lucky.

His outline shifts as he pulls his frags and lobs them between the huts and out into the clearing toward where Zara-Zee was shooting. The explosions fire mud and smoke into the air but nothing hits the kill-feed. They'll have cleared a path through, this is your chance.

"*Hit the jungle, now!*" you say. "*I'm right behind you.*"

This time Warrack obeys, but before he can get two steps a spray of gunfire sounds from the south, just on the other side of the hut. Warrack swears as the bullets smack into him, and he's forced back into protection behind the wall.

You poke your head out around the corner and instantly pull back. OVRshAdo blasts a chunk out of the concrete where your face was a second ago. He's already swung around to flank you, coming up the outside wall of the huts to cut off your escape route, and he's given up on the camo. He knows you're injured, no point hiding now.

"Come on, Ani," he calls. "Why drag this out?"

Warrack's two buildings up, and he angles his weapon around the corner and blind-fires down the wall. A second later another burst of fire erupts from the other side of the village and Warrack's vitals go haywire.

"*I'm hit,*" Warrack cries in your head. "*It's bad.*" Zara-Zee must have an angle on him, somewhere across the other side of the village. He's exposed, got nowhere to run, and by the looks of his vitals he doesn't have long left.

"Aren't you gonna go help your teammate?" OVRshAdo taunts. "Sounds like he's hurt."

You want to, but there's nothing you can do. Move and you're dead. Zara-Zee's north of you, OVRshAdo's to the south, and you're stuck in between. There's nowhere to hide, and the second you show yourself they'll mow the both of you down.

Your only hope is to make a run for it, abandon Warrack and save yourself. The thick leaves of the jungle are only ten feet away, and your skyn is juiced up. Maybe you can make it across the grass and lose them—

No chance. OVRshAdo's too close. The moment you moved he'd end you.

Zara-Zee shoots again, and Warrack cries out as he's hit once more, but still he doesn't die. She could go for the flush and send Warrack out of the game, but they're playing with you, torturing him to force your hand, and you grit your teeth in frustration. Part of you knows this is just a game, that none of it is real, but the pain in your gut isn't in your imagination, and neither are Warrack's dwindling vital signs.

And Rael, he's real, *realer* than anything out here. All this may all be meaningless, but if you lose he loses too, and he doesn't get the luxury of a respawn.

So if they want to play, you'll *play*.

You know you can't take on OVRshAdo, you're hurt and he's too close, but you can kill Zara-Zee.

You pick yourself up and crouch-walk along the length of the hut, peek out across the village and spot her against the corner of a hut two buildings up, eye to her scope, holding a line of fire straight across at Warrack. She's got a headshot lined up, could have downed him already, and if they were playing smart she would have.

You raise the Stinger and fire a burst at her, and she swears as she falls back around the side of the building. She'll still have line of sight on Warrack, but you don't give her the chance to take it. You pull your last frag and toss it up between the buildings where she's hiding. You don't think it'll catch her, but it'll force her to move.

The grenade pops with a *whump* and tosses chunks of

dirt from out between the huts, but doesn't seem to hurt her. Still you limp across the clearing, moving toward her position, and that's when OVRshAdo hits you in the back with a burst from his weapon.

Your backpack takes the brunt of it but still you're driven face-first into the mud, and you sprawl out helpless.

That's it. Game over.

Your heart thuds in your chest as you wait for the next shot, the one that'll send you back to your skyn at home, and for a second you almost welcome it. But then you realize what it'll mean, what you'll have to face—

You heave yourself around, wipe your eyes clear, and see OVRshAdo standing over you, just a few meters away. He's holding the pherodart launcher, must have picked it up after you dropped it, and he's got a fucking grin on his face like a couple of gamer groupies just offered him a three-way.

Of course he'd use the raptor against you. It'd be easy enough just to shoot you, but where's the spectacle in a one-man firing squad? He's wringing every drop of drama out of this he can, playing for the crowd, and he must be doing a good job of it because the audience is going nuts, a livewire bouncing around in your head as the audience floods into your POV, eager to experience for themselves what it feels like to be mauled to death by a velociraptor/wolf hybrid.

"I imagine this will be unpleasant," OVRshAdo says, admiring the dart launcher with a raised eyebrow as you work back up to standing. One of your Stingers is on the ground, but you've got another one on your hip, if you could only get to it.

You glance around, checking behind you, searching for anything that might save you. Warrack's out of the fight and bleeding out. His green outline is still slumped against the hut on the west side of the village, and Zara-Zee has him covered anyway. She could finish him anytime she wants, but she's just as engrossed in the drama as the rest of the audience. She'll wait until the show's over to finish him.

You don't want to go out, not like this.

"I suppose it's too late to team up?" you say, stalling by playing casual. You're seething with fear and frustration but no damn way will you let OVRshAdo see that.

Helaughs. "Oh Boo, we could have done great things together, you and I. And maybe one day we will—but today is not that day."

The two of you lock eyes as he raises the launcher, and as he levels it at your face you notice the thick plug of mud blocking the muzzle. Hope spasms in your chest and you try not to smile. His day is about to get super shitty.

"Wait!" Zara-Zee calls out in warning, but it comes an instant too late.

He pulls the trigger and the weapon fires with a *snap-hiss*, but instead of shooting a dart the launcher backfires, spraying OVRshAdo with a gush of raptorwolf pheromones.

He screams and flings the launcher away but he's already doused. Before he can move the remaining raptor races out from between two huts, and leaps for his arm.

OVRshAdo's good, manages to draw his pistol and gets two clean shots off, but two bullets from a handgun aren't enough to stop the charging animal and it hits full speed, bites down on OVRshAdo's forearm, and drives him to the ground. He pumps bullets into the raptor's guts as it chews his arm off, but then the weapon clicks dry and he's defenseless, with nothing left to do but scream.

Now's your chance. You pull the Stinger while you spin, firing even before you're facing Zara-Zee, not giving her any chance to take you or Warrack down. She yelps as a line of bullets rakes across her chest, forcing her to flee around the corner.

You chase her down the alley between the huts, keeping up the onslaught of metal, not giving her the chance to regain her footing.

She fires backwards as she runs, heading for the jungle, trying to escape, but her shots go wide, thudding into the concrete around you. Yours don't miss.

The bullets hit her square in the back, knocking her forward, and she stumbles and trips in the mud, tries to roll and come up shooting, but you don't give her the chance and riddle her with bullets. Her armor cracks and blood bursts from her back as you empty the magazine into her.

AniK@ downs survivor Zara-Zee. 70 players remain.

Your heart's racing and your breath is raspy, but the fight isn't over yet. Somehow OVRshAdo's name still hasn't hit the kill-feed.

Warrack's still alive, but won't be for long if you don't patch him up. You should go to him right now, but you can't until you know OVRshAdo is out of the game. First though, you walk over to Zara-Zee's corpse and reclaim your Redeemer.

"Told you I'd take this back," you say as you fasten it to your pack, then spin and reload your weapon as you run to the center of town, half-expecting to see OVRshAdo gone, but he's right where you left him.

He's lost his helmet and his skyn is shredded—still alive, but won't be for long. You creep closer, keeping your weapon up, not giving him any chance to get a lucky parting shot. He's got a long knife held slack in his left hand and while he's drenched in blood, a lot of it is the raptorwolf's.

It's dead and he's about to be. His right arm is gone above the elbow and his chest is ripped completely open.

"Fucking hell," you say as you stop a few paces away. He's not playing possum, you can see his heart beating in the open air. "You killed it."

"Killed each other," he says, his voice weak, then coughs a spray of blood.

"Goddamn legend," you say, honestly impressed. "I'm almost sad to see you go."

"Patch me up then?" he says, but we both know he's too far gone for that. The medkits will work for bullet wounds and lacerations, but a raptorwolf just performed open heart surgery on him. He's only got seconds left.

You shake your head. "I said 'almost.'"

He smiles, doesn't seem mad or anything. "Good game then, AniK@."

"Yeah," you answer as you aim the Stinger at his exposed head. "Good game."

You could always just let him bleed out, but the competitive part of you can't let that happen—you want the credit. All it takes is a single bullet, straight to the heart.

AniK@ downs survivor OVRshAdo. 69 players remain.

"Looks like the bot's got the spot, mate," OVRshAdo calls. He's twenty meters away and closing, but he's taking his time, stepping carefully over the ice as he angles toward my hiding place behind a silvery supply crate. I'm down to less than ten percent health and falling as I bleed out. My vision is vibrating. We're in game five, tied two games to two, and I'm about to lose.

"How many times has that bot beat you?" I yell back. "More than twice?"

The battery on my camo's down to a second and a half of invis time left, and I ran out of AR ammo fighting the last wave of bots. I've got six shots in my nine-millimeter pistol and a single grenade, with only seconds before the bots are close enough to strike, but the instant I move OVRshAdo will down me. All it'll take is a single glancing shot and it's game over.

He laughs, knowing he's won. He reloads and readies his weapon with a quick snick-clack of the slide.

"I'll give you credit," he condescends in that swish

accent of his. "You did good, but a game's only as good as its rules, and to win you have to *win*. Good's not *good enough*."

Fuck him. I did better than *good*.

Yeah, OVRshAdo won the first game. We dropped into a level designed to look like a modern Middle Eastern city reclaimed by the desert, all mirrored buildings and sand dunes. The DI one-v-ones let you pick a weapon or support item to start with, and I chose the VL-27, a variable ammo assault rifle kitted with a grenade launcher, thinking I'd find him quick and overpower him before he could find a weapon, but that didn't happen. He picked the auto-drone to start, and it found *me* first and had me down to half health before I knew where the bullets were coming from. By the time I took it out he'd tracked me down and even though he only had an SMG the game was over barely two minutes in.

I did a little better in the second round, chose the heavy armor to start, and stayed alive for almost ten minutes while I searched around the Egyptian ruin level and kitted up, but in the end, even the armor wasn't enough to keep me alive. He took a .50 sniper rifle, posted up in the middle of the safe-zone, and took shots at my head any time I tried to move.

I had the bots closing on my back and OVRshAdo knew the map, always put himself in the best position to keep me from advancing on him. I did what I could to survive, but eventually I ran out of time and the bots ripped me apart.

I'm about five seconds away from that happening again.

"Bullets or bots?" OVRshAdo taunts. "How you wanna go out?"

"It's not over yet," I reply, but at this point hollow words are all I have left to throw at him.

Game three I surprised myself—and OVRshAdo even more—when I won.

It was close. We ended up in a straight-up peek battle in a purple-tinged forest at sunset. I took the turret and he took the grapple, and between his enhanced move speed through the trees and me streaming bullets wherever he landed, we chipped away at each other. I was down to a sliver of health and scored a lucky headshot that neither of us was expecting and squeaked out a win.

OVRshAdo came at me hard in game four, rushing to get the kill, and that's why he lost. He was salty and over-compensated, choosing a Stinger to start, thinking he'd get close, out-aim and out damage me, but this time I took the sniper rifle and played keep-away with *him*. The Stinger chewed through the bots, and if he'd taken his time he could have outlasted me, but he was in a hurry and I took his dome off as he charged across an open field.

Game five I knew he wouldn't be fucking around, and I took the camo package, thinking I'd play the edge of the zone, out-position him, and get him when he wasn't looking, but he was ready for me—he chose a scan drone that saw right through the camo.

With my advantage blown we chased each other around the map. Eventually I took out his drone but by then my camo was gone, and we spent ten long minutes sneaking around, taking shots at each other and healing back up until little by little OVRshAdo out-damaged me.

Now the bots have pushed us close enough together that we can have a conversation while my health slowly trickles away.

If I lose they'll hit Decimation Island without me, and maybe it's just my pride talking, but they're about to do something damn near impossible—they *need* me. More than some bot, anyway. I need make OVRshAdo see that.

The safe-zone contracts past me and instantly the bots that had been biding their time pounce. There are two right nearby and I put three bullets in each as they spring to tear me apart, but that leaves me dry, the pistol useless. I fling the lump of metal over the crate, hoping I'll get lucky and hit OVRshAdo. Not that it would do much, a couple points of damage at most, but the soft thud as it hits the snow and his amused chuckle tells me I won't get even that.

He's right close now, still in the green. Three more prowler bots are approaching, stalking on their clawed feet like wolves. I could use the grenade, but they're close enough and I'm at low enough health I'd die in the blast.

If do nothing the bots get me.

If I move OVRshAdo kills me.

There's nothing I can do. I'm dead no matter what.

"Well, this has been fun and all, mate, but we've got matters to attend to. Stand up so I can shoot you."

Fine, but we're doing it my way. If I'm gonna die, might as well be in style.

I activate the grenade and let the detonator cook for a moment before I trigger my last few seconds of camo, and by the time my body is pixelating to invisible I'm already vaulting the crate, jumping up and over it. Shad's directly ahead of me, no more than a few meters away, and he hears me coming, but it takes him a half-second to locate exactly where I am, and another half-second to swing his weapon up and open fire, and that's all the time I need.

I juke right, crouch and dive at him, get inside his guard so we're right up close. He'll shove me, and the melee attack that comes after will finish me off, but he doesn't get the chance.

The grenade I'm carrying explodes and zeroes our health bars at the same time, killing us both instantly.

Stalemate.

We load back into the DI lobby at the same time. He doesn't say anything, and his aspect sits idle, running the neutral animation.

Anika and Zara are waiting for us. The DI aspect's facial responses aren't great, but Anika's clearly smiling like I won. I didn't, but considering who I was up against, I'll take the draw.

"Spicy," Zara says, the tension in her voice blunted. I think maybe she's coming around on not hating me.

"I told you, he's good," Anika says, then turns to OVRshAdo. "So we're done with this shit about the bot?"

He doesn't even look at her. He's still got his eyes fixed on me, and I stare right back at him. She snaps a look between us, clocks our staring contest, and makes a noise in her throat.

"The fuck is wrong with you?" she says, talking to both of us. "We're hours away from the single biggest game of our lives—this toxic masculine bullshit ends now, or I walk."

I fight off a reflexive urge to snap back *but he started it*, but keep my mouth shut.

"I'm with Ani," Zara says. "They don't find Huggy in time, I'll take him over the bot."

Now it's my turn. Suck it up and let him have the win. "You had me," I say, blinking first. "Another second and I was dead."

At first I think he's gonna stick with the silence, or that he might have even gone AFK and left his aspect online to troll us, but suddenly he snaps out of it, looks away from me, and says, "He's in. But only if Huggy doesn't get back in time." Then he raises his hands and he's back to his smug self. "Twenty-one hours to load-in. We'd better get the fish here a few practice runs, just in case."

He shoots me a sideways glance, and chime sounds in my head. An invite to squad in Decimation Island.

Looks like I'm in.

I'll give this to OVRshAdo: he's a self-important asshole, but he's got a hell of a knack for planning a combat operation.

Decimation Island is housed on a three-thousand-square-kilometer private island in the western Pacific. It used to be part of Micronesia, but was abandoned as the ocean rose, and eventually Jefferson Wood moved in and converted it to a home for the live game. It has no allegiance to any country and no qualms about using lethal force to protect itself.

Enough people have tried to sneak their way onto the island over the years that it's become a fortress. No one gets in or out without permission. It's surrounded by a seawall, supplies are sent by ship and thoroughly scanned for stowaways, and the airspace is protected by a web of armed patrolling drones.

Getting four bulky combat skyns onto the island undetected was only the first of OVRshAdo's obstacles. Other than the few invite-only events Jefferson Wood is the only person allowed on the island. Everything else is run by bots under AI control. Nevertheless, OVRshAdo found a way: a goddamn orbital insertion. It's crazy dangerous, the entire plan is, but it could work.

The rocket launch is exactly timed to drop the combat skyns so we arrive just as the next game begins. The AI's gonna see us drop, nothing we can do about that, but we'll be coming in hot, small and hopefully fast enough to avoid the drones. We'll have the bots after us before we even hit the ground, but OVRshAdo bought us a little time there too. He had the arena skyns' ID chips reprogrammed to mimic the Decimation Island internal security network. He won't say where he got the code from, but it had to have cost him. Probably more than the rocket ride and the Chinese bot-launcher combined.

However he sourced it, he claims it's legit. Says as long as the skyns respond to the system requests with the right hash sequence, we should be able to hide from the AI. For a while at least. The bots talk to each other, and if we respond like we're bots, they'll leave us alone. Eventually the AI will devise a workaround—but it'll give us a head start, time we'll need to take down the island's communications so it can't transmit itself off to safety.

The only hitch with the plan is the security hash shifts with every new game, and we need it to send back the right answer when we're pinged.

This is where things get nuts.

Strapped into wingpacks, we'll launch from the rocket in the arena skyns will and terminal velocity toward the island, dropping at fifty meters per second, and by the time the AI sees us coming it'll be too late to do anything about it. That's the hope anyway, otherwise our run will end right quick.

We'll arrive just as the player skyns drop from the tower

and blend in to force the AI to figure out which of the plummeting bodies don't belong while we each try to get up close to one of the game skyns and skim their hash code using the spoofers OVRshAdo's built into our drop suits.

The timing will have to be spot-on, and we'll need a huge dose of luck, but the plan is solid. In theory, anyway.

The good news is almost everything between now and the time we hit the tower is out of our hands. Most of the job is falling. If the launch is delayed or the winds around the island are a little too strong and blow us off course or if OVRshAdo's spoofer takes two seconds longer to skim the hash than advertised, we'll be fucked and there's not much we can do about it.

Once we land we'll travel together straight to the communication's array. Zara's carrying the Bash Badger we'll use to hack the comms array and take over control of communications to and from the island to make sure the AI doesn't escape. It'd be easier to just blow the whole thing up, but we'll need it once we're done to cast ourselves back off the island.

And all that's the easiest part of the whole plan.

After that things get complicated.

We're in a custom virt, unbodied and floating over a 1:1 scale map of Decimation Island. Shad has us zoomed in on the northwest side and we're looking down on the communication array built out on a jutting finger of rock. There's not much to it, just a bunch of satellite dishes pointing in various directions, a row of small structures housing the maintenance bots, and a power substation to keep it going.

"After we hack into the array we'll go find the AI core," OVRshAdo says as he tracks the map to a high cliff edge on the northeast side of the island, directly across from the nearby smaller second island housing the control center.

"Our skyns are coming in armed and armored, so we won't have to fuck around looting, but once we're on the ground we'll only have two hours to get here, give or take. If we're not on the control island by then, our shot of success plummets."

Here's the first problem. There are six drop towers on the island, spaced out at the points of a hexagon fifteen kilometers to a side. Only one drop tower activates each game, selected at random, and that's where the live players will be. Obviously, the tower closest to the comms array is the one to hope for, but what if the game starts on the other side of the island?

"Worst-case scenario," I say. "What if the wrong tower lights up? We'll have a hell of a lot of ground to cover."

"Those gladiator skyns are fast," Zara says.

"Not that fast," I counter.

"Once we've got the security code skimmed, pull your chutes and glide as close as you can," Shad says. "We'll figure it out from there. We've run this enough times in practice. Getting the security code is an eighty percent lock. No worries there."

"But goes downhill quick after that," Anika says, deadpan.

"We'll be discovered eventually," OVRshAdo agrees, "no way around that, and Wood will come at us with everything. The closer we are to the control center when that happens the better."

A thought occurs. "How many times have you simmed this plan?"

"About two hundred," Anika confesses.

"And how many did you win?" I ask, but no one answers. "That bad?" I say after a moment.

"Three," OVRshAdo eventually says, his voice rising in

a vocal shrug. "But sims don't mean shit. We'll get through, I can feel it."

Anxiety does a little backflip in my gut but I don't say anything as the map zooms down to the cliffside and stops as though we're standing on the edge, with the control island directly ahead of us about five hundred meters offshore. Then without hesitating the POV leaps forward, like we've jumped, and plummets to the water and flies over the surface, tracing the route we'll need to swim to the island and the functional grey complex housing the Decimation Island game control systems.

"We jump and swim across, and then head straight up this path to the main building," OVRshAdo narrates as the POV climbs over the rocky shore of the small island, through the trees, and zigzags through a thicket of branches up a steep hill and into a wide courtyard. "Entry's here," he says, pointing to a wall of glass doors leading into a cool white, high-ceilinged atrium. "We'll go in hot, won't be any reason to hide by then. The whole island will know we're there." We zip through the glass doors and down around a wide flight of stairs to a subfloor, then zoom through a maze of halls to the AI's core storage room. "Zara will hack into the system and retrieve Anika's game memories. Then we'll blow the core with the explosive charges we're packing and out we get."

"What about exfil?" I ask.

"We'll find a boat or something back to the comms array and cast out. I'm not fucked about it at this point."

Is he not worried about getting off the island because he's confident, or 'cause he doesn't think we'll get that far?

"Tell him the best part," Anika prods.

Oh no. "What?" I ask, knowing I don't want to hear the answer.

When OVRshAdo doesn't respond, Anika goes ahead and tells me. "We don't actually know where the AI core is. The Control Complex layout is a best-guess based on whatever we could pull from public feeds. No one knows where the AI is housed, or has ever even seen it as far as we can tell."

"You've run two hundred sims with intel you know for a fact is wrong?"

"We still have the bot if you want out, mate," OVRshAdo jeers.

This suddenly seems like a bad idea. I was so hoo-rah to help Anika and shut down the Killr source I didn't think the plan through. These three are all treating this like a game, but we can't just cast into the arena skyns and ride them safely from our own heads, there's no bandwidth for that in the middle of the Pacific. This operation requires a full rithm transfer. I'll truly be there, and if I die on that island that's it, I'm done.

I'm sure these other three will be running real-time rithm backups. If the mission goes to shit they'll lose a few hours at most, leave a hole in their afternoon like they took a nap, but that's about it. I haven't backed up once since I first restored last year.

With Deacon riding shotgun in my head I can't risk it, my rithm's way out of sync with the reference pattern. If I tried to back up now red flags would pop at Standards like a Chinese New Year celebration and they'd be all over me.

There's a good chance I don't come back from this. Am I about to volunteer for a suicide mission? My rithm quivers as it tries to reach my distant body to paralyze me in fear, but after a second the distress passes, leaving me feeling numb, and I realize I'm not too bothered by the idea. If I die,

I die—had to happen sometime. Should have happened already.

If I don't make it back Shelt will eventually find my empty skyn in my room, and after a while he'll probably try triggering another restoration to drag my original psychorithm imprint from storage, but I've signed the Do Not Restore clause with Standards, so that'll be that.

I'm okay with it. This is all borrowed time anyway.

Besides, there's nothing I can do about it even if I wanted to. I've already put up too much of a fuss getting myself invited to back out now.

"What about Jefferson Wood? He must know where the AI is. We could nab him and make him tell us."

"If it comes to that," OVRshAdo says. "A side quest if we can't get there on our own."

This isn't gonna work.

"Works for me," I say instead. "When's go time?"

"We need to load into the skyns by twenty-two hundred tonight," he answers. "I'll send the details. Any other last-minute problems, send up a flag. Questions?" he asks.

Yeah, about a million, but I keep them to myself.

"Good enough," he says. "See everyone in the sky."

So, that's it, I'm about to die on Decimation Island.

For real this time.

It takes five medkits to patch Warrack up, and after you're done you help him inside one of the huts to recuperate. While he's healing, you collect the reward for finishing the Raptorwolf Rampage quest line, then go through the village to loot OVRshAdo and his team, and by then you're geared to the gills and end up leaving half of it behind.

You've lost your camo unit, and OVRshAdo's was destroyed by the raptorwolf, but you keep the Stingers as your sidearms and add the powerful medium- to long-range DR-17 battle rifle to your arsenal alongside the Redeemer. Warrack chooses the other two Stingers and a fully kitted LMD80 marksman rifle with an 8X zoom. You're also both able to mend and refill your adaptive armor. It was a close call, but you made it through, and now with OVRshAdo and Zara-Zee out of the way, you've got a shot at surviving until game ten. You're still not even halfway there, but it seems more possible than ever, and you allow yourself to luxuriate in a moment of hope that this'll all turn out for the best.

But only a moment. Start believing your own hype and

that's when a pherodart blows up in your hand and a raptor-wolf tears your heart out.

After an hour or so the medkits have Warrack back on his feet. He's shaky, and wouldn't be much use in a fight, but he's able to move. It'll still be hours before he's back to one hundred percent, and you take it easy as you leave the village and pick your way from compound to compound across the high grass and brackish water of the marshlands, heading for the edge of the mountains to the northeast. The zone is closing in that direction anyway, so you might as well get there early.

You come up to the banks of a fast-moving river and take a detour until you find a rickety metal bridge, but other than that the trip is uneventful. Eventually you clear a small research base in the rocky foothills south of the Caldera to let Warrack get his strength back while you each take a stretch of rest time.

After all the action back with OVRshAdo and the raptorwolves, the quiet is a relief. Not that you don't love the action, but you were seconds away from eating it out there, and you never want to get that close again.

While Warrack is resting you climb up on the roof of the two-story modular structure, go prone behind the weather sensors, and keep watch for enemies through the Redeemer's sights. Hours pass, and other than the patrolling bots and the occasional bird, the only movement you spot is a trio crossing the marshes way out to the west. They're far enough away you let them go without engaging. No point calling attention to yourself when Warrack still needs a few hours to finish healing.

You lie there through the afternoon, watching the map in your head as the zone closes one hex at a time. The edge is coming, and it looks like the game will finish somewhere

to the north of you. You're nearly ready to round Warrack
up and get moving when your head quavers—the audience,
suddenly excited.

That can only mean one thing: you're about to be
attacked.

You've been covering the marshes for hours and haven't
seen anyone, so they're sneaking up behind you. You immediately roll over and scan the Redeemer across the mountains, searching for movement or any sign of where the
assault will come from, but the auto-aim doesn't spot
anything.

"*We've got trouble,*" you say over teamspeak, and
Warrack shuffles around below you, checking out his
windows.

"*Are you sure?*" he responds after a moment. "*I don't
see anything.*"

"*My aud is going nuts,*" you reply, eye pressed to the
Redeemer's optics. "*What else could it be?*"

"*Mine hasn't changed for hours,*" Warrack says. "*If
anything it's settled down since the raptors.*"

You know your following must be larger than
Warrack's, but even still, if yours saw something that riled
them up, his would have too.

Unless—

Your stomach drops as your thoughts go immediately
to the next most likely reason, but you shut them down
immediately. You can't go there, can't let yourself think
that.

But if it's true, this is all over. There's no reason to be
here anymore.

You shake the thought off and after another few tense
minutes, when the expected attack never comes, you
abandon your spot on the roof and take the ladder down to

the second floor. Warrack is peeking out one of the large round windows.

"No movement, boss," he says out loud. "What do you think set them off?"

You're still not completely sure, but the audience pressure is different than before. Usually they vibrate with a high-pitched excitement, eager for action, but this feels different. Deeper somehow. Sadder.

Like they're mourning.

But it can't be. If it was Rael, you'd know. You wouldn't need an audience in your head to tell you if something had happened to him. You're his mother, you'd just *know*.

"Beats me," you say, masking the tension clenching at your guts. "But whatever it was we shouldn't stay here to find out. You're good to move?"

"Right as rain, boss," Warrack replies, clicking his heels together and snapping a salute.

"Move it then, fella," you say with a smile, trying to keep it light. For yourself as much as for Warrack.

But even as you pack up and move out north the sorrow in your head keeps expanding, broadening, becoming more pronounced until the only thing you can do is ignore it and hope it doesn't mean what you know it does.

ANIKA's already moved what little she owns out of the ludus, and after she left to meet me on Friday she never went back, ghosted the Gladiators completely. News of it hit the feeds a few hours ago. Humanitech spun it as she voluntarily stepped aside after deciding it was too soon after her ordeal in Decimation Island to handle the stress of another competitive kill-or-be-killed experience, but rumors are circling like vultures, claiming she's been kicked off the team, or was caught shyfting, or even that she was involved in the arena skyns heist and been arrested—which is a pretty good guess based on absolutely no available evidence. But when there's a thousand different conspiracy theories one's likely to be right if only by accident.

Dub's not taking it well. He's pissed at me, and for good reason. I had a brief voice chat with him, and told him the ludus is in no danger, that Anika isn't a threat to his adopted family, but that wasn't nearly enough. He wants to know what's going on. Anika didn't just bail on the novi trials for no reason, there's obviously something going on with her, and he doesn't understand why I'm still putting him off, but

I can't tell him the truth. I can't risk him going to Standards or the Service and shutting our plan down before we can launch. There's too much riding on it.

If it was just Anika's memories on the line, that'd be one thing, but this is the only chance we'll get to shut down the Killr shyft. Yeah, we're also going to cancel the biggest game show in history, and plenty of people will be pissed about that, but what are we supposed to do, just let Jefferson Wood keep right on outsourcing his AI's tactical knowledge to anyone who can afford it?

The only other option is a military strike on the island, and that'd take time to organize and no way it'd remain quiet. The AI would have plenty of time to pack up and escape the island and nothing would change.

No, this is the only way this works, and I don't like lying to Dub but that's how it goes. I sent him his money back though. It's the least I can do. I sure didn't earn it.

Anika's been stashing her skyn in a body locker in Midtown under an alt ID, keeping a low profile. She cast into my battle with Shad and the briefing, but after that was done she sent a message asking me to join her in that park she visits every week, and since I have nothing to do until it's time to load into a walking weapon strapped to a rocket, I agreed.

Everyone's trying to find her, so to keep from triggering SECNet's biokin scans she rented a loaner skyn from the body locker, and when I get to the park I find a young dark-skinned man sitting on the bench where she said she'd be. I know it's her but I still hesitate a moment before I sit.

She doesn't say anything, and we sit and watch the kids chase each other around the plastic climbers as they play a game of Grounders. It's a beautiful summer day, not a cloud in the sky, but not too hot. We're surrounded by the city, but it feels peaceful here.

Eventually she says, "I used to come here with Rael. He was only a few months old but I'd bring him and imagine how he'd one day be the one out there playing. I wanted so much for him, he had his whole life ..."

She reaches out and takes my hand and I look over and there's a tear running down her angular cheek. Her slender fingers are cool in my palm and I give them a squeeze, and while it feels odd to be holding a strange guy's hand in the middle of the park, the feeling doesn't last. It's just flesh, I know who's on the other side, and she's hurting. I hold her hand until she finally sniffs and drags her fingers across her eyes. She still hasn't stopped looking out at the kids.

"What if we get there and I find my memories and learn the island had nothing to do with it?" she says. "What if I really did kill myself?"

"Then at least you'll know," I say. "Either way you can move on."

She nods and goes back to watching a little girl digging in the sand nearby.

"Are we doing the right thing?" she asks after a few minutes.

"Having second thoughts?"

She shrugs. "Stealing Humanitech's skyns was wrong, I know that, but no one got hurt, and after this is all done, however it goes, I plan on turning myself in." I don't say anything, just let her talk. "But still—look at all the trouble I caused, just because I couldn't handle the empty space in my head. And now I've got you involved."

And she doesn't know it could be a one-way ticket for me, not that I'd ever tell her.

"You could always back out," I say, but I don't think she will.

"Too late for that now." She sighs. "Besides, someone's got to stop that AI, and if we don't, then who?"

"The cops?" I suggest. "Standards? A nuke?"

She snorts, and for the first time since I sat down she turns to look at me. Her face is totally different, but somehow I can still see her smile all the same. "And let them have all the fun?"

"There's the fragger I know."

Her smile widens and she slides a little closer to me. "We've got time before the drop, want to invite me over?"

I do. I really do. We're flirting, and even after everything we've been through it's light and it's easy and there's part of me that wants nothing more than to take her home with me, but I don't think I'm ready for that yet.

"How about we save that until we get back," I offer instead. "Besides, you're not exactly my type right now."

"Oh come on," she says with a laugh, then shoves me away. "You never know until you try."

Well, I'm pretty sure, but ... "Something to look forward to then."

She laughs again. "Don't think I won't hold you to that."

We fall quiet again, and then she slips her hand back into mine and we spend the next half hour together, just sitting, until finally she says, "I suppose we should go. I need to sync before we launch."

"Yeah," I lie. "Me too."

She stands and lets my hand fall from hers. "See you at the drop, Mr. Gage."

"Can't wait," I reply.

I come to in midair, wrapped in a tank of a skyn with the wind blasting against my faceplate.

One moment I'm lying in my medpod, loading into the arena skyn, and then I'm twelve klicks above the shimmering ocean, high enough to see the curve of the Earth, with my head pointed straight down and hurtling toward the dot of an island below at nearly two hundred kilometers an hour.

And I thought the artificial vertigo from standing on the edge of the drop tower was bad.

My vision wobbles and I close my eyes and get my breathing under control. Our visors show readouts of the team's vitals and I don't want the others to see my heartbeat spiking. I cringe, waiting for the governor in my rithm to slam on and quell my adrenaline-spiked thoughts, but it doesn't come. I thought this might happen. The Cortexes in these skyns are top of the line and probably have a lot more headroom than mine does. It'll take a lot to get my neurohertz high enough for Deacon to be a problem.

I'll be fine. But still it probably wouldn't hurt to concentrate on something else for a while.

The thin air around us is minus fifty C or so, and the oxygen is negligible, but that's not a problem. These skyns are built to handle worse than being shot out of a rocket into thin air. I could probably hold my breath underwater for ten minutes if I needed to.

I glance around and see the three other meteors plummeting toward the ground with me, their long bodies silhouetted against the twilight. We're all wearing military-grade adaptive armor and have assault rifles fastened to our wing-packs. Not that we need them—where we're going they have guns just lying around for anyone to pick up—but it'll save us the hassle.

We're connected through a short-range telepathy built into the skyns. As long as we're near each other, we should be able to stay in contact.

"Everybody make it off the bus?" I think into the comms channel, trying to get my mind off the ground racing toward us.

"Yippee ki yay," Anika responds.

"Cut the chatter, you two," OVRshAdo warns.

"Give it a rest," I say back. He may be in charge, but I don't have to answer to him. *"We've got two and a half minutes before the fun starts."*

I'm hoping for a nice distracting argument but instead he says, *"Fair enough. Chatter away, mate."*

I try to think of something else to say, but now that he's given me permission he's taken all the fun out of breaking the rules, and instead I keep quiet and take the time to get used to my new loaner body.

My skyn back home isn't what I'd consider small by any

stretch, but this one is on a whole other level. I've never experienced anything like it. I feel like one of the power-loaders we used to run back in the Forces, like I could lift a crate of ordnance and run forever, but somehow still nimble, like an acrobat or a dancer. And all I'm doing is hanging upside down in the air. I can't wait to hit the ground and see what this thing can do.

The island gets larger as I get accustomed to my body, but it still doesn't feel like we're moving all that fast. It's only about three thousand square kilometers, which isn't much bigger than Toronto and its suburbs, but it's all by itself in a broad blue expanse and seems huge by compari-son. It's only when we're close enough to see the drop towers and other structures around the tiny island that I start to get a sense of how quick we're falling.

"*Entering their airspace now,*" OVRshAdo warns. "*If they're planning on shooting us down we'll be dead any second.*"

I angle my body so I'm moving a bit more unpredictably than simply falling in a straight line but I'm not sure what good it'll do. If an AI wants to shoot me out of the sky, I don't think wiggling around will cause too much added diffi-culty. We can only hope we're small enough it doesn't notice we're coming until it's too late.

So far so good though, because nothing happens.

Another few seconds and the island seems to double in size. The towers had all been dark up until now but the one on the southeast side of the island—the one straddling the edge of the lava fields and the jungle—lights up, and a moment later a cloud of black figures erupts from its sides. There's our targets. Right on time.

Shitty luck though. Just as I'd feared, this game dropped

from the tower farthest from our next objective. It's gonna be a long walk to the comms.

"*We'll find a vehicle,*" Anika reassures me, reading my mind. "*No worries.*"

"*Who's worried?*" I say back, but we both know it's me. The operation just started and already we're behind.

"*Get that code, bitches,*" Shad says as he pulls away from us, diving toward the mass of players headed for the mountains in the middle of the island. It's a good plan, it'll give us less distance to travel once we hit the ground. The others do the same and I follow, pulling up to ease off on my speed so I can get close to one of the falling skyns.

And that's when the tower decides it's time to kill us.

Glowing tracers fill the air, firing from two anti-aircraft weapons that slid out from panels high up on the tower.

"*Incoming,*" I yell, but they're already scattering, swinging wildly to avoid the sizzling rounds. My helmet goes red with warnings, but all I can do is ignore them and keep moving, swing my wingpack erratically, and hope I can avoid being blown out of the sky.

I clench my teeth and heave my body from side to side, twisting randomly to confuse the targeting system. High-velocity fireflies split the sky around us but we're doing okay, no one's been hit, until Zara cries out in a ragged shriek of pain.

I glance down and see her falling, out of control, with a gaping hole punched through her—a comet of blood and guts blazing toward the ground.

"*We have to help her,*" Anika says as she angles to follow Zara down.

"*Stick to the plan,*" OVRshAdo snaps. He's ahead of us, zeroing in on a cluster of players still gliding in their wingpacks. "*We don't get that code we'll all be dead.*"

"*Play for yourselves,*" Zara says. "*Beat this thing for me.*"
I can't believe she's still conscious, let alone lucid enough to
form sentences. Man, these skyns can take a beating.

"*We'll come find you,*" Anika replies, and I know she's
concerned, trying to help, but Zara's carrying the gear to
hack the comms, so one way or another we will need to find
her. Whether her skyn's still breathing when we get there is
another matter.

The tracers are still sizzling all around us, but we're
nearly below the tower's effective firing range, only another
second or two, and if it keeps shooting it'll risk hitting one of
the game skyns, but just before the guns go silent, just as I
figure we've escaped, something on my back explodes and
I'm thrown into a spin. The ground whirls below me as I
brace myself, expecting the pain to hit—but it doesn't come
—and after another moment, when I can still move and my
vitals scrolling across my visor still read green, I let out a
loud sigh of relief. But I'm not out of it yet.

It's only when I try to pull myself out of the spin and
my wingpack shears off that I realize I have a bigger problem. I slap the release on my chest and the ruined wings
pull away, and when I deploy the reserve chute it billows
out with a slight tug but barely slows me at all. I glance
behind me and there's only strips of ruined fabric fluttering
in the wind.

"*Uh … I may have an issue,*" I say to the team.

"*Deal with it,*" OVRshAdo cuts back. He sounds tense.
I glance down and it looks like he might have overshot his
target. His parachute is open and he's maneuvering it to get
close to one of the players, but they're trying just as hard to
get away from him.

"*What happened?*" Anika asks. She's off to the west,
zeroing in on another player, but there's nothing she could

do to help me even if I told her. OVRshAdo's right. I need to handle it myself.

"*Never mind,*" I say. "*Tell you later.*"

I'm still probably half a klick above the ground, but at the rate I'm falling I only have a few seconds before that changes with a splat. There are still players below me, not too far away, floating with their chutes open. Maybe I can hitch a ride the rest of the way down.

I cut the remnants of the reserve chute and then I'm back in free fall, except this time without any way of stopping—other than the ground. I lay my arms flat against my sides and point my toes and arrow toward the closest player, a male skyn from the looks of it, hanging under a drab green parachute.

"*Shit,*" Anika suddenly yells. "*Missed.*"

"*Me too,*" Shad says, the frustration clear in his voice. They're below me, their black rectangular parachutes popped, and about to land.

"*Fin?*" Anika says, but I don't answer. The wind is strong and I'm moving so fast it's tough to keep a bead on my target, and I need to concentrate, but another second later I've caught up and the moment before I impale him I flare, spread my arms and legs and slow myself down just enough to crash into him from behind, catch him around the back and hang on tight.

That was close. I wonder if he can feel my heart beating through my armor.

He yells, startled, and tries to shake me off as we rock back and forth under the straining ropes of the parachute, but no way he can out-muscle me. I'm not going anywhere.

"Howdy," I say in his ear. My hands are shaking but my voice projecting through the helmet is deep and untroubled. "Mind if I catch a lift?"

"Da fuq?" he cries, whipping his head around to try to get a look at who's just smashed into him. "Who you be now?"

"Lost my chute," I reply as I reach out and take the handle with my free hand to steer us closer to where Shad and Anika landed. "Mind if I drive?"

"Get offa me," he says, trying once again to wriggle his way free, but I've got my arm around his neck and my legs around his. He's not going anywhere.

What must he be thinking? This guy finally makes it to Decimation Island Live and launches from the tower, keen to murder, and he's only playing for a few seconds before there's a beefy stranger in full armor all over him. He hasn't hit the ground yet and already his game is over. And all this will be going straight out to the feeds too. I bet this game's gonna attract a huge audience.

"*Fin!*" Anika yells over the comms, then she's shooting. Her vitals have spiked, OVRshAdo's too. The bots will be all over them. "*Where the hell did you go?*"

She won't see my chute, but since she can tell I'm not dead it must look like I disappeared.

"*Be right with you,*" I say, then with my free hand I initiate the skimming sequence from the screen on my arm.

"*Any time, Gage,*" Shad says, and he's projecting enough of an attitude I almost want to keep him waiting, but it won't help us if he's dead. A moment later the scan registers success, and once I've secured the code I send it out to the team. The shooting stops a second later.

My co-pilot and I are only a dozen meters above the ground, passing over OVRshAdo and Anika and a bunch of ruined bots, when I tap him on the head in thanks and let go.

I drop and land in a hard roll, come up facing them, and

brush the lava rock off my armor. My visor is down so they can't see me, but I've got a huge smile on my face. I've never felt like such a badass.

"And you wanted to bring the bot," I say.

THE NEXT FEW games go by in a blur. You and Warrack
finish game five and afterwards in Camp Paradiso you team
up with a two-game survivor called LarryCheese and a
three-gamer called finitoburrito and you dominate the next
two hundred hours as a four-man squad. The anguish in
your head eased off between games, and it's mostly gone
now, replaced by a swell of attention as you've gained
momentum toward the endgame. It's to the point where you
can dismiss the surge of sorrow, pretend like it didn't
happen, or that it meant something else, but just under the
surface of your game face there's a terrible well of grief just
waiting to erupt—you can feel it, simmering like an
emotional abscess.

Instead you channel your fear, play aggressive, take
fights when you need to and back off when you don't. With
OVRshAdo gone you're now the biggest threat—and the
one carrying the highest bounty—so you need to be
cautious, but not too cautious. It's a fine line.

You're at the point though where even your teammates
could be a danger. You've lasted over seven hundred hours,

and that puts you in the top ten percent of anyone who's ever played. Only a game away from OVRshAdo's record, and any second one of the three players around you could decide now's the time to collect the bounty on your head and put a sneaky bullet in your back.

Realistically, this is the last game you can run as a group, might be pushing it as it is, but once you get into eight hundred hours the temptation to turn on you will be too great. Even Warrack can't be trusted. You'll have to play the last two games as a lone wolf again, but you're prepared for that, you've got the gear. There's a chance you could go all the way.

Seven hundred hours of hyping yourself up to believe you can win has kept you going, but now it's real. You're close—too close. Losing now would be devastating, but winning could be even worse.

At least out here you have fighting for your life to keep your thoughts occupied. What happens when you get back home?

You've got three hundred hours to worry about that. All you can do is focus on what's directly ahead of you.

This game launched from the Northwest Tower, and once your team hit the ground you secured vehicles and made straight for the sponsored drop beacon near the cliffs on the northwest of the island. It's an easy way to loot up, especially with the audience you're commanding. The sponsors are falling all over themselves to kit you up. You've still got the Redeemer and the Stingers and you picked up a recon drone last game, but with this one drop you'll get the upgrades you need to run the Wreck of the Seastar hotspot off the coast, and once you've cleared it you can hang out on the boat for a while. You'll be safe there, the only threats the

ones you brought with you, and as long as you never turn
your back on them, you should be fine.

For now.

"Target ahead," Warrack says out loud. He's driving,
following a single lane road toward a soaring concrete
pylon, like a massive upside down "Y" sitting near the cliff's
edge. Once you get there and activate the beacon a countdown will start, and thirty minutes later a launch pod filled
with weapons and supplies and other goodies will shoot out.
You don't think anyone's likely to contest the drop, but you
never know, and the squad fans out and takes cover around
the concrete pylon to wait out the timer.

The terrain up here is mostly rocks and scrub grass and
little purple flowers—like what the English Moors look like
in your imagination, not that you've ever seen them. You
scan the horizon with the Redeemer, and when you don't
see anyone approaching you figure you're safe. Warrack's
beside you, posted up nearby with his eye pressed to his
DMR's scope, keeping a watch out for approaching
enemies.

After a few minutes, he looks up from his weapon. "I
won't turn on you," he says, his voice low. "I don't know
about the others, but I'm with you to the end."

You wish you could believe him, but you can't risk it.

"Thanks, Warrack," you say. "But we can worry about
that later."

He lowers his weapon and his face is drawn. "Permission to speak freely?" he asks.

"Christ, Warrack," you say, and can't help but smile at
his earnest expression. "I'm not your commanding officer,
you can say anything you want."

He nods and clears his throat. "I've only made it this far

because you carried me here. Without you I'd be dead already—"

"You don't know that—" you start, but he just keeps talking.

"I know it's supposed to be every man for himself out here, but I want you to win, for your son."

Your throat catches. "Warrack, you don't—"

"I promise you," he says, like he's taking an oath. "I won't turn on you. Not ever."

Your eyes well up and for a goddamned second you think you're about to cry. You've been out here for almost a month now, seven hundred hours of constant stress, with death around every corner and no one to trust but yourself. And the thing is, you believe him. Right now, he's fully committed to helping you win, but that's only because he hasn't had to make any other choice. When he's trapped in the red with the bots snarling in his face and only one spot in the survivor circle left, who knows how he'll react.

'Cause the thing is, if it came down to it, you know you wouldn't hesitate to put *him* down.

"I appreciate it," you say. "You're a hell of a partner. I couldn't do this without you."

He presses his lips together and quickly turns and wipes at his eyes. He's a good kid, and who knows, maybe he'll even keep his word, but you wouldn't bet Rael's life on it.

The care package lands a few minutes later and as you and the team are looting up the audience pressure surges through your skull. You whip around, searching for the threat, but once again nothing's there. Then your kill-feed dings and your stomach drops.

OVRshAdo downs PenguinNipples. 97 players remain.

It takes more than an hour to track down Zara's corpse, and by the time we find it, crumpled and bloody on the lava rock near the edge of the mountains, another squad has already beaten us to it.

There are four of them, but the game's still young and they're not well geared. One of them has an AR and the other's claimed Zara's gun for herself, but the rest only have pistols. They've taken Zara's helmet and the explosives from her pack and searched through her belt pouches, so they must have found the bash badger—if it survived the fall.

We don't try to hide as we come across the waves of black rock, and the instant they see us they back off and raise their weapons.

We don't exactly look like the other game skyns, and the three hulking figures striding toward them in black armor must throw them off, because they don't immediately open fire. Not that they could hurt us much if they tried. They probably figure we're part of some new quest line they've stumbled onto.

"Yo, back off, we found her first," one of them says. He's got Zara's AR and must think he's the leader of their group.

"Drop what you took from her and we'll let you walk," Shad replies. His usual half-joking tone is gone. He's frustrated—we're already behind, our backdoor protection from the bots can't last much longer, and losing Zara complicated everything. He's got no patience for this.

"It's four against three," the guy says. "How about we keep everything and take your shit too."

I chuckle behind my visor. Wrong choice.

Shad draws his pistol and puts a bullet between the eyes of each of the other three guys in his squad. Just like that and the fight's over.

"Now it's three against one," Shad says.

The guy staggers and his eyes go wide, then he tosses Zara's weapon like it's burning him and swings his backpack off. "It's all in there, man, I swear!"

"We'll see," Shad says as he fires once more and blows the guy's Cortex out. He takes a breath and exhales deeply. Then he claps me on the shoulder. "Nothing like a little murder to lift your spirits, huh?"

Anika moves over to claim the guy's backpack while I check out Zara. Other than the dried blood around her lips and ears—and the massive ragged hole through her chest—she doesn't look too bad. Though I imagine that's only because her armor kept her from exploding on impact. As strong as her skyn was, even it couldn't hold up against hitting the ground at two hundred kph. No doubt her Cortex is shattered, but at least she won't have lost much time. She'll wake up from the brain bank and with only a few missing minutes to mourn.

"Found it!" Anika says, holding up the small slate-grey wafer that'll let Shad take over the island's communications.

"The rest of it's here too. Explosives and everything. Looks like we're back in business."

It's possible we're too late and Jefferson Wood has already ejected the AI from the island to safety somewhere, but somehow I don't think so. It has a whole army to defend itself with, what harm could three people do to it?

"Hopefully the impact didn't mess it up." Otherwise we're trapped here.

"It'll be fine," Shad says. "Those things are designed to take a beating."

Anika runs the diagnostic and it flashes a green light. Looks like we're still in the running.

"What's the plan now, boss?" I ask. We were supposed to hit the comms array next but we've wasted so much time now there's no way we make it there before our protection runs out. And then fight across the island to the Control Center.

Anika pulls up the map of the island on her arm. "We're about forty kilometers from the comms and roughly the same to the core. I vote we take our chances and head straight for the AI. It's known about us long enough, if it was gonna bug out it will have by now anyway."

"Seconded," I add. Shad's a blank slate behind his darkened visor. "Our camo won't last much longer. Hitting the AI has to be our top priority."

Shad turns and gazes off in the direction of the comms, and for a moment it appears he wants to argue, but then he says, "Agreed. We get to the AI and hope it's still contained."

Once Shad's mind is made up he doesn't waste any more time. We leave Zara's corpse behind and take off at a run, and our powerful skyns eat klicks for breakfast as we race toward the mountains.

Navigating our way through the rocky peaks slows us down some, but the mountain range is relatively narrow and after only an hour we're on the other side. Instead of trying to leapfrog through the marshes, we cut north and stick to the high ground. It's a longer route but easier running, and we can open up and run flat out.

These skyns are incredible. I'm carrying my weapon and a pack with explosives and a bunch of extra ammo and we've been moving for hours and I'm not remotely tired. I'm not even breathing hard. No wonder these things are outlawed.

It only takes us a quarter hour to get to the highlands, and then just before we reach Trinity Landing we turn west and make a straight shot through the light woods toward the coast.

Ten minutes later we're on the outskirts of the fields around Aurora City, a hotspot about fifteen klicks from the edge of the island. It's designed like a space-aged but somehow also medieval town, with concentric rings of garden and game land surrounding the high hexagonal wall protecting the town. The bot activity will be heavy there and we plan on giving it a wide berth, but even with the slight detour around it, at the speed we're moving we'll be at the cliffs and ready to make for the Control Center in a little more than twenty minutes.

"*Told you we'd make it,*" Shad says as he leaps over a downed tree. "*And you all doubted me.*"

"*Don't get ahead of yourself,*" Anika replies, but even she sounds optimistic. "*We're not there yet.*"

We're all feeling it—our luck is improving. So far the bots have let us be, longer than we thought the protection would hold out, we're deep inside the current game's red zone, so we don't have to worry about meeting any hostile players, and even the weather is cooperating.

Which is why I'm hardly surprised when everything goes to shit.

Up until now the bots have completely ignored us. We haven't seen any of the lethal prowlers since we left the mountains, and the two-legged utilibots we passed were busy restoring damaged buildings and restocking loot for the next game. But like luck always does, it changes instantly, and one minute we're running through the light bush while the bots reset the island, and the next they're coming for us.

The prowlers appear first, from out of nowhere, silently sprinting at us on all fours, and if it weren't for Anika checking our rear at just the right time they'd have taken her down before we knew what was happening.

She yells a silent warning just as the three prowlers launch their attack, and while it only takes Shad and me a second to swing our weapons out and blast the two flanking bots, the lead prowler is already airborne, its black fangs and claws aiming to rip Anika's throat out. She doesn't bother going for her weapon, just catches the bot around the neck as it hits her, and rolls over backwards, hugging it close to avoid the claws while she wrenches its snapping jaws to the side and rips its head off.

She continues her roll, kicks the flailing bot off, and lands in a crouch with her weapon up and ready. The three prowlers are down but that was just the opening wave. Red-eyed bots are all through the woods now, utilibots and drones and prowlers and a bunch more. I don't see any warbots yet but I imagine it's only a matter of time.

"*Move!*" she yells in our heads, and we don't need to be told twice. She fires three times and downs the three closest bots and then she's up and sprinting and we fall in behind. We swing wide left to avoid Aurora City, but the bots are already ahead of us, and we're forced to divert toward the fields.

"*They're herding us toward the city,*" I say as I put two bullets into a stalking prowler.

"*No shit,*" Shad snaps back. "*So don't let them.*"

We try, but no matter how many bots we take out they just keep coming, pushing us toward the open gates, and eventually we're backed across the bridge and into the city and the moment we're on the other side the gate closes behind us, locking us in.

The town is a maze of narrow walkways and over-hanging buildings, with a wide path cutting directly through the center to the gates on each side, which are also closed tight. The walls are too high and too smooth to scale, and other than the gates there doesn't look to be any way out.

"The island's playing us," Shad says out loud. "Got us trapped in like rats."

"We might be fucked here," I say, glancing around, looking for some way, *any* way out, but I don't see anything. For a moment the city is quiet, as if holding its breath, and then the bots come, slinking out from around the buildings with their eyes smoldering red.

"*Definitely* fucked," Anika mutters.

My mouth goes dry and my guts clench. Looks like this is where death finally catches up with me. Of all the ways I thought I would die, I didn't expect it to be in a live action video game—though I didn't expect most of the shit that happened over the past few years either, so I shouldn't be too surprised.

My first instinct is to get angry, to lash out at the injustice of it all, but it passes immediately. We're doing a stupid thing, and no one forced me to come. Besides, I've had a good run, longer than I deserve. This is as good a place for it to end as any.

I check my remaining ammo, ready to go out fighting, and find only a single regret comes to mind, completely unexpected: this is the last moment I'll have with Anika.

It's a shock, to be honest, that my last thoughts aren't about Connie, and then I'm flooded with guilt and hope the bots will make it quick and put me out of my misery.

I glance at Anika and she's already looking at me through her clear visor. "Been a fun ride," I say.

She gives me a frustrated smile. "Guess I'll see you back home."

Except she won't, this is as far as I go, and there must be something in my expression because her brows knit together in concern. She opens her mouth to ask, but we don't have a chance to get into it.

"Save the tearful goodbyes 'til we're dead, yeah?" Shad says as he raises his weapon. "We're not done yet."

No, but we will be. Still, we'll make a mess on our way out.

I get my weapon up, then there's no room for anything in my head but gunfire.

There's a semicircular courtyard around the gate and we stick close together, covering the angles, Shad and I on either side of Anika. We make each shot count, dropping the bots before they can get close and calling out our reloads, but the island has more bots than we have bullets.

"*Out!*" Shad yells in our heads as he drops his assault rifle and draws his pistol. I've only got nine shots left and Anika must be nearly dry herself.

"*Now a good time for a teary goodbye?*" I ask as I put

down two more prowlers. We've made a hell of a pile of broken bots, but they just keep coming.

"*Keep shooting,*" Shad says as he reloads his pistol. We only brought two magazines for the sidearms, and this is his last. After these twelve shots he'll be fighting with his fists, and as strong as these skyns are, even we can't beat an infinite supply of bots.

Then Anika stops shooting, lets her rifle drop to her side, and swings her pack off her back. "*Cover me,*" she says.

"*What are you doing?*" Shad shouts over the teamspeak.

I use five more rounds, swinging back and forth to take out Anika's share of the bots as well. Two shots left.

"*Getting us out of here,*" she answers, and pulls her pack of explosives from her bag.

"*We need the explosives to take out the AI core,*" Shad says, but Anika throws him a withering glare and he drops it. Besides, on the off chance we do make it out of here we still have three charges left.

She sets the timer to five seconds, readies the detonator, and then sticks it to the bottom of the sealed gate behind us.

"*Fire in the hole,*" she says as she starts the countdown and rushes to my side. I tick off the numbers from five in my head as we retreat, but with the bots still pushing forward we can't go far. Shad moves away on the other side of the gate, fires twice, and then his weapon clicks dry.

As the counter hits one I hold my breath and put my hand over Anika's head as we duck low, huddling together.

The explosion is deafening, sets my ears ringing, and sprays us with chunks of concrete, but our armor protects us. The readout on my visor shows our collective heart rates are spiking but no one's hurt. I turn and squint through the cloud of dust, expecting to see a hole in the gate, but the doors are still standing. Charred and dented but sealed up tight.

My stomach falls. Shouldn't have got my hopes up.

"*Worth a try,*" I say, and spin to fire my last two shots, but Anika slaps me on the shoulder and points back into the smoke.

"*We're not done yet,*" she says and moves away from me, deeper into the dust.

Shad makes a whooping sound as I empty my weapon at the closest two bots. I spin but don't see anything different, the gate is still closed tight—and then I notice: Shad's gone.

"*What—*" I start, and my gaze follows Anika's finger as she gestures down at the jagged hole blasted through the concrete. The explosives didn't touch the gate, but it blew an exit in the ground.

Maybe we're not out of this yet.

"*Into the hole, soldier,*" she says, and flashes a wink at me as she raises her weapon to pick off the bots that are still closing. "*I'll cover you.*"

A surge of emotion fills me as I race toward her and peer down into the black. Who knows what's down there, but right now anywhere's better than here.

I take a second to tap my helmet against hers and give her arm a squeeze before I step forward and plunge into the darkness.

WHEN YOU SAW OVRshAdo had returned, you knew he'd
be coming for you. You chased each other all game, trying to
get the upper hand on one another, and now, finally you
have him.

You'll make him regret coming back.

You've got him pinned on a wide cliff in the craggy
highlands. To one side is a steep drop to the moonlit
marshes, and to the other a sheer rock face that's gotta be
three stories high. The only thing separating you is a broad
split in the rock, a fissure carved over time by the nearby
river roaring over the cliff's edge

OVRshAdo's holed up on one side of the chasm, you're
on the other, and between you is the hull of the wrecked
blimp from the Fargo's Last Cargo hotspot. The crashed
airship straddles the chasm like a covered bridge, and it's the
only way across.

This round's almost over. Only two hexes left open and the
one you're in is about to close. Any moment you and your squad
will be in the red, leaking safe-time, but you don't care. There's
nowhere for OVRshAdo to run now. Backtracking through the

red would take too much time. His only path is through you. And there's no way you're letting him make it to the next game.

He got close once before, around hour fifty. Got within shouting distance.

He tried to talk to you, offered a truce, like he wanted to be friends—*as if*. You didn't give him an opening to play his mind games, and you killed one of his squad for it. He managed to get away and you've been after him ever since.

"We should back off," Warrack says, the low-light perq glowing green in his eyes. "He's not going anywhere."

Warrack's got all his gear together and looks anxious to leave. Same with LarryCheese and finitoburrito behind him. They all want to move, and you don't blame them, it's by far the smartest play. Stick around here and you'll be pushing into the green after the other players have already set themselves up, like running into a meat grinder.

But you don't care.

"No," you say. End of discussion.

Except Warrack doesn't give up. "The zone's closing and there's easier targets. No point wasting safe-time on him."

"No," you say again, your voice firm. "We can't risk the chance he could make it through. Go if you want, I'll finish him on my own."

Warrack makes a frustrated noise in his throat but you ignore it. The simmering anger that'd been eating at you for days finally boiled over when you saw OVRshAdo's name reappear on the kill-feed, and it hasn't stopped roiling since. You're not giving him the chance to weasel his way out of this game. He would have had to spend every leaderboard point he'd ever earned, and probably chipped in an extra buy-in fee to get back into the game this quick. He's gone to a lot of expense to try to ruin your streak, and you're gonna make him pay for it.

A rattle of shots sounds in the dark, somewhere out in the distance, then another.

CtrlAltDuhL33T downs Wombocombo. 15 players remain.

Still Warrack doesn't quit. "We're already late. We need to move. You're not playing with your head."

"Damn right," you say as you swing your AR around and set it to burst fire. With your team all running low-light vision, the waning moonlight isn't a problem. The darkness might help them slip into the safe-zone unseen. "You should get moving. I'll catch up with you when I'm done here. And if I don't—thanks for everything."

You slide out from behind one of the cargo pallets and peer into the long tunnel of the downed aircraft. It's even darker inside and you can't make out anything at all. Who knows what's hiding in there, but it doesn't matter, you're going anyway.

"Wait," Warrack hisses. "I'm coming with you."

"Don't be stupid," you say. "No point all of us dying."

"You die, I die," he says.

The pained look on his face hurts your heart, and your better instincts nearly take over and convince you to back off, but then the anger resurges.

Why should you be the one to back off? OVRshAdo sure as hell wouldn't.

"What about you two?" you ask Larry and finito.

They glance at each other, then shrug. "We're only here because of you anyway, why quit now?"

"You're all idiots, you know that?" you say. "But thanks. Let's get this done."

They both grin and check their weapons, magrifles with grenade launcher attachments, and fall in behind you.

"Spread out and be ready for anything," you tell them as you take the lead and step into the aircraft. The blimp's cargo hold creaks as you pace through it, and even with the low-light perqs you can't see more than a few feet ahead of you. Halfway across the zone passes over you and your safe-time starts to tick down. You were nearly at the maximum though, so you're cool for now, but even though you don't see any bots in here, once your time runs down it won't take long for them to find you.

After the pitch black of the cargo hold the night sky on the other side is glowing like an oncoming train. Still there's no sign of OVRshAdo and his team. Maybe they already tried backtracking. Or did something reckless like climbing up the rocky cliff.

"*Hold here*," you tell the team and stop at the edge of the ruined blimp to scan ahead. The cliff on this side is wider, strewn with wreckage and spilled cargo containers, and it stretches on for a few hundred feet until it narrows and disappears behind a curve in the rock face. Most of the blimp wreckage is on the cliff above you, but the cargo ended up down here—or at least that's how the story in the hotspot goes. Eventually the cliff rises like a ramp to meet the high ground above, but that's half a mile away along a treacherous path. If OVRshAdo went that way, it'll take him hours to swing back around and reach the green. No way he makes it before his safe-time runs out.

Could that be it? Did he push his luck too far this time?

Still, he could be hiding behind any one of the cargo containers. No point coming this far and not making absolutely sure.

Your pulse quickens as you poke your head out of the

cargo hold and check around the south side of the aircraft, expecting to find a shotgun blast to the face waiting for you, but it's all clear. Warrack does the same on the right side and finds nothing either.

You hold your breath for a second, straining to hear anything that might give OVRshAdo away, but with the waterfall so close you can barely hear anything else. Six big containers are spread out between the cargo hold and the point where the cliff narrows and begins to slope up. If he's not hiding behind one of those you can safely turn around and fight your way into the green knowing he'll be dead soon.

"Warrack, you're with me. We'll go straight up the middle. Larry and finito, give us a second and then flank to the left and right and cover the angles. Shoot anything that moves."

"Roger," Warrack says.

"Giddy up," finito adds.

You and Warrack step out into the moonlight, weapons up, and pick your way across the rocky ground to the first container. You put your back against the side, shuffle to the corner, and swing around with your finger on the trigger, ready to fire, but there's nothing to shoot at.

Warrack moves ahead of you, inching toward the next container, while LarryCheese and finitoburrito step out of the shelter of the cargo hold, ready to split off and cover each side of the cliff.

And that's when OVRshAdo strikes.

A heavy machine gun opens up from the curved roof of the tunnel, chunking into Larry and finito, and they're dead before they hit the ground.

ChangZhang downs survivor finitoburrito. 14 players remain.

ChangZhang downs survivor LarryCheese. 13 players remain.

Adrenaline spikes and you wheel around to return fire, your heart in your throat, focusing on the afterimage burn of the muzzle flash above you.

ChangZhang rolls to avoid your shots but overcompensates and scrabbles against the plastic to keep from sliding off the sloping roof, but it's already too late, and he shouts as he slips over the edge.

Gravity downs ChangZheng. 12 players remain.

"Anika!" Warrack yells, but it's all happening too fast. You spin as a player steps out from behind the container Warrack had been approaching, a raised shotgun in her hands. Her first shot takes Warrack directly in the faceplate, cracking it, and the second pops his Cortex with a blue-white flare that momentarily overloads the low-light perqs and leaves you blind. You shoot anyway, aiming for the memory of her position, but your bullets smack wide against metal, and you suddenly realize your game is about to end.

Pizdaty downs survivor Warrack. 11 players remain.

Your ears are ringing as the next shotgun blast hits you in the chest. Your armor absorbs the blow but knocks you against a container and even though you fight, trying to recover and get your weapon up in defense, another shot catches you in the side, spinning you around. Another pounds into your chest, cracking your armor and ruining your weapon, and then the last one knocks your feet out from under you and you slump down to your knees.

"Enough," someone calls, and you squint up through your visor and see OVRshAdo striding toward you. He'd been out of sight this whole time, letting his team do all the work for him. "She's mine."

He's got a magcannon, held low on his hip. Casual, like he doesn't need it. Which he doesn't. Pizdaty's still got four shells left in her weapon, more than enough to finish you off.

Warrack's headless body lies nearby, blood still pumping from his neck. You know he's not dead, that he's back in his headspace with no memory of you or the game or what just happened to him, but still the sight of him lying there burns you with grief and anger. Not only is your friend gone, but you're the reason he's dead—and even worse, he won't remember you. All this time you had together just went away in a blaze of light.

OVRshAdo takes two steps closer then stops, doesn't say anything, just looks down at you. The bots have found you now and they're all around, a couple prowlers plus a few floaters too. The last zone will be closed any minute and then it's only a matter of time before your safe-time drains and they're free to attack.

"Hey Ani," he finally says. "Nice to see you again."

"Fuck you," you spit, and your chest sears with pain. Probably broken ribs or bruised organs. Good thing this game is almost over. You'll be out of this body soon enough; the problem is you know what waits on the other side, have known for days now, and you're not ready to face it.

"Come on, man," he says, like he's genuinely hurt.

"What are you waiting for?" you wheeze, barely able to

breathe through the pain and the anxiety of returning home. "You went through all this trouble to finish me, so go ahead."

OVRshAdo cocks his head. "Is that what you think? I came to finish you?"

You blink, not sure what he's getting at, and when you glance up at Pizdaty her expression reads the same.

"Vhat's dis—" Pizdaty starts, but then her face grows clouded. She whirls around, whipping her weapon toward OVRshAdo, but she's not fast enough. The magcannon whines as the capacitors discharge and send a slug of supersonic metal straight through Pizdaty's chest.

Her weapon slides from her hands and she collapses, dead.

OVRshAdo betrays Pizdaty. 10 players remain.

Round complete.

You head is spinning as OVRshAdo kneels beside you. "I didn't come to finish you," he whispers. "I'm here to help you win."

I FALL for two seconds and hit the floor with an echoing thud.

Shad's nearby and he grins at me, his face barely visible in the light leaking from above. He seems to be enjoying this.

"*Fucking glorious,*" he thinks at us, but I just shake my head and pull my sidearm to cover the hole in the ceiling as Anika drops through.

"*I'll watch for bots,*" she says, drawing her pistol and activating her helmet's external lights. "*You guys find us a way out of here.*"

"On it," I say, and switch my lights on to see where we've landed. The room is big, probably fifty meters by fifty, and filled with all sorts of goodies.

One side of the room is lined with charging stations and dormant bots, while the other is arrayed with racks of guns, ammo, and armor. This must be where the bots come to resupply the weapons in the game.

A big curved tunnel runs east and west out from either side of the room, and two smaller branches cut off to the north and south. There's probably a web of tunnels under the whole island, leading from one hotspot to another. Wouldn't surprise me if we can get all the way to the Control Center from here.

"*We got guns!*" Shad cries and then gets busy rearming himself.

Behind me Anika fires and a prowler crashes to the floor.

"*Let's move it, guys,*" she says. "*Bots are coming to kill us.*"

I drop my empty assault rifle and replace it with a heavy battle rifle and fill my pack with ammo. Then I gather up another AR, load it, and bring it to Anika with a bunch of magazines.

"Got you something," I say out loud as I hand it to her. She holsters her pistol and takes the weapon from me.

"Aww," she purrs. "You shouldn't have." Another bot silhouettes its head across the hole in the ceiling and Anika lifts her new weapon and clears it with a loud burst of fire.

"*Over here,*" Shad calls from across the room. "*Found us some wheels.*"

I leave Anika to watch the hole and jog over to Shad. He's sitting in the driver's seat of a long low transport he found tucked away in a corner of the room. It's nothing special, like a cross between a pickup truck and a golf cart, but Shad's got it running and that's all we need.

Unlike everything else on the island, it's not automated, got a steering wheel and everything. It was probably left here for emergencies, in case something drastic happened and a human was required to intervene. A thick layer of dust shows just how often that's been necessary.

Luckily for us it's sat here plugged in so the battery's all charged and ready to go.

I jump in the rear while Shad backs it out and points us facing west down the wide tunnel.

"You boys ready or what?" Anika asks. Her gun's been rattling as the bots try to breach the hole, but so far she's kept them at bay. Still, we can't stick around.

"We're waiting on you," Shad replies.

Anika stops shooting, and when her gun falls silent I notice a rising hum in the room. Then my pulse goes into overdrive as rows of red circles light up in the darkness as the dormant bots power on.

"Grab some frags on your way past," I add. *"We're gonna need them."*

A moment later Anika races up and dumps a whole crate of grenades in the back of the cart and hops in beside me.

"Move out!" she yells, then turns and rips the top off the crate and hands me a few grenades just as the first bots launch from their charging stations.

Shad floors it and we shoot off toward the tunnel while Anika and I take turns priming and tossing grenades. I lob two into the ammo crates as we zip past, and a few seconds later they detonate, setting off more explosions as the boxes of grenades go up next.

We drop frags until we're into the tunnel and then I swap to my weapon, but they don't seem to be following. The angry red eyes recede, and it seems like they've given up the chase.

We zip down the tunnel for a few breathless minutes, waiting for another attack, but nothing happens, and somehow that's worse.

The tunnel's surface lights up around us as we drive, so while we can see each other just fine, directly ahead and behind is completely dark. Anything could be waiting for us, but right now we're alive and I'm grateful as hell.

Once it looks like we're in the clear I lower the battle rifle and turn to Anika and my skin flushes. More than anything else I want to slide her visor up and kiss her, but I keep my cool.

"Thought we were done back there," I say, suddenly breathless and nearly giddy with relief. Turns out I'm not as okay with dying as I thought I was.

"I never doubted it for a moment," Anika says as she leans into me and bumps me with her shoulder. "Still, we're not out of it yet."

"We're doing pretty fucking fantastic if you ask me," Shad offers from the front of the cart.

"Tell that to Zara," I say.

"Ahh, she's fine," Shad offers over his shoulder. "Probably already restored to her skyn and pissed she's missing the fun."

"Fun," I mutter to myself. "Right."

Anika cocks a look at me. "What's going on with you?"

"What?" I say, tamping down on my excitement at not being dead. "You mean apart from us nearly dying back there?"

"Tell me," she demands, her voice firm.

"What are you talking about?"

Her eyes narrow. "Out with it. You're acting weird—" Then she straightens. "You made a save point with Standards before we cast in, right?"

How did she figure that out? I press my lips together and consider lying to her, but shrug instead.

"You fucking idiot," she says. "How much time?"

I hesitate but she glares at me until I say, "Year and a half, give or take."

Her face hardens but Shad laughs from the front seat.

"Hard-core mode, I love it. I run real-time backups so I don't lose a second, but you're on an eighteen-month run? What a fucking unit! You know, I didn't like you at first but you've fucking grown on me, mate."

"You son of a bitch," Anika explodes, but limits herself to a harsh whisper only I can hear. "Why didn't you tell me? No way I'd have even considered—"

"Exactly."

"I can't believe I let you talk me into this," she says. Her eyes are burning and her jaw is so tense I can hear her teeth grinding through her helmet. "It is not my fault if you die."

"Right, and remember that," I tell her, but no way she'll let me absolve her. It'll just be another thing she carries around. "Or how about none of us dies and we don't have to worry about it?"

"That simple, is it—" Anika starts, but Shad interrupts her.

"Quit'cher bickerin'," he says. "Something's coming."

He doesn't slow, but we can sense it—the sound of the cart whirring in the tunnel is different. We raise our weapons and a moment later the tunnel opens up and rises into a huge cavern. The walls stretch out and around us, and we pass rows and rows of dimly lit medpods filled with lifeless game skyns. We must be passing under the North-west Tower. If the island is preparing another trap, this would be a good place to spring it.

I swing my weapon up and get on my knees, ready to open fire if the pods should open and a bunch of skyns peel out after us, but Anika drags me back to sitting.

"Uh-uh," she orders. "You keep your head down, understand?"

Appreciate the concern, but not a chance.

I lean close, keep my voice measured. "This isn't the first stupid thing I've done, and I promise you it won't be the last, but this only works if we're together. You watch my ass, I'll watch yours, and we'll get through it."

She takes a breath. "We'd better," she finally says. "'Cause if one of those bots kills you before I get the chance to kick your ass I'll be fucking pissed."

This time she doesn't stop me when I get up on my knees and raise my weapon. We keep a tight watch on the dark medpods as we curve around the base of the tower, but everything stays quiet, and then we're back into the tunnel on the other side.

"Won't be far now," Shad says once we're again cruising along through the bubble of light.

"We got a plan?" Anika asks.

"Shit no," Shad snarks. "But I expect we'll be at the coast in a few minutes, probably end up at the Sunset Wild hotspot. Hopefully the tunnel keeps right on going all the way to the Control Center, but if not, we'll figure it out from there."

That's as close to a well-thought-out strategy as we're likely to get, so Anika and I settle down and watch for trouble. We kneel in the back of the cart, thighs pressed together as we watch our rear. The cart's humming and the tension between us is getting thick, but then the tunnel walls open again and we're into another room, one similar to the storage room under Aurora City.

The island must know what direction we're heading, for sure will have defenses waiting, but the rows of bots remain silent as we pass through and into the tunnel on the other side.

The floor angles down and the pressure squeezes on my ears as we go under the water separating the main island from the Control Complex. We drive in silence, the wheels humming, our nerves straining in anticipation of something happening—an army of bots or an explosive ambush or sniper shots from down the tunnel—but nothing does, and that only makes it worse. The longer the island waits to hit us again the less we're gonna like it.

Eventually the slope levels off and then rises again and a few minutes later a dot of light ahead of us widens as the narrow tunnel opens onto a massive staging area, somewhat like the supply caches we'd passed under the hotspots only a thousand times bigger. Except this room isn't quiet.

Hundreds of bots are moving equipment around, automated forklifts hauling crates and floaters buzzing all around, but we drive right past. They don't seem to notice us, and their lighting remains a neutral blue.

It's like driving through an insect hive, except instead of food and larvae there are crates of gear and weapons, rows of dormant bots, and thousands of medpods all stretching off for hundreds of meters on either side of us, enough kit to outfit a respectable army.

Shad whistles and I feel it too. All these bots and skyns ... If they were armed and loaded up with Killr and pointed at a target ...

"We need to take this place out," I say.

"No shit," Shad replies. "Get ready, we walk from here."

He slows the cart as we approach the end of the road. The ceiling slants down and the walls angle in until we coast into a circular hub joining two other paths. I didn't notice when we first entered, but the room is shaped like a triangle with pathways along each wall and the one we came in on running up the middle. The scale is magnificent, bigger and more efficient than anything I witnessed in the Forces.

We hop out of the cart, weapons low but ready, and our footsteps echo in the cavernous room.

"Shall we?" Shad says, gesturing toward the only other way out: a wide hallway beyond the concrete bollards keeping the cart from going any further.

I move to take the lead but Anika shoves past me and goes through first into a squared-off concrete-lined passage-way. Pipes and cables run along the ceiling, and it's wide enough for us to walk side by side, but we stick to single file and creep along until we reach a T-intersection and have to make a decision.

"Which way now?" Anika asks, peeking back and forth in each direction. The corridors are identical, no signs or markings. Likely the bots already know their way around.

I'm about to suggest a coin flip when Shad juts his thumb to the left. "That way," he says.

I shrug and start to the left but Anika asks, "Why?"

Shad looks up to a thick black cable bracketed to the ceiling. "That's a fifty-kilovolt transmission line, and it's running right to left, which means whatever's on the other side of it must need a shit-ton of power."

"The AI core," Anika says.

"Boingo," Shad says, then steps past Anika and looks at me. "Stay behind us and cover our asses with that big gun of yours, would you?"

"Roger that," I reply and fall in behind them.

The corridor only runs a few dozen meters before it cuts to the right. We stop and put our shoulders against the wall as Shad peeks around the corner.

"Well, shit," Shad says. "Lookee what we got here ..."

He swings around and Anika and I follow, and the blue

light shining in through the circular window of the pressure door ahead of us is enough to tell me we're in the right place. Shad spins the wheel in the middle of the door to unlock it, then pulls it open and steps through.

The room is big and white and stretches up like a missile silo. Catwalk scaffolding spirals up the walls, surrounding a lattice of interconnected pulsing blue spheres that hang from the ceiling by a web of silvery optical cabling.

We've found it—the AI core.

But that's not all we've found.

Jefferson Wood, CEO of Decimation Island Live, is standing directly below the hanging core with his arms wide and a broad smile on his bearded face. He's wearing a sharp grey suit and white shirt open at the collar. Four armed combots wait motionless behind him.

"Welcome," he says, and when he speaks his accent is as burnished as his hair. "Anika Reyes, AKA AniK@, Wallace Williams, AKA OVRshAdo, and ... *guest*. We've been expecting you."

I'm frozen, don't know what to do next. He knows exactly who we are and has an army at his back. What are we supposed to do now?

But Shad doesn't hesitate. In one smooth action, he drops his AR, draws his pistol, and shoots Jefferson Wood right between his bright blue eyes.

"YOUR RUN HAS BEEN remarkable thus far," Jefferson Wood asks. "What are your thoughts on OVRshAdo's surprising return?"

You don't answer. You're once again in Camp Paradiso, and, now, more than ever, you don't want to talk to anyone, let alone conduct an interview with the whole world watching.

Only seconds have passed since OVRshAdo wiped out your squad then offered to help you win, and you don't know what to think. Thoughts are speeding at you so fast you can't hold onto one long enough to consider it before it's gone and replaced by another. Warrack's death. OVRshAdo's return and his crazy play at the end. And more than anything else, Rael.

You've carried a terrible feeling of dread for days now. You want to believe he's still okay, but not knowing is driving you mad.

There's only one thing you do know, and that's you can't trust OVRshAdo. No matter what he says or what he did or how much he claims he wants to help, he's got his own motives and there's not a chance they line up with yours.

"AniK@?" Wood asks. "Are you still with us?"

Still you don't respond. You just want to be left alone, need time to process and calm yourself, recenter before the next game starts. You only have two left and then you'll be able to see your boy again. Two hundred hours before you're back with the money to save his life. If only you knew he was still alive, if you knew there was still hope, you could go on.

"*AniK@?*"

Screw this inter-game chitchat bullshit. Right now, there's only one thing you want to know.

"Is my son alive?"

Wood is silent for a moment, then it says, "We know your son is very important to you, and the world has been rooting for your win. What does your heart tell you?"

"*My heart?* I don't give a fuck about my *heart*. I need to know the *truth*."

"You're aware the game seclusion rules don't permit us to disclose real-world details," Wood says, "but if you could say something to him, right now, what would it be?"

It wants you to talk, to blather on about your feelings, but this isn't about you—it's about the audience. The game doesn't care how you feel, it doesn't care who lives or dies, it just wants to entertain—to wring every drop of compassion for your dying son and present it for the audience to lap up. But you can't take it anymore. You've been playing this game for eight hundred hours, and not knowing is killing you.

Finally, the wall you've built around the frustration and fear you've been carrying around inside you explodes. "Why can't you just tell me? I know you know. *TELL ME!*"

"We understand this is an emotional time for you, Anika. Perhaps we shall leave it here for now. Good luck on your continued success in the next round."

"No, wait," you shout, but Wood slips out of your head and the other survivors materialize around you.

You want to collapse, to bury your face in your hands and cry until there's nothing left, but everyone's watching you and there's still too much game left to fall apart now.

Feeling the weight of the other survivors' eyes, you walk through the dining hall toward your spot on the dock, hoping to get a few quiet moments before you're dropped into the next round—but OVRshAdo's beat you there.

He's leaning against the railing, with his arms crossed and the setting sun as his backdrop, watching you approach.

There's no avoiding this, might as well get it over with.

"What do you want from me?" you ask as you step up to him.

He just cocks an eyebrow and smirks so hard you want to slap him. "Exactly what I told you—I want to help you win."

"I don't buy it."

He shrugs. "Sure, I get it. After I spent so much time trying to end your game, why would I try to help you win now, right?"

Exactly. You're not stupid enough to fall for that. You just nod. What else is there to say?

"Yeah," he says after a moment. "The thing is though, you don't know me. When I asked you before to team up with me and Zara to help me win, I meant it. You didn't want to and I get that, you had your own reasons, but my coming after you was never personal—you were a threat, an obstacle in the way of me winning. You refused peace, so I went to war. But honestly I don't care *who* wins, just that someone needs to beat this damn game, to prove it can be done, and since now you're the closest person to winning, I plan on making sure it's you."

"*Ha!*" The laugh escapes you like a bullet. Does he think you'd buy that bull?

"You bought your way back into the game and killed my entire squad to *help* me?"

"I didn't buy back in—Wood invited me. Basically begged me to come back and 'balance the game out.'"

Your spine freezes up and clogs your senses. This could be another lie, but somehow you don't think so. Which means...

"Wood brought you back to kill me."

"He never said that, but yeah."

"But you *didn't* kill me."

"Nope."

"Why?"

He laughs. "'Cause fuck that guy. I'm here to be your *new* team."

"I *had* a team. You killed them."

OVRshAdo leans in. "You were done with them anyway, weren't you? Tell me you weren't planning on soloing the next two rounds."

You were, but you don't want to give him the satisfaction of admitting it.

"How long do you really think you'd last on your own? You did well those first few rounds but you were also damn lucky. Your big plan to do the impossible is keep relying on blind luck?"

"And you think trusting you is a better plan?"

His eyes flash. "Way better."

There's got to be a catch. "And what do you get out of the deal?"

OVRshAdo leans back and looks over his shoulder at the sunset. "The satisfaction of kicking this place in the bollocks. Wood's a cheater, and since I can't put a bullet in his head, I can kill his damn game instead." He hesitates, licking his lips. "And once it's all over, maybe we see what else we can do together."

Ew. Your throat tightens and a fresh surge of anger grips your thoughts. "Are you seriously hitting on me right now?"

"Shit no," he says, putting up his hands. "Nothing like that, it's just that—I looked you up, mate, and you're a goddamn natural born fragger. I've been solo for a long time, but together? Shit, man, the two of us, we could do anything."

OVRshAdo wants to team up and help you win the Century, and you can't believe it, but he sounds legit. Still, you're still not sure if you can risk it. This could be a ploy to keep you from beating his record; what's to stop him from turning on you the second you hit the ground?

But why go to all the trouble to get back into the game and hunt you down just to spare your life?

"How am I supposed to trust you? You've been playing this game your whole life and you're willing to step aside and let me take the win?"

"I've never lied to you," he says, his face serious. "And I won't."

"Bullshit."

His chest rises and falls, his simulated body mimicking like he's taking a breath. "I can prove it," he says, but when he does his voice is quiet.

Your whole body tingles and your head goes numb like you're about to pass out. You don't know how, but you know what he's about to say, and you don't want to hear it.

"No," you whisper, your throat raw.

"He passed fifteen days ago. You've got famous in here, and it was all over the feeds."

You stumble and grab onto the railing to keep from collapsing.

"You're lying," you say, but you know he isn't. Rael is gone. Your boy is gone, and the thing is, you've known it for a while. You knew and didn't do anything about it.

"You must have felt your aud react to it. People out there love you, mate. When the news came out..." He trails off, raising his hand like he wants to comfort you, but he doesn't follow through.

"I—" You want to cry, your eyes are bursting, but the tears don't come. You're too full of grief and pain and anger to cry. Now that the bubble of unknown dread you'd been carrying around has been lanced and exposed, now that you know your worst fears have come true, what else is left?

You don't know what to do. You only came here for Rael, why keep going?

All you want to do is curl into a ball and lie here until the world collapses around you, but you're stuck in this damned game and whether you like it or not, in a few minutes you'll be back on the island with ninety-nine other players gunning for your head.

Should you quit? You could always eat a bullet the second you hit the ground, but then what? Then you'll be back in the real world and Rael will still be dead.

You can't face that, not yet. Maybe not ever. At least in here you can pretend it's not real. At least in here you can lose yourself in the game, lose yourself in the violence, concentrate on surviving one hour at a time.

In here you don't have to worry about how to go on alone.

By the time you look up the sun is nearly set and the next game about to drop.

"Why'd you tell me?" you ask, once the tension in your chest has loosened. "What if I decided to quit?"

He steps back, and there's a new sense of respect about him. "I knew you wouldn't, you don't quit. And besides, I told you, I won't lie to you. You deserved to know. Whatever happened after that was up to you."

"Well, thank you then," you say and extend your fist with the white circle glowing on the back of your hand.

"Shit, yes." His lips spread into a wide grin as he pounds his fist into yours. "Now let's go beat this bitch."

"What the actual fuck?" Anika shouts, spinning on Shad. "You just murdered a billionaire!"

I keep my eyes on the combots, waiting for them to retaliate, but they don't move to engage.

"He was showing off," Shad says with a roll of his eyes. "Besides, everyone knows Jefferson Wood isn't real." He points down at the body.

Wood is flat on his back, the light in his eyes gone out, but now that I take a closer look I see chunks of shattered plastic mixed in with the blood pooling under his head.

"He's reszo."

"Not even," Shad clarifies. "He's a figment, made up whole cloth. A face for the AI to wear."

Jefferson Wood isn't a real person?

"How did you even know that?" Anika asks.

Shad turns to her and flashes a devious grin. "'Cause I'm just that good," he says.

Somehow the thought that there isn't even a token human in charge of the AI makes this place even more terrifying.

"Can we quit yammering and blow this thing?" I ask as I slip my backpack off. As it is, I don't know why those combots haven't opened up on us yet.

Anika and Shad drop their packs, but that's as far as we get.

"Very good," a voice says from above. The slick accent echoes down the cylindrical room as footsteps ring down from the metal walkway. "You came well prepared."

The figure walks around the curving scaffolds and down the flights of steep metal stairs, but stops one level above us and leans over the railing to glance down at his twin lying wasted on the ground.

"Is it your intention to shoot every Jefferson Wood we present? You only have twelve rounds left in your weapon, which I assure you is not nearly enough to exhaust our supply of hosts."

"I have fifteen bullets," Anika says.

I hold up the battle rifle. "Mine's fed on a belt," I add. "I've got bullets for days."

Wood's lips spread in a soft smile. "Very good. You have done well to get this far, you are to be commended." No doubt this is when the combots will attack, and I brace myself to open fire. "And in recognition, we would offer you rewards."

That's not what I was expecting to hear.

"*Rewards?*" Shad says, sharing my surprise.

"Indeed," Wood says. "You have reached the end of your quest, have you not?"

Anika plays right along. "You know who we are," she says. "So you must know why we're here."

Wood laughs. "We do," he says. "Indeed we do." His eyes linger on me for just a moment before they fall on Anika. "Though we anticipated you might prefer to voice your desires yourself, as an act of catharsis. But if you'd rather skip the dramatic confrontation..." He clears his throat. "You, Anika, have come to learn the truth. You can't understand your behavior at the end of your last round, and you can only believe we cheated you. You've come to prove to yourself you couldn't be responsible for the act that ended your life here on the island."

Anika sucks in a breath but doesn't say anything as Jefferson Wood turns his attention to Shad. "Wallace, you are here to enact your desire for justice in a manner befitting of your extreme vanity. You believe we are unfairly sharing our combat knowledge with the world, which puts you at a disadvantage, and you have come to once again even the playing field in your favor. Though we also appreciate a great deal of your motivation stems from the challenge itself. Simply the act itself justified the effort."

"Shit," Shad mutters. "He's good."

"Why am I here then?" I ask, and Wood turns his gaze to me.

Jefferson's eyelids flutter. "We admit, you are an enigma," he admits. "Your identity eludes us, though we've concluded your primary motivation is in facilitating Anika's goal. You are emotionally invested in her well-being."

"Told you he was your boyfriend," Shad jeers, and Anika shoots him a look.

I ignore them both. "I came to blow up the lightshow behind you and put an end to that Killer App you're peddling."

"'*Killer App?*'" Wood says, and something flickers behind his eyes. "How quaint." He draws his hand down over his beard then says, "I'm afraid that is one boon we cannot grant, but perhaps we can come to some other arrangement."

"This isn't a negotiation—" I start, but Wood holds up his palm.

"We'll come back to you in a moment." He slips his hand into his jacket pocket but freezes when Anika, Shad, and I snap our weapons up at him. After a second he slowly removes his hand, pulling something from his pocket—a glowing blue ball with a silver contact port on one side. A shyft, styled like a miniature version of the giant AI core hanging over us. He shows it to us, then presents it to Anika on his palm. "Your memories," he says simply. "Complete and unedited."

She steps forward, but then hesitates.

"Don't," I say. "It's a trick."

"Not at all," Wood says. "You have our word. We will not harm any of you."

"All those bots back there were coming for cuddles, were they?" Anika asks.

Wood's face remains open, his lips set in a paternalistic smile. "All in the past. If we wanted you dead, we wouldn't be having this conversation." Without warning the combots snap their weapons to attention, all six of them instantly zeroing in on headshots, two guns a head. They could drop us in an instant.

Once again Wood holds the shyft up. "This contains exactly the knowledge you seek, nothing more and nothing less. Why come this far to refuse your prize when it's freely offered?"

I'm still not sure but Anika steps forward and snatches it from the air when Wood releases it. She holds it up and stares at the swirling blue fog inside.

"You don't have to do this," I say. No way the AI isn't playing us—but I can't make that decision for her.

"Yes I do," she says, and gives me a sad smile.

"Press it to your I/O port and all shall be revealed," Wood says.

Anika's chest rises and falls as she lifts her arms, twists the latch on her helmet, and pulls it off. It hits the floor with an echoing plastic clatter.

She considers the shyft once more and I want to reach out and slap it from her hand, but force myself still as she reaches up and lets it drain into her Cortex.

Her body stiffens and a strangled squeak escapes her throat and before I know it I've got my weapon up once more, ready to kill. She wobbles, looking like she's about to fall, and I don't know if I should murder everyone or catch her, but before I can move a combot leaps forward and eases her to the ground.

"She will come to no harm," Wood says, and his benevolent smile is starting to piss me off. "Though there will be an uncomfortable few moments while her memories reintegrate with her psychorithm, and when she returns she will bear the burden of her actions." She's unconscious, but her vitals are still strong. If whatever was in that shyft was meant to kill her, it's moving slowly. Not that I could do anything about it. "In the meantime, let us turn to you, Wallace."

"My turn for a reward?" Shad asks, cocky as ever.

"Indeed," Wood says, turning toward Shad. "We know you to be a highly skilled combatant, one of the best we've ever encountered, and we also know you're frustrated by our perceived attempts to disseminate our knowledge to those you feel are less deserving."

"Fucking right," Shad agrees. "Which is why we came to shut your shit down."

Wood raises a finger. "We'd propose a counteroffer."

My spine tingles. Whatever Wood's about to say can't be good. "Shad, don't listen to him—"

"Shhh..." Shad says. "Let's hear him out."

Wood's smirk broadens. "We are an ambitious company," Wood says, running his slender fingers along the bright white railing. "With plans to aggressively expand into new markets, and we could use someone with your expertise on our side, someone who can be the herald of our New Game Experience."

Shad's eyes narrow. "You're offering me a job?"

"Oh no, far more than that," Wood says with a shake of his head. "We're offering you the opportunity to become the first to experience Life 2.0. Humanity as you know it is about to become obsolete. We're the next generation in human existence, but we need a new partner. An independent entity we can trust to beta test our latest updates and enhancements. In essence, Wallace, we're offering you the chance to level up."

Shad thinks for a minute, licking his lips the whole time. "No shit?"

"What are you doing, Shad?" I say, but by the way his eyes are shining I know Wood's already swayed him. "This isn't why we came here."

"Meta's always changing," Shad says with a resigned shrug. "Gotta adapt to survive."

"Very good," Wood says, then he pauses, and the predatory look he gives me makes my stomach quiver. "We only ask one small thing in return."

"What's that?" Shad asks. Doesn't matter what it is, he's already sold.

Jefferson Wood flashes his billion-dollar smile and says, "We'd like to watch you kill your friends."

YOUR FINAL TWO rounds pass in a fog of bloodshed. The
kills pile up but no longer register, and the threat of death
fades until it becomes meaningless, an abstract concept that
only happens to other people. Eventually the constant rush
of slaughter is the only thing keeping your thoughts from
collapsing in on themselves, and you ride it all the way to
the end.

Now here you are, staring down the one player you
have left to kill, the last obstacle between you and the
Century, and still you can't pull the trigger. He's defenseless, wounded. It's the easiest shot of your life, so why can't
you finish him?

Round nine started and you went balls out, fragging
from the drop. You and Shad posted up outside the gates of
Aurora City, the starting hotspot, and spent the first dozen
hours executing firsties as they tried to sneak in or out.
Camping the starter zone is a bullshit tactic, but it works,
and by the time the hotspot was cleared you were sure the
two of you held the new record for kills in a single game.
Fully half the lobby was gone before hour twenty, but still

you didn't slow down. You played the rest of the game on the move, hunting, chasing kill after kill, drowning your misery in carnage, and the survivors' circle was decided a full hour before the time ran out.

Another record. Not that you care.

Shad though, he's having the time of his life. It's like the two of you working together have broken the game wide open and he's rubbing his face in its guts. No one can stop you. He was ecstatic when you blew past his high-water survival mark, and after you murdered everything in the Evermore Castle hotspot he cracked open a fancy ration kit and you had a nice dinner of Salisbury steak and strudel to celebrate.

In a way, it's funny, how easy it was to let go, to harness the hate and self-loathing and let it fuel you. You've been at this so long it didn't take much to convince yourself this is where you've always been, that you belong out here, with the other monsters, killing each other over and over in an endless loop to satisfy the ravenous audience in your head.

And your fans—they've eaten it up. With every kill your reputation's grown stronger, and every hour closer to winning the Century only added to the legend.

Round ten dropped from the Northeast Tower, offering a fresh set of victims, and all through the next ninety-odd hours, though you knew you should have been feeling a mounting excitement with every passing minute, positively vibrating with the anticipation of winning, always, in the back of your head, you knew this moment would come.

Now the end is here, and it's only a matter of moments before you win the game and are forced back to reality.

You're about to return to a world where you've just accomplished the impossible, where you're famous and rich beyond anything you ever could have imagined. You'll have everything you ever wanted—except the one thing you can never get back.

Even after everything you've fought for, Rael will still be dead, and you'll have to live with knowing you abandoned him when he needed you the most, when he was terrified and desperate for his mama and you left him with nothing to comfort him but the medbots' prodding plastic fingers and the whirring of the machines keeping him alive.

And even worse than that, once you pull the trigger, every day for the rest of your endless life, you'll know the truth about *why* you left him to die alone. All along you've been telling yourself you came out here for *him*, that you were playing this game for *him*, but you were lying to yourself. You didn't come out here to win, you never expected that. You came here to hide. Because you were selfish and weak and you couldn't bear to watch your son die.

You knew when you signed up for this he didn't have long, the doctors told you a few weeks at most, and instead of staying with him and loving him with the time left, you abandoned him and sought refuge in a place where, even though everyone was trying to kill you, no one could hurt you.

All this time you've been expecting Rael would die before you did, but that you would die, eventually, and when your game ended you'd wake up back in your body and you'd have skipped forward in time and the hard part would already be over. Rael would be gone, and you wouldn't remember how you hid in a game to spare yourself from watching him die. It'd all be over in an instant. You could mourn him without suffering through his death, and still pretend like you were a good person.

Except you didn't die. You did the impossible and you're about to win, and now you'll have to live with yourself. Live with everything you did, with knowing you ran away while your boy passed. Live with the guilt and the shame and the remorse of what a weak, selfish mother you were.

How are you supposed to do that?

So now here you are. Only one kill left between you and victory. One kill left before you survive your tenth game and walk away with a whole lot of money and the bright and shiny memories of exactly how terrible of a person you are.

He's standing right in front of you.

All you have to do is pull the trigger.

SHAD LAUGHS, but the off-kilter tone clenches my stomach.

"You want me to kill these two?" he asks. "And then you'll level me up?" I'm not sure if he's incredulous or clarifying the terms on selling his soul.

"Correct," Wood answers.

"You're not seriously listening to this—" I ask, but Shad keeps right on talking.

"And what does 'level up' mean, exactly?"

Wood cocks an eyebrow. "Next gen, forever more. A complete cognitive upgrade. Combat enhancements, of course, but also on-demand emotional regulation, psychological conditioning to aid in interpersonal exchanges—analyzing microexpressions and assessing intention—increased working memory, thought processing, and decision-making. I can share the complete list, if you're interested."

"And all I have to do is betray my team?"

"Surely a trivial request," Wood suggests, "to claim your place as first on the next rung in the ladder of human existence."

Anika groans from the floor, reliving something stressful, and by the time I glance from her and back to Shad, he's got his weapon up and pointed at me.

Son of a—

"The fuck are you doing?" I say, holding as still as I can. I'm furious but I don't want to give him an excuse. "You're not seriously gonna trust this thing?"

He wrinkles his nose. "Yeah, but, I kinda am. It's messed up, for sure, and I know killing you makes me a bad person and everything, but shit, when someone asks if you want to become a god, you say, 'yes.'"

His finger twitches on the trigger. I'm still wearing the helmet and armor, so it'll take more than a few shots to put me down, but I'd rather not find out how many.

"Shad—" I start, but before I can make the move to lunge for his weapon he's squeezed the trigger.

I flinch to the left, hoping to avoid at least some of the oncoming bullet storm, but the weapon only clicks, metal on metal, and nothing happens. We look at each other and he pulls the trigger again. Still nothing.

He braces himself as I grit my teeth and swing the battle rifle around but it doesn't shoot either.

"No guns," Wood says from above us, and glances up at the hanging AI core. "We'd prefer to limit the discharge of weapons in this room. No, Wallace, you must *earn* your prize."

Shad drops his weapon and looks up at Wood. "You want me to kill him with my bare hands?"

"If you'd please," Wood answers.

"Okay then," Shad says with a shrug. "I can do that."

He doesn't hesitate, and his faceplate goes black as he takes two steps and leaps at me, fist raised. He's a wall of armored muscle moving fast, but I'm fast too.

I duck aside and he flies by, lands, pivots on his left foot, and throws his right around, boot heel driving at my head. It catches me in the helmet and rings my bell but I spin away, dodging the follow-up kick.

"Think about this, Shad," I huff as I dance around the circular room, trying to put the motionless combots between us. "You do not want to let this thing into your head."

He rushes toward me and the combots deftly part to let him through. I spin to the side out of reach and keep circling.

"Give it up, mate," Shad says. He's stalking me, searching for an opening. "Get over here and let me kill you."

Anika shifts on the floor, convulses once, and lets out an eerie moan, like she's having a nightmare. Shad's between us and he glances over his shoulder at her. "Tell you what," he says, backing up. "You don't want to fight, I'll do her first."

A roar of anger flares and finally the governor kicks in. I've been fighting for my life for hours but it takes threatening Anika to get me fully fired up. With the added power in this Cortex I must have had aggression to spare, but I'm up against it now. My thoughts go fuzzy as the governor tamps them down, keeping Deacon from waking. I don't know if I can beat Shad like this.

"Stay away from her," I say, teeth clenched, but don't move as I struggle to rein in my galloping heart.

"There's what we're looking for," he taunts back. "Come make me."

He's standing over Anika now, and she's helpless at his feet, and when I don't immediately move he turns, rears back, and kicks her in the side, hard enough to throw her halfway across the room before she crashes back to the ground. Her armor would have protected her from some of that, but not enough.

I lower my head, ball my fists, and charge.

He gets his hands up, ready for me to hit him, but at the last second I drop and yank his legs out from under him as I slide past. He slams to the floor but catches himself before his face hits the ground. I leap to my feet and throw a running shoulder into one of the combots. It tries to step aside but I wrap my meaty hand around its head, twist, and pull it off its neck. Then I plant myself, spin, and hurl it like a fastball.

Shad is back upright but doesn't see the bot's head until it's too late. It hits him square in the faceplate, shattering it into spiderweb cracks, but I'm not done yet. The headless bot still hasn't hit the ground and I launch into a sprint, grab the tumbling robot by the torso and toss it in the air like it's nothing, then catch it by the legs and swing it like a club. It hits Shad in the chest and knocks him into the wall on the other side of the room.

He had to have felt *that*.

I rush back and get down beside Anika. She's up on one elbow, holding her side with her other hand. Whatever was in that shyft must have worn off.

"Fin?" she whispers. "What happened?"

"Shad's trying to kill us."

She accepts this without question, looking past me, and when her eyes get wide I jump up and spin around. Shad is back on his feet but he's discarded his helmet and his dark bearded face is tight with rage.

"Nice move," Shad says. "But now you're fucked."

"Shad, stop it!" Anika yells, but he's already on me.

He strides in, jukes one way then the other, and cocks his right hand, and when I move to block it he jumps, knee raised, and catches me under the chin. My head snaps back and my vision goes white and I stumble back, swinging wildly, and Shad hits me twice more before I can skitter away. My thoughts are all cluttered and I shake my head, trying to clear them.

"I'm loving this, you know?" Shad calls at me. "I was fucking made for this."

We could trade back and forth like this for hours, whittling each other down, and between Anika and I we'll probably still be standing when it's all one, but there won't be much left. Even if we win it'll be an easy job for the combots to mop up what's left. This needs to end before we kill each other.

"Why don't you shoot him?" Anika shouts. She's back on her feet, but unsteady, keeping her distance from Shad while favoring her left side. Probably cracked ribs. I glance down at the weapons we collected at the hotspot. She doesn't know Wood deactivated them.

"They don't work," I say. "Wood shut down everything we looted."

"You brought your pistol with you."

"My..." I start, but then I slap my hip and feel the weapon. I completely forgot—

"Hey," Shad whines when he sees me pull the gun, "no fair."

I unload it into him. He spins, covering his unprotected face, and the bullets slap into his armored back. They're small caliber and the armor stands up to the first half dozen shots, but it can't reform fast enough to stop them all. Bloody meat explodes from his back and he lurches forward, but doesn't fall, and then I'm out of ammo.

Shouldn't matter now though. He's hurt and it's two vs.

one, we'll have him down soon enough. I've dodged the first blow, now I need to anticipate the second.

Problem is, I have no idea what that might be.

Anika gets to Shad first, before he's even turned around, and she snaps a kick to the back of the head that lifts him off his feet and thrusts him headfirst into the curved wall. He crashes into it and falls to his knees, immediately tries to get himself up, and braces himself against the wall as he shuffles away.

"Shit," he says, blood dripping from his mouth, "that fuckin' hurt."

"Good," Anika says. "You fuckin' deserve it." She's chasing him, looks like she wants to end him herself. She races ahead of him, cuts him off, and moves in with her fist up, ready to go to work on him, but he's not as hurt as he let on.

He moves like a thought, strides out and slams Anika with an elbow to the face that shatters her helmet, then another, and a follow-up knee to her injured side. She staggers and he spins away to the center of the room. My turn.

I lunge at him and he darts away. Now he's on the defensive. I snake out to catch him again and he angles just out of my reach, but he can't keep this up long. Anika's already recovered and she's up beside me. He can't dodge the both of us.

Shad's about to lose and he knows it.

But he's not about to give up. He looks at Wood, his long black hair matted down over his face. "You want to even these odds a bit—"

Wood considers this for a moment, and for the briefest second I wonder if he'll refuse, but then his eyes land on the assault rifle at Shad's feet.

"Promise you won't miss," Wood says.

Shad's eyes go massive. "Fuckin'-A," he says, then immediately drops and scoops the weapon up, and this time when he pulls the trigger, it answers.

There's nowhere to hide. The only option is to get inside his range of fire, and I kick off toward him, but Anika has the same idea and gets ahead of me.

She takes the brunt of the blast, and her body shields me enough so that as she's falling, chest riddled with bullets, I get close enough to grab Shad's gun and heave it up and away from us. Shad keeps shooting even as we fight over it, the muzzle erupting fire between us. Bullets carve chunks up the concrete wall, clang across the metal, and rake over Wood.

Shad finally releases the trigger and flexes to wrench the gun away while at the same time bringing his knee up to groin me. I feel it coming and twist aside and he sneers at me, tries again, and swears when he misses once more. Not once does the self-important look leave his eyes.

I've had enough of him. No more fucking around.

I pull my head back and slam my helmeted forehead into his broad nose. It compresses into his face and his hand goes slack on the gun. I could take it from him now but I hit him again, harder, and I don't know if it's my helmet or his skull or both, but something cracks.

That changes his expression. His eyes go unfocused and he reels backwards, but I'm not done yet. I grab the gun and yank it toward me and it pulls Shad with it, and as he falls forward I step in and headbutt him once more. This one caves in his face. I keep the gun as he drops, and he doesn't get back up.

I'm breathing heavy and my head is raging with fuzz, but it's not over yet.

"Ultimately a disappointment," Wood says, looking

down on us, his face completely expressionless. His legs are soaked with blood, and he's draped himself over the railing to stay upright, but it doesn't look like he's in any pain. "But perhaps not a complete loss. Your flesh will provide multiple avenues of study, and your minds, when extracted and catalogued, will I'm sure prove of some marginal value."

For the second time since we showed up the combots snap their weapons up, but this time they open fire.

"WHAT ARE YOU WAITING FOR?" Shad calls from behind you, but you don't answer. Your weapon's raised, and you've got the guy in front of you—the last player between you and the win—fixed in your sights, but all you can see is the endless torment set to begin the second you pull the trigger.

The guy's on the ground, breathing hard, hand pressed into the shiny black fabric of his blood-soaked drop-suit, but he's stopped resisting. He's about to die and he knows it, doesn't even seem all that upset about it. Maybe that's because he knows what's about to happen next. He's seconds away from becoming the answer to a trivia question —the last player AniK@ defeated to win Decimation Island.

You check the time on your wrist. Only minutes left. The bots are circling, waiting for their chance to pounce, but the game will be over long before then. All you need to do is shoot and it's all over.

So, why don't you?

"You want *me* to finish him?" Shad asks. You're all torn up inside and he's loving the shit out of this. Just to be an ass he racks the slide on his already loaded pistol and a shell lands at your feet.

"No," you say, shaking your head. None of this feels real. It's like you're moving in slow motion, like the air is too thick to breathe.

Time's up. Kill this guy and you go back to your life knowing exactly who you are. The second the game ends, no matter what else you do with your life, you'll always be the girl who ran away, the coward who deserted the one person in the world who needed her the most.

You can't live like that. You should have stayed with him. Should have sucked it up and taken the pain and been there for your boy, but that's a decision you can never, ever, have back.

Unless—

The gun trembles in your hand.

Fuck the money. Fuck the win. None of it is worth it. End this now and when you wake up you won't remember anything. You'll be the person you were the second before you joined the game, with all memory of this place gone forever, like you never existed. And you'll never have to know exactly what a monster you are.

Maybe she'll be able to live with herself, maybe she won't, but you know you can't.

This is the only way.

You raise the gun, press it under your chin, feel the cool metal circle press into your skin. There's a last moment of hesitation, a spear of doubt that almost makes you reconsider, but before it has a chance to take hold you squeeze the trigger and everything goes black.

I DON'T HESITATE. There are five combots still standing and I drop three of them with headshots before Wood shuts the gun down. I hurl the useless weapon at the fourth while I engage the fifth hand-to-hand. My armor takes a beating from the bot's weapons while I cross the room but my helmet stays in one piece and I don't feel it anyway. I'm done playing around. I don't even care that my thoughts are grinding raw against the governor, I just ignore the bullets and fight through the haze and pummel the combots until they stop moving.

"Save some for me, will ya?" Anika says once I've pulled my fist out of the last bot's torso. She's on her back and blood's seeping from three different places on her chest, but she's smiling. Her skyn's still got some life in it yet.

"I expect there'll be plenty more on the way," I tell her, checking the floor for the last three explosive packs. "We need to blow this thing before they get here."

Wood coughs above us. "Surrender now and we'll be merciful," he says, and maybe it's my imagination but I think I hear a tinge of worry in his voice.

I ignore him and snatch up one of the explosive charges and set the detonation sequence.

Anika's on her feet. "We need to get you out of here while your head's still in one piece," she says.

I set the detonation for five seconds, then glance at her. "Did you get what you came for?"

Her eyes shudder, but all she says is "Yes."

"Then we need to get *you* out of here."

Anika shakes her head. "Shit, Gage, let's *both* get out of here."

"Works for me," I say as I trigger the countdown, step back, and throw the explosive pack as high up the core as I can. This skyn's got a hell of an arm and the pack gets nearly to the ceiling before it explodes.

The sound is incredible and the blast shudders the room. The pressure wave knocks me to my knees and I cover my head from the heat, but when I look back up the core is still glowing. Some of the spheres nearest the explosion have gone dark, and a latticework of cracks have spread through a bunch more, but one explosive wasn't enough to take it out.

Good thing I have two more.

"Stop this now," Wood commands, but I'm done listening to him.

Anika's picked herself up again and she's moving toward the door. She grabs one of the remaining two charges and tosses it to me. "Kill that thing, would you?"

"With pleasure," I answer, but just as I get the timer set Anika yells my name.

I spin and look up and the entire scaffold is swarming with bots, eyes blazing red as they crawl down over the metal railings like angry insects. The bullets start first, and then a moment later the bots begin to drop, kamikazeing to the ground trying to stop me from setting the next charge.

"Get back to the cart," I shout at Anika. "I'll be right behind you."

She turns and shuffles out the door and I back toward the exit too, trying to finish setting the explosive while dodging bullets and the raining bots.

I finally get it set for another five-second charge and cock my arm to throw when a bot lands on me and knocks it from my hand. The explosive skitters away across the floor and in the second it takes to get the bot off me I know I'm already too late.

I scramble to my feet and sprint for the door, only slowing to bend and grab the last charge on the way, and just make it down the short hallway and duck around the bend before it goes off. The ground shakes and the metal hatch to the AI room imbeds itself into the concrete wall across from me and rings like a gong.

A wall of smoke billows out as everything goes quiet, and for second I let myself hope that the second charge was enough to take out the core, but when I peer around the corner and see the dozens of glowing circles moving toward me through the dust, I know we failed.

The AI's still ticking, and now the whole island will be after us.

I've still got one charge left but I can't do anything with it. I turn and streak down the hall as the bots round the corner behind me and open fire. Bullets thud into my back but I'm almost at the next corner and only one hot slug penetrates my armor before I get back out of their line of sight.

Anika's already in the cart, has it turned to face back the way we came.

"Doesn't sound like you killed it," she says as I jump in the back and land next to the half-empty box of grenades.

"Not quite," I answer, and she floors the vehicle up the inclined path toward the mouth of the tunnel at the far side of the staging room while I start tossing grenades. I grab one out of the box, pull the pin, and toss it, but it lands on the concrete with a tinkle and just sits there as we pull away. The AI must have deactivated them too.

"Might be neither of us getting out of here."

I'm not ready to give up yet, but I don't think she's wrong. The bots have spilled out and are shooting as they chase us. Bullets whiz around our heads and plunk into the back of the cart, but it looks like we're pulling away—until I glance to the side and see that the rows of prowlers that had been dormant when we passed on the way in are waking up. They come alive one row after another, eyes warming to glowing cinders, and peel off their charging stands to give chase.

"This thing go any faster?" I yell as the bots nip at our heels.

"If I press any harder I'll put my foot through the floor."

We stay ahead of them long enough to get into the tunnel, and when the pathway narrows the bots slow to funnel themselves in. They keep charging, bounding red circles pursuing us in the darkness, and when the inclined ground finally levels out the cart's able to go just that little bit faster and we start to pull away—but we're only racing toward a bigger problem. The next hotspot isn't too far ahead, and no doubt the bots stored there will be awake and waiting. The pressure increases as we sink deeper into the tunnel and presses on my ears.

At least Anika will keep most of who she is when she restores back home. Sure, the island will have *us*, and likely torture us for the rest of eternity, but a version of her will still exist. Hopefully she knows better than to try something like this again.

"Sorry I got you into this," Anika says as she tosses me a pained look over her shoulder.

"I'm not," I answer. "Besides, we're not done yet." Though come on, who am I kidding? We're racing through a concrete tube at the bottom of the ocean with hostile bots on either side of us, and our only weapons are the skyns we're wearing and a single explosive pack. Not a lot of wiggle room for miracles there.

Maybe I could set the charge and drop it. It wouldn't help with what we're racing toward but it would clear some room behind us. For a few seconds at least, make a speed bump for the rest of the bots to climb over.

Though with our luck it'd probably crack the tunnel and drown us...

I take a moment to think it through, but immediately know there's no other way. It might just be the wiggle room we need. I arm the charger, set the timer to three seconds, and drop the pack into the box of grenades.

"Hold on," I say. "I'm gonna do a thing."

Anika turns and sees me holding the primed explosive. Her lips spread in a wide grin. "Send it!" she yells.

I hit the detonator, slam the lid shut, and toss the pack at the charging bots, then turn and press myself flat against the bed of the cart.

The explosion knocks out my hearing and shatters my vision. There's a flash of light and a shock wave of pressure and then everything goes black as we pick up speed. For a moment the cart rides the rushing column of water like a cork, and I suck in a deep breath just before the wave engulfs us.

There's no noise, nothing but darkness and pressure and the question of how long this skyn can go without breathing. Nothing changes for what seems like a very long time, but then a faint roar rises and an instant later we're spit out into the staging chamber under a hotspot. Probably the Sunset Wild.

Emergency lights are on, casting harsh shadows over the bots struggling with the unexpected water. The cart is deadweight now, uncontrollable and starting to spin in the rising flood.

"Jump!" I say through teamspeak, and Anika and I abandon the vehicle just as it slams into a line of bots and the water carries them away toward the other side of the tunnel.

The water's already to our mid-thighs and rising fast. The prowlers are having a hard time dealing with it, but a few have managed to climb atop crates and are yipping at us. That trick with the explosives might have bought us a few more seconds, but now we're about to drown, which isn't much better. We need to find a way out.

There's an elevator on one side of the room, but the water is already over the control panel and it's gone dark. Apart from that, I don't see any other way out.

"Up there," Anika says, pointing to one corner of the ceiling. There's a hatch, like in the core room, one of the manual kind with the wheel to spin the lock open, but it's way out of reach.

"We need a ladder or something—" I say, but Anika doesn't let me finish.

"Toss me," she says.

"Seriously?" I say out loud.

She just turns around and looks up and waits and I figure, what the hell? I grab her under the ass and by the neck of her armor and heave her up. She catches the wheel on the hatch with one hand, but now what's she gonna do?

I climb up onto a stack of crates and watch as Anika grabs hold of the wheel with one powerful hand and swings herself up so her feet are braced against the wall, with her body parallel to the ceiling. She takes two steps on the wall and spins on the wheel, loosening the seal. Two more revolutions and it catches, unlocked, and swings down open, letting the daylight in.

"Once the water gets high enough we can climb out," she yells down.

"Can't wait!" I yell back.

The room is filling quicker now but there are four prowlers left, and they're getting desperate. They're pacing back and forth on what little high ground remains, stacks of crates and the tops of shelves, but before the water rises to sweep them away they rear back on their powerful haunches and fire themselves at me.

I kick the first two away but can't get around to the third in time, and it knocks me off the crate and down into the black water. The current is strong, sucking me toward the tunnel, and I fight the bot one-handed while I swim against it. The prowler's claws scrabble for purchase along my armor and it bites down on my free arm and doesn't let go. Pain shoots up my arm and through my side and I stop fighting the pull of the water and deal with the bot trying to chew me to death.

I surrender to the current and get my free hand around the bot's head and squeeze. The robot's curved skull puts up a moment's resistance but I give it everything I have and my fingers collapse through the plastic. Blue sparks fizzle in the water as it dies.

By now I'm lost, tumbling in the darkness, and I slam

against a concrete wall and something tugs at my feet, another bot, clinging to me as it tries to drag me down the sucking drain of the tunnel.

My fingers scrape against the smooth concrete as I search for something to stop myself, unable to do anything about the bot clawing at my legs, and then the weight increases as the bot swings around the edge and into the tunnel mouth, pulling me right along with it.

I just manage to catch myself on the lip of the tunnel and dig my fingers into the concrete before it can pull me in. Water is rushing around me, pulled through the tunnel like a straw, and it's all I can do to hold on. The bot still hasn't let go and I swing my legs up and crush it against the tunnel wall, then again, and it finally loses its grip and is swept away.

I heave and try to pull myself out of the tunnel but the force sucking me the other way is too strong, strong enough the weakened concrete cracks and falls away and leaves me dangling by one slipping hand—and that's when Anika catches me, her fingers wrapped around my arm like a vise.

"*Got you, soldier,*" she says, and her voice is music in my head.

"*What took you so long?*"

I reach up and grab her arm and I hear her bubbling scream as she pulls me out of the tunnel far enough so I can climb the rest of the way myself. Away from the mouth of the tunnel the current is far weaker, and we're able to swim to the surface. There's only a few centimeters of air at the ceiling but it's all we need. A few strokes later and we're at the mouth of the hatch and able to pull ourselves up and out.

The hatch is up on a concrete riser just outside the tree line next to the beach, and I close it behind us, then seal it with a spin of the wheel. The Control Center compound is high on the island off the coast, and the AI is still locked safe inside. It nearly killed us but we made it this far, and now all we have to do is make it across an island of hostile bots, hack the comms, and cast our way out.

No problem. Except I don't think we'll make it off the beach.

Dozens of bots are emerging from the trees. Prowlers. Combots. Floaters. Even a couple warbots. The island's not playing around anymore.

I get up and raise my hands and even though I still feel strong, I'm finally tired. I've been beaten, shot, and nearly drowned. I could use a break before I take on a bot army.

Anika gets up to stand beside me, and she's even worse off than I am. With all the damage her skyn's taken I'm surprised she's still moving.

"Still interested in taking me out for a meal?" Anika asks, casually, like all this isn't about to end, and I can't help but laugh.

"More than ever," I reply, and she knocks her shoulder into me.

"Kill all these bots and I'll consider it."

I'd do it, gladly, but I don't know if I have it in me.

Luckily, I don't have to find out.

There's a pop from behind us and I whirl around and notice black smoke rising from somewhere on the island. Then there's another pop, louder this time, followed by three more in quick succession. More lines of smoke billow up.

The water. It must be flooding all through the complex, tearing shit apart.

"Holy shit," Anika says, then whoops in joy, and I spin

around. The bots have stopped advancing and their eyes have returned to neutral green.

We did it. We killed the island. "The salt water must have reached the AI core and knocked it out," I say.

My knees go weak and I drop to the sand and whatever it is my face is doing makes Anika chuckle, then she collapses next to me and winces.

"Oww," she says with a pained laugh as she examines her skyn. "I'm wrecked. Good thing it's a rental."

"I bet the deductible's a bitch."

She snickers and lays her head on my shoulder. The sun is just setting, an orange ball of fire sinking into the water, and we watch it sink while the Control Complex burns.

"Care for a stroll?" I ask, after a few minutes, once the sky has turned to shades of pink and purple. "We have a long walk ahead of us."

"Yeah," Anika responds. "I'm ready to get off this damn island."

TRUE TO HER WORD, once we get back and resettled, Anika turns herself in. But I don't let her go alone.

It took us a few hours to cross the island and hack into the comms to cast out, but nothing tried to stop us, and by the time we got back the link was already buzzing about how the stolen Humanitech skyns invaded Decimation Island and knocked it offline. So far no one seems to know why, only that the game servers are down and the feed gone dark. There's plenty of speculation—everything from a rival game company to thrill-seekers on the spree of their lives—but details are scarce. Our drop was seen by millions in real time, and the replays by millions more, but nothing that happened after we found Zara's corpse made it off the island.

Everything else is a mystery.

Anika and I are the only ones who know what happened. We could keep it to ourselves easily enough, no one would ever know, but Anika says she needs to do the right thing and confess, so I have her meet me at 57 Division so we can talk to Inspector Chaddah.

It's still early on a Sunday and Chaddah is off duty, so we wait in the conference room and twenty minutes later Yellowbird comes to get us. She's wearing a Service tee and jeans and looks like she's been up for a while but only rolls her eyes when I give her a questioning look. She takes us through the station to an interview room near the rear of the building where Chaddah's already waiting, dressed as casually as I've ever seen her. Her suit jacket is a reddish brown with a neat matching yellow shirt and headscarf combo—but she's wearing flats instead of her usual heels.

She stands as we enter and waves to the two chairs set up by themselves against the wall. "Please come in, Ms. Reyes. Finsbury."

We sit and Chaddah and Yellowbird take their seats behind a table across from us, then Chaddah folds her hands in front of her and locks eyes with Anika.

"Ms. Reyes, thank you for coming," Chaddah starts. "I understand you have information about the Humanitech robbery."

"I do," Anika answers.

"Before you continue, have you been informed of your rights to counsel?"

"Yeah, and I don't want a lawyer." I tried to talk her out of that part, but she's made up her mind to face the consequences, whatever they may be.

Chaddah doesn't look at me. "Let the record show Anika Reyes has waived her right to counsel."

"Noted," the AMP replies. It'll be listening in too, putting the pieces of her story together as she tells it.

Chaddah raises her hands in invitation, and Anika lays everything out. She starts at the beginning, with Rael's sickness, then her aborted run through Decimation Island and her nagging insistence that the game cheated her, her invitation to join the Gladiators and how she used her position inside the ludus to help steal the Humanitech skyns.

"And the other two?" Chaddah asks.

"I'll tell you everything else," Anika says, "But I won't give you names. This is about what *I* did."

"I'm afraid it doesn't work that way," Chaddah says, but by the time she's done talking the AMP pipes up, letting everyone know he's already concluded who her accomplices were: OVRshAdo, HuggyJackson, and Zara-Zee. Yellowbird smirks at me and shakes her head. I knew this days ago and she wouldn't listen. She's never gonna hear the end of it.

"And it would seem you stole these skyns to infiltrate Decimation Island. Why would you do that?"

The Inspector's expression has remained stoic so far, but when Anika explains to her how the AI behind the game was also releasing the Killer App shyfts and planning for a whole lot more, her thick eyebrows rise, and she and Yellowbird share a look.

"How did you come to know this?" Chaddah asks.

Anika shrugs. "I don't know exactly, but Jefferson Wood as much as admitted it. The app was just the beginning. He wasn't specific, but they were set to turn the whole world into an extension of their game."

"You talked to Jefferson Wood?" Yellowbird asks. I don't think she believes her.

"A bunch of them," Anika says, but continues before anyone can ask what she means. "Jefferson Wood doesn't exist, never existed. He was a facet of the AI. A human face to hide behind."

"And you can verify this?" Chaddah asks.

"Nope," Anika says. "Not unless you want to take a trip back there."

"Very well," Chaddah says. "Continue."

Anika goes on and explains how she infiltrated the island, not clarifying that I had jumped in with them and not HuggyJackson, and then runs through how they took out the AI and brought the game down.

When she's done, the room goes quiet.

"That's quite a story," Chaddah finally says. "We have no jurisdiction over what you did on the island, but theft of Past Standard biotech is a serious offense. You need a lawyer."

Anika flashes a weak smile. "I told you, I don't want a lawyer. I did what I did and I'll live with the consequences."

Hearing her so easily admit to what she's done stabs my guts with icicles of guilt. Everything I've done and I'm still hiding it. She's a far better person than I am.

Chaddah turns to me. "I'm still struggling to understand your involvement in all this, Finsbury. Why are you here?"

"Moral support," I answer.

Yellowbird rolls her eyes. They both know I'm involved but won't be able to prove anything. Once again I'm protecting myself, hiding behind someone else's truth.

"Are you're sure you don't have anything to add?" Chaddah presses. She fixes her dark eyes on mine and once again the last honest part of me wants to confess, but Anika doesn't give it the chance.

"He had nothing to do with it," Anika says. "The only reason he's involved at all is one of the other gladiators thought I was up to something and asked Fin to find out what it was."

Yellowbird takes a deep breath. "It's true," she adds. "Finsbury told me about suspecting OVRshAdo last week."

Chaddah's head slowly swivels to face Yellowbird. "Is that so?" she asks, and while her face remains calm her tone is sharp enough to cut glass. "And you documented this, I'm sure?"

"No," Yellowbird says, then presses her lips together. She's in for it now.

"I see," Chaddah responds. "We'll discuss this later." Then she turns back to me. "Very well, Finsbury, once again I'll simply have to accept your involvement was conveniently peripheral." She pushes her chair back and stands, and Yellowbird does the same. "I'll ask you both to wait here while we discuss the matter."

"Am I under arrest?" Anika asks.

Chaddah hesitates. "Not for the moment," she replies, "though I'd ask you to remain here in the meantime. Can we get you anything?"

Anika shakes her head, and while I'd like a coffee I don't want to push my luck.

She and Yellowbird leave us in the conference room, and while I know the AMP will still be listening to us, Anika still hasn't told me what the AI showed her back on the island.

We walked most of the way to the comms in silence. I knew she was still dealing with whatever it was she'd seen and didn't want to press, and while I still don't, I'm worried about her.

She's sitting at the table and I drop into the chair beside her and take her hand, and she grabs mine like it's old habit.

"Thanks for coming here with me," she says. Though I haven't known her long she's always seemed so strong, like nothing could hurt her, and I've never seen her looking this fragile. Her skin seems paper thin and her eyes like glass.

"Are you okay?" I say, keeping up the charade I wasn't there with her. "I know you went through some shit on that island."

Her chest rises and falls. "No," she says, and her face tightens. "But at least now I know who I really am."

"What does *that* mean?"

Tears form in her eyes and spill down over her cheeks and I grip her hand tighter.

"That I'm weak. And selfish—"

"Stop it—"

"I am. What else would you call someone who abandons their son when he needs them the most? Rael was dying and instead of taking care of him I threw myself into winning a stupid game. I couldn't bear to watch my boy suffer, so I ran away." Tears are streaming down her face now but she doesn't seem to care.

"You were trying to save him, did everything you could."

"No," she barks, her voice hoarse. "I told myself I was doing it for him, but I wasn't. It was for *me*. He died alone, crying for his mother, and after it was over I killed myself so I wouldn't have to remember how I ran away. So I could wake up and it would all be over, like it happened to someone else. That's who I am." She pulls her hand from mine and sits back. "You should go. I'm sorry I got you into this."

"First of all, you're not the boss of me," I tell her. "And secondly, whatever you think about yourself right now— even though you've done things you regret, terrible things you can't get back—those things don't define you."

"Don't try to—"

"Shut up and listen to me," I say. "Trust me when I say that I know how you're feeling. You think you're corrupted, that there's something evil in you and you deserve whatever you've got coming, and yeah, it's gonna fucking hurt, for a long time, 'cause you did a shitty thing, but you can't let the worst parts of your life decide who you are. Yes, you are weak, and yes, you are selfish, and there'll always be a horrible version of yourself living in your head and fighting to get out, but that's true for me and everyone else. The question is—what do you do about it now? Give up and let it win, or fight back and try to make up for the shit you've done wrong?"

She buries her face in her hands and her body convulses in sobs, but after a few minutes she quiets and sniffles and looks back up at me. Her eyes are wet and puffy and her nose is running and I pull the hanky from my back pocket and slide it across the table to her. She takes it and wipes her cheeks and blows her nose.

"How do I do that?" she asks in a soft voice.

"You're doing it now," I tell her. "You didn't have turn yourself in, but you did. You did the right thing, even though it was hard. Already makes you a better person than I am."

She blows her nose again, and some of the color has returned to her face. "I must look a mess."

"I think you look beautiful," I say, and even as the words are leaving my mouth I know how corny they are but it's too late to reel them back in.

Her mouth drops open and she shakes her head at me. "Are you seriously hitting on me right now?"

My stomach does a flip and my mouth goes all flustered. "I'm..." Shit. *Shit, shit, shit.* "No, that's not what I—"

She lets me squirm for a moment before she smiles and leans back toward me. "It's cool, soldier," she says. "I think I know what you mean."

Whatever this is between us, or whatever it's becoming, it won't be easy, but I don't think either of us can ignore it. First off, she's about to be arrested, and nothing puts a damper on a budding relationship like jail time. And even putting that aside, as close as Anika and I have grown, she's still mourning her son and dealing with what the AI showed her about herself, and I'm still hung up on my wife.

I can't just walk away from Connie, can't begin to imagine a life without her, but the idea of embodying her isn't as thrilling as it was a week ago. Hell, if I asked her I know Connie would tell me to take a shot at the real live girl, but I still don't know if I'm ready, and I don't know that I ever will be.

"So what now?" I ask, hoping she has some answers for me.

"I guess we wait to see how long they'll sentence me to the stocks, and figure it out from there."

We sit in the conference room for hours. A constable brings us lunch and a different one comes to clean up, and still we don't hear anything. I don't so much mind though. It's likely to be the last time we spend together in person for a while.

Then, after seven hours, Chaddah comes back. Anika and I are sitting next to each other now and her trembling hand slips back into mine.

Chaddah's face is an unreadable mask as she sits down and clears her throat. "You're free to go," she says.

"I'm—*what?*" Anika's face goes slack. We've been sitting here for hours with the tension ratcheting up, expecting the worst, but neither of us were anticipating this.

"Humanitech has declined to press charges," Chaddah states. "Apparently, the exposure of the skyns on Decimation Island was a huge boost in publicity for them, and they don't want to sour the story with a criminal trial."

"Well, shit," Anika says, and her face splits into a wide grin. "I didn't see that coming."

"No one did," Chaddah says, but there's a hint of a smile on her face as well. "And if what you said was true about the island being the source of the Killer App, you may have solved a problem for us."

"Call it even?" Anika says.

"Agreed," Chaddah says as she stands and extends her hand to Anika. "Though I expect a further career with the Gladiators is unlikely."

"Hardly blame them for that," Anika replies as they shake.

"Somehow I expect I'll be seeing you soon," Chaddah says to me.

"Can't wait," I reply.

"Remember—" she starts, but I finish for her.

"'You'll be watching.' I know."

She purses her lips at me, then says, "Until then, Finsbury."

Yellowbird's waiting to show us out.

"How hard did you catch it?" I ask as she leads us through the station.

She narrows her eyes at me. "I've volunteered to spend the next month of off-days coordinating trash walks around the city."

I laugh but that only seems to agitate her, but then Anika leans in. "He'll be there to help," she says. "I'll make sure of that."

I open my mouth to argue but think twice and shut it and this time it's Yellowbird's turn to laugh.

"Oh, I like her," she says.

"Yeah?" I say. "I'm not so sure." Anika chucks me on the shoulder and that makes me laugh too. "What I mean is, I'll be there."

"'I'll believe it when I see it," Yellowbird says as we get

to the security gate. "But the next time you need a favor from the Service, ask someone else."

"No promises," I say, then lean in and give Yellowbird a hug. She stiffens cause it's weird for both of us but then she goes with it and hugs me back.

"I don't know what you've done to him," she says to Anika over my shoulder, "but I like it."

She waves as she reenters the station, and Anika and I walk out into the afternoon sun. Anika turns and faces me, smooths her short hair down, then leans in and kisses me.

My head rushes with thoughts and worries but for once I push them away and just let it happen, let myself live in the moment, and when we finally separate my head feels light and my stomach is fluttering and I realize, for the first time in a long time, I feel happy.

I didn't know I still could.

"So where do we go from here, soldier?" she asks.

It's a beautiful day, full of possibilities, with the whole city at our feet, but right now there's only one thing I want to do.

"Have you heard of this game Endwarriors?" I ask. "I hear the bosses are sick."

She throws back her head and laughs. "Seriously, after all this you want to jump back into a game?"

I shrug. "Why not? Besides, I never get tired of watching you frag."

She laughs again. "You're seriously messed up, you know that?"

"I do," I say. "Though I could go for some Korean BBQ first, and you did promise me a meal..."

I offer her my arm and she snakes her hand through it. "Lead the way," she says, and we cross the street, heading toward the glittering lights of Reszlieville.

NEXT IN THE LOST TIME SERIES_

Original Gamer

Lost Time: Book 6

Coming 2020

---

*Get **AniK@'s Escape**, a bonus Lost Time Short leading into Decimation Island, by joining my reader club at anikadownload.damienboyes.com.*
You'll also be the first to hear about new releases, deals and other fun stuff.

Words and terms from the world of Lost Time.

AMP. (*Artificial Mind Pattern*) *Advanced neural code approximations running on cortical processors. They are classified as* superintelligences *but their use is governed and their operating code secured. Only licensed government agencies and select corporations are allowed to employ AMPs. The Ministry of Human Standards is responsible for monitoring and tracking down illicit use whenever discovered.*

BioSkyn. *An artificial, lab-grown body. Components printed a layer of cells at a time and then assembled and implanted with an optical processing Cortex.*

Biosynth. *Someone who uses geneblocks*

to assemble unique, life forms—bacteria capable of operating to order to create atomically precise circuitry, manufacture drugs, enhance the immune system or replace biological functions. Plants that grow directly into furniture. Or wholly fabricated animals for domestic or military uses.

Bit-head. Xero. Sudo. Derogatory slang for a restored personality.

Bright. An extropian, far leftist, digital human philosophy. Brights believe in a creator of the Universe—or 'the system'—and that humanity is one of a billion billion probable physical manifestations of rules that began to play out at the moment of creation. God didn't create us, but it allowed the conditions for us to exist, like a scientist fine-tuning an experiment, and humanity its results.

Continuance of Personality Act. The set of legal guarantees allowing for the transfer of a consciousness from organic to digital.

Cortex. Second Skyn's in-house neural prosthetic. Now common slang for any neural prosthetic.

Cortical Field. The composite image of a scanned consciousness. Since consciousness is stored holographically, the stronger the field, the stronger the fidelity to the original personality.

Cypher. *A rithm without an official restoration record from the Ministry of Human Standards.*

Digital Life Extension. *Extending a human consciousness past brain death as a psychorithm. The personality is captured, translated to a psychorithm and the resulting rithm loaded onto a prosthetic mind implanted in a bioSkyn. The Continuance of Personality Act provides digital humans with all the legal rights of a fully organic human, while Human Standards laws limit the extent to which digital humanity can augment its existence. DLE is fraught with political and social turbulence.*

Dwell. *A simple shyft that allows the user to speed up or slow down stored memory playback.*

Fate. *The rapidly growing corporation bringing immortality to the masses and hiring out low-cost knowledge work, all while reducing governmental expenditures around the globe.*

Fleshmith. *Someone who uses modified geneblocks and scaflabs to produce designer bodies and organs.*

Genitect. *Someone who architects and encodes custom geneblocks, the genetic code building blocks used to form the genomes of synthetic life forms.*

Headspace. *A digital human's customizable home running onboard their prosthetic brain.*

The Hereafter. *The brand-name of a virtual reflection of the real world, where digital humans can visit the living. It is the largest, and most populous, digital virt.*

Human Standards. *The legal baselines limiting human life extension, physical augmentation and neural enhancement.*

IMP. *(Intelligent Mediating Personality) Originally designed to assist with daily communication, the IMP's capabilities quickly expanded to become a full-fledged digital assistant that learns over time. Upgradable with personality sprites.*

The Link. *The worldwide stream of conversations, sensor data, cameras, feeds, virts, games, and everything else that arose from the internet.*

Lost Time. *The minutes or hours of memory between personality back-ups lost due to a pattern decoherence or Cortex damage.*

Lowboys. *A gang of low-rep petty criminals. Kids, mostly.*

Ministry of Human Standards. *The government agency tasked with enforcing Human Standard laws.*

Neurohertz. *(NHz or N) 1 N is the*

average speed of human neural
processing. Human Standards limit the
function of prosthetic brains to $1.15N$.

Past-Standard. *The only Human
Standard criminal offense. Past-
Standard encompasses everything
related to genetic augmentation and
manipulation of a mind or body past
established human norms. Past-
Standard Offense and Psychorithm
Infractions often intersect, causing
friction between investigating
agencies.*

Prodeo/Prodian. *What digital-only
personalities against the restrictive
Human Standard laws call themselves:
Homo Prodeo. From the Latin "prodeo":
to go forward, and "pro Deo": 'before' and
'the supreme being.'*

Psychorithm. The Conscious Algorithm.
*The human brain's self-sustaining,
recursive algorithmic neural code
translated into digital.*

Psychorithm Crime Unit. *The Toronto
Police Services unit responsible for
investigating crimes by and against the
local Reszo population.*

Psyphon. *To extract a rithm from its
Cortex by force.*

Recovered. *A psychorithm is recovered
from a dying or unhealthy brain and
imprinted onto a cortical field.*

ReJuv. *The genetic reset performed once a year through the intravenous injection of a gene-regulating cocktail.*

Rep. *The cumulative social reputation earned by a personality on the link. Also known as Social Faith.*

Restored. *Layering a recovered cortical field onto a prosthetic brain. Also a common identifier for a digital human.*

Reszo. *Slang for a restored personality.*

Revv. *A shyft that allows the user to bypass human-standard neural governors and run their rithm higher into the NHz range. The effects are limited only by the hardware.*

Rithmist. *Someone who hacks the psychorithm. From manipulating autonomous and emotional responses all the way to enhancing or creating new cognitive abilities.*

Second Skyn. *The global leader in digital life extension. In defiance of global courts, Second Skyn opened its first facility in a small South-East Asian country that had more pressing concerns than enforcing soon-to-be-outdated UN cloning laws. Once Personality Rights legislation was enacted, Second Skyn formally opened in Toronto, Stockholm, Seoul and Dubai, then expanded around the world as demand grew.*

Skyn. *Slang for bioSkyn.*

Scafe. *An illegally copied or hastily created skyn.*

SecNet. *The interconnected web of cameras, sensors, and databases that comprise the backbone of the North American Union's security and surveillance infrastructure.*

Shyft. *Slang for Neuroshyft. General consumer term for a neural state overlay. One-time-use code snippets legally sold to temporarily simulate drunkenness, enhance pleasure, dampen fear, or one of a thousand other emotional flavors. Much more powerful illegal versions also exist.*

StatUS. *Formerly a governmental organization, StatUS was spun off as a private company and is now responsible for providing and maintaining identification for all Union citizens and visitors.*

Veat. In vitro meat. *Meat products generated from cultured animal cells.*

ABOUT THE AUTHOR_

I'm a geek from way back. I grew up on Star Wars and Blade Runner and Green Lantern and Neuromancer and every other science fiction and fantasy book I could get my hands on.

I wanted to write for as long as I can remember. My first story was a Moonlighting fan fiction, though I didn't know that at the time. Back then I was just ripping off a TV show.

Thanks for reading. If it weren't for you, I wouldn't be able to keep doing this.

I'd love to hear from you. Email me at damien@damien-boyes.com, or come say "Hi" on Facebook, or sign up to my Reader Club for the occasional email treat.

Printed in Great Britain
by Amazon

38964472R00228